PRAISE FOR THE NOVELS OF WENDY WAX

"[A] sparkling, deeply satisfying tale."
—*New York Times* bestselling author Karen White

"Wax offers her trademark form of fiction, the beach read with substance."
—*Booklist*

"Wax really knows how to make a cast of characters come alive. . . . [She] infuses each chapter with enough drama, laughter, family angst, and friendship to keep readers greedily turning pages until the end."
—RT Book Reviews

"This season's perfect beach read!"
—Single Titles

"A tribute to the transformative power of female friendship. . . . Reading Wendy Wax is like discovering a witty, wise, and wonderful new friend."
—Claire Cook, *New York Times* bestselling author of *Must Love Dogs* and *Time Flies*

"If you're a sucker for plucky women who rise to the occasion, this is for you."
—*USA Today*

"Just the right amount of suspense and drama for a beach read."
—*Publishers Weekly*

"A loving tribute to friendship and the power of the female spirit."
—*Las Vegas Review-Journal*

"Beautifully written and constructed by an author who evidently knows what she is doing. . . . One fantastic read."
—Book Binge

"A lovely story that recognizes the power of the female spirit, while being fun, emotional, and a little romantic."

—Fresh Fiction

"Funny, heartbreaking, romantic, and so much more. . . . Just delightful!"
—The Best Reviews

"Wax's Florida titles . . . are terrific for lovers of women's fiction and family drama, especially if you enjoy a touch of suspense and romance."
—*Library Journal Express*

The
Break-Up
Book Club

Wendy Wax

Berkley
New York

BERKLEY
An imprint of Penguin Random House LLC
penguinrandomhouse.com

Copyright © 2021 by Wendy Wax
Readers Guide copyright © 2021 by Penguin Random House LLC
Penguin Random House supports copyright. Copyright fuels creativity, encourages diverse
voices, promotes free speech, and creates a vibrant culture. Thank you for buying an authorized
edition of this book and for complying with copyright laws by not reproducing, scanning,
or distributing any part of it in any form without permission. You are supporting writers and
allowing Penguin Random House to continue to publish books for every reader.

BERKLEY and the BERKLEY & B colophon are registered trademarks of Penguin Random
House LLC.

LIBRARY OF CONGRESS CATALOGING-IN-PUBLICATION DATA

Names: Wax, Wendy, author.
Title: The break-up book club / Wendy Wax.
Description: First Edition. | New York: Berkley, 2021.
Identifiers: LCCN 2020035472 (print) | LCCN 2020035473 (ebook) |
ISBN 9780440001454 (trade paperback) | ISBN 9780440001461 (ebook)
Classification: LCC PS3623.A893 B74 2021 (print) | LCC PS3623.A893 (ebook) |
DDC 813/.6—dc23
LC record available at https://lccn.loc.gov/2020035472
LC ebook record available at https://lccn.loc.gov/2020035473

First Edition: May 2021

Printed in the United States of America

1st Printing

Book design by Nancy Resnick

This is a work of fiction. Names, characters, places, and incidents either are the product of the
author's imagination or are used fictitiously, and any resemblance to actual persons, living or
dead, business establishments, events, or locales is entirely coincidental.

To my husband, John.
I miss you more than I can say.
It's way too quiet here without you.

And to our sons, Kevin and Drew,
who have grown into such amazing adults.

Dear Reader,

I finished writing *The Break-Up Book Club* in early 2020, just before the coronavirus took over our lives and we found ourselves in the kind of isolation that belongs in a science fiction or horror novel, not in the lighter, more upbeat novels I write.

That August, my husband of almost thirty-five years succumbed to this virus. During the month he spent in the hospital, growing weaker and ever less responsive, I was not allowed to visit him. I couldn't hold his hand, tell him how much I loved him, or advocate for him in person. Like all long-married couples, we had experienced our share of tough times, but nothing came close to this. I hate that he battled this horrible disease alone. That I could only have eyes on him via FaceTime or if a nurse held a phone to his ear so that he could hear my voice.

I have set this novel pre-COVID, because I couldn't bear to include it. This book, like the others I wrote before it, revolves around friendship and laughter and women who take whatever life throws at them and become stronger because of it. I refuse to write dark and heavy just because the world sometimes feels that way.

I hope that as you read this novel, we have found a vaccine and beaten this virus into submission, and that we are once again living in a world we recognize.

That friends and family can hug each other whenever they want to, that we don't need masks to protect ourselves and others, and that book clubs, like the very special one in this novel, are once again meeting in person.

Warmly,
Wendy

One

Judith

Favorite book: *The Red Tent*—yes, still!

I read somewhere that the very first "book club" (female discussion group) took place in 1634 on a ship sailing to the Massachusetts Bay Colony when a "religious renegade" named Anne invited a group of women—no doubt exhausted from the voyage and in dire need of a break from their husbands and children—to talk about (and apparently critique) the sermons given at weekly services. (Which was nowhere near as relaxing as, say, a conversation about *Bridget Jones's Diary* or *Where the Crawdads Sing*.)

They continued these discussions when they reached land (because how else did you get out of the cabin to hang with your friends?). It seems this didn't go down too well with the Bay Colony's general assembly, because they condemned the gatherings and banished Anne to Rhode Island. Which seems a bit extreme and, frankly, confusing. Perhaps they believed that the state was too small for a worrying number of women to gather?

Women have bravely faced the threat of banishment to Rhode Island ever since, gathering in reading circles and salons and literary clubs and societies. They were aided and abetted by the Book-of-the-Month Club, galvanized by Helen Hooven Santmyer's *". . . And Ladies of the Club"*, and ultimately validated by Oprah, whose meatier/weighty exploration of dysfunction and unhappy endings put the concept on the map. And perhaps introduced the need for wine at book club meetings so as not to lose hope completely.

Our book club was started in 2004 by Annell Barrett, who owns Between the Covers Bookstore, which takes up the bottom floor of the historic home she lives in. It sits just OTP, which is Atlanta shorthand for Outside the Perimeter, aka I-285, the highway that encircles the city—kind of like the early settlers' circling of the wagons—and separates the city folk and the suburbanites.

Annell, who is a practical sort of woman, never saw a reason to give the book club a name or confine it to a single genre. She just wanted more readers in the store, and so she picked a book she thought people would like, wrote the title up on the chalkboard behind the register, and offered a twenty percent discount to anyone who joined the book club. Then she promised there'd be wine. (The food to soak up the wine and allow members to drive home legally came later.)

There were five of us, including my friend and neighbor Meena Parker, at that first meeting in the carriage house behind the store, to discuss *The Secret Life of Bees*. The next month there were ten for *The Jane Austen Book Club*. *He's Just Not That Into You*, requested by then twenty-five-year-old twins Wesley and Phoebe, who kept falling in love with the same commitment-phobic guys, took us to fifteen members.

I chose this club over the one that started in our neighborhood because I love everything about Between the Covers and the carriage house behind it, and also because my neighbors liked to talk about one another more than the books. Plus, a few doors from home is not far enough away to avoid coming back for an especially messy meltdown, a lost cell phone, or a science project that is suddenly and inexplicably due.

Over the last fourteen years, we've read one hundred and fifty-four books, which Annell has duly recorded in an official book club binder that she keeps at the front desk. The group swells and shrinks. We've had two different sets of siblings. Mothers and daughters. Best friends, work friends, and the occasional frenemy. Some members have left, never to be seen again. Others have come back. One member joined as Carl and transitioned to Carlotta, and both of them totally rocked their skinny jeans in a way I've always dreamed of.

We've tried out nearby restaurants and bars, but we always end up back at the carriage house. It's a reassuring and comforting constant in a world that can take you by surprise.

Like the day I realized that Nathan, my husband of thirty years, had been rewriting our personal history. At first the revisions were so small I barely noticed. A minor detail reinterpreted. A tiny triumph appropriated and then repeated until it became an undisputed part of our marital history.

I never made a conscious decision to allow it. But I didn't call him on his embellishments, either. (Which in case you're wondering is the emotional equivalent of faking orgasms and then being doomed to nonorgasmic lovemaking for the rest of your married life.) This is how he became the star of our life together and I became the supporting player.

At the moment, he's packing the things I laid out for him into the suitcase I left open on the bed. I started letting him think he was actually packing way before the creators of pre-packaged meals began putting just enough premeasured ingredients in a box to convince the person assembling them that they were actually cooking.

The first time I did this, the suitcase was made of cardboard, the mattress it sat on was lumpy, and the red-and-blue-striped tie I bought him for his first sales trip came from the sale rack at T.J. Maxx.

"Thanks for picking up the dry cleaning." Nathan stops long enough to flash me a smile. At fifty-eight, his hairline is in retreat and his features have begun to blur, but his dark eyes still crinkle at the corners when he smiles, and he can still make a person feel like the most fascinating being on the planet.

"No problem." I don't bother to explain that I haven't dropped off or picked up the dry cleaning for a good ten years now. Because really, how can he not know this?

"Have you seen my lucky . . . Ah, there it is." He lifts the red-and-blue-striped tie—now an Hermès that I reorder from Neiman's as needed. "Can't close a deal without this baby."

"Oh, I'm sure you could close a deal in your sleep if you had to." The words of reassurance are automatic, but they barely fit through my lips. Because no amount of smiling is going to change the fact that he's leaving for Europe to introduce the Chickin' Lickin' chain of "Southern fried chicken" to key cities. And he did not invite me to go with him.

"I know you wanted to come, Jude, but I'm going to be racing from one meeting to the next. You'd be bored to death."

"I'm pretty sure I could have found a few things to do in Paris and Rome on my own." I think about those magnificent cities all lit up for the holidays. The Christmas markets. The department store decorations. The Louvre and Musée d'Orsay. The *presepe* in St. Peter's Square.

He slips his Dopp kit, upgraded over periodic Father's Days, into the corner of the Tumi suitcase. "You know I'd love to have you with me, but I'm going to be completely focused on business. I can't afford to get distracted."

Somehow, I manage not to ask if he's ever heard of multitasking. Nor do I point out that he might never have been anything more than a semi-successful salesman if I hadn't been there to push and encourage him, to entertain potential franchisees and the company brass, while keeping a sharp eye on our finances.

We never talk about the fact that I'm the one who kept us on a spartan budget so that we could buy our first Chickin' Lickin' franchise. Or that I put every penny my parents left me into a second franchise. All while running our home and our lives, serving on every PTA at every school our kids attended, being room mom and team mom and field trip chaperone and . . . it makes me tired just to remember it all.

"I heard from the children today," I say, because hearing from Ansley and Ethan, now in their mid-twenties and working in different cities, is always a treat and because I'm determined not to pick a fight before Nate leaves town.

"Oh?"

"Yes. Ethan thought the interview for the new sales position went really well."

"Like father, like son." He nods approvingly as he tucks the last few items into his suitcase.

"And Ansley and Hannah have picked a date over Labor Day weekend."

Nate's shoulders stiffen, but he makes no comment. I'm happy that our daughter has found someone to love and share her life with. Nate can't quite accept that Ansley is in love with and wants to marry a woman.

I'm proud of both our kids. Thrilled that they're happy in the paths they've chosen. That's a parent's job, isn't it? To help prepare their children to stand on their own two feet. Wherever those feet lead them.

It's not their fault that that independence has left me in the cheering section of their lives without a game of my own.

"Are we ready for the McCall dinner on the Thursday after I get back?" He zips the suitcase and lifts it from the bed. "And the cocktail reception at the club?"

"Yes. Of course."

"You're the best, Jude," he says as he turns and walks toward me to drop a kiss on the top of my head. A friendly pat on the back follows. The kind you might give a teammate. Or the family dog. "I can't imagine how I'd survive without you."

I follow him to the foyer, my smile frozen at the compliment that still somehow manages to be all about him. As he glances out the double glass doors to the black car waiting in the driveway, I swallow back the hurt and anger.

Nate is going to Europe where he'll be on the run, surrounded by people, and fully occupied doing business while I . . . another swallow of unpleasant reality . . . I'll be filling my time with tennis and yoga and lunch with friends. Extra volunteer shifts. Unneeded mani-pedis. Finishing the book we'll be discussing at our January book club.

"Well, then." I swallow one last time. "Have a good trip."

"Thanks." He gives me a peck on the cheek and reaches for the doorknob. But then he hesitates.

"You know what?" He turns, and my heart picks up a beat. Maybe he's going to come back and give me a real kiss. Or maybe he's going to tell me to throw some things in a suitcase and come with him—because there are plenty of shops in Paris and Rome. Or perhaps he'll invite me to join him when the meetings are over so that we can have a few days together.

"What?" Hope surges in my veins as I look into the eyes that used to spark with love and adoration.

"I have dinners every night, and the time difference is always a pain. So, I'll just text you in the mornings to organize a convenient time to speak, okay?"

My mini fantasy, and the hope it fueled, evaporates.

"Yes. Of course." I smooth my face into a pleasant, unperturbed mask even as I wonder if he's expecting some sort of thank-you for fitting me in to his day. "Whatever works best for you."

The sarcasm flies right over his head as he walks through the door, eager to go forth and conquer. While I remain behind. Like a faithful hound you leave off at the kennel on your way out of town.

After Nate leaves, I drink a couple glasses of wine to smooth out the angry edges, then watch HGTV reruns until it's late enough to get in bed without feeling completely pathetic. There I sit up watching *The Tonight Show Starring Jimmy Fallon*, then *Late Night with Seth Meyers*, mostly so that the house doesn't feel so big and quiet and because I'm angry in a way that's new and unfamiliar and that keeps me from falling into a real sleep.

Tired and grumpy, I down a first cup of coffee in the silent kitchen the next morning, then carry a second into the bathroom, where I shower in an effort to wake all the way up. Wiping steam off the mirror, I stare at my reflection and wish someone would hurry up and invent a way to apply makeup with your eyes closed. I actually google this, but so far no one appears to have attempted it. I am left to dry my hair and trowel on the makeup with my eyes wide open.

I putter around the house until it's finally time to dress for my early lunch at Rumi's Kitchen with Meena, but no matter how many times I check, the only message from Nate is a brief text announcing his safe arrival. There's nothing from the kids, either, though I don't necessarily expect daily communication. I have discovered that sometimes no news is the very best news of all. But this does not apply to husbands.

I'm the first to arrive at Rumi's, which is named after a thirteenth-century Persian poet, and I'm shown to a table for two in the center of the rapidly filling restaurant. I'm sitting down when Meena, who has a tendency for tardiness, texts that she's almost there.

Meena and Stan and Nate and I used to hang out together. We moved into the neighborhood around the same time and had children who were about the same age. Stan and Nate played golf together. Meena and I carpooled, made a fair doubles team in tennis, and often drove to book club together. The kids were in and out of our houses. Not long after we became empty nesters, Stan and Meena downsized to a two-thousand-square-foot condo in a Buckhead high-rise. We stayed put.

It turns out it's hard to hide from each other and each other's annoying habits in that kind of square footage. (Which is undoubtedly why even the least-expensive homes in the Atlanta suburbs are so massive.)

They separated just over a year ago. Stan and Nate still play golf. Meena and I still get together, and see each other at book club, but she's become a little less available now that Stan is out of the picture. They're not the subject of gossip they were when news of their split surfaced, but it's generally assumed that although Stan was always a bit of a jerk and a cheater, Meena, now single in her fifties, must be miserable.

This is the first time we'll be together since their divorce became final two and a half months ago. I'm braced for anger and/or unhappiness and prepared to offer sympathy. A bottle of pinot noir sits open and breathing on the table, and I've instructed the hostess that the bill is to come to me. But when Meena arrives, there is nothing pitiful about her.

"Wow! You . . . you look great!"

"Thanks." Her smile takes up most of her face. "I *feel* great."

I study her. She's lost weight and her face is . . . it's not just the smile.

Meena laughs. "You're trying to figure out if I've had something done."

"Maybe."

Another laugh. "I may have had a little tightening around the eyes. A filler or two."

She does not mention a boob job or tummy tuck, but the transformation is stunning. So is the smile on her face. "I wanted to look good for my online dating profile. I hired this adorable young girl to shoot photos for me." She pulls out her phone, and within seconds I'm looking at absolutely gorgeous shots of Meena, both posed and candid.

"You have an online profile, and you're . . . are you really dating?"

"I am." She pours us both a glass of wine and lifts hers to mine. "And it's so much more fun than I ever imagined." She laughs this light, happy laugh. "I wanted to be prepared in case I'm ever naked in front of someone who didn't know me before I had children."

I cover my gasp as the waiter approaches to take our orders, then down my entire glass of pinot and start on a second as Meena chatters on about swiping right and swiping left. "It's this incredible validation to see how many men find you interesting when your husband has barely looked at you in years." She scrolls and taps her phone. "This is Frank. We've been out a few times. He's a very successful software sales rep. His office isn't too far from my condo." She angles the screen toward me, and I see a smiling, clean-shaven man with even features, a squared chin with a comma of a cleft in it, and bright blue eyes. His dark hair is threaded with gray. He looks to be in his mid-sixties.

"He's cute. And he has a really nice smile." I feel an actual rush of what may be jealousy as we finish off the bottle. "Did things get settled all right financially?"

"Better than all right." She leans forward. "I was completely freaked out when Stan first told me he wanted a divorce, but I had the greatest attorney. I absolutely loved her, and honestly, it was inspiring to see a woman kick butt like that."

We finish our meals and contemplate the dessert menu. Meena's the one who orders the dessert and a glass of champagne for each of us. When the bill comes, it's delivered to her.

"Oh, no. I invited you for lunch. It's definitely my treat."

"No, it's mine. A lot of my friends beat a hasty retreat when Stan and I broke up." She toasts me with what remains of her glass of champagne. "Your friendship means the world to me."

When we walk out to the valet to retrieve our cars, she's still smiling. She seems confident, taller somehow, as if a weight has been lifted from her shoulders. We hug and promise to see each other at book club in January. She flashes me a wink and a last smile as her car arrives. I realize the weight she's lost is named Stan.

Two

Jazmine

Favorite book: *Becoming*—because isn't that what it's all about?

I was ten years old when Oprah started her book club. My mother watched her show every day no matter what. Me, I just loved that Oprah! often had an exclamation point attached to her name and that she didn't have to sing or be sexy to become a one-namer. Just smart and determined.

Determination is something I know something about. It's why I'm walking through the double doors of the intentionally impressive offices of StarSports Advisors in Atlanta as its first and only female sports agent and not as the next Serena Williams I once hoped to be.

My eyes are on my phone as I nod to the receptionist at the front desk and head for my own glass-walled corner office. I slow as I approach my assistant's desk and almost stumble when I see the stranger sitting at it.

"Good morning!" The voice is as bright and perky as the blonde who jumps up to hold out a small, slim hand. "I'm Erin. Erin Richmond. Louise had a family emergency, and Larry, er, Mr. Carpenter, asked me to fill in while she's gone."

My assistant, Louise Lloyd, is a formidable woman in her

early sixties with a no-nonsense manner that no one, including the most arrogant athletes our firm represents, has ever attempted any nonsense with.

This tiny blonde with her bright-blue eyes and pale skin is the antithesis of Louise, who took me under her wing when I joined the firm three years ago. On a good day, Louise would no doubt fuss over the girl at her desk just like she fusses over me. On a bad one, she'd eat her for lunch.

"I was told to let you know that Louise will call you when she can. She's on her way to Memphis because her mother fell and fractured her hip."

I know how close Louise is to her mother, and I understand why she's on her way to her side. What I don't know is where this girl came from or why she ended up behind Louise's desk.

"Would you like me to send flowers to the hospital? Or food to the house? Or . . . something? Her mother's address is right here. And I have the name of the hospital."

"I'll give her a call, but flowers to the hospital would be good." I study the girl more closely—she can't be more than very early twenties. She looks like a bit of fluff. But she also looks familiar.

"How do you know Larry Carpenter?" Larry founded the firm twenty years ago, when he signed a good part of the Atlanta Braves pitching rotation. He's built the agency into a powerhouse, with sixty-five clients and three hundred million in contracts spread throughout the NFL, the NBA, and MLB.

"My, um, fiancé, Josh Stevens, is a client of his, and I interned here over the summer."

"Ahhh." Mystery solved. Stevens has a 101 mph fastball and a wipeout slider. The Braves took him in the first round two years ago and have just called him up from Triple-A.

"So, you have experience in sports management?"

"Just the internship. But I do have a degree in sports management from UGA, and I've been shadowing Marc Sutton's assistant for the last three months." She takes a breath. "And I know sports, especially baseball. My three brothers played through college. And I've known Josh since we were kids." It's clear she's nervous, but she holds my gaze. "And I'm super organized. Kind of borderline OCD according to my brothers." Her chin lifts. "When I heard they were looking for someone to work for you, I went to Larry and asked for the opportunity."

I don't point out that it's me and not Erin who should have been given the choice, but I wouldn't leave any young female in Marc's office—or at his mercy—under any circumstances. The man is the very sort of troglodyte who made the #MeToo movement necessary and who has not learned a single thing from it.

"Okay, then." I look down at my phone and pull up the day's schedule. "I'm going to be out most of the day. Do you have any questions?"

Her fingers fly over the keyboard in front of her, her eyes on Louise's monitor. "It shows Ron Collier for lunch at Le Bilbo-quet at one. Then you have a call with John Prentiss in Detroit at two forty-five. Which you can take while you're in the car on your way to drinks with Tyrone Browning at the InterCon-tinental." Erin looks up. "There's a note from Louise reminding you not to let him have more than two drinks or you'll never get out of there."

"Too true." I learned that one the hard way when I was first wooing the three-hundred-pound defensive lineman who'd had one too many lemon drop martinis. When he face-planted in a plate of ravioli, I had to figure out how to extract him without attracting undue attention.

"And your father called a few minutes ago to say that he'd pick up your daughter from school—her name's Maya, right?"

At my nod she continues reading from the screen. "He said he can drop her off at tennis, but he won't be able to stay and bring her home." The girl—it's hard to think of her as a "young woman," whatever PC demands—drops her eyes to the schedule. "But I see your appointments take you north on Peachtree so that you won't have far to go to get to the Chastain Park Tennis Center."

"Yes." I skim back over the timing of the day's appointments. "I should have plenty of time to return calls and get over to the courts for pickup."

"At six thirty. On the dot this time." Erin winces. "Sorry. That's a direct quote from your father."

"I thought I recognized the tone." I sigh because when you're giving face time to an athlete you're eager to sign or trying to keep happy, it's hard to jump up and leave if they aren't ready to go. "All right."

"Please don't worry about leaving me here. I promise I'm capable of keeping things going until Louise gets back. People have underestimated me my whole life—just because I'm short and blond. I think it's unfair to make decisions about people just because of how they look."

I flush as the point hits home. How many times have I been discounted just because I'm female and black? "Noted. Can you get me Matt Fein at the Hawks office? The numbers are already programmed in to . . ."

She's already scrolling through the on-screen directory before I finish. "I'm on it. Should I buzz you when I have him on the line?"

I nod and walk to my office. When I drop into my desk chair the GM is already on hold.

The morning flies by without any noticeable missteps from my temporary assistant. By the time I head out to my lunch appointment, I'm no longer totally shocked not to see Louise behind the desk outside my office. Still, I slow for one last coaching session. "Just text or forward anything that feels serious or that you're not sure what to do with. I'll check in when

I can. If you need help here in the office, your best bet's probably Cameron. He's Jake Winslow's assistant." I point toward the third desk to Erin's right. Then I make myself leave.

One long lunch and a conference call later, I'm being shown to a prime table at the Bourbon Bar inside the InterContinental. Tyrone is already halfway through a very pink drink decorated with a striped straw and turquoise paper umbrella, and garnished with fat red cherries. The glass disappears completely in his ham-size hand as he lifts and drains it. The drink might be on the girly side, but Tyrone's eyes are hard and angry.

I slide into the chair across from him and raise a hand to summon the waiter. When he arrives, Tyrone orders another drink that I hope is only his second. I order a Pellegrino and appetizers to help soak up the alcohol he's consuming.

"What's going on?" I ask, although I'm pretty sure I don't really want to know.

"I thought you told me that endorsement deal with Verizon was as good as signed."

"It is. I just spoke to them last week."

"Well, somebody's lyin'. And I don't think it's *Sports Illustrated*."

"What?" It's all I can do not to shout the word as he holds up a shiny, new copy of the magazine that won't be on shelves for another ten days. A wide receiver named Luther Hemmings takes up most of the cover. His arm is slung around his agent's shoulders. Both men are grinning.

"Luther got the damn deal." Tyrone and Luther played together in college and hit the NFL draft at the same time. Their relationship teeters between love and hate, with a side of jealousy thrown in. "Five million dollars for five years." He gestures wildly, sending the pink liquid sloshing and the turquoise umbrella flying. "That's twenty-five million dollars. I told Lucy we were set. I told my friends it was a done deal. You made me look like a fool or a liar, and I'm not sure which one I hate worse."

I had begged him not to say anything until the contracts were signed. But that wasn't really the point.

I look at the agent on the cover. Rich Hanson is one of the most successful sports agents in the business and a prick of the first order. "I'll give Dan at Verizon a call and see what's going on."

"You can read what's goin' on right here, girl." He tosses the magazine at me. "And it ain't me."

"Let's just have a bite and talk this through."

"Ain't nothin' to talk about. I signed with you cuz of the way you went after things for Mo Morgan when he didn't get signed. I knew you got yourself a law degree. And I heard good things." He drains the last of the pink concoction and slams the glass down on the table. "But I don't have no time for people who don't deliver."

His accent gets increasingly and belligerently Southern. He has conveniently forgotten the position I helped him hold on to after an altercation with a teammate. The false paternity suit I saved him from and which he told me saved his marriage.

The waiter arrives with the appetizers and places them on the table. For the first time since I've met him, Tyrone ignores the food completely. He scrapes back his chair and gets to his feet, intentionally towering over me and the table.

I stand to face him. I'm five-eleven barefoot. Today's kitten heels take me to six-two, and I still have to look up to meet his eyes. "I'll find out what happened. And I'll make it right."

He snorts.

"Have I ever broken a promise to you?"

He loses some of the glare. "No. Least not that I know of. But this whole thing sucks."

"It does. But I *am* going to find out how this happened.

And then I'm going to get you an endorsement deal that will put this one to shame."

A small, grim smile appears on his lips. "You do that. Or I'm gonna be exercising that escape clause from our contract faster than you can say, 'Where'd he go?'"

I continue to stand as everyone in the place watches him storm out. Then, although I'm not a particularly heavy drinker, I order a Tito's on the rocks and sip it while I read the article in the magazine Tyrone left behind.

These deals don't happen overnight. Which means while I was negotiating in good faith, Rich Hanson somehow snuck in and claimed the prize for his wide receiver. This is not the first time Hanson has appropriated something that was meant for one of my clients. What I don't know and clearly need to find out is whether I'm his only target or just one of many.

I've completely lost my appetite, but I sip the drink, hoping it will calm me down. When I feel able to speak without the heat of anger, I start making calls, beginning with the fringe of people who might be involved in Rich Hanson's schemes and working my way toward the epicenter of the deception. I know from experience that it pays to be thorough. I didn't make it to where I am now because I'm more talented than others but because I consistently outwork the competition.

My fury builds as I realize how deftly Hanson has outmaneuvered me. I drain the last of the drink I've been nursing and glance down at my Apple Watch, which is telling me to breathe and suggesting I stand up. It also tells me it's 6:25 P.M. *Shit.* Chastain Park isn't far, but there's no way I could get there in five minutes even if it weren't rush hour.

I fire off a text to Maya that I'm on my way, but by the time I pay the tab and the valet hands over my car, it's 6:40. When I screech to a halt in the tennis complex parking lot, the temperature has dropped. My daughter and her instructor stand beneath a streetlight, bathed in its glow. It's 7:05.

Maya, who just turned thirteen and is already closing in on six feet, doesn't even try to hide her irritation. One size 11 tennis shoe taps impatiently. Her high cheekbones, honey skin tone, and wide-set brown eyes are duplicates of mine, but at the moment those eyes are angry. The wide, mobile mouth, a near replica of her father's, twists into a frown. With a flip of a box braid over one broad shoulder, she glares at me. If looks could kill, I'd be a chalk outline on the concrete right now.

Kyle Anderson, with whom Maya has been working for close to a year, appears more resigned than angry. This is not the first time I've been late, and no matter how often or sincerely I promise to do better, we all know it's unlikely to be the last.

I'm out of the car and striding toward them before the engine comes to a full stop. "I'm so sorry. I had a work emergency."

Anderson, tall and lanky with sun-streaked blond hair, a perennial tan, and the requisite zinc oxide–covered nose, nods a greeting.

"It's sports, Mom, not brain surgery," Maya snaps. "Your clients are always having emergencies." She air quotes the last word. "You'd think they'd be old enough to take care of themselves."

If only. "I get paid to take care of those emergencies. It's what I do. And you know it's never been a nine-to-five job." And certainly not a career path I ever planned on.

I'd been nearing the end of my senior year at Georgia Tech, where I'd gone on a tennis scholarship, only months away from graduation, the sports media already referring to me as the "next Serena Williams" even though Serena Williams was still very much a force. I was poised to join the women's pro tour and madly in love with Xavier Wright, point guard for the Atlanta Hawks. My entire life, everything I'd dreamed of and worked so hard for was within my grasp.

All of it was blown to pieces when a rusted-out Mustang spun out of control and slammed into us.

When I awoke in the hospital with a career-ending crushed pelvis and a broken kneecap, Xavier was dead. The blood test I'd been given before treatment could commence revealed a pregnancy so early I hadn't even been aware of it.

"I'm really sorry," I say to the instructor. "Thank you so much for waiting."

"Couldn't leave her standing here on her own in the dark, now could I?" He looks so all-American that the British accent always takes me by surprise. He's smiling, and his voice betrays no disrespect, but the set of his jaw telegraphs his disapproval.

But then Anderson is single and, as far as I know, has no children. It's easy to disapprove of others when the only person you have to look out for is yourself. And how stressful could teaching tennis be? I shake my head. God, what I wouldn't give to smack the hell out of a tennis ball right now, ace a serve at ninety-five miles an hour, drop a shot over the net that my opponent can't get to. What I'd really like to do is wipe the court with this guy. But although I can still hit a tennis ball pretty much wherever I aim it, I can't move fast or well enough to play the game.

"As I said, I am truly sorry. It won't happen again."

If he notices how tight my voice is or how much I wish I could show him up on the court, he gives no indication. "See you next time, Maya. Don't forget to work on those drills." He turns and heads for the only other car in the lot, a low, sporty, penis-shaped convertible.

"You promised you were going to do better," Maya says as she slams the passenger door of my more practical and less phallic BMW. "It's humiliating to always be the last one standing here. Poppy is never late."

"Your grandfather is retired. He has all the time in the world. And thank God for that." It's my father who first took me out on the public courts near our house when I was five. He did the same for his granddaughter.

"I hate how everything else is always more important to you than me."

"That's not true. And it isn't fair."

"Ha! Aren't you the one who's always telling me that life isn't fair and that I'd better get used to it?" My daughter unerringly chooses to hurl at me the one thing that I should never have said.

I take a deep breath, searching for the calm adult tone I know the situation calls for. But I've been jangling since Tyrone Browning dropped that damned *SI* on the table. My heart's still pounding from the race to get here. So is my head.

Maya shoots off a text—no doubt a complaint about me—then turns to stare out the passenger window.

Fine. Even without a reminder from my Apple Watch, I breathe for a full minute, both hands gripping the wheel, my eyes straight ahead. As my thoughts begin to clear, it comes to me that this moment calls not only for deep breathing but for acknowledging the positive.

Traffic has thinned, so I take Wieuca over to Peachtree. Ignoring Maya's huff of impatience when I fail to make the light, I acknowledge the top three in my head. One—I have a healthy, and clearly uncowed, daughter. Two—I have a successful, if stressful, career. All working mothers, especially the single ones, have to juggle way too many balls for comfort. Three—My parents. Having them nearby and a part of our lives is about as positive as it gets.

At Peachtree I head north to Dresden, then sneak a peek at Maya, who's staring out her window as if she's never seen the Brookhaven MARTA station before.

"I hope you're hungry," I say to the back of her head. "I've got a whole bunch of appetizers from the InterContinental for dinner."

There's no response. And no sign of thawing.

I'm about to reprimand her for ignoring me when I realize that my daughter's silence is a great big positive at the moment. So is the fact that I'm not going to have to make dinner. There. How's that for determined, positive thinking?

Three

Sara

Favorite book: All of them—I can't help it!

The bathroom doorknob jiggles. "Sara? Are you in there?" My mother-in-law's voice is as brisk as her knock, easily reaching me where I sit. On top of the closed toilet seat. Reading. Hiding.

I consider staying silent, but the door is locked, and my car is parked in the driveway. There's no way I can pretend that I'm not home. "Yes?"

"Are you planning to come out soon?" Dorothy, never Dottie or, God forbid, Dot, moved in three months ago after hip replacement surgery that didn't go smoothly. Although the home health care workers are now gone and she is, according to her doctor, fully mended, she's still here and in no rush to move back to her home in Greenville.

My husband, Mitchell, has no problem with this, primarily because he got a new job and has been working in Birmingham for the last six months and comes home only on weekends. This makes Dorothy, who has always made me feel that I am not good enough for her son, my responsibility.

Each month, our three-bedroom, two-bath home—the very first I've ever been able to call "mine"—gets smaller. There's virtually nowhere left to hide. Including, it seems, the master bathroom.

"Yes. Of course." I wait for Dorothy's footsteps to recede, but my mother-in-law stays put. I glance around the bathroom looking for an escape route, but the lone window that overlooks the backyard is small. I've always been almost painfully thin, but I wouldn't lay money on being able to squeeze through it. And even if I managed to wriggle out, I'd have to come back at some point.

"Any chance it'll be this millennium?"

I curse myself for not locking the bedroom door, even though barging into a closed bedroom and knocking on a bathroom door is a stretch even for Dorothy.

"Are you all right?" I ask in case this is an emergency.

She doesn't answer. I listen intently, but there's no ragged breathing, no body crumpling to the floor. I set my book on the vanity countertop, reject the instinct to flush the unused toilet just to prove I've been doing something legitimate, and open the door. "Is something wrong?"

"No." Dorothy's puff of thin white hair is deceptively grand-motherly and looks freshly washed. She's wearing makeup. Her purse hangs over one bony shoulder. "I just wanted to see if you'd heard from Mitchell."

My parents left me in a rest stop bathroom on the Florida-Georgia state line when I was three years old. I have virtually no memory of them, but highway rest areas still make me queasy. I grew up in foster homes—six of them—before I finally aged out. After that, I worked multiple jobs to keep a roof over my head and pay for night school until I finally got my teaching degree. Meeting Mitchell Whalen at a friend's birthday party was the most exciting thing that had ever happened to me. I'd never had a boyfriend. The fact that he'd never known his father and I couldn't remember either of my parents gave us something important in common. When he asked me to marry him, I felt as if I'd won the lottery; I was going to have a husband *and* a mother. Unfortunately, what warmth Dorothy has is reserved for her son. I have tried my hardest, but it's impossible to have a relationship all by yourself.

"No, I haven't. But he must be on his way."

The drive from Birmingham is just over two and a half hours, but Mitch doesn't drive home on Friday nights for fear of rush-hour traffic, nor does he jump out of bed early on Saturday mornings. Normally, he rolls in around noon, which is when I typically leave for my weekly Saturday afternoon shift at Between the Covers. I check my phone. It's eleven thirty.

"I'm sure he'll be here any minute and ready for your lunch date." This is the one-on-one time Mitch gives his mother each week. We share him Saturday evening. Once she goes to bed, he's all mine; we tiptoe past her bedroom and into ours like naughty teenagers. There we make love (as quietly as possible), then curl up together to watch *Saturday Night Live.* It's my favorite part of the week.

He heads back to Birmingham on Sunday afternoon so that he won't have to fight rush hour getting out of Atlanta on Monday morning. "Did you call him?"

"No." A former efficiency expert, Dorothy does not engage in idle chitchat, at least not with me. If she's ever poured her heart or thoughts out to her son, I've never witnessed it and he's never mentioned it. "You know I don't like to bother him or distract him if he's driving."

I hit speed dial. Mitch picks up on the fourth ring sounding oddly out of breath for someone sitting in a car.

"Hi. Where are you?"

"Home." He pauses. "I mean, in the apartment. I've got some kind of bug. I'm, uh, not going to be able to get back this weekend."

The bathroom is small, but I manage to turn away from Dorothy. "When were you planning to let us know?" I whisper as the disappointment seeps through me. "Your mother's expecting you." *And so am I.*

"I'm sick, Sara. It happens." He coughs loudly. A less charitable person might say unconvincingly. This is not the first time he's bailed at the last minute.

"It's only a couple hours' drive," I point out. "I'm not scheduled to work at the bookstore today. I'll make a great big pot of chicken soup, and you can lie in bed and be waited on."

"Sorry. But I can barely get out of the bed I'm in," he says. "Besides, my mother's had surgery. I promise neither of you want to be around these germs."

The anger gurgles up from somewhere deep inside of me. It's an emotion I rarely give in to. One of the keys to surviving a lifetime in other people's homes is tamping down your feelings and not making waves.

"Hang on a sec. I want you to explain that to her."

"Oh, no. You can't . . ."

I hand the phone to Dorothy. Unable to get by her in the tight space, I'm forced to watch her face fall as she listens to her son's excuses. Her lips quiver as she hands my phone back.

I feel like crying, too. I love my husband and I want him *here*, not in some furnished corporate apartment two hours away. And if I have to be here when he's not, I don't want to be left with this woman who barely tolerates me while she waits for his appearance on the weekends.

Since I'm not getting either of those things, I want a pint of ice cream. And I want to eat it lying in bed reading a novel that will take me somewhere else. Let me *be* someone else. Books are what got me through the foster care system and every other situation that I've had no control over. Don't get me wrong, I like to read when I'm happy or even just okay, but books—and the words that form them—have gotten me through a lot of things I'd like to forget. If I'd relied on ice cream alone, I'd be the size of a barn.

Dorothy, who's normally puffed up beyond her diminutive size, looks small and shriveled.

Before I can think it through, I ask her if she'd still like to go out for lunch.

Dorothy sniffs. Her eyes are moist with tears that don't dare to fall. "I can make myself a sandwich." She looks at me suspiciously. "Assuming there are things in the refrigerator." Like her son, Dorothy chooses to believe that grocery elves come in to stock it while she's asleep.

"We could make grilled cheese or peanut butter and jelly sandwiches, but I wouldn't mind picking up a few more things. I think we should go out and have a bite together."

"Why on earth would we do that?" She looks as horrified as I feel.

"Because I know you were looking forward to going out. And it might make us both feel better."

We do a bit of a stare down. Her gray eyes are identical to Mitch's, only without the warmth. I will my green ones—they've always been my best feature and help to cancel out my stick-straight carrot-red hair and ghost-white skin—to telegraph sincerity even though I already regret the offer.

"If you like." Her tone is grudging, and I have to remind myself that I'm doing a nice thing and that is supposed to be its own reward.

"Anyplace you'd especially like to go?" I ask.

She shrugs.

"Okay. How about the Brooklyn Café? They have good salads. Then we can stop by Between the Covers. I want to pick up the book club book even though we won't be discussing it until January. Then I can run into Whole Foods."

She nods glumly.

We get into the car, and I back it out of the driveway. As we drive to the restaurant, I attempt to fill the silence. I tell her about how I first started working at the bookstore where we'll be stopping after lunch, on Saturday afternoons and then over school holidays and summer break. (I'm a reading specialist at Eastend Middle School.) Then I go on to tell her about how Annell Barrett, the owner of Between the Covers, first formed the book club, how long it's been in existence, and that it takes place in a carriage house. Just thinking about book club and how warm and welcoming a group it is, I feel lighter.

Dorothy doesn't ask a single question, so I ramble on about how the book club's on hiatus over the holidays because everyone's so busy. (Present company excepted.) I'm an introvert by nature, and when I'm uncomfortable (which is always around Dorothy) or nervous I develop logorrhea. In case you're wondering, that's

> log·or·rhea
> lȯ-gə-'rē-ə
> *noun*
> Origin: Greek, early 20th century.
> 1. uncontrollable talkativeness
> 2. a tendency toward overly complex wordiness in speech or writing
> Ex: "If I'm not careful, my logorrhea leads to foot-in-mouth disease."

As we enter the restaurant, it's clear I'm going to need not just the new book club book but a LOT of ice cream to get me through this weekend.

At the table, I order an appetizer to share and a glass of wine. At her sniff of disapproval, I say, "Normally, I don't drink until after five P.M. But it's got to be five o'clock somewhere, right?"

She doesn't crack a smile and only tastes the appetizer when I push the plate toward her and ask her to tell me what she thinks.

"Not bad. If you like roasted brussels sprouts. I didn't realize that was a thing."

"I love them," I admit. If I knew who thought of seasoning and roasting them this way, I would send a thank-you note.

My mother-in-law harrumphs. I didn't realize until she came to live with us that harrumphing was still a thing. I met Mitch twelve years ago and have been married to him for ten, but I could probably count the number of times I've been alone with Dorothy on one and a quarter hands. Although she's very attached to her son, I've never witnessed a serious display of affection between them. When I ask Mitch about his childhood, he says, "It was fine. Pretty ordinary. Virtually no drama." This, I have learned over the years, is how he likes it.

I think now about how restrained Dorothy is, and for the first time, I wonder why.

"Did you and Mitchell argue?" Dorothy looks up from the panini and salad she's been picking at. "Is that why he's not coming home this weekend?"

I blink in surprise. Has she really just blamed *me* for Mitch's absence? His fake cough and lame excuses are on the tip of my tongue, but I pop another brussels sprout in my mouth and remain silent.

"You should be living in the same city, not forcing him to drive back and forth every week."

I put down my fork. "You might want to mention that to Mitch. He's the one who didn't want to sell the house or uproot me until he was sure he was happy with the new company."

"What's not to like?" she counters. "He has a bigger title, and he's making more money. I would have thought you'd want to be with him."

"Of course I want to be with him. But there's nothing wrong with taking it slowly."

She raises an eyebrow. "If you'd had children, he might not have been so quick to leave you behind."

I blink against the automatic press of tears. It takes everything I have not to push back my chair and run out of here at the injustice. "Mitch has never wanted children." He'd made that clear before he'd asked me to marry him, and I'd been so in love, so happy and grateful that someone loved me and wanted to marry me, that I'd believed I could make him change his mind. Only that never happened. "And he didn't 'leave me behind.' I've filled out an application for the Birmingham Public School System, and I'm watching the postings. Real hiring for the next school year usually starts in March."

She gives me an oddly knowing look, but this woman knows nothing about me or my relationship with her son.

Although my appetite is gone, I force myself to finish my salad, and for some reason I don't understand but am going to blame on logorrhea, I can't let myself give in and eat in silence. So, I ask her about the work she used to do as an efficiency expert, how she ended up in Greenville, all the things I should have already known. Anything to keep her talking about something besides me and Mitch.

She picks at her lunch and gives short, succinct answers while I chew and swallow food I no longer taste.

When our meal is finally over, my mother-in-law sits in the car while I run into Between the Covers.

"Are you all right?" Annell, for whom I'd give my right arm and all the roasted brussels sprouts in the world, hands me a copy of *Educated*, by Tara Westover, along with a look of concern.

"Mitch is sick and isn't coming home for the weekend, and my mother-in-law can be a bit much."

"Poor thing." Annell, who barely reaches my shoulders, steps out from behind the counter and wraps me in a hug. Though she has never, to my knowledge, given birth, she is the mother I wish I'd had or been given a chance to be. "Shall I come out and explain to her just how lucky she is to have you for a daughter-in-law?"

"Tempting, but I think I'll survive." The sincerity of the offer and her obvious affection give me the strength to force myself back outside to the car when I'd much rather hang out here in the place I love, around people who are more like family than my husband's mother has ever wanted to be.

At the grocery store, Dorothy once again remains in the car. I pick up staples and sandwich makings and easily assembled meals like the good "elf" that I am.

Then I go to the freezer section, where I fill the rest of the cart with teetering piles of pints and quarts and gallons of ice cream.

Four

Erin

I've been filling in for Louise for a week now. I really hope that her mother gets better. I do. It's just—well, I'm kind of hoping Louise stays in Memphis long enough for me to prove myself here.

The agency will close for the holidays, and while support staff will be in the office right after New Year's, agents like Jazmine with NFL clients will travel most of the month. January's their "busy" season.

Josh and I are getting married on New Year's Day. Yeah, I know. A lot of the guests will be watching bowl games on their phones and watches while I'm walking down the aisle. But we picked the date because friends and family will still be off work and school for the holidays. When we get back from our honeymoon in Turks and Caicos, I'll finally move out of my parents' house and into the gorgeous thirty-seventh-floor Buckhead condo Josh bought for us. We'll have six whole weeks together before he reports to spring training in Florida.

Footsteps sound on the marble floor, and I look up to see Josh, who has a meeting with his agent. He shoots me a wink as he passes, and even after all these years I can't quite believe he's really mine.

I was six the first time I watched him pitch at one of my brother Tyler's Little League baseball games. I fell in love with Josh—and how hard he could throw a baseball—at seven. When I turned eight, I decided I was going to marry him.

Laugh if you want, but I just knew. And my determination to make him love me back kept growing while I trailed behind Josh and Ty through elementary and middle school, even though I wanted to cry every time he called me "squirt" or ruffled my hair.

Other girls started developing in middle school, while I stayed short and flat. I prayed for breasts every single night, and while it wasn't exactly a miracle on the order of the Virgin birth, my prayers were finally answered that summer before I started high school.

I think I prayed a little *too* hard, because they turned out a lot bigger than I was expecting.

I only have brothers, and their idea of dressing up is athletic shorts that have been worn for only two or three days, so I had to scour fashion magazines for the kinds of clothes that would emphasize my new best features without revealing too much of them. Ditto for the most flattering haircut for my too-narrow face, the right shade of blond to compensate for the dishwater shade I was born with, and makeup that made my eyes bluer and my lips poutier.

Josh had been away playing ball all summer, so when I put myself in front of him as if by accident on my first day at Walden High School, he actually stuttered in surprise. "I . . . jeez, squirt . . . is that really you?" His dark brows shot up. Confusion clouded his beautiful brown eyes.

"Of course it's me," I said in the matter-of-fact tone I'd been practicing. "We all have to grow up sometime." And then, although I honestly don't know how I pulled it off, I gave him a small, friendly smile and walked away.

After that, I went out with every guy who asked me (especially to places Josh might see me) and most especially to the high school baseball games, where I made a point of treating him like a brother. (Think comfortable old couch.)

When he finally asked me out, I made him wait for six weeks before I said yes.

From then on, we were Joshanerin. God, I loved that. And him.

A lot of high school romances end at graduation, but I tended ours. I even graduated early so that I could study sports management at UGA while he worked his way up in the pitching rotation.

"Hey." He flashes his killer smile at me as he leaves Larry's office and walks toward me. "Ty's waiting downstairs. The rest of the guys are meeting us at the airport." Josh and the guys are headed to Las Vegas for his bachelor weekend.

"Have a good time." I look up into his eyes. "Just not too good."

"Back atcha," he says automatically. "Don't forget to wave your left hand around while I'm gone so everybody knows you're taken."

I glance down at the two-carat emerald-cut diamond engagement ring that takes up most of my ring finger and part of my knuckle. (Women who top out at five-four don't have long, elegant fingers.) "I don't see how anyone could possibly miss it," I tease, holding it up and admiring it as the overhead light sets it flashing.

I sense someone walking up behind me.

"Hi, Josh. I'm . . ." Jazmine's voice sounds over my shoulder.

"Yes, ma'am. We met back when I first signed with Larry. I've been hearing great things about you lately."

I blush, but it's the truth. I've learned more in the week I've been working for Jazmine Miller than in college, my internship, and the last three months put together.

"That's good to hear," she says.

He flashes the friendly yet confident smile that first slayed me when I was six. Then he leans down to give me a quick peck goodbye.

"I'll text you when we land." He nods and smiles at Jazmine. His long legs eat up the distance as he moves through the office.

"There are tall women all over the world hating on you right now for unnecessarily taking a six-foot-plus male out of the dating pool."

I shrug. I have always hated being the runt of the litter—all three of my brothers are way over six feet. I wish I was tall and *lithe* (I have always loved that word and wished it could be applied to me) like Jazmine. But I honestly don't see any reason why short women should get stuck with short men, who often seem to have a chip on their small shoulders.

Josh turns and gives me one last smile before he turns the corner, and I know I'm the luckiest girl alive. Or maybe I'm just the best planner.

Judith

It sounds so old-school now, but I left all the important communication to Nate back when we first started dating. The first I love you. The first conversation about being exclusive. The first mention of marriage, even though I was already planning our wedding in my head.

I thought we were going on an adventure together, and in a way I guess we were. There was the first pregnancy. Our move out to the swim and tennis neighborhood in the suburbs, where the public schools were better and where we were surrounded by other couples starting families and raising children.

Like all the neighborhoods around it, River Forge was a place where the first day of school required a moms' brunch hosted by a mother sending off a child for the first time, and Halloween meant a pre-trick-or-treating party at the clubhouse that had been turned into a haunted house. Easter included a neighborhood-wide Easter egg hunt, and the Christmas holidays featured a cookie exchange and an adults-only party at somebody's house. The entire neighborhood resembled a ghost town over spring break.

When we first moved to River Forge, there were a few older neighbors whose kids were grown and who seemed vaguely out of place. It never occurred to me that I might become one of them someday, but the school schedule no longer means anything to me, and I'm often surprised when I hear the school bus rumbling down the hill toward our cul-de-sac. When the neighborhood kids show up selling Girl Scout Cookies, or pine straw, or wrapping paper, I often don't know or recognize them.

Nathan believes your home is your castle and there's no reason to ever move, but most of the neighbors who moved into River Forge around the time we did have already left and downsized like Meena and Stan did. Even the holdouts have their houses on the market or are thinking about it.

Which is why we are now the old farts, the sick and dying animals left behind when the herd moves on.

Today this old fart is making meringues to take to the neighborhood cookie exchange. I'm known for my meringues—what my kids used to refer to as "cloud" cookies because of their free-form shapes and sugary airiness. Ethan liked them stuffed with chocolate bits. Ansley considered the chocolate bits intruders, so I always made her a separate batch unsullied with chocolate. Out of habit, I continue to make them both ways and will put some of each kind on the tray I'll take to the exchange and into the gift tins that I'll fill for Nate's key employees, as well as the lawn guy and the mailman. I'll make fresh batches just before the kids come home for Christmas. Can it really be just two weeks away?

I whip up the meringue and mix the chocolate bits into the batter. As I drop rounded spoonfuls onto the baking sheets, I think about Meena and her move ITP (Inside the Perimeter). How vastly her life has changed. How much mine has stayed the same. At least on the surface.

Once the trays are in the oven and the timer is set, I go down to the basement, where I wrestle the Christmas decorations out of storage and drag the artificial tree toward the stairs. When I hear the lawn mower start up and see Gabe mow past the basement windows, I run out and ask him if he can help me carry up the tree.

"Sure, Miz Aimes, no problem."

At my direction, he carries it upstairs and places it in a corner of the family room not far from the fireplace. While he goes back down for the decorations, I place some still-warm meringues in an open tin and give it to him along with the envelope with the holiday card and the cash we give him every year.

"Have a happy holiday."

"Thanks, Miz Aimes. You, too."

The last of the cookies are cooling on their racks and the holiday tins are open and laid out all over the kitchen counter and island when my phone rings. I know it's Nate because I hear Frank Sinatra belting out "My Way": a newly assigned ringtone that is not intended as a compliment.

Given how little I've heard from him this trip, I consider not answering. But just before it goes to voice mail, I do. "Hello?"

All I hear is ambient sound. The hum of conversation. Cutlery on china. Nate's voice and another that is heavily accented.

"Nate? Helloooo??"

Being butt-dialed is so insulting. Especially given his lack of communication. I've been the recipient of the occasional text, a picture of the Eiffel Tower. Another of the Colosseum. Not a single "Wish you were here."

"Damn it, Nathan. Are you there or not?" I'm about to hang up when his voice rises above the ambient background noise.

"Congratulations on your anniversary." Nate's voice is hearty.

The clink of glassware follows.

"Grazie." The voice is male and Italian. "Grazie mille."

Glasses clink again.

"How long have you been married?"

"Otto anni," the Italian replies. "Eight years."

"That's nice," Nate says, and I know what's coming. Sure enough, he adds, "Before I got married, my father told me that the first forty years are the most difficult." Nate has shared this tidbit a million times. It always gets a laugh, and today is no exception.

"And how long have you been married?" the Italian asks once he stops chuckling. "Was he correct?"

"Thirty years," Nate says with the cadence I know is leading to his punch line. "Only ten more years to go."

There is more laughter.

"At this moment, thirty years sounds like a . . . very long time," the Italian says. "A . . . how is it called in your country? A life sentence, I think?"

Nate guffaws.

"And has your marriage been a . . . happy one?" the other man asks.

A silence follows. Suddenly, I'm afraid that the unintended call will disconnect before Nate answers and equally afraid that it won't. We've never actually discussed our relative degrees of happiness. More and more I find myself feeling irritated or put-upon, and like any other couple, we occasionally snap at each other and argue. But it has never really occurred to me that he might have complaints of his own.

"Sure. I'd say we've been pretty happy."

I would relax now except Nate's answer is off-puttingly off-hand. "My Judith's a good egg."

"Che cosa?" His companion has apparently never heard this expression.

"You know, a good sport," Nate explains. "I don't think I could have picked a better helpmate and mother."

I blink back tears. The compliment is for himself and the choice he made. It's all about the things I do for him, the role I play, not who I am or how he *feels* about me.

"I mean you can't really expect passion to last forever, right?" my husband continues. "At first it's all about being in . . . love. Then you have children and it starts to change. Your wife's exhausted. Short-tempered. Pissed off that she can't lose the baby weight. Everybody's on a hamster wheel, working, running, juggling."

More background restaurant noise. Something in Italian I can't hear. Then . . . "Even if you aren't flat-out in love anymore, you stay because you made a commitment. She's the mother of your children. You know each other, what to expect. And then the years fly by. The kids are grown and you're both still there. But you're just kind of going through the motions."

His voice trails off. Even without a soundtrack, I can see the shrug that follows. His casual dismissal of me and the life we've been leading is a punch to the gut. I turn off my phone before he can say something that will make me feel even worse. Though I'm not sure that's possible. Tears blur the racks of cooling cookies all around me. My reflection in the glass of the microwave door is equally blurry.

Oh no, you don't, I tell my reflection. *You will not cry. You've raised two great human beings. Helped this ungrateful man who's just "going through the motions" build a business. Thirty years is not something to sneeze at. Nate's opinion does not define you.*

My chin goes up as I straighten. Indignation courses through me. If this is the thanks I get for spending most of my adult life trying to make him happy, the time has come to stop.

Good egg, my ass.

Five

Jazmine

We're at my parents' for Sunday dinner. As usual, the table groans under the weight of the platters of fried chicken and honey baked ham, the baskets of corn bread and biscuits, all of which are surrounded by bowls of mashed potatoes and every vegetable a Southern garden can be coaxed to produce.

I am full to bursting from my mother's deservedly famous fried chicken, the corn bread I can never resist, and the butter beans and collard greens that I tell myself are still vegetables and therefore healthy, no matter what they've been cooked in. Surely, God wouldn't allow her to create such an incredible feast and then penalize us for eating it.

From where I'm seated, I can see the decked-out Christmas tree twinkling in the next room. There's even a smattering of presents underneath it, a stark reminder that I'm behind on pretty much everything to do with this holiday that is inexplicably less than two weeks away.

Somehow, I find room for a slice of warm apple pie with vanilla ice cream melting on it.

Maya and her sixteen-year-old cousin, Carmen, have their heads together over a cell phone, even though phones are supposed to be banned during family meals. Lord knows I'm having a hard time not looking at mine. My older sister,

Thea, motions to her daughter to put the phone away. My father is holding forth on today's sermon, which I will confess to sleeping through, and cradling his latest grandbaby in his lap. The baby's father, my younger brother, Stephen, shovels food into his mouth just like he's always done. "Mama, I'm telling you, nobody makes corn bread as good as you. Nobody."

My mother's food deserves every bit of praise it receives, but I listen with half an ear to the talk all around me. I'm still stewing over Rich Hanson's theft of the endorsement deal I spent so long teeing up for Tyrone and worried about what else he might have up his sleeve. I'd call him to tell him to cut his shit out, but I don't want to let him know he's getting to me.

"Jazz?"

"Hmmm?" I look up and realize the table has gone quiet. Even Maya and Carmen are looking at me rather than the phone that is most likely in Carmen's lap. "Sorry. Did you say something?"

"I sure did." Thea, who is not one to beat about the bush, looks straight at me. "I said, there's a fine-looking man who just joined Jamal's firm. He's single and new to Atlanta."

"That's nice." I'm careful not to roll my eyes or ask what this has to do with me. Because apparently every eligible man, especially every single, professional black man, has something to do with me. My sister, my mother, and pretty much every married woman I know, including my assistant, Louise, refuse to believe a woman can be truly happy without a man.

I look down and push a few butter beans around my plate. "I appreciate you thinking of me, Thee, but I don't really have time for dating."

"You don't think you could make the time to spend one evening getting to know someone? Or to show a newcomer around Atlanta?"

"I'm sure I could *make* the time if I had to. But dating is not a priority for me right now."

My sister's eyes narrow, a signal she's not going to give up on this.

My mother sighs. "Girls." She motions to Maya and Carmen. "Please take the leftovers into the kitchen and wrap them up. We'll clear the table in a few minutes and join you."

The girls depart with furtive glances over their shoulders.

My father reaches out and nudges my brother. "There's a problem with the furnace. I'd like you to come take a look."

"I'm going to feed Eugene now. Then I'll put him down for his nap and help the girls with the dishes." My sister-in-law, Renata, jumps up, puts the baby over her shoulder, and follows my father and brother out of the dining room.

I am left with my mother, my sister, and my brother-in-law, Jamal, who's been around so long I almost can't remember our family before he was a member.

"You'd like Derrick. He's a great guy. Smart. Successful. Good sense of humor." Jamal is an attorney, and he knows how to make an argument.

"Thank you very much for thinking of me. I'm not interested right now." I can barely keep up with everything I already have on my plate. How am I supposed to deal with a man, too, let alone a potential husband?

"Right now?" My sister huffs. "It's been fourteen years since the accident, and you've barely dated. Don't you think it's time to take a risk and let someone in your life again?"

"I am not afraid of letting someone in."

"You know we just want you to be happy." My mother's eyes are moist with tears. "And what about Maya? Don't you think she should have a father?"

"She has Poppy and Jamal and Stephen in her life. That's way more father figures than a lot of kids have." My mother has been lobbying for me to find Maya a father practically since she was born. "And I'm perfectly happy with my life as it is." Happy enough.

They make no comment, but my mother's face is all twisted up. No one does silent agony like she does.

"You have so much to offer. And you deserve to be in a happy and loving relationship," my sister says.

"I do *not* need a man to complete me." Okay, that came out a little more Gloria Steinem than I was going for, but I do not want to be backed into this corner. "And between work and Maya, I really don't have the time."

Jamal's look says, "Liar, liar, pants on fire!" but he remains silent. My mother sighs in a way that speaks volumes.

"I think you better look at making the time to make the time," Thea bites out. "Because before you know it, Maya's going to be in college." Their son, Michael, is a junior at Auburn, so she says this with great authority. "There's no guarantee that there will be an army of single men worth having lined up and waiting when you finally decide you have the time."

"Thanks for your concern. I appreciate it." I have learned that this is a great conversation ender, so I do not add how much I don't appreciate her sticking her nose in my business or the reminder that I'm getting older by the second. "Now, if you'll excuse me?" I stand and begin to gather dirty dishes, acting for all I'm worth as if I'm not at all bothered by the fact that she's probably right.

Judith

By the time Nate gets back from Europe, I've decorated the tree, the house, and pretty much everything that doesn't move. I do this partly because I know the kids will enjoy it but mostly because I need somewhere, anywhere, constructive to channel the hurt and anger coursing through me.

But no matter how forcefully I bake and decorate and clean, I am nowhere near over Nate's assessment of me and our marriage. At the grocery store where I stock up on the kids' favorite foods, at the mall where I plow through slower, happier holiday shoppers to buy last-minute gifts and stocking stuffers, even at the salon where I seethe through a cut and color followed by buffing, waxing, and tweezing, Nate's damning praise reverberates in my head.

No woman on earth aspires to being "a good egg." Sexy, lovable, irresistible, my life, my rock, my salvation—yes. Good egg—absolutely not.

Still, it's not as if I overheard him having sex with another woman. Surely, no one has ever ended up on *Snapped* because she overheard her husband describing her as "meh." Nonetheless, I can barely look my butt-dialing husband in the eye. Smiling in his presence feels like lying. But I can't quite settle on a plan of attack. Or even a way to make him understand how he's made me feel.

It turns cold and windy the day before the kids come home. Heavy clouds scud across the sky. The meteorologists are beside themselves with glee at the possibility of a white Christmas, and I watch the Bing Crosby / Danny Kaye movie of the same name twice in an effort to get into the holiday spirit, but I just can't seem to get there.

I've already told you why I'm not in favor of faking orgasms, but I'm totally prepared to fake holiday cheer for my children. Which is why I make sure we shake presents under the tree and try to guess what's in them, go to a candlelight Christmas Eve service, then come home to sip hot chocolate and eggnog and watch *National Lampoon's Christmas Vacation*, shouting all the dialogue. (A tradition Ansley's fiancée, Hannah, who's small and thin with an elfin face, has clearly been prepping for.)

"We want to keep it small. Just close friends and family," Ansley says when I ask about their wedding plans. "There's a beautiful spot right on the lake near our house. A good friend of ours is an ordained Universal Life minister." Ansley's arm goes around Hannah's slim shoulders. Her eyes fill with the bottomless love I thought I'd always feel for her father. That I thought Nate and I would always feel for each other.

In bed that night I stare up at the ceiling reliving our years together. Trying to see where I took the wrong turn. The warning signs I missed. When I convinced myself that all relationships were about compromise and it didn't matter if one person (me) did most of the conceding. Or whether the spark was supposed to last a lifetime.

I feel the earth shifting and moving under my feet, and not in the uplifting Carole King way. I teeter on the edge of a precipice: dying to speak my mind and demand to know whether he really meant what he said on the phone, afraid I'll go too far and say something I can't step back from. My husband doesn't seem to notice anything's amiss.

Christmas morning dawns to the same dark clouds that have so far shed no snow.

Tired from lack of sleep but committed to making the holiday feel as normal as possible, I pull on a robe and drag myself downstairs. The fire is blazing in the fireplace, the turkey and ham are in the oven, and I'm drinking coffee and setting out coffee cake and donuts when Nate comes down an hour later looking well rested.

"Merry Christmas." He hands me a small gift box wrapped in gold paper. "I picked this up for you in Paris."

Normally, the fact that he's chosen a gift for me that doesn't require an electrical outlet would be enough to improve my mood, but that butt dial and my "good egginess" refuse to recede.

"Thank you. It's very pretty." The delicate gold bracelet is, in fact, extremely pretty. It's also about as far from the bold, chunky jewelry that I've always worn as he could get. Which proves it is in fact possible to live with, and ostensibly love, a woman for more than a quarter of a century and still have no idea what she does and doesn't like. A fact I've become used to but can't seem to accept or shrug off today.

As Nate carries his coffee out to the living room to sip in front of the tree, I want to stomp over there and remove his gifts that I thought so long and hard about. If Amazon had a lump of coal that could be delivered in the next two hours, I'd order it now. But I do none of these things. Because it's Christmas and I will do everything humanly possible to spare my children the odd mixture of ugliness and despair that's taken root inside me.

Hannah comes down just as I'm debating whether it's too early to wake Ansley.

"Merry Christmas!" She pours herself a cup of coffee, then pitches in peeling potatoes and dicing onions, proving that she knows her way around a kitchen and that someone somewhere has taught her how to be a good houseguest. When the orange juice is poured and another carafe of coffee brewed, she gives me a warm smile. "Ansley will be down soon. She promised to make sure Ethan gets up, too." Her smile is so loving when she says my daughter's name that it takes several swallows to clear my throat of the emotion that clogs it before I can speak.

When everyone's downstairs and at least partially caffeinated, we carry coffee cake and donuts out to the living room, and the gift opening commences. As family tradition prescribes, we hold up presents to be photographed and put on mittens and scarves and other wearable gifts to form impromptu gift-laden tableaus, which also get photographed.

As the morning progresses, coffee gives way to eggnog. Nate becomes increasingly jovial. He even starts to loosen up with Hannah. This should be a relief, but his happiness is gasoline on the fire of my discontent. Every smile and laugh is a fresh insult. The way he sits and simply expects to be waited on makes me furious, though I have no doubt a jury of my peers would point out that I'm to blame for letting him get away with it all these years.

"Are you okay, Mom?" Ansley asks, her forehead wrinkled in concern.

"Of course, sweetheart." I swallow and pull tightly on the ragged edges of my anger. "I was just trying to figure out whether we need to peel more potatoes."

Hours later, when Christmas dinner is ready, Nate slices the turkey and ham onto the serving platters, bowing as if expecting applause for this lone contribution to the meal. I keep myself from snorting by picturing Meena rolling her eyes.

"You know, Jude," he says when I pass him a plate with wedges of homemade pumpkin and pecan pie for dessert, "I think this may be our best Christmas ever."

The smile freezes on my face, and I clamp my lips shut. Christmas is a day for making happy memories, not spewing hard truths. If I open my mouth now, I'm afraid I'll tell him and our children what I really think. And exactly how I feel.

This is not the time to rain my hurt and anger and disappointment down all over him. This Christmas needs to be one we'll all remember as happy. Because after the kids leave, Nate and I are going to have our own very personal come-to-Jesus meeting.

For the first time, I realize that if that doesn't set things straight, this could be our very last Christmas together.

Six

Erin

The morning after Christmas used to feel anticlimactic, with all the excitement of the holiday over (if you didn't count the after-Christmas sales that my parents treated like a call to battle) and too much time to kill until we went back to school.

But this December 26 I'm barely a week away from finally turning the dream I've been dreaming all these years into reality. Once I walk down the aisle at the historic Primrose Cottage to become Mrs. Joshua Stevens, Josh and I will finally get to eat, sleep, and live together. This beautiful condo that we chose and decorated will become *our* home.

I pull the covers up around us and snuggle in against the heat that Josh always generates. Happiness floods through me. He's the only guy I've ever loved. The only one I've slept with.

I finger the delicate rose-gold necklace with its graffiti-style heart and arrow Josh gave me for Christmas and that I slept in and that I never plan to take off. It's the only thing I'm wearing, and each time it moves against my bare skin, I actually feel like the sex goddess Josh calls me.

I rub my face against his chest, and its cover of dark hair tickles my nose. His scent is both heady and comforting. The way he moves, his reactions, are as familiar as my own. I don't know whether humans imprint the same way animals do, but everything about him feels exactly right.

I keep my eyes closed because once I open them it'll really be morning and I'll feel like I have to get out of bed and do something, when all I want to do is lie here next to Josh. Maybe Sleeping Beauty wasn't really poisoned but just sleeping in until Prince Charming arrived. Feeling wicked and bold, I climb on top of him and let the necklace and my breasts brush against him.

He moans softly and hardens beneath me. He may be the only person I've ever slept with, but I've learned the things he likes, and I know how to tell just how much he likes it. But this time when I start to move against him, he puts his hands on my waist to stop me.

"Hold on."

I laugh because I know he has to be kidding. He's always wanting me to be bolder, to take the initiative. "Are you okay?"

"Yeah." His eyes are open now, and he looks way too serious for someone who talked me into all those wicked things last night. "But I . . ." He lifts me off him and sets me gently on the bed. "I, uh, need to pee. Be right back."

I pillow my head in my hands and look up into the tray ceiling, letting myself imagine him waiting for me, looking lovingly up the aisle as I make my way toward him. When he comes back, he's wearing sweatpants that hang low on his hips. "Here." He hands me one of his T-shirts. "Put this on."

I sit up, confused. He has never, ever asked me to put clothes *on*. I'm not very experienced, but I know it's not good when a man, especially your fiancé, asks you to get dressed. "Okay, now you're starting to freak me out. What's going on?"

"Please. Just . . . sit up. Here." He takes the T-shirt back and yanks it down over my head, holding it there until I push my arms through the short sleeves, which hang to my wrists.

"Okay." He swallows. "I um, let's . . . maybe we should go in the kitchen. You'd probably like a cup of coffee, right?"

Before I can answer, he reaches for my hand and pulls me out of bed. In the kitchen, he leads me to a barstool, then puts a K-Cup in the machine. When he sets the steaming mug in front of me, he stays on the other side of the counter and doesn't meet my eye. I shiver, but not because I'm only wearing his T-shirt.

"There's something I've been wanting . . . that I need to tell you."

Butterflies start kickboxing in my stomach. I don't want to hear whatever put that hitch in his voice.

Now he meets my eyes, and his are filled with panic, which is something a big-league pitcher never shows.

If he's about to confess he cheated on me, I don't want to hear it. Not today. Maybe not ever. Confession might be good for the soul, but I don't think it's good for a relationship. And it's definitely not good for a bride to hear from her groom one week before their wedding.

"No." I put out a hand to stop him. "Don't." I shake my head. "Because once you say it . . . you'll never be able to take it back. And I'll never be able to unhear it."

When he clasps my hands between his, I tell myself it's okay. That we all make mistakes. Though I'm pretty sure cheating is technically more of a sin than a mistake.

"I'm sorrier than I can ever say." His voice shakes with emotion. "But . . ."

"Oh, God." I close my eyes and tell myself that it doesn't matter who *she* was. I don't need details. And I don't want to know her name. All I have to do is listen to his apology so that I can forgive him. And at some point, I'll find a way to get over it. *Unless it's someone I know. Or a close friend. Or . . .*

His hands crush mine. My heart is a drum trying to beat its way out of my chest.

"I can't marry you," he blurts. "I wish I could, but I can't."

"What?" My eyes fly open. I drag a breath of air into my lungs, but with all the blood whooshing in my ears, I must not have heard him right. "What did you say?"

"I said, I can't go through with the wedding. I'm not ready to get married."

I rip my hands out of his. My head moves back and forth in denial.

"Think about it, Erin. We've been together for so long. Don't you ever wonder what you've missed? What you might miss in the future?" His pleading look is an arrow through the heart. A slap across the face.

"No." My head is still wagging back and forth. "No, I don't. Not ever."

"Well, you should. You're only twenty-three, and you've already spent your entire life with one person."

The anger is sharp and clean. It's all that keeps me from collapsing in a heap on the floor. "Don't you dare act like you're only thinking of me. You said you loved me and wanted to marry me. You said you wanted to have children, build a family."

"I do love you. But getting married? Having children right away? That was your dream, not mine. I didn't want to lose you."

"And now you can't wait to be rid of me."

"That's not true. But if I'm going to live up to my potential, make the most of the incredible opportunity I've been given, I've got to focus on my pitching. On development."

"And what about me? What about what I want?" My voice breaks.

"You should be focused on your own development, too, Erin. You're smart and driven. You can do anything you set your mind to." He swallows. "Up until now that's mostly been me."

"I know you don't mean this. You can't." My heart is racing so fast I'm afraid it's going to jump out of my chest. "It's normal to have cold feet—especially for guys. It's probably just nerves. I'm sure it'll pass."

He's the one shaking his head now.

"I know. Maybe we just need to give each other some space this week." I'm pleading now. "Let the anticipation build. We could go talk to Father Ryan."

His hands retake mine. His eyes are filled with regret, but there's not a trace of indecision in them. "No. I feel like we've been on this runaway train. I need to get off."

Something warm and wet and salty lands on my tongue. I'm crying. "But a hundred and fifty people are coming to see us get married. You can't do this."

"I'm sorry. I know I should have said something sooner. But I didn't want to ruin Christmas . . ."

The fact that he spent what I thought was such a beautiful holiday working up the courage to have this conversation is its own mushroom cloud of pain. "Are you frickin' kidding me? You've ruined everything!"

I spring to my feet and race out of the kitchen and into the foyer, where I scoop up my purse and car keys and sprint out the front door.

"Erin! Come back! You can't . . ."

The elevator door closes. I only notice that I'm not wearing shoes or anything but Josh's shirt when I step out of the elevator into the unheated garage. Worse than the cold air swirling up my bare legs is the moment I press the key fob and Josh's Maserati beeps in response. *Crap.* There's no way I'm going back upstairs, so I slide my bare ass across the cold leather seat. Once I figure out how to move that seat forward far enough to reach the gas pedal, I fire up the engine and back out of the space.

I drive too fast and sob so hard that it's a miracle I don't get pulled over or cause a pileup. Somehow, I make it to my parents' and am desperately grateful that their car isn't there. I'm even more grateful that my brothers' aren't, either.

After turning off the engine with shaky fingers, I lay my forehead on the steering wheel while I try to stop crying, gather my thoughts, and un-hear the things Josh said. Only I can't manage any of those things. I don't know how long I sit there before I finally find the strength to get out of the car and make my wobbly way inside.

In my bedroom, I pull off Josh's T-shirt, stomp on it with my dirty bare feet, and throw it in the trash. Then I pull on my ancient plaid flannel pajamas and crawl into my childhood bed wishing I'd never woken up this morning, that everything that's happened today was nothing more than a bad dream.

But no matter how far I burrow under the covers, no matter how hard I shake and cry, no matter how much I try to pretend Josh never called off our wedding, every word he said is now seared into my brain. So is the fact that I never, ever imagined that I wouldn't be enough for Josh when he's been everything to me.

For such a long-term planner, I have certainly turned out to be exceptionally shortsighted.

Seven

Jazmine

My sister Thea's personal mantra is "never give up, never surrender," a line from the *Star Trek* spoof *Galaxy Quest* that we watched ad nauseam when we were kids. Normally, I admire her drive and determination. Except when it's aimed at me.

When she calls, I'm at the Mercedes-Benz Stadium where the Chick-fil-A Peach Bowl is about to start. I have my eye on a running back who'll be a senior next year.

"I'm working," I say when I answer my phone.

"Girl, if I only reached out when you weren't working, we'd never talk at all."

I don't argue, because there is some truth to this. Plus, if I argue, this call will last way longer than it needs to. Because as I believe I mentioned, my older sister is more Mack Truck than Machiavelli. She does not back down. Ever.

"I just wanted to let you know that Derrick Warren is coming to our New Year's Eve party and he *really* wants to meet you."

I wonder for about a second whether Derrick Warren *really* wants to meet me any more than I *really* want to meet him. But at least I have a legitimate excuse this time. (Yes, I've made some up in the past, mostly to avoid becoming roadkill beneath her wheels.)

"That's nice to hear," I say as sincerely as I can. "But I'll be in Tampa. I've got a QB in the Outback Bowl that I'm about to sign." This, happily, is true. There've been lots of bigger agents buzzing around him, including "he who must not be named," but I have an inside track. That inside track is his mother, Beverly, who appreciates the fact that I have firsthand experience with the pressures of being a college athlete and that we are both single mothers.

"Can't you come to our party and then fly down to Tampa on the first?"

"No. I can't. Because I'm having dinner with the QB's mother on New Year's Eve, and I'm not about to take a chance on letting anyone else get close to her right now."

"But Derrick might . . ."

". . . meet somebody else? That's a risk I'll have to take. And if he's as new to town as you say, he *should* meet as many people as possible. I'm not exactly the only single woman you know in Atlanta."

"No, but you're the only one who's my sister."

"I'm willing to meet him when things slow down," I say more to get Thea off my back than anything else.

"I'm taking that as a promise, and I'm holding you to it."

This is not an idle threat, but there's no point in worrying about forces of nature like my sister. I have more immediate issues.

The Peach Bowl is a nail-biter that South Carolina, ultimately, loses. Which makes the running back slightly less cocky and a lot more eager to sign.

Three days later in Tampa, Beverly Sizemore and I spend a fairly quiet New Year's Eve at Bern's Steak House. With its red velvet and brocade decor, old-school waiters, homegrown beef, and deservedly famous wine cellar, it's the perfect place to dine with clients and potential clients. And I'm not the only agent making the most of the ambience. I freeze for a moment when

I spot who I think is Rich Hanson slithering out of the bar and toward a private dining room.

"Jazmine?" Beverly leans across the table. "Are you all right?"

"Yes. Sorry." I glance back toward the bar, but there's no sign of the snake. Nonetheless, I don't leave Beverly alone, not even to go to the ladies' room. Just in case you-know-who wasn't an unpleasant figment of my imagination.

"Has anyone else approached you lately about representing Kaden?" I ask as we finish up coffee and dessert and receive our individual bills. (I have never disobeyed NCAA guidelines, and I'm not about to start. There will be plenty of opportunities to treat Beverly to meals once Kade turns pro.)

"Does a bear shit in the woods?" She snorts. "I'll be glad when tomorrow's over. Once Kade officially signs with Star-Sports Advisors, I assume the sharks will finally stop circling?"

"Well, the most predatory sharks have to keep swimming or die. But I hope you know that I'll protect and represent Kaden as if he were my own flesh and blood."

"I do. In fact, I'm counting on it." She reaches out and places her hand on mine. "Otherwise, I wouldn't be sitting here right now. I'm not just here for the steak."

Sara

Having Mitch home for the whole week of Christmas reminds me just how much I've missed him and our life before Dorothy's surgery and his new position in Birmingham. I've spent the last several months telling myself I'm fine on my own. But the truth is, life is so much better and brighter when he's here.

Even Dorothy seems happier. Or at least less unhappy than usual.

It's almost midnight now. The new year is about to start.

Dorothy went to her bedroom a couple hours ago, and I'm sa-voring this rare alone time every bit as much as the bottle of champagne that we're in the process of finishing. The TV over the fireplace is muted so we can watch the ball drop in Times Square. Jazz plays softly in the background.

Mitch refills both our glasses and lifts his to mine. "Here's lookin' at you, kid."

"And you."

We both take a long swallow. The champagne bubbles down my throat.

"I know these last months have been hard on you," Mitch says softly. "But I really appreciate how great you've been to my mother. She isn't always the easiest person to have around."

I blush at the compliment and grow warm under his gaze. "I know it must be difficult to be alone and getting older. The surgery was hard on her."

"You're a saint. Knowing she has you looking out for her means a lot to me." He places a kiss on the top of my head. "Having you here to come back to means even more."

We drain our glasses and look into each other's eyes. My husband has always acted as if he sees me as a "Titian-haired goddess," not the carrot-haired woman with too many freckles that stares back from the mirror.

He leans in and presses his lips to mine.

"Ummm. You taste like champagne."

"And *you* taste like heaven." The way he looks into my eyes as he says this makes me feel as fizzy as the champagne.

"I miss you when you're gone all week."

"And I miss you." He leans in and kisses me again, more slowly this time.

"But I . . . I do worry what spending so much time apart could do to our relationship."

"And here I was thinking it adds a little extra spice to things." His eyes darken. The look he gives me is so intimate it makes my pulse skitter beneath my skin. "You know what they say about absence and the heart . . ." He lowers his head and nuzzles my ear. "I feel myself growing *fonder* by the second."

My arms loop around his neck. He pulls me into his lap.

"Are you happy with the new position?" I ask.

"Oh yeah." He repositions me so that I feel every inch of his erection. "I absolutely love it."

"Very funny." I nibble at his lip and wriggle in his lap. Because how can I not when he makes me feel so sexy? So not my usual self? "But you *are* happy with the new job?"

"I am. But you know what would make me even happier?"

I wriggle further onto his lap and raise an eyebrow in question.

"Definitely that." He unbuttons my blouse, palms a breast, then skims his thumb across my nipple. "And a little bit of *this* . . ."

I shiver as he carries me half-naked and fully aroused to our bedroom. Where he proceeds to make us both deliriously happy.

I wake the next morning with Mitch's body wrapped around mine.

My eyes slit open. Morning light streams through the bedroom window and splashes across the wood floor.

This is the first and only house I've ever owned. Mitch and I bought it right after we got married and have spent the years since putting our personal stamp on it. For someone who moved from foster home to foster home and then apartment to apartment, owning this house, knowing that I couldn't be removed from it or sent elsewhere, meant everything.

Mitch's breath is warm on the back of my neck. His arm

folds over my waist. His presence fills up the house and makes it "home" in a way I can't manage on my own.

I smile and snuggle closer. I feel loved. Protected. Happy.

Agreeing to give up this home, my job, the friends I've made, so that Mitch could take the new position he was offered was one of the most difficult choices I've ever made. In appreciation of that sacrifice, he insisted I finish out the school year before we even put the house on the market or begin to look for a new one in Birmingham.

But this morning, the promise of the new year crooks its finger. I'm eager, even impatient, to get started.

I ease out of bed, pull on a bathrobe, and pick up the clothes strewn across the floor with a wicked sense of satisfaction.

There's no sign of Dorothy as I pad into the laundry room to drop the dirty clothes in the basket. Soon I'm sitting at the kitchen table sipping coffee, watching squirrels toboggan down the tree trunks while birds land and take off from the rim of the frozen birdbath.

I've been a busy elf. There are eggs to scramble, bread to toast, and bacon to fry. A bottle of syrup tucked in the corner of the refrigerator turns my thoughts to French toast, which used to be a favorite weekend treat. In that moment, I'm inspired to make the kind of breakfast I rarely bother with for myself and that Dorothy has never seemed interested in.

As if conjured by my thoughts, she comes into the kitchen fully dressed and made up, no doubt in honor of her son's presence. "Oh." She looks decidedly disappointed when she realizes it's only me.

"I didn't have the heart to wake him."

She sniffs. "It's almost ten o'clock."

"True. But it's a holiday." And the surprisingly stellar start of what I hope will be an equally stellar year. "Happy New Year, Dorothy."

"Thank you." Another sniff. "The same to you." She offers the pleasantry as if expecting a lightning bolt or clap of thunder. When neither of these things happen, I begin to crack eggs into a bowl. She pours herself a cup of coffee.

"I thought French toast might be more fun than the traditional black-eyed peas and collard greens."

She nods and sips her coffee tentatively as I beat the eggs and open a loaf of bread. The pan is heating over the flame when the sound of our bedroom shower reaches us. I grin as I dunk slices of bread in the mixture, then lay them in the pan.

Mitch has almost always come home on the weekends, especially since his mother has been living here, but maybe I could go to Birmingham next weekend so that we can start looking at houses and I can see the schools I'm applying to in person.

The egg-coated pieces of bread sizzle merrily in the pan. I flush with memory of last night's lovemaking and am careful not to look Dorothy in the eye when I ask her to please cut up some fruit. She hesitates just long enough to make me regret asking, then sighs in a beleaguered way when she pulls open the refrigerator door.

When the first pieces of French toast come out of the pan and new ones are sizzling, I set the table thinking that maybe Mitch can have a talk with her after breakfast. If we buy a house in Birmingham and create a timeline for a move there, surely that will help Dorothy commit to her own move back to Greenville.

Dorothy sets the bowl of fruit on the center of the table with a huff that I ignore. I'm checking the last pieces of French toast when I hear a buzzing in the laundry room. When it doesn't stop, I follow the sound to where I find a cell phone vibrating madly against the bottom of the laundry basket.

"All right already!" Impatient to get back to breakfast before it burns, I raise the phone to my ear. "Hello?!"

There's no response. I'm about to hang up when a little boy's voice pipes, "Is this Mitchhull Wayleb's pone?"

I pull the phone away from my ear and am about to hang up when I realize that although the cell phone isn't one of the pair we bought together, it can only belong to Mitch. The only person on the planet who scoffs at password protection.

"Who is this, and to whom do you wish to speak?" I ask in my teacher's voice.

"This is Mitchhull, too," the child replies. "An I wanna speak to my daddy!"

Eight

Sara

I'm in the bedroom with no idea how I got there, stalking into the bathroom where Mitch is standing in front of a steamy mirror, shaving cream covering his face, naked except for the towel around his hips.

I barely wait for him to turn around before I'm shoving the phone at him. "It's for you!"

"Hey! What the hell?" Mitch glances at the phone, then up at me. "Where did you get that?" He grabs the phone. "What have you done?"

"I should be asking you those questions," I hiss. "I *am* asking you those questions."

He wipes the shaving cream off his face, but he doesn't speak.

"There's a little boy named *Mitchhull* on the line. He wants to speak to his *daddy*."

The color leeches from Mitch's face. His eyes close in what looks like pain. Any shred of hope that I've misheard, that this is a prank or, please God, a surprisingly serendipitous wrong number, is ripped away. When his eyes open, they're pinned to mine.

"You have a cell phone I didn't even know existed." Disbelief is etched in every word. "And unless this is some bizarre, tasteless joke or we're on the reimagined version of *Punk'd*, you also have a child."

I wait for him to deny it. To reassure me that this couldn't possibly be true. Instead, he turns and walks calmly into the closet. I follow him far less calmly, dogging his heels. "After all these years of refusing to even consider getting pregnant, even though you know why it matters so much to me, how could you have a son?"

Mitch's eyes flit around the closet as if considering avenues of escape. He drops the towel and steps into underwear and jeans, then pulls on a long-sleeved T-shirt as if getting dressed is the only thing on his mind. As if the phone call never happened. As if I haven't asked him the most important question of our married life. As if that marriage isn't suddenly and inexplicably on the line.

I follow him into the bedroom and plant myself in front of him as he shoves the phone in his pocket. "Answer me, damn it! Answer me or . . . or get out!" I point toward the bedroom door.

He sets his jaw, pulls his suitcase out from under the bed, then begins to stuff clothes into it. He stalks into the bathroom and comes out zipping his Dopp kit in harsh, jerky movements.

"You're going to leave without answering?"

"You told me to get out." His reasonable tone is even more incendiary than his silence.

"No, I asked you to explain what's going on. You *owe* me an answer!" I cry. Even though we both know that not denying this monstrous possibility is its own answer.

"There would be absolutely no point in trying to explain anything given the state you're in."

"The state I'm in?" My "state" could incinerate an entire city.

He yanks his suitcase off the bed.

"You're not really going to turn and run?" I ask even as he strides out of the bedroom and through the house.

The front door slams. His car roars to life. He is gone.

Rooted to the floor, I sway, trying to absorb what's happened. When I finally make my way into the kitchen, Dorothy pounces. "He didn't even say goodbye to me. What did you do? Why did you run him off?"

"Did you know that Mitch has a child?"

"Don't be silly," she scoffs.

"A little boy called on Mitch's phone and asked to speak to his 'daddy.'"

"That's ridiculous. It must have been a wrong number and you've jumped to the worst possible conclusion." Her arms fold across her chest. Her eyes narrow.

"No, it wasn't. It was a phone I've never seen before. He said his name is Mitchell, too. He sounded about three, maybe four."

"Rubbish." The word is a curse and an indictment.

"Mitch didn't deny it."

"Of course he didn't deny it. He must have been crushed that you could accuse him of such a thing. I can't imagine what you were thinking!" She turns and marches out of the kitchen.

My heart aches so badly I think it might actually be broken. With a sob I run into the bedroom, slam the door, and throw myself on the bed that still smells of champagne and sex and the already broken promise of a sparkly new year.

Jazmine

I've been on the road the entire first week of January. Today I'm popping into the office to plot out the rest of the month and check on Louise, who's decided to move to Memphis to take care of her mother full-time.

"Happy New Year!" Louise says as I approach. "I almost forgot what you looked like."

"Ha!" I say as we hug. "What was your name again?"

She follows me into my office and drops into the chair in front of my desk on which mail and messages are neatly arranged in Louise's signature "from urgent to when you have time" order.

"Ah, bless you." I sit down behind my desk. "Are you absolutely sure you have to move to Memphis?"

"I am. My sister's with Mom now, but she's using up all her vacation days and every bit of sick leave to give me time to help you find and train my replacement and get my house on the market. I've got exactly five weeks. I've already put together a list of possible replacements."

She hands me a stack of résumés with her comments affixed on sticky notes. I know without asking that they're arranged in order from "would not hesitate" to "definitely good enough."

I leaf through them. "These look interesting, but I've pretty much decided to offer the job to Erin. She did a great job under difficult circumstances. She's a quick study. And she's not as ornery as you are. I'd like you to reach out and see how soon she can start after she gets back from her honeymoon."

Louise shoots me a look of surprise. "That girl didn't go on a honeymoon."

"What are you talking about?"

"She didn't go on a honeymoon because they didn't get married," Louise states with certainty. "I just found out this morning, but I . . . well, I assumed you already knew."

"What happened?"

She lowers her voice. "He called off the wedding."

"Oh no!" I remember Erin's excitement. Her certainty, since childhood, that she and Josh were destined to be together. And although the circumstances are different, I know exactly how it feels to have a longtime love snatched away just when your real future together is about to begin. "I didn't see so much as a peep in the press or a post on social media."

"Apparently, Josh didn't want Erin embarrassed. And Larry didn't want Josh to look bad," Louise says. "Especially not over the holidays, when things are slow and something like this could blow up."

I can imagine how many favors were called in to keep this quiet. "Let me guess. A release is going out today stating that it was a mutual decision. That they'll always be the best of friends. Yada, yada . . ."

Louise nods. "And we have all been reminded that is the only acceptable comment."

I close my eyes in memory. If it hadn't been for the baby growing inside me, I might not have survived the loss of the man and the sport that I loved. If I hadn't had the need to support our child, I doubt I would have found the strength to pursue a law degree, which allowed me to help the unsigned Mo Morgan, which led me to become a sports agent. Without a purpose, something to hold on to, it's too easy to spiral into the pit of grief and never find your way back out.

"Please get Erin on the phone for me, so I can offer her the job."

Louise sighs.

"Why are you looking at me like that?"

"Because this is probably the last place that girl wants to work right now. And I doubt Larry's going to think she should."

"I am contractually able to hire anyone I choose. That's the advantage of being an attorney and drawing up your own employment contract. I don't need Larry's permission."

"You may not need his permission, but it couldn't hurt to have his blessing." Louise gives me her most persuasive smile. The one that bends lesser mortals to her will.

"Fine. Will you . . ."

". . . I'll check and see if he's in."

Louise goes to her desk. Two minutes later, she buzzes me. "He can see you now. Oh, I almost forgot. There's something else you need to know . . ." she begins.

I'm already on my feet and headed toward her desk. "I'll be right back. We can catch up then, and you can get the paperwork started. The more time she has to train under you, the better."

"But . . . I need to tell you that . . ."

"Back in a few." I stride past her and move quickly down the corridor. After a nod to Larry's assistant, I rap on his open door.

"Jazz. Happy New Year!" Larry beams.

"You, too!" I drop into the chair across from his desk and beam back.

"And congrats on signing Kade Sizemore and locking up that running back from South Carolina. What a great start to the new year."

"Thanks. I have some thoughts about that shortstop I told you about. I've made plans to head down to spring training in February. And I've been wanting to talk to you about that shit that Rich Hanson pulled with Tyrone Browning's endorsement deal."

"Yeah, there's something we have to clear up about that," Larry says. "I . . ."

"Before we get to that, I wanted to tell you that I'm planning to hire Erin Richmond to replace Louise. I'd like to bring her on as quickly as possible so that Louise can help get her up to speed."

"You must not have heard about her and Josh," Larry says.

"Oh, I heard. The boy changed his mind. He's entitled. But I'd say this would make Erin all the more eager to lock up a full-time job in her chosen field. She's smart. And she catches on fast."

"That *boy* is an important client," Larry replies. "With a hundred-plus fastball and a huge future in front of him. I wouldn't want him to be *uncomfortable* at the agency he's chosen to represent him."

"Uncomfortable?"

"Think about it, Jazmine. That girl has to be upset with him for calling off their wedding. We don't want him to feel he has to avoid coming by the office or interfacing with me or anyone else here."

"So, you're suggesting that she can't work at StarSports Advisors in any capacity because *he* decided not to marry her?"

"Yes."

"That's like being put in the penalty box for the opposing team's penalty."

"Josh Stevens is our client. Our goal, our job, really, is to keep his career and his life running smoothly."

I try to clamp down on my anger. There's nothing to be gained by calling out the founder of the firm on his antiquated thinking. But passing up the candidate I've chosen because a twenty-five-year-old athlete might suffer a minute or two of embarrassment feels wrong on every level. I want to hire Erin because of her abilities. And because this job will give her something to hold on to, a reason to get out of bed in the morning.

I'm about to enumerate Erin's qualities when a knock sounds on the office door. Before Larry calls out for the person to enter, Rich Hanson strolls in.

Larry doesn't look at all surprised to see him. I, on the other hand, am stunned. I meet the hazel eyes that are an odd mix of brown and gold and framed by dark lashes. He's just over six feet with a loose-limbed, lightly muscled body. A winter tan has deepened his pale skin and gives his angular features a healthy glow. His blond hair is sun-streaked and just shy of shaggy.

"What on earth are you doing here?"

"That's what I wanted to tell you," Larry says. "Rich has joined the firm. Brought quite a lot of major-league talent with him." He stands and claps Rich on the back. "He's going to head up our football division and help look for new opportunities."

This is a nightmare. Only I'm wide awake. "He's a snake. He can't be trusted."

"Maybe as a competitor. But he's our snake now," Larry replies, unperturbed. "You two are going to have to find a way to work together. As in, I expect you both to play nice."

"I've never understood what you have against me." Rich smiles.

"You mean besides your overweening aggressiveness? The need to win at all costs? Your glee at poaching from other agents?"

"Goodness, but I seem to have made a strong impression." Hanson is still smiling. He even flashes a dimple.

"Yes. Kind of like cholera. The plague. A knitting needle in the eye."

Hanson just laughs. As if we are engaging in banter and not opening hostilities.

"Rich brings a lot of years of experience to the table," Larry says. "Say, Rich, what do you think of Jazmine hiring Josh Stevens's former fiancée to work for her?"

"The one he dumped a week before the wedding?" Hanson shoves his hands in his pockets. "I'd advise against it. We wouldn't want Josh feeling uncomfortable."

The two men smile at each other, completely at ease with their draconian view of the world.

"Well, then." I get to my feet as casually as I can. "I guess it's a good thing that I don't need anyone's approval or permission to offer the job to whomever I choose."

I nod politely at Larry. I don't even glance at Rich Hanson. Because if there's still a smile on his face, I will have no choice but to wipe it off.

Nine

Sara

It's been just over a week since Mitch fled. I am going through the motions of my life, but nothing really penetrates the heavy fog that has settled around me.

My calls and texts to Mitch's cell phone have gone unanswered, so I still have no idea what's going on in Birmingham or how my husband could possibly have a child old enough to make a phone call without me having known of his existence.

I tell myself this child is the result of some meaningless one-night stand, a single transgression that has suddenly popped up to haunt us. That it's only Mitch's shame preventing him from talking to me. But that doesn't quite explain the secret cell phone. Or how this child, who claims his name is also Mitchell, had access to it.

School's back in, and I can't imagine making it through another day trying to pretend that nothing's wrong. Despite all my years attempting to appear happy and well-adjusted and "no trouble at all" in front of foster parents, I'm just not that good an actress. I need to sit down with Mitchell face-to-face and make him tell me what the hell is going on.

On Saturday morning, I get out of bed early after a sleepless night and begin to dress for the drive to Birmingham.

I'm not a religious person, but I've spent the last four days praying that I'm not going to discover that the woman Mitch impregnated has also resurfaced. Or that he's taken advantage of living in another city to sleep with a string of women who are young and beautiful, or outgoing and entertaining; in short, all the things I'm not.

Because when you're tall and thin and plain, with a mop of stick-straight red hair that conjures comparisons to Anne of Green Gables and Pippi Longstocking (or a very tall version of Raggedy Ann), you live in fear that the person you love will discover they can do better. Or maybe you fear that they've always known that and have nonetheless unaccountably opted for available and grateful.

Dorothy's at the kitchen table, clutching a cup of coffee and staring morosely out the window. She's become even quieter since Mitch's New Year's Day declaration if you don't count the condemning looks and tragic sighs. She also looks older and frailer, but then so do I.

"I'm driving to Birmingham to see Mitch. Do you want to come?"

"But it's Saturday. I thought maybe he'd be coming home. Like he always does." Her gaze turns accusing. "You know, once he'd had time to get over the unfortunate ruckus you started."

"That I started?" Dorothy is clearly in denial. But then Mitch and I have almost never argued because I do not make waves. Or "start" things. I excel at giving in and smoothing things over. But a heretofore unknown child? Even the most careful, nonconfrontational person would have trouble staying calm after that kind of revelation. "He hasn't returned any of my calls. We haven't discussed what happened in any way." This in itself is almost as alarming as the "ruckus" Dorothy alluded to. I have no idea what state of mind he's in. Or how he might be dealing with this mess. "I don't see how he could just show up as if nothing has happened."

She sighs another beleaguered sigh. "Does he know you're coming?"

"No."

My mother-in-law stares at me as if I've lost my mind. Which is entirely possible.

I'd planned to be on the road long before Dorothy got up, but I've been dragging my feet because I have no idea what's going to happen when I get there. And it occurs to me that she has as much right as I do to find out what her son is up to.

"You're joking."

"No." I seriously doubt I have a scintilla of a sense of humor left.

"And your plan is?"

I shrug even though my stomach twists. A plan would be good. But so far all I've come up with is showing up at his apartment and forcing him to tell me what's going on.

"You must have a plan of some kind. Something you hope to gain from showing up unannounced." Her tone manages to be both disapproving and matter-of-fact. As if she's still the efficiency expert demanding a clear and concise accounting of what each move is meant to accomplish.

I doubt there's anything to be gained. I'm not even sure there's anything to salvage. All I know is that my husband needs to explain himself and his actions. "He has a child, Dorothy."

"He didn't say that," she replies stubbornly.

"But he didn't deny it. I need to know what's really happened and what it means."

"It can't mean anything," she snaps.

"How can you say that?"

Her chin juts. "Because for better or worse, *you're* the one he's married to. *You're* his wife. Although you haven't been acting like it, staying in another city like you have, not knowing what's going on."

The blow lands way beneath the belt. If we were in a ring, I'd be staggering to the mat. "Did *you* know what was going on?"

Her face reveals her fury, her disappointment, frustration at her impotence. All the things I feel. "No. No, I didn't."

"Well, then. I'd think we'd both want to understand what's going on. And if you do have a grandson"—my lips tremble on the word—"I'd think you'd want to meet him."

Her lips clamp shut. Exactly the way her son's did. Only she doesn't run.

We make the trip in silence. I keep my eyes on the road and my hands on the wheel, as if being a safe driver will somehow protect me from whatever is about to happen.

We stop at a grocery store about a mile from Mitch's apartment, and I call his cell phone one last time while Dorothy downs a bottled water. When he doesn't answer, I leave another message that doesn't include the fact that we're in Birmingham. For all I know, he might flee the building. Or perhaps he already has.

In the grocery store restroom, I splash water on my face and put Refresh drops in my eyes. Then I apply makeup with a hand that's almost as shaky as my stomach. I really wish bathroom vending machines included emotional armor along with tampons and sanitary napkins.

The condominium complex caters to corporate clients, and though it's not designed for high rollers, it's well maintained. I helped Mitch move into his fifth-floor apartment, which overlooks the swimming pool, but haven't been back since.

"Does Mitch know we're coming?" Dorothy asks for what I think is the fourth time as we ride up in the elevator.

"I called and texted saying that we need to talk," I answer yet again. "He still hasn't responded."

"And if he's not here?" she asks, her voice hushed as we step off the elevator.

"We'll wait. Or I'll go down and ask the manager for a key. I *am* on the lease. And as you pointed out, I'm his wife. Worst-case scenario, I ask the manager to text Mitch. Maybe that would get his attention." My voice sounds less than matter-of-fact.

Outside his apartment, I raise one fist, but I can't quite find the strength to knock.

If Dorothy weren't standing beside me with her chin up and her eyes laser focused on the door, I might already be sprinting for the elevator. Instead, I knock briskly. I do not give in to the temptation to yell, "Police! Open up!"

Dorothy and I stare at the door for what feels like an eternity. I don't think I'm the only one of us willing it to open while praying it stays closed.

I'm about to give up and find the office when the door opens.

Mitch stands in the opening. I wasn't expecting him to throw his arms around me, but I wasn't expecting the look of horror on his face, either.

I also wasn't expecting the adorable little boy who has not only Mitch's name but his face. And I sure as hell wasn't expecting the beautiful and hugely pregnant woman standing next to him.

> speech·less
> 'spēCHləs/
> *adjective*
> unable to speak, especially as the temporary
> result of shock or some strong emotion
> Ex: "I am speechless at this proof of my hus-
> band's infidelity."

Erin

You know that thing people say about how when the going gets tough the tough get going? I always thought I was one of the tough ones; the kind of ordinary person who steps up in an emergency. That even though I'm small, I could tap into some sort of superhuman strength if I had to pull a stranger from a burning building or foil a kidnap attempt.

Now I think I'm way more wuss than Wonder Woman. Because ever since Josh called off our wedding, I've been lying in my childhood bed feeling sorry for myself.

Other than trying to tempt me with food and urging basic hygiene, my parents have mostly left me alone, believing I just need time.

The group chat that Katrina Hopkins, my best friend and maid of honor, set up the day, practically the minute, Josh and I got engaged pings constantly with validation and encouragement . . . You're the best . . . he sucks . . . what a dick . . . drinks??? . . . wanna do brunch? . . . here if you need me . . . But I don't have the energy to respond.

My brothers Ryan and Travis have offered to maim or kill Josh. Tyler offered to do both, in whichever order I choose. Only I'm too tired to think about revenge. I've loved Josh my whole life, and I don't know how to stop. Pathetic, right?

I'm lying in bed scrolling mindlessly through Instagram posts of people who have *lives* when a knock sounds on the door. "Honey?" my dad's voice calls out. "It's me."

Unlike my mother, who has never let a closed door stop her, my dad usually goes away if I don't answer. Today he walks in and sits down on the chair next to my bed. He's way too tall for the chair, which is made to fit me, and his long legs stick way out. Kind of like a male Goldilocks trying to cram himself into Baby Bear's chair. His calm, concerned presence and the worry lines creased into his forehead make fresh tears leak out of the corners of my eyes.

"You know I can't bear to see you cry."

"I know. But I'm having a hard time finding the off switch." My nose starts to run.

"It's not good for you to lie here crying." The pain in his blue eyes is clear.

"I know," I say through trembling lips. "But I don't really know how to stop."

He swallows. "You know that frown needs to get turned upside down," he says in exactly the way he used to when I was little. "Those lips were made for smiling."

Josh used to say the same thing. Only he told me they were made for kissing, too.

I close my eyes against the tears, but some still manage to squeeze out. I think of my wedding dress, perfectly tailored to fit my body alone. The one I'll never get to wear.

Then I think about the humiliating visit when Josh came to see me and I'd let myself believe he'd come to say that he'd just been nervous, that he'd come to his senses, that he couldn't possibly live without me. But he'd only come to apologize and to offer to pay for everything. I told him where he could shove his money and his lame apologies.

A sob slips out.

"It's all right. Hush now. I know you're upset. Anyone would be." My father's on the edge of his seat, his face panicked. As much as he loves me, it's clear he'd rather be anywhere but here.

He smooths a large hand over my hair and cups the side of my tearstained cheek. "Your mother didn't want me to say this, but even though his timing was truly awful, you don't want to be married to someone who isn't ready. I always thought you set your heart on Josh way too young." His smile is crooked. His eyes are filled with love. "You're only twenty-three, Erin. You have your whole life ahead of you."

"Oh, Daaaad . . ." I use what little energy I have left to crawl into his lap, where I lay my head against his chest and grab a fistful of his shirt to, hold on to just like I did when I was a toddler. It's a wonder I don't suck my thumb. His heartbeat under my ear is just as strong and steady as it was then.

"But I had such a good plan. And I stuck to it. Only everything has turned out so disa . . . disa . . . p . . . pointing."

I squall into his shirt like a child while he pets my head and makes soothing noises. "It's all right, Erin. Everything's going to be all right."

He repeats this until I finally get myself under control.

"You can't lie here forever," he says quietly. "You're going to have to give some thought to what you're going to do next."

My eyes tear up again.

"I know how much you enjoyed working for Jazmine. And you do have a degree in sports management," he says. "Maybe you should give her a call and see if she still needs help."

My head goes up. Everybody has to know by now. I don't see how I could walk into that office and face everyone. "I don't think I'm ready for that. Not yet." I might never be ready. Maybe I'll just lie here, trying not to cry, until I get really, really old. Like until I'm forty.

"I know you, sweetheart. You're strong and smart and resilient. I have every confidence that you can do anything you put your mind to."

"Except marry Josh," I say, releasing a fresh flood of tears.

"Love and marriage aren't things you *make* happen. And no amount of planning or scheduling can control the universe. In my experience, love most often happens when you're not looking for it or planning it."

He stands up easily with me in his arms, then sets me down gently on the bed. "Good night, honey. Try to get some sleep."

"G'night, Dad."

I lie there both comforted and alarmed as the door snicks closed. Because if love is something that just "happens," that means you have no control at all . . . The tears are back, riding on a wave of hopelessness.

How am I supposed to figure out what to do next when I can't even figure out how to stop crying?

Ten

Jazmine

It's the last Tuesday of the month, and the parking lot at Between the Covers is almost full by the time I arrive for our first book club meeting of the year. I considered skipping tonight because I've been away so much, but I managed to read *Educated* by Tara Westover while I was on the road, and I never feel completely "done" with a book until I've discussed it here at book club.

On the bright side, my year is off to a good start: two new clients, one verbal agreement, and opening conversations in my hunt for a new endorsement deal for Tyrone—things I would have once run by Larry but now keep completely to myself for fear that the backstabbing, client-poaching, thunder-stealing Rich Hanson may catch wind of something. When I'm forced to share a conference table with him, I sit as far away as possible and keep my interactions brief. Even a curt nod in the hallway feels too friendly.

On the somewhat dimmer side, Louise has forced me to waste almost two and a half of her final five weeks interviewing additional candidates instead of hiring Erin like I wanted to the day I marched out of Larry's office.

I've lost track of the number of times she's reminded me that just because I *can* hire someone Larry objects to doesn't mean I should, but so far none of the applicants come close to Erin in focus, organization, and initiative, the three things I value most in Louise. And, of course, Erin and I have both had our lives ripped apart by the loss of the person we planned to spend that life with. I want to take her under my wing and help her become the badass I think she could be. And, okay, it would be a bit of a "fuck you" to Rich Hanson, who weighed in against her. And to Larry, who brought him into the firm.

I huddle into my coat as I cross the parking lot, my eyes on the warm, welcoming light that spills out of the store windows. The buzz of conversation and the smell of polished wood and books greet me when I step inside.

My shoulders relax, and I'm pretty sure my blood pressure goes down even before Annell throws her arms around me. "Happy New Year!" Her hug is followed by a kiss on both cheeks—an official invitation into what has always been a no-stress, no-judgment zone. "Did you and Maya have a good holiday?"

"We did. You?" Her voice as she fills me in is warm and soothing. I love this store and its full-to-bursting bookshelves, which are broken up by reading nooks and conversation areas defined by brightly patterned rugs and well-placed sofas and chairs. Book posters signed by their authors cover the walls. A hand-lettered sign warns, DON'T JUDGE A BOOK BY ITS MOVIE! Charm, who's worked for Annell as long as I've been a customer, smiles her hello from behind the register.

A children's section stretches across one side of the room with child-size tables and chairs. The story corner where Annell reads to a gang of children every Saturday used to be Maya's favorite spot. A spiral staircase winds up to Annell's home, which takes up the entire second floor.

Annell leads me back to the refreshments, where most of the regulars and several newcomers are already mingling and munching. "We have veggies and dip and fruit kabobs for the people who are still keeping their New Year's resolutions." She motions to the first table. "Judith brought brownies and her world-famous cloud cookies for those who've fallen off the wagon. Or never got on."

"I had to get them out of the house," Judith says as I lean in for a hug from her and from Carlotta, formerly known as Carl. "Otherwise I'd eat every one of them myself."

"I put the dangerously tempting stuff in the freezer," Carlotta says as she plucks a grape from the bunch on her plate.

"People always say that, but I have yet to meet a frozen chocolate thing I couldn't eat," Judith replies. "And if it needs a little softening, isn't that what microwaves are for?"

"Yes, I believe that's why they were invented," I agree as she piles brownies and meringues on my plate. "Thanks, Judith."

"You're welcome." She watches me pop the first meringue into my mouth. "I'm trying my hardest not to be jealous of your age and your metabolism, but I am so tired of trying to make 'good choices.'" Her voice goes up oddly on the last words.

"Sex is a great calorie burner," Carlotta points out. Carl was a very attractive man when he first started coming to book club, but Carlotta is truly stunning. I assume she's burning lots of calories whenever she feels like it.

"And it's a lot more fun than the gym or even my Peloton," Judith's longtime friend, Meena, adds as she joins us. When I first met Judith and Meena, they were stay-at-home moms, raising children, volunteering, and playing on their neighborhood tennis team. When they found out I'd played at Georgia Tech, they began asking for tips and pointers. Every now and then they show up at one of Maya's local matches. They make a significant two-person cheering section.

"Of course, calories burned may vary," Meena says with a wicked smile. "Based on energy expended." Judith smiles, too, but there's an edge to her laughter, as if she's trying just a little too hard to appear lighthearted and happy.

I sigh with pleasure at my first bite into the fudge center of my brownie. "These are sooo good." I moan my way through the brownie as Judith fills someone else's plate. "I know I've said this before, but you could totally give Mrs. Fields a run for her money."

I'm still savoring the brownie when Angela McBride, tall, blond, and leggy, appears at my side and wraps me in a hug. "Hey, girl. Are you done traveling yet?"

"Mostly."

"You look like you could use some wine."

"That's funny, I was about to say the same thing about you."

"Ha!"

We step up to the drinks table and fill our glasses.

Angela is the person who first invited me to this book club, for which I'll always be grateful. Her husband, Perley, and Xavier were friends in college before Xavier went pro. I met them both when I first started dating Xavier, and even though they were a bit older and already married, we've been friends ever since. Perley and Angela were rocks that I leaned on when Xavier died. Every year on the anniversary of Xavier's death we visit his grave together then go chow down at Xavier's favorite pizza place where we consume an XX Large "Everything But the Kitchen Sink" Pizza in his honor.

We're in the middle of catching up when Annell claps her hands together like the middle school teacher she once was. "It's time to get started. Please bring your food and drink with you and take a seat." Annell ushers us through the breezeway and into the carriage house.

The walls of the carriage house are a soft seafoam green. The trim, including the partially vaulted ceiling, is white. There's a small kitchen in one corner and a bathroom in another, but the rest of the space is bright and open. A second wrought iron staircase winds up to a loft that serves as Annell's office.

The original double barn doors have been replaced with sliding glass that opens onto her garden. Opposite is a row of windows with a white wooden window seat covered by paisley velvet cushions. Folding chairs are arranged in a semicircle across from the window seat. Small tables hold our drinks and food.

Angela and I claim spots on the window seat. Judith is on my other side, with Meena beside her.

For the first time, I notice that Sara isn't here. This is highly unusual because Sara Whalen is a bookworm of the first order and rarely misses book club. When Annell can't make it, Sara leads the discussion. I lean over and ask Judith where she is.

"I'm not sure," Judith replies. "Annell said Sara hasn't been able to work the last few weekends. I think something happened with her mother-in-law."

Once everyone's situated, Annell raises her hand and the crowd falls silent.

"As most of you know, I'm Annell Barrett. I own Between the Covers, and I'm very glad you could join us tonight to discuss Tara Westover's *Educated*.

"Now." She flashes a smile. "How many of you have read the book?"

"Wonderful," she says when all hands go up. "One of our main rules is that you're always welcome even if you haven't. But we will not tiptoe around the details of any book. There *will* be spoilers."

She looks around the circle. "Since we have some new faces here tonight, let's run around the circle so that we can all introduce ourselves."

Twins Wesley and Phoebe pop up in unison. On the verge of forty, they share the same wiry build, even features, and dark wavy hair. They also share an apartment and, on occasion, clothes. "This is my brother, Wesley," Phoebe says. "He was a computer geek before there was such a thing. And he's a really awesome graphic designer."

"And this is my sister, Phoebe," Wesley says. "She knows her way around a computer pretty well herself, but she works part-time as an activities director at the Sandy Springs Senior Center, so if you're looking for a game of Monopoly or balloon volleyball or Name That Tune . . ."

". . . I'm your girl. We read everything . . ."

". . . including cereal boxes," Wesley continues. "But my favorite genre is urban fantasy."

"I like romance, especially historical with time travel," Phoebe adds. "Especially . . ."

". . . Diana Gabaldon. Don't ever get between Phoebe and her *Outlander*."

"We've been members for a long time," Phoebe says. "But recently we've started thinking that it might finally be time . . ."

". . . to give the book club a name."

They sit. No one seems sure whether to applaud or agree.

"Hmmm . . ." Annell says. "I've never wanted to curtail what we read or who might enjoy it, but maybe it's time to consider naming ourselves. I'll put a box at the front for suggestions."

I'm not too worried about the group having a name, but I wouldn't mind being able to communicate as clearly and effortlessly with Maya as Wesley and Phoebe do with each other. Or even with Thea, who will not let go of how much I need to meet Derrick Warren. And marry him. And have his babies.

Carlotta stands and introduces herself with a twirl that shows off a circle skirt in a bold geometric pattern that is one of her most recent designs. "I have loved too many books to have one favorite. But I did especially appreciate *Middlesex* and *Trans-Sister Radio*. Oh, and *The Martian*." She shrugs. "Variety *is* the spice of life."

Meena is up next. "I'm Meena. I'm recently single and am currently experimenting with online dating. I found a great photographer if anyone ever wants to do new profile pictures. My favorite book at the moment is *121 First Dates*, which sounded kind of daunting at first but is actually a really great 'how-to' manual. I will be happy to share my newly gleaned information with anyone who's interested."

Judith sways slightly as she stands. "I'm Judith. I still live in the suburbs even though my nest is empty. My daughter is getting married over Labor Day weekend. And my favorite book is *The Red Tent* even though it doesn't contain dating advice." She looks at Meena. "Yes. Still."

The young man who stands next appears to be in his late thirties. "I'm Chaz. I'm an EMT, and this is my first time here." He smiles, seeming completely unbothered that he and Wesley are the only males present. "Is that *Red Tent* book tied to *Red Sonja* in any way?" he asks. "I heard there's a remake of the film finally happening."

"Um. No. Not really," Judith says.

Meena snorts.

As I look around our circle, I'm glad that we have always been a mix of ages, occupations, genders, and ethnicities. And that newcomers are welcome. It's part of what attracted me to the group in the first place.

When it's my turn, I stay seated and say only that I'm a sports agent with StarSports Advisors. Ever since a former book club member tried to convince me to look at her ten-year-old daughter who'd pitched a no-hitter in her church softball league, I try to downplay what I do.

Angela stands and smiles her always-sunny smile. "I'm Angela and I'm an accountant." She laughs lightly. "Okay, that sounded a little more like an AA intro than I intended. I'm not actually trying to quit being a CPA. In fact, my husband, Perley, and I own our own firm. We have three daughters." She pauses and gets that happy smile that accompanies any reference to Lyllie, Mollie, and Kerina. "Even after all these years and books, my favorite is *Little Women. Pride and Prejudice* is a close second." She pauses. "And though she failed to mention it, Jazmine's is *Becoming* by Michelle Obama. I think we should consider reading it."

There are nods and murmurs.

The dark-haired woman sitting across from Angela jumps to her feet, sending a pair of golf ball earrings swinging. Despite the cold January temperatures and the fact that it's dark outside, she's wearing a golf visor with the Masters logo on it. "I'm Nancy Flaherty and I just moved to Atlanta. I'm originally from Charleston, but more recently from Florida. I'm a receptionist at a real estate firm here in Sandy Springs. My favorite book of all time is *The Greatest Game Ever Played*. Ditto for the movie. I'm a 16 handicap, and I spend as much time as possible on the golf course." She hesitates and turns to me, her smile freezing on her lips. "Do you know Tiger Woods personally?"

"Sorry. No." I shake my head. "I don't handle golfers."

The smile unfreezes. There's a small sigh of what might be relief. "Well, I do. Very personally." She winks, then takes her seat with a brisk nod and swing of her golf balls.

As the last introductions take place, Judith picks up a bottle of red wine and one of white and walks around the circle topping off glasses. Back at her seat, she tops hers off, then sets the bottles within reach.

"So," Annell says with a smile. "What did we think of the book?"

"I liked it," Angela answers quickly. "But it was hard to read about how vulnerable the narrator was. As a mother, I couldn't understand how her parents could have left their children uninoculated and uneducated."

"I could hardly read the parts when she had to do all those horribly dangerous jobs because her father made her." Carlotta shudders.

"Those kids got maimed. And the mother, too," Chaz the EMT says. "It's hard to imagine refusing to see a doctor or go to a hospital."

"Remember when she sees the term 'bipolar' for the first time and realizes that's what her father was?" Phoebe asks.

With that we are off and running. Whenever discussion slows, Annell raises another point or question. It's a very different thing to have someone directing the conversation and keeping it flowing. It's another reason I enjoy the group so much.

Judith makes the rounds again with the wine. "Are you sure you're done?" she asks when I cover my glass. Her eyes look a little unfocused. Her smile's reached the Cheshire Cat stage.

"Afraid so. I've got to drive home."

"Too bad. That's why I B-BUbered . . ." She laughs. "I mean, Ubered. Because I kind of need the alcohol tonight."

I'm not sure what to say to this. "Is everything all right, Judith?" I ask quietly.

"No, not really. But it will be."

Eleven

Judith

I zip my coat all the way up as Meena and I walk out to the parking lot, calling out our goodbyes, in plumy breaths. It takes a few tries to open the Uber app on my phone and set home as my destination. I'm fairly certain it's because my hands are frozen and not because I had too much to drink. Or it could be the small print.

"Forget Uber," Meena says. "It's freezing out here. I'll run you home."

"Don't be silly. You live in the opposite direction."

"I think I can go a little out of my way for a friend. And you won't even have to plug in an address."

"No, I really don't think . . ."

"Stop arguing and come on." She links her elbow with mine and leads me toward her car.

"All right. But you really don't have to do this."

"I know."

In the car, I fumble with the seat belt until she reaches across me and clicks it together.

"What's going on?" she asks.

"What do you mean?" I blow on my hands while the heater blasts on and begins to defrost the windshield.

"I know you. You didn't drive. You drank like you were screwing up your courage for something." Meena starts the car and backs out of the parking space.

I stare straight ahead as we drive the two-lane street that leads to Johnson Ferry Road, which will wind into East Cobb, where River Forge is.

"Fine," I say finally. "I had an appointment with your divorce attorney yesterday. Thanks for getting me in, by the way. I had no idea that the busiest time of year for divorce filings was immediately after the holidays."

"There are lots of suicides right after the holidays, too," Meena says quietly. "Clearly, it's not always the holly, jolly time it's cracked up to be."

"Yeah."

"How did it go?" Streetlights illuminate Meena's face, then cast it back into shadow.

"I liked her. She laid everything out, what would happen, the retainer, gathering financial information. How she'd position me."

The scenery flies by. The suburbs are quiet at ten P.M. on a Tuesday night. Some stores and restaurants are still open, but the parking lots are mostly empty. There are very few cars on the road.

"What made you decide to see her?" Meena asks.

"Nate didn't invite me to Europe. And then he butt-dialed me from Italy, and I was forced to hear him tell a total stranger that our spark died a long time ago and that he's just 'going through the motions.' And FYI—none of those motions include sex. I almost wish he'd been screwing around."

"No, you don't," Meena says.

"You're right. Sorry. It's just . . . the kids aren't really kids anymore, but I don't think either of them is ready for their family to cease to exist. And . . . I mean it all feels so . . . final."

"It is." Tonight, Meena is my confessor and advisor.

"Have your kids forgiven you?" I ask, not sure I want to hear the answer.

"More or less. I think they've come to understand that the divorce has made things better. At least for me. Now I have my own relationship with them, and I have to remind myself I'm not responsible for making sure they have a relationship with Stan. I'm not his spokesperson. Or his promoter.

"I'm polite when we're all together, but Stan likes to pretend that everything was fine and I just got bored." She shrugs. "I'm happier than I was in a marriage that wasn't working, but nothing's perfect. Sometimes I feel lonely. I even miss Stan now and then. But I know I did the right thing. For me."

We turn onto Upper Roswell as she continues. "The way I see it you have three choices: Suck it up, stay married, and make the best of the situation. You can spend more time with friends, take trips he's not interested in on your own, live as separate a life as you need to without actually leaving.

"Or you work on your marriage and try to make it better. Of course, that takes cooperation on both sides." Meena's gaze lands on my face. "Maybe if Nate knew he was going to lose you, he'd try harder. Stan didn't, but Nate could be different."

She stops for a last red light. "Or you file for divorce and commit yourself to creating the life you want."

"I'm fifty-five years old." At the moment it sounds like one hundred.

"I know," Meena replies. "Fortunately, there's no age limit on happiness. You could live another forty years, Jude. Are you willing to *settle* for four more decades?"

My mind swims with visions of what forty years of settling might feel like. What it would do to me. Could I even survive it?

We turn into River Forge, driving past the clubhouse and pool and the perfectly flat street where Ansley and Ethan learned to ride their bikes.

As we drive down the neighborhood's main street, our former lives are everywhere. Meena's mouth tightens when we enter the cul-de-sac we shared and cruise past her former house, on our way to mine. The Parkers' house was always part of the view from our master bedroom. Any trip to the mailbox included a quick glance to see whether Meena's Volvo was parked in their garage. When the kids were still in school, no one ever closed their garage door until the entire family was in for the night. Nowadays, I pull in and close the garage door behind me as soon as the car is off.

"God, it seems like a lifetime ago that we moved into the neighborhood," Meena muses. "I remember you coming over with homemade brownies the day we moved in."

"Yeah. Me, too. There are new versions of us moving in every day." I look at my old friend. "I wish Nate had been open to moving. Maybe we would have had a better chance at adapting somewhere new."

She's kind enough not to remind me that a new home didn't save her marriage. When we reach my house, she pulls into the driveway and stops, leaving her engine running. "So. What now?"

"Well, this afternoon I shaved body parts I didn't even know I still had. I'm going to go inside, put on my sexiest negligee, which would be my only remaining negligee, and seduce my husband." I don't add that one of my biggest fears is whether I'm still desirable enough to pull this off. "I think that falls under your marital option number two. I'm hoping that it will remind us both who we are and what we once had."

"And then?"

"Then, once he's completely relaxed, I'm going to explain that I'm tired of being taken for granted and that things have to change if we're going to stay married. I don't actually know what he'll choose, but either way, things are going to change."

Meena reaches out and squeezes my hand. "Good luck. Let me know how it goes."

The front porch is brightly lit because the lights are on timers. Inside it's pitch-dark and quiet. I flip on lights, pushing back my irritation that my husband hasn't even left a single light on, because that would require a moment of thought about someone other than himself. In the kitchen, I pour a final glass of courage, which I carry upstairs.

Nate's already in bed. He's on his back, his arms flung wide. His snores are loud and ragged. This, of course, is not exactly a turn-on. But I am a woman on a mission.

In the bathroom, I remove my clothes and slip the neatly pressed negligee over my head. If I squint and angle my body just right, I do not look too old for sex. At least not in this light.

The expensive "date night" perfume is buried in the back of my medicine cabinet covered in dust. I spritz it in strategic spots, then slather on moisturizer that my skin sucks in like a desperate woman downing a last cocktail at closing time.

I don't let myself think about how long it's been—it's like riding a bike, right? I especially don't think about exactly what I'll say afterward or how things might turn out. I want the sex to be good. Proof that we can still "connect," that the spark can still be ignited.

In the bedroom, I walk to where Nate is sprawled and snoring and pull back the covers. His chest is bare, the hair that covers it more white now than dark. His pajama bottoms are bunched below his stomach; his legs are windmilled. The pajama placket gapes open.

I wait for him to wake and look up, but his eyes remain shut. The snoring continues.

"Nate?" My voice is low and husky. "Na-aaa-te?" I coo as provocatively as I can.

The only thing moving is his chest. Air whistles through his lips as he snores.

This is not the response I was hoping for. But I do not retreat. I crouch between his legs and contemplate what lies before me. His penis flops out of the placket and curls wormlike against his thigh.

I remember an ancient joke that asks, What do you get if you have a large green ball in one hand and another large green ball in the other? Complete control of the Jolly Green Giant.

With a small smile, I take him in my palm. His eyes remain closed, but the body part I'm holding thickens.

"Nate?"

"Hmmm?"

"What would you like to see happen here?"

His eyes open. There's a weariness in them I'm not used to, but his lips quirk upward.

"I don't know. I've been dragging something awful all day. I feel like I might be fighting off the flu. But at the moment I'm tempted to just leave myself in your hands."

"Very funny," I say.

His eyes flutter shut mid-smirk. I consider my options. I could give up on pleasuring either of us and table the conversation until tomorrow. But I know this man almost as well as I know myself. He's a lot more likely to be receptive to what I have to say once he's lolling in postcoital satisfaction.

"Hang on, then. I've got this." With a smirk of my own, I hike up the negligee and position myself above him, rubbing up and down until I'm wet and he's hard. Slowly, I lower myself onto his erection. He groans, his head rolling from side to side, as I settle myself. His hands cup my buttocks when I begin to ride. They drop away as I find my rhythm, raising and lowering myself, seeking out the friction, reveling, forgetting everything including my mission as the delicious tension builds. My eyes close. My head falls back. I let myself remember the first time we made love, the look in his eyes when he asked me to marry him, the day we brought Ansley home from the hospital. Then

I lose myself in the motion, in riding him, feeling the tension mount to that exquisite breaking point just beyond the edge of reason.

His body goes rigid. He spasms, bucks. His wordless shout spurs me on as he erupts, catapulting me over the edge, into the stratosphere. Into free fall. Until I collapse on top of him, both of us slick with sweat. His heartbeat beneath my ear is a runaway freight train.

"Wow." We're both trying to catch our breath as I drag myself off him. Nate's still gasping on the bed when I throw the covers up over him and stagger to the bathroom, where I pull on a robe, wash my face, and brush my teeth. It takes some time to calm down and remember what I wanted to say.

When I get back to the bedroom, Nate's still lying flat on his back but is no longer gasping for breath. He appears to be staring up at the ceiling. Since he's not snoring, I assume he's awake.

"Nate?"

I climb into bed, my back against the headboard. I still feel warm and tingly from the orgasm and hope Nate does, too. In truth, I'd rather go to sleep—maybe even curled up in his arms—than talk, but I'm not sure I *can* sleep without getting everything off my chest.

"Nate? Are you listening?"

He doesn't answer, but his head lolls in my direction.

"Fine. Just listen, then. There are things I need to say." I draw a breath. "First of all, you butt-dialed me from Italy. Do you have any idea what it feels like to hear your husband tell a total stranger that he's 'only going through the motions'?"

Again, no response. But I can see the edge of his eyelashes, so I assume his eyes are open.

"Well, it sucks. And I am not a 'good egg,' damn it! I'm a person. A woman. Your wife. And what we just did together proves that there's still a spark. Only we both have to fan it to keep it alive."

I'm on a roll now. I get out of bed. Eager to lay it all out, to persuade him, I begin to pace the room on my side of the bed, ticking the points off on my fingers. "I believe we can find a way to regain what we've lost. We just have to *want* to. I need you to understand who I am. And care about what's important to me." I reach the end of the bedroom with its view of what used to be the Parkers' house and turn. "We're comfortably off, the kids are self-sufficient. This could be the best time of our lives. If we want it to be. But we have to share ourselves and take care of each other." I swallow. "I wasn't put on this earth to take care of you and make your life run smoothly. I should never have acted like that was all I was capable of or wanted. And you shouldn't have let me."

I stop and turn at the head of the bed. Once again, I wait for him to comment. To agree or disagree. To tell me he loves me and that he'll try harder, do better. Or even that he's done. But he just lies there.

"I can't believe this." The hope I've been nursing begins to evaporate. I thought that sex might rekindle the spark and facilitate this conversation, but I'm the one who's turned an orgasm into something more than it was. "I'm pouring my heart out here and you have nothing to say?"

I stalk over to where he's lying, talking the whole time. "How like you to not even listen. I'm telling you how we could save our marriage and avoid a divorce, and you don't even care enough to pay attention!

"I'm talking to you!" I lean over and poke his arm as hard as I can. His head still hangs to one side. I climb onto the bed to look into his open eyes. They're glazed and vacant.

"Nate?" I grab his shoulder and shake him. He's limp and unresisting. "Nate!"

I lean in until my face is only inches from his. This is when I realize that his chest is not moving up and down.

I race to the nightstand and grab my phone. I punch in 911. Praying that they really can trace a call to its location, I yell, "Help! My husband isn't breathing!" Then I shout our address into the phone and throw it down so that I can drag him onto the floor, kneel beside him, and frantically start performing CPR.

"Oh no, you don't!" I shout as I begin the compressions on his chest. "You are NOT allowed to die while I'm yelling at you!"

Twelve

Judith

I cower in the bedroom chair while the EMTs attempt to revive Nate. My vision blurs and stretches as if I'm staring into a funhouse mirror. A dull roar fills my ears as they insert a breathing tube and hook up an IV. I try to breathe deeply and calmly, like I learned in yoga, but I can't seem to catch my breath. Worse, I keep remembering the sound of Nate trying to catch his. Gasps that I assumed were of a sexual nature.

You know it's been too long since you last had sex when you can't tell a heart attack from an orgasm.

"Does your husband have a heart condition, ma'am? Does he take medication?" one of them asks while the other begins a much steadier, controlled version of CPR than the frantic version I'd managed.

"No. No medication." The answer is automatic. We belong to a concierge practice that includes yearly physicals and wellness visits. When asked, Nate brags that he has "great genes" and "the ticker of a much younger man." Then he grins and adds, "I hope he doesn't want it back." I never asked for details.

A policewoman materializes in the doorway. She scans the room, the rumpled bed, Nate on the floor with the EMTs working over him. Me in my robe and bare feet rocking in the bedroom chair. "Mrs. Aimes?"

I nod but can't take my eyes off Nate. His chest still hasn't gone up or down on its own. My own breathing is ragged.

"I'm Officer Vetrano. Is that your husband?"

"Yes." It's a whisper. My eyes are pinned to the EMTs who are putting pads on his bare chest. Connecting wires. A mechanical voice starts issuing instructions. I hold my breath as Nate's body jolts.

"Can you tell me what happened?" the officer asks.

"I don't . . . I don't know." I don't want to look at Nate's jolting body or the measured compressions that one of the EMTs performs in between. But I can't tear my eyes away. "I . . . I . . . he . . . he's only fifty-eight."

The EMTs talk calmly, their movements practiced and efficient. The machine's voice tells them to "get clear of the body" before sending another jolt of electricity through Nate's body.

"Shouldn't we be going to the hospital?" I cry at them. "Can't we take him to the hospital now?"

Neither of them answers.

"Can you tell me what happened?" the policewoman asks, trying, I assume, to distract me as another current is sent through my husband's body.

"Mrs. Aimes?" She leans closer, drawing my gaze back to her face.

"I . . . we . . ."

"Clear!" The EMTs lean away from Nate at the mechanical voice command.

I sneak a peek at Nate, who is still unresponsive. "We . . . were in bed and . . . he . . . he was gasping . . . He couldn't seem to catch his breath."

"Were you asleep?" she asks. "Did the gasping sound wake you?"

"N . . . no . . ." I flush at the memory. Riding Nate like a jockey hell-bent for the finish line. The burst of pleasure. My retreat to the bathroom. "No. We . . .

"We were . . . we had . . ." There is no way I can say this. Not to this stranger. Not in front of the EMTs who are now conferring quietly over Nate's body, their sense of urgency gone.

"Intercourse?" she asks in the same tone she might ask whether we were playing chess.

"Yes." The word comes out in a rush. "And then I went into the bathroom to . . ."

One EMT puts two fingers to Nate's neck again, then shakes his head slightly. The other nods, pulls out a cell phone, and steps away to make a call.

A sob escapes my lips as the two men begin to disconnect the wires from the pads attached to Nate's too-pale chest and stomach. This is my fault. I wanted Nate to love me more and to show it. If I hadn't been so angry, so focused on myself, I might have understood what was happening in time to save him.

The EMTs look to me. "I'm sorry," one of them says. "We weren't able to sustain a pulse or heartbeat."

I sob harder as they unfold a sheet they've brought and pull it over Nathan. This is my fault. I did this. I want to throw myself on his body—his body!—and beg his forgiveness for letting my anger and resentment blind me to what was happening. I am too wracked with guilt to do anything but cry as I watch the EMTs pack up their equipment.

"Do you have family or friends nearby?" the officer asks when we're alone. "Someone I can call?"

At first, I don't understand the question. When I do, it takes time to find an answer and even longer to express it.

"The medical examiner's office will send someone to pick up the . . . your husband. From there, he'll be released to the funeral home, if you have one."

She leads me into the living room, where I sob louder and hold tightly to myself. Nate had never been one for grand gestures or the romantic surprises I craved, but he had always been prepared. His twentieth wedding anniversary gift was not platinum jewelry or crystals but joint burial plots. He had made sure our wills were updated periodically and that all of us knew where to find the important paperwork in the event of . . . *this*.

I rock and cry as memories bombard me. Not the things he didn't say or do that I've held against him, but the care he took with the details of our lives. The servicing of the cars, the life insurance policy, the investment portfolio meant to protect and support us in our old age. An old age that Nate will never see.

I'm still rocking and blubbering when the policewoman answers the door and Meena rushes in.

"Oh my God, Judith. Are you all right? What happened? Is Nate . . . is Nate really . . . gone?"

I nod and cry as she throws her arms around me.

"I'm here. I'm here for however long you need me. Just tell me what you want me to do and who you want to call."

Once the hugging and swaying dies down, the policewoman stands in front of me. "I'm very sorry for your loss." She hands me her card. "I'll be filing a report. If there's anything you'd like to add to what you've already told me, please be in touch."

Everything that follows moves in slow motion. The kids come home, and I'm way too freaked out to adequately cushion the blow. I have always put them first, but what I've done is too big to be pushed aside or shared. I was seriously contemplating divorcing their father. Then I let him die while I was issuing ultimatums. I made his last minutes all about me.

"Will you be all right?" Ansley asks. "I can't imagine you without each other. Whenever one of my friends' parents got divorced, I felt so sorry for them. I knew you and Dad would be together forever." Tears stream down her cheeks. "I just assumed you'd have longer."

Hannah rubs her back. "They were lucky to have each other as long as they did. Not everyone finds their soul mate."

Now I'm crying, too. Hot, salty, guilty tears. The last time we were together as a family, I was angry that their father went to Europe without me, disappointed in the gift he gave me, furious at being dismissed as a good egg. Pretending to be happy for their sake.

"You gave us an example of what marriage could be," Ethan says. "Most of my friends spent years watching their parents fight and their families come apart. They got shuttled back and forth and had to deal with stepparents and stepsiblings. Running all over the place on holidays. I always felt so lucky that you and Dad had such a great marriage. It made me feel secure, you know?"

I'm having trouble breathing now. But I'm grateful for the scrim of tears that keeps them from seeing not only my shame but my relief. That I did not destroy their childhood memories by tearing our family apart. That they didn't have to see their father as I came to see him.

"He loved you both so much," I say, confident that this at least is true. "And he was incredibly proud of you."

Is it wrong to be glad that they came home for a funeral rather than a divorce?

The church is full for Nate's funeral, an impenetrable blur of bodies and faces. I try to listen to the service, but the roaring in my ears remains, and I stare numbly at the casket. I know Nate is wearing his favorite blue suit and lucky tie, but I can't stop seeing him naked, with his head lolling to one side.

After the service, Ethan, Ansley, Hannah, and I are ushered into the funeral home's black limo. In it, we follow the hearse, clutching one another's hands.

At the graveside, I try to focus, but I keep imagining my

husband trapped in the casket, being lowered into the ground. Covered with dirt. Where he will lie alone in the dark. Forever.

Our house is packed with people by the time we arrive. Meena orchestrates the receiving and arrangement of the casseroles, without which no one in the South is allowed to mourn, and charges Stan with tending bar and lubricating the guests, beginning with me.

I accept condolences from old neighbors and a smattering of new ones, from Chickin' Lickin' store managers and longtime employees. From tennis partners and golf buddies. From the kids he helped coach on Ethan's soccer teams.

I cry at each accolade and memory. But even as I mourn Nate and our life together, my sorrow is laced with fear that my guilt will show through. That people will see it in my eyes, hear it in my voice. That they'll know that Nate was only "going through the motions" and that I had consulted a divorce attorney and was attempting to draw a line in the sand while Nate was gasping out his last breaths.

The long-standing members of book club are there in full force. Each in their own version of mourning. Wesley and Phoebe wear matching black blazers. Carlotta has on the perfect little black dress.

Sara looks like she's in mourning herself. Annell embraces me and tells me how sorry she is. Stan refills my glass. Each time he gives me a hug and says, "I can't believe he's gone."

Meena brings glasses of water to counter the alcohol and treats me as if I might break. She gives no hint that she knows exactly how Nate died, that I am drowning in guilt, that I am not the typical grieving widow. *Widow!*

Angela and Jazmine serve as Meena's "seconds," taking and retrieving coats, replenishing food platters, ushering drinkers to the bar. They join the ranks of those making sure I have food and drink even though I'm only interested in the alcohol, which blends with the Xanax and allows me to listen to other people try to say the right things while I attempt to do the same.

But inside the fog that fills my brain, it's still all about me. My loss. My anger. My guilt. My mistake.

"Your marriage was such an inspiration," Dolly, a member of the neighborhood ALTA tennis team, says. "It's rare to see people so happy."

"Oh, God. I . . . I can't . . . I'm sorry. Please . . . excuse me." I bow my head to try to hide the tears and race from the room.

Murmurs of concern follow me as I pound up the stairs.

For possibly the first time in my adult life, I am forced to abdicate even the illusion of control. There's nothing I can do about what has happened. There's nothing to arrange or choreograph. But I feel as if there's an awful lot to hide.

Sara

Judith's husband is dead. Apparently, he suffered a heart attack at home in his own bed. A prime example of "here one minute, gone the next," which is, I believe, how we'd all like to go.

I went to his funeral yesterday and spent most of the service wishing it was Mitch in that casket.

At least Judith's husband didn't choose to die. And he had the good manners to do it in his sleep. Probably with a smile on his face.

I haven't smiled in weeks. Because my husband is in another city procreating. As if he has every right to live as many lives as he likes while I take care of his mother and keep the home fires burning.

Judith is allowed, even expected, to mourn, while I'm consigned to living in limbo. Still married in the eyes of the law and pretending that all is well. That Mitch is just commuting for work and not living another life that includes children he refused to have with me.

It's been weeks since the surprise visit to Birmingham, and although I've been too hurt and angry to even attempt to reach Mitchell, I've overheard Dorothy leaving angry messages. Exhortations to at least "do the right thing," by which I think she means coming to get her and divorcing me, which she actually described as "setting the poor woman free."

I'm in the bathroom putting on makeup for my afternoon shift at Between the Covers when I hear his car pull into the drive. He doesn't park in the garage—maybe he's afraid he won't be able to get out fast enough—and since I'm behind a locked door, I take my time getting dressed and straightening my spine. Deep breathing follows.

When I leave the bedroom, I do not sprint for my car like I want to but follow the sound of voices into the kitchen, where Dorothy is staring across the table at her son, her chin quivering.

Mitchell stands and walks toward me. I resist the urge to fall back. "Why are you here?"

"I came to say I'm sorry. I never meant for any of this to happen." He says this quite sincerely.

"So, you accidentally impregnated a woman twice and are accidentally living with her and your son"—I can barely get the word out—"while pretending that we're still married and sharing a life?"

"We *are* still married," he replies.

"No. Not as far as I'm concerned, we're not."

"Legally, we are."

"Maybe on paper. But I plan to take care of that as soon as possible." My own chin quivers. "You're living the life I begged for. With another woman."

"Her name is Margot."

I shudder at the sound of her name and the way he says it. "I don't care what her name is. I don't want to know anything about her. If you came for your clothes, things that actually belong to you, be my guest." I wave my arm in the direction of the bedroom. "It'll save me the trouble of throwing them out in the yard and stomping all over them when I get back from the bookstore."

"Like some wronged heroine exacting a clichéd revenge?" His mouth quirks in amusement. "This isn't one of your romance novels."

"No, it certainly is not." I settle my purse strap over my shoulder and head for the hall closet to get my coat.

"I made a mistake," he says, following me. "And I'm here to apologize."

I yank my coat out of the closet and pull it on. "One child might be a mistake. Two—two is not a mistake. You're a father, and you clearly have a longtime relationship with that . . . that woman." I don't intend to ever speak her name. "How could you come home on weekends and make . . . have sex with me . . . and then go back to her and to your other life?"

"I didn't mean for it to happen. I slipped up and had an affair." His voice turns pleading.

"That boy . . . your son . . . has to be close to four. And she's pregnant again. You obviously have feelings for her. Do you have any idea how it makes me feel? I *begged* you to have children, and you had no problem saying no."

"Yeah, well." He shoves his hands into his pockets. "She never asked."

This sucks the air right out of my lungs. Dorothy gasps, too, from wherever she is in the kitchen. Listening. Hanging on to every word of this miserable conversation.

"Things just got out of control. I had to support him, didn't I?" Mitch says. "And she had morning sickness the whole time. And then she couldn't afford childcare, so she had to stay home with him."

Each admission is a gunshot to my chest, a hole in my heart.

"I just . . . everything spiraled all to hell. And . . . I love you. I'm still attracted to you." He offers this as if it's some great gift, then steps closer. "I can fix this."

I slap him with every ounce of fury and hurt I possess. "You have clearly lost your mind. I'm done. *We* were finished the minute you started sleeping with her, only I didn't know it." For once, I am too angry to cry. "Clear out your things. I'll be changing the locks after work."

He looks shocked to the core. I have never spoken to anyone this harshly or with this much certainty.

His mother gasps in the kitchen.

"Come on out, Dorothy," I call.

When she limps out to the foyer, I look at the two of them. "I'm pretty sure your mother is expecting you to take her with you. Or at least back to her own house."

I nod to my mother-in-law. "You always made me feel like I wasn't good enough for your son. But it's your son who isn't good enough for me."

I'm about to make my exit when Mitch says, "I, um, can't take her with me."

"What?" Dorothy and I Greek chorus.

He shifts uncomfortably from foot to foot. "There's no room for her in the Birmingham apartment. And I'm a little short on funds, so I can't take a bigger place."

"Then take her home."

He winces and gets this odd hangdog look on his face. "I can't do that, either."

"Why not?" Dorothy and I chorus once again.

"Because I had to stop making her mortgage payments so that I'd have the cash to support Margot and Mitch Junior without you finding out." He swallows and drops his eyes. "I . . . the bank has foreclosed and I . . . there's nothing I can do about it."

Dorothy's face reveals every bit of horror that I feel. Mitch cosigned the mortgage when Dorothy refinanced her home, and agreed to make the monthly payments until he'd paid back the money he'd borrowed from her.

"Are you telling me that you've lost your mother's home and now you're planning to just walk away and leave her here? What in the world is wrong with you?"

a·ghast
/ə'gast/
adjective
filled with horror or shock
Ex: "I am aghast at how ugly and self-centered my husband has proven himself to be."

Thirteen

Jazmine

On the first of February, the snow everyone was forecasting for Christmas arrives, and everything, including Hartsfield-Jackson International Airport, raises its hands and surrenders. Every time it snows here in Atlanta, we embarrass ourselves on the global stage. Frankly, I think everyone, including the equally inexperienced former Southern Californian Rich Hanson, needs to cut us some slack.

I point this out to him when he laughs at the tiny amount of snow required to shut the city down. IMHO, expecting Atlanta to have snow-moving equipment waiting for the rare snowfall that sticks is like expecting Yakutsk, Siberia, to be perfectly air-conditioned on the off chance it hits ninety for a couple of hours one day.

I tell myself that nothing Rich Hanson says can bother me. Because Sony is begging me to get Tyrone Browning to sign a multiyear endorsement deal that will, in fact, put Luther Hemmings's five million in the piggy bank range. I believe this until I run into him coming out of Larry's office, where he seems to spend an inordinate amount of time.

"Saw a picture of your new client and his girlfriend," he says, referring to Kaden Sizemore, who happens to be the MVP

QB of the Outback Bowl. "She's not exactly destined to hit the list of Hottest Athlete WAGs."

"Really?" WAGs is shorthand for wives and girlfriends. Certain troglodyte sports writers still like to debate (and continue to write about) which athletes have the hottest girlfriends and wives. "You think the fact that he doesn't *need* a showy girlfriend makes him weak?"

"Everyone knows it indicates a lack of confidence," he replies.

"Only dinosaurs think that way. And we all know what happened to them," I say. "I have a helluva lot more respect for a man—and athlete—who doesn't need a model to boost his confidence."

I look him up and down. "Do you ever have serious relationships with *real* women who can string whole multi-word sentences together?"

"Me?" Hanson asks. "I think the pot may have just called the kettle black. At least from what I hear."

I clench my jaw to keep from calling him all the names that are springing to my lips. When my phone rings, I answer it without looking. I'd rather listen to a telemarketer right now than Rich Hanson.

"Wow. I can't believe you picked up," my sister says. "I was going to leave you a message. But since I've got you, I need you to agree to a double date with us and Derrick Warren on Friday night."

"This Friday night?" I let a pleased smile curve my lips. "You know I'd love to, but I'm afraid I'm already committed. How about the Friday after that?"

Thea is stunned into silence by my sudden capitulation but recovers quickly. "That's the twelfth, Jazz, and I'm holding you to it."

"Wonderful. I promise it'll be worth the wait." My voice is

almost a purr as I hang up. I give Hanson an innocent look. "I'm sorry, what were you saying?"

When he turns and stalks silently away, I barely resist the urge to fist-pump. I'm smiling as I sail to my office. "Louise, please get Erin on the phone for me."

"But I thought you were still . . ."

"I've spoken to your entire list of candidates, and we're running out of time. The job is Erin's if she wants it."

"Yes, ma'am." I know Louise is not happy when she 'ma'am's me, but this is my decision after all. By the time I'm at my desk, she has Erin on the line.

"Erin?"

"Yes. Hello." Erin's voice sounds a bit like Judith's was at her house after the funeral. But then loss is loss, as I know too well.

"I'm calling to offer you the job as my assistant."

This is the third stunned silence in under ten minutes.

"You must not have heard about Josh and me. He . . ."

"I heard. And I'm truly sorry, Erin. You got a raw deal. Life, and this business in particular, is full of them. But if you're in the market for a job, I'm offering you one."

"But . . . everyone there will know. I'll have to face Josh."

"Yes," I agree, not entirely sure if she's speaking to herself or to me. "It won't be easy. But then I wouldn't be offering you this position if I didn't think you could handle difficult situations."

The silence on the other end crackles. I imagine I can hear her thinking, weighing. But as much as I'd like to have her on my team, I'm certainly not going to beg.

"So, what's it going to be, Erin? You're my first choice, but there are plenty of qualified candidates."

"Yes, I know," she says quickly. "I can't thank you enough for the offer and for your faith in me."

I feel an odd smile tug at my lips. I honestly can't tell whether she's about to accept or decline.

"Is tomorrow too soon to start?"

Erin

It feels pretty great to have an actual reason to get out of bed, take a shower, wash my hair, and put on makeup. Not crying while I do those things feels even better. I arrive at the office embarrassingly early, something I plan to blame on yesterday's snowstorm if anyone comments. (Hey, we got a whole inch, and everyone's still freaking out.) Tyler told me Josh is out of town, so at least I don't have to worry about running into him. Still, I hang out in the lobby for a while and let several elevators go without me while I work up my nerve. When I check in at the front desk, eagle-eyed for any sign of pity or surprise, Gayle, the receptionist, just smiles and tells me that Louise is expecting me.

There are brief hushes followed by murmurs as I pass by the assistants and agents-in-training that sit outside their bosses' offices, but although my legs feel Jell-O-y, I'm here because Jazmine chose me. I manage to keep my chin up, a vague smile on my lips, and my eyes straight ahead.

"Good morning," Louise greets me when I reach the relative safety of her desk. "Why don't you hang up your coat and go get yourself a cup of coffee before we get started."

"I'm all set, thanks," I say as I remove my coat and hang it on the nearest peg. "I'm completely caffeinated and ready to go to work."

Her expression says she knows I'm afraid to walk the gauntlet again and will starve before I brave the break room, but her tone is more motherly than drill sergeant. "So, here's survival tip number one: When you work in a shark tank, you need to learn how to master your fear. Or at least mask it. Otherwise you'll get ripped apart."

"Got it." My chin goes up another notch so that I'm practically staring at the ceiling. My shoulders go up around my ears. "No sudden moves. And no flailing or thrashing."

This wins me a smile. "All right, then. Let's get started. I only have nine workdays to turn you into me."

We go over Jazmine's schedule—despite the snow, she's in the air and on her way to Indianapolis for the NFL Scouting Combine, which will last all week. Next week, she'll attend a number of smaller pro days around the country. After that, Louise explains how Jazmine likes information laid out and delivered. How important it is to anticipate Jazmine's every need. We scroll through her list of clients, which is way bigger and stronger than I realized and contains notes on their likes and dislikes, parents, spouses, children, girlfriends, birthdays, anniversaries, et cetera.

"Just to be clear, this is confidential information," Louise says. "It is never to be shared with anyone, or even hinted at. Your lips are sealed. You are the Sphinx. Sometimes, despite best efforts, there are leaks. None of those leaks can come from you. A breach of any kind in this regard is grounds for immediate dismissal. Clear?"

"Crystal." I cross my heart and hold my hand up as if I'm swearing fealty, which, of course, I am. Jazmine has given me this once-in-a-lifetime opportunity, and I am going to prove her confidence in me.

"A few statistics to bear in mind: Only five percent of certified NFL agents are female. The forty-one women with active certification represent a fifty percent increase since 2010. Only twenty-one had a client signed to an NFL contract in 2017. Jazmine has two and has just signed what she's convinced will be a future high-round draft pick. A lot of women took a lot of shit so that you could have this opportunity. You need to prove your worth and pay it forward as you rise."

I nod because I know that women have been knocking on these doors for a long time even though they rarely opened.

"'No' is a word you're going to hear a lot," Louise continues. "You will have to get used to it or find another line of work. You can't turn that 'no' into a 'yes' if you fold up your tent every time someone puts an obstacle in front of you.

"Jazmine is all about outworking the competition. She does not offer lip service or make false claims, and neither can you. If she makes a promise to a client, she finds a way to keep it. She is not about setting unrealistic expectations." Louise raises an eyebrow.

"Got it."

"Client prospecting is crucial, and this requires gathering player intel. Part of that is assessing a player's online presence. What is and is *not* on social media can provide important clues."

She hands me a stack of printouts. "Here's the list of athletes Jazmine wants you to look at this morning. Please prepare a report on each of them. I'd like those reports on my desk by noon. We've got a hell of a lot of ground to cover."

"Yes, ma'am." I manage not to salute. But I am ready to absorb every last bit of knowledge she's willing to share. I'm going to impress the hell out of Louise *and* Jazmine or die in the attempt.

Jazmine

You're not really holding me to this double date thing r you? I text my sister from the Dallas airport just before I board the plane back to Atlanta on Thursday afternoon more to yank her chain than to try to get out of the blind date with Derrick Warren.

I'm going to get this out of the way so that Thea will stop bugging me about it once and for all.

I am. Yes is yes. 8PM. Mission + Market.

Yep. Got all 6 confirms.

Ur in town right?

I will be.

Good. No emergencies, contingencies, excuses. Zero wiggle room. Pick u up or meet there?

I'm almost shocked to be given this choice, and know I have Jamal to thank. C u there.

There's a hesitation, and I know she's debating whether to remind me one more time that if I don't show she will come hunt me down. Wanna pick out my outfit, too?

Just make sure u wear ur smile!

Erin

I have just completed nine long, some might say brutal, days attempting to become Louise Lloyd's clone. Or at least as close as a heartbroken twenty-three-year-old white girl can get.

Louise is a miracle of thought and efficiency who can get more done in thirty minutes than most of us can do in a day. If you look up "impressive" in the dictionary, I'm pretty sure her picture will be there.

We have been the first ones in and the last to leave each day. As far as I can see, she has two basic settings—motherly but professional and bulldozer—and she can switch between them faster than most people can breathe. Most impressively, she does not take one single ounce of shit from anyone, including the CEO, catered-to clients, and Rich Hanson. Who has a tendency to loiter around Jazmine's office an awful lot for someone whom Jazmine can't stand the sight of.

Today is Louise's last day. Jazmine is back in town and acting for all she's worth as if it's just another workday, but underneath her game face she looks kind of shaky.

At noon, the two of them leave for a two-and-a-half-hour lunch that Jazmine doesn't return from. Louise says something "came up," but I'm guessing Jazmine just couldn't bear to watch Louise leave for the last time. For the record, despite how glad I am to have Louise's job, I'm not looking forward to watching her leave, either.

For the rest of the afternoon, I answer the phone and handle what has to be done while StarSports employees from Larry Carpenter down to the lowliest interns stop by to say goodbye. A lot of them bring small gifts, which I wish I had thought of. The ones who know her best bring chocolate. For such a no-nonsense person, she is surprisingly beloved.

I bite back a whimper at exactly five P.M. when she shrugs into her coat, hefts her bag of gifts, and smiles a final mother lioness smile—one that both threatens and protects. And though her voice is not quite as deep as Mufasa's, her last words of advice are worthy of the Lion King himself. "Remember," she says with quiet certainty, "inner strength has nothing to do with size or age or color. It comes from meeting things head-on. You are smart and quick and resilient. Own up to your mistakes and learn from them. And never, ever let them see you cry."

Jazmine

I totally respect Louise for wanting to be there for her mother, but after our goodbye lunch, I spent most of the afternoon trying not to think about how much I'm going to miss her. I distracted myself by contemplating the clothes in my closet. I briefly considered taking my sister at her word and doing a Lady Godiva and wearing *only* a smile. Then I considered dressing down in some kind of mousy brown wren thing that would render me uninteresting, but it turned out my ego wouldn't allow it. Plus, my sister would probably kill me.

Ultimately, I arrive at the restaurant in my leopard print Louboutin booties with the black leather trim and a black wool Alexander McQueen minidress that hugs my curves and that I plan to wear until it falls apart.

Heads turn as I'm shown to the table. It's impossible to go unnoticed if you're a female over six feet. I learned early not to slump or try to shave off even an inch. My height and muscle mass were huge assets to my tennis game. They've served me equally well in my current profession, where the worst thing that can happen to you is to go unnoticed.

Jamal and Derrick stand when I arrive, and I'm surprised to discover that I have to look up to meet Derrick's eyes and his smile, both of which are friendly and easygoing.

My sister's smile carries a whole lot of "I told you so."

When Derrick shakes my hand, then pulls out the empty chair beside him, she adds an approving nod.

Under cover of drink ordering and opening conversation, I check the man out. His hair is closely cropped, and his face sports that five-o'clock shadow that says he cares about his appearance but doesn't try too hard. His features carry a hint of something exotic, and his voice holds the faintest trace of the islands. There's a bit of twinkle to his dark eyes.

"So, at last we meet," he says.

"They are a persistent duo."

"Yes. But clearly they did not exaggerate. You are most beautiful." His gaze lingers in an appreciative but not icky way. "I understand that you are a sports agent?"

I laugh. "They didn't send you my complete résumé?"

"Just a brief bio, I'm afraid."

"Shocking."

"Yes. I believe they were attempting to show restraint. But I did not require urging. I trust Jamal's judgment in most things. And he and Thea have been truly wonderful. As a newcomer, I appreciate the hospitality and the occasional home-cooked meal."

I blush at my own lack of hospitality and at how hard I resisted even the idea of meeting this man.

"It's unusual to be so firmly adopted. And your sister is quite a good cook."

"She is," I admit. "I'm more of a dine-out and order-in person." I look up and catch my sister watching us. Trying to hide her excitement that we seem to be hitting it off.

"We all have our individual strengths and weaknesses." His laugh is rich and inclusive. His smile is infectious. How ironic that I might not have agreed to this date if I hadn't been trying to put Rich Hanson in his place. One day, I'll have to thank him.

"If you don't stop all that smiling, Thea will have us picking out wedding china," I warn even though I'm smiling, too. "She's very upset that I never married."

"She loves you and your daughter very much," he says.

"And we love her right back. Only Thea thinks everyone has to be married in order to be happy." I shoot a glance at my sister, who is hanging on every word. "The thing is, I have a lot on my plate, and men like Jamal aren't that easy to find."

"This is true," Derrick says, seemingly unoffended.

"Are you talking smack about me?" Jamal asks.

"And if we were?" I reply.

"Just remember that I've known you since you were a difficult and somewhat homely child. And I've got pictures to prove it."

"Ha! Derrick here was singing your praises. I told him that's just because he doesn't really know you yet."

There's laughter, then Derrick deftly changes the subject. "So, what were you doing in Dallas?"

"I have my eye on a running back out there. I went to watch him work out. Everyone thinks he's too small. But with most teams using a two running back system, I think he could be a great addition for some team. He's got an incredible work ethic for someone his age."

Derrick asks intelligent questions. Most men I'm around try to impress me with their sports knowledge and fandom. Derrick admits that while he enjoys watching baseball and football, and originally left Jamaica to play basketball at Vanderbilt, he'd rather be on a beach or out on a lake than inside watching sports on television.

I like that he knows how to show interest without making a big deal of it and has no problem giving a woman the floor. In fact, he asks just enough questions about my work to demonstrate that he's interested. But he doesn't overdo that, either.

It's a comfortable meal, and I realize with some surprise that it's eased some of my angst at losing Louise. I'm enjoying the evening, if not my sister's overjoyed expression.

When dessert has been ordered—I never miss a chance at Chef Ian's bread pudding—my sister stands and gives me a look. "Jazmine. Can you come help me with something?"

"You need me to come with you to the ladies' room?"

She rolls her eyes. "Yes. I, um, ripped my hem when we were coming in. I need some help pinning it up."

"Wouldn't it be better to wait until . . ."

"Now." It's a command and it is accompanied by a steely-eyed gaze that I've obeyed since childhood. "Let's go so we can get back before these two polish off all the dessert."

Jamal and Derrick pretend not to notice the exchange, but we all know what's going on here.

"If I just admit that Derrick is far nicer than I was expecting and that I'm glad you forced, er, organized, this outing, can I stay here and drink my coffee?"

Derrick grins.

"She got you there!" Jamal crows to Thea.

"All right. Fine," Thea huffs. "But I taught her better than that. There's no need to take all the fun out of being right."

Fourteen

Sara

Throwing Mitch's things in the yard (the side, not the front, because—neighbors!) and watching them deteriorate in the slush hasn't been anywhere near as satisfying as it seems in books and movies. Neither was changing the locks, since he hasn't been in any hurry to come back to face me or his mother. But I had to do *something*.

So far Dorothy and I have had no meaningful conversation. We nod. Say good morning, good afternoon, good night. Both of us are still reeling from Mitch's actions and their consequences.

I know Dorothy would love to reframe her son's actions in some way that will make them less heinous or at least more palatable, but as difficult as she's always been, I believe she's intrinsically honest. Even if she could devise a suitable defense for her son twice impregnating a woman who is not his wife, I doubt she's going to excuse his robbing her of her home in order to support that secret family.

I have my fury and my job along with a retirement account and credit cards in my own name. My car is old but paid off. He has stolen her largest and most important asset.

Although I have helped to feed and take care of her, we have no experience in comforting each other. We have been two planets orbiting her son while attempting not to collide. Now we are the collateral damage of his appalling lack of character.

I am, of course, dealing with the demise of my marriage the same way I've gotten through so many things in my life: by withdrawing as much as humanly possible and escaping into books. Of the six I've read over the last three weeks, the one I enjoyed most was Elizabeth Gilbert's *City of Girls*. The lone bright spot in my immediate future is that we'll be discussing it at book club next Tuesday night.

I'm looking for my copy when I walk into the kitchen and find Dorothy at the kitchen table, staring out the window at the bare-branched yard and the empty street beyond. *City of Girls* sits on the table.

"I wondered where I left that book. I can't seem to remember anything right now. Or maybe I'm just trying so hard not to think about what happened that I can't think at all."

Dorothy's lips twist, but it's more grimace than smile. "My brain doesn't seem to be up to much, either." The grimace fades. "I can't understand how the child I gave up so much for and assumed I'd taught right from wrong could have done this."

"I know. It's . . ." My voice trails off. I simply cannot find the vocabulary required.

Dorothy's eyes meet mine. For the first time, hers is not the look of an impatient mother-in-law to an unwelcome and unworthy daughter-in-law but one betrayed woman to another.

I pick up the book. "You're welcome to read this if you like. I thought it was very good."

"It is." An odd, almost timid look steals into her eyes. "I hope you don't mind, but I read it yesterday."

"You read the entire book in one day?"

"Yes."

"All four hundred eighty pages?"

She nods. "It's hard to believe it was written by the same woman who wrote *Eat, Pray, Love.*"

I blink in surprise. I have never seen Dorothy with a book or e-reader in her hands. She's never mentioned a title that she loved or hated. Has never commented on the fact that I'm a reading specialist or that I work part-time in a bookstore. She's never set foot in Between the Covers, never asked for a recommendation. Though now that I think about it, I have sometimes found books I'm reading somewhere I didn't remember leaving them.

She looks me straight in the eye. "I've always been a bit of a *closet* reader."

"Why?"

"When I was growing up, my parents believed that anything that wasn't educational or uplifting was a waste of one's time." She raises one eyebrow. "So, I would hide, sometimes in an actual closet with a flashlight." Regret tinges her voice. So does anger. "My parents have been gone a long time, so I don't typically resort to closets anymore. Or bathrooms." She spears me with a look. "But I rarely read in public."

I have read in many hidey-holes in order to escape real life, but the idea of parents shaming their own child into reading in a closet may be one of the saddest things I've ever heard.

"I've especially enjoyed the *Outlander* series," Dorothy admits quietly. "And anything by Mary Balogh or Maeve Binchy." Her eyes almost twinkle. "Back in the day, I was an avid fan of Kathleen Woodiwiss."

"Wow." My mouth gapes slightly. This is the equivalent of someone who has never been caught listening to anything but Mozart admitting that they're a Kanye West fan.

I smile at the sheer unexpectedness of it. "I guess there are a few things we don't know about each other."

"It would seem so," she concedes.

It's enough to make me wonder whether any of the things we think we know about each other are true.

Erin

As of today, I've completed six days on my own as Jazmine's full-time assistant. Following Louise's advice to the letter, I march into the break room for coffee first thing every morning nodding and smiling at everyone I see. Then I nod and smile my way back to my desk, where I open Jazmine's calendar on the desktop computer, my iPad, and my iPhone so that I can track her movements and access whatever she might need every minute of every day, under any and all circumstances.

Today begins like all the others. It will end when the "homemade" chocolate chip cookies that she will take to her book club are delivered at six thirty so that they'll be fresh when she arrives at the bookstore at seven.

I eat the lunch I brought from home at my desk. Getting things done. Nodding to everyone who passes as if I don't have a worry in the world.

Thanks to Louise, I know who is who, who to be careful of, who to trust, who wanted this job and didn't get it, and who to never turn my back on. I'm vigilant but no longer waiting for the bogeyman to pop out from around the corner. Or for a call that will require me to do something I have no idea how to do.

Everything's going so smoothly that at four P.M. I go into the break room and treat myself to an afternoon latte.

When I get back to my desk, there's a newspaper clipping in the center of it. I set my latte down, lower myself into my chair, and reach for it, assuming someone dropped it off for Jazmine. But there's no note on the clipping, which looks like it's been ripped from one of those tabloids you see at the grocery checkout.

The black-and-white photo is of Josh in a bar, surrounded by his teammates. A tall, beautiful brunette is wrapped around him as if she's a pole dancer and he is the pole. Despite the crappy image quality, I can practically see the hunger in her eyes and smell the sex wafting off her. Josh is grinning like he just pitched a no-hitter.

My eyes blur with the very tears Louise warned me not to shed under any circumstances. I don't want to look at this picture a second longer—there's a reason I've been avoiding Instagram except to scroll through occasionally to give myself some semblance of normalcy, but this is the moment I've been dreading. *Ugh.* I know I should bunch it up and throw it in the trash where it belongs, only I can't quite bring myself to touch it or stop myself from memorizing every single pixel.

I sneak a look around. I don't know who put it here, but the only reason anyone would is to make me feel like shit. It's working.

I'm screwing up my courage, swallowing back tears, and reaching for the photo when someone clears his voice.

My head snaps up.

"Are you all right?" Rich Hanson asks.

"Of course."

"Are you sure? Because you look like you're about to cry." He pushes the box of Kleenex Louise always kept on her desk toward me.

"I am not crying." I push the Kleenex back. Rich Hanson is pretty attractive for an old guy—right around six feet, runner trim, blond hair, hazel eyes. But he's at the top of Jazmine's "do not turn your back on" list. Which puts him at the top of mine.

"I'm just trying to help," he says. "Really. I only . . ."

"Thank you. But I'm fine." I sniff and try to look efficient. "How can I help you?"

He looks at me.

"Did you have a message for Jazmine?"

"No. I was just passing by and thought I'd have a word with her. Then I noticed that you looked upset."

"I am not upset."

It's clear he knows I'm lying. But he doesn't call me on it again.

When he doesn't speak, I stand, palming the photo in one hand and grabbing my phone with the other. "I . . . excuse me. I, um, I have to . . . go."

Somehow, even with his eyes glued to my back, I manage to walk away without spilling a tear or letting out a single sob. Once I've turned the corner, I racewalk to the ladies' room, where I lock myself in a stall and sit on the toilet seat lid, not allowing a single tear to fall until I've made it ten full minutes without hearing a footstep or flush or squeak of a stall door.

I wish I'd known I was capable of that kind of control when I was blubbering in my childhood bed.

Jazmine

When I arrive at the office that afternoon, Erin's not at her desk. I'm on my way to my own when someone comes up behind me.

"If you're looking for your assistant, she's in the ladies' room," Rich Hanson says.

"What?" I ask as I turn slowly to face him.

"I was talking to her when she bolted. I'm a little concerned. She's been in there for a while."

I fold my arms across my chest. "What did you say to her?"

"Me? Nothing." If you're not careful, you can be pulled in by the friendly sheep act and forget that there's a wolf inside. "I'd stopped by to talk to you, and I noticed that she was upset."

"And she was upset because . . . ?"

"I'm assuming it was because of the photo of Josh in the *National Enquirer* that hit the shelves today. He was in the company of a former Miss Florida turned reality TV star."

"And you made it your business to make sure she knew about it," I say, trying not to think about the fact that this is the very kind of thing Louise warned me about when I chose Erin.

"Why would I do that?" Hanson's tone is sincere.

"Who knows why you do what you do? Because you didn't think I should hire her in the first place? Because you like to cause trouble? Because you tortured small animals as a child?"

He shakes his head. "I may have a no-holds-barred approach to my work, but I have never intentionally upset a young, vulnerable girl."

I continue to meet his gaze.

He sighs. "I came over here to talk to you and found her staring at the photo, trying not to cry."

"And how did that make you feel?"

"Crappy." His voice is surprisingly quiet. "She's been through some serious stuff, and while I didn't think hiring her was a good idea, I respect the fact that she's still standing. I take no pleasure in seeing innocent people suffer. I find it in winning for my clients. In besting competitors. Equals who can hold their own."

I turn and lead him into my office, letting the compliment pass. "So, what was it you wanted to talk to me about when you got distracted by Erin's unhappiness?" I ask as I sit behind my desk and motion him into the chair opposite.

"I saw a player—a wide receiver—at a pro day over the

weekend that needs better advice than he's getting. And I thought of you."

"So now you're trying to get other people to steal other agents' players for you?"

"No, not at all. I just feel like he's being pushed to declare too early. I can't take him on, but he needs someone to convince him to stay in school and get a degree while he works on his game."

"So, you thought of me." I can't quite figure out his angle, but I'm sure there has to be one.

"Yes. We've had our differences, but you're good at what you do, and I think you have your clients' best interests at heart." He sighs. "Your assistant fled before I could leave a message."

"Well, seeing as how I'm often tempted to flee your company as quickly as possible, it may have just been her survival instincts kicking in. Or a stomach bug." I've seen Rich Hanson's killer instinct at work too often to ever completely trust in the earnestness he's displaying.

He spreads his arms wide. "Believe what you will. I came to offer an olive branch. At some point, we're going to have to figure out how to work with each other. Or one of us"—his tone infers that the one of us is me—"could get shoved out."

"Thanks for the warning. And your *concern* for Erin. But she is a strong, professional woman and doesn't need it."

Then I stand. As soon as he's out of sight, I turn and head for the ladies' room as if I'm not the least bit worried about what I might find when I get there.

Fifteen

Erin

I'm not sure how long I've been in the bathroom when I hear Jazmine's confident, long-strided click of high heels.

"Erin?"

"Yes?"

"Are you all right?"

I'm pretty sure the fact that I'm basically hiding in a stall requires me to say no, but I didn't cry and I *am* functional. It's just that the longer I stayed in here, the harder it got to leave.

"If you're sick, you should go home." There's a pause. "And if you're hiding here because you're too upset to work . . ."

"But I *am* working." I unlock the stall door and step out with my hands up, like some criminal who has to prove he's not dangerous. One of those hands clutches my cell phone. "I only came in here because Louise told me I should never let anyone see me cry. And I was kind of afraid that I might."

Her head tilts at an angle, and her arms cross over her chest. "First of all, I'm not loving the fact that you have been conducting my business from a ladies' room. Second, if Louise told you not to let anyone see you cry, she actually meant do not cry. Period."

"But I haven't," I say almost proudly. "I just didn't want to go back to my desk until I was completely sure I had it under control."

"You do realize that when you stay in a bathroom long enough for people to notice, they assume that you have some horrible and possibly contagious intestinal problem. Or you're goofing off. Or you're crying."

My cheeks heat with embarrassment.

"I have no doubt odds have been laid on exactly how long you'll be in here." She pauses. "I wouldn't be surprised if there's also a side bet on whether or not you'll still be working here after today."

Holy crap. I offer up a prayer that I haven't thrown away this incredible opportunity over a stupid tabloid picture. "Are you firing me?"

"No." Jazmine's eyes close briefly. Her exhale is long. "If you don't want to work for me, you're going to have to say so. In the meantime, here are a few things to consider:

"One—chances are the photo in the *Enquirer* was set up by someone's publicist or a publicist attached to her reality show. You need to learn how to tell the difference. Two—someone put that on your desk to hurt and embarrass you. To see if they could make you cry. It was a test of your strength, and you failed. Louise advised you not to cry because a woman's tears are often used as proof that women are weak, too delicate for this work. The same applies to running and hiding."

My shoulders sag. It's all I can do not to hang my head.

"Do you think Rich Hanson instigated this?" Jazmine asks in a tone that sounds as if it's meant to be casual but isn't.

"No. He said he came to talk to you. I just . . . He offered me a Kleenex, and I left because I didn't want to take a chance on crying in front of him."

Jazmine's sigh is long and jagged. "Bottom line, Erin, that

photo is nothing compared to the things you'll have to put up with if you intend to succeed in this business. You will encounter lots of oversize egos and tons of jealousy. Ulterior motives and agendas will abound. You will need a backbone and a poker face. No matter what happens, you'll have to keep your head up and walk tall. This is not a business for sissies."

I roll the newsprint into a ball and drop it in the trash. "I'm not a sissy."

Jazmine looks down, her eyes taking me in. I'd give anything to tower over people like she does.

"All right, then. Let's go. There's work to be done."

"Yes, ma'am," I say as firmly and positively as I can. If I didn't think she'd take it the wrong way, I'd salute.

"You do know that you don't have to *be* tall to walk tall," she says.

"Technically, yes. I get the concept. But people do judge by appearance. Small is weak, blond is frivolous." I straighten with resolve. "Which just means I've got to show them they're wrong."

"Exactly," Jazmine says as we move toward the bathroom door. "You can't be such an open book. It makes people think they're free to rip out your pages or try to break your spine."

We stop at the door. One of her dark eyebrows arches up in silent question.

I take a deep breath and nod.

She pushes open the door. Together, we stride out into the corridor. Or rather I stride out and she pulls back so that we move together.

"I really should have told you not to eat that PayDay bar Louise left in her desk. Someone gave it to her as a joke years ago. I'm surprised they didn't have to carry you out on a stretcher." She pitches her voice just loud enough for the people we pass to hear.

A text dings in on my phone. "Perfect timing on that book

analogy," I say with an overlarge smile. "Your cookies have arrived. Although my mother's book club brings cookies and
treats they bake themselves."

"So do some of the members in mine," Jazmine replies with
an even wider smile. "Unfortunately, baking isn't one of my
talents. And I'd rather bring something people will actually
eat and enjoy and that won't make them sick."

"Yes." This time my grin is real. "I've heard that stomach
pumping can suck a whole lot of pleasure out of an evening."

Jazmine laughs. "It's not at all conducive to an in-depth
book discussion."

We're still smiling and chatting when we reach my desk. I
have a crick in my neck from looking up at her, but I'm truly
grateful that she got me out of the bathroom without embarrassing me any more than I'd already embarrassed myself. All
I want to do right now is go home and crawl into bed. Maybe
binge-watch a couple episodes of *Insecure*.

"You know what?" Jazmine says. "I think you should come
to book club with me."

"Hmmm?"

"I'd like you to come to book club."

"Oh. Wow   at's really nice of you. I'd love to, um, do that
sometime. M   nother really loves her book club." And all the
older women who are in it.

I pause and sneak a casual peek around. Only a few desks
are still occupied. No one is close enough to hear what we're
saying.

"And thanks again for . . . well, for not firing me." I nod and
smile, only it feels a little bit like a boxer's bob and weave.

"Right." Jazmine flashes a bright smile. "Do you want to
follow me there? Or should I just share the address? Between
the Covers is on your way home."

I wonder briefly why she's still performing when there's
hardly anyone left to perform for. Then I realize she's not.

"Book club always cheers me up," she continues. "Plus, nobody there will know anything about what you've been through unless you choose to tell them. It's a great group. Sometimes my friend Angela's oldest daughter, Lyllie, comes when she's home from college."

I am caught flat-footed. And speechless.

"And there'll be wine and some truly killer cookies."

"You could just give me a cookie or two to take home with me."

Her look stops this line of defense and has me searching for another. "I mean, I haven't even read the book."

"That, fortunately, is not a requirement," she says smoothly. "I think you should come. It'll give you something to do besides trying to figure out who put that clipping on your desk."

I look up and meet Jazmine's eyes.

This woman gave me a job when no one, including Louise, thought she should. And she has just rescued me from a bathroom stall. There is only one acceptable response to her invitation.

"Sure. That would be great. I've already got the address in my phone, but I'd be glad to follow you."

Judith

I ignore the doorbell, and whoever's leaning on it, for as long as I can. When I finally yank it open, Meena is standing there. Her arms are filled with the mail that I haven't bothered to go outside to retrieve. Her expression is a mixture of fear and irritation.

"Why haven't you returned my calls? I've been trying to reach you all week. I've been worried about you."

"Sorry." I step back to let her enter. "I just . . . I haven't been able to make myself talk to anyone but the kids." I don't mention how seldom they've called or how stilted those conversations have been. Mostly because I'm afraid they'll somehow sense my guilt. Or ask questions that I will never be able to answer. "I don't have the strength for any more awkward condolence calls." My eyes tear up. "And if I ever see another casserole, I won't be responsible for my actions."

"You don't look so good," Meena says.

"I'm pretty sure you didn't come all this way to tell me I look like shit."

"No." She cocks her head and studies me. Doesn't even try to hide her wince. "I came to take you to book club."

My snort of laughter is pure reflex. I haven't been dressed in days and can't remember the last time I showered. "There is no way I'm going to book club."

Her eyes land on the empty bottle of wine on the living room cocktail table. One used wineglass sits beside it.

"Why not?" she asks, as if this is a reasonable question.

"Because I practically killed my husband. And I'm in mourning."

"You did not kill your husband," Meena says, following me into the kitchen where the sink is filled with more dirty wineglasses. Which I will wash and reuse when I run out. "You had sex with him and then you tried to get him to agree to work on your marriage."

"While he was either having a heart attack or already dead!" The words reverberate in the silent house.

"You didn't know that." She states this as if it's a fact, but I'm no longer sure what I did and did not know.

"Because I was completely absorbed in myself and what I wanted."

"It's not a crime to try to save your marriage." Her voice and face reflect a quiet certainty I wish I felt. I don't know whether

I was trying to save my marriage or looking for an excuse to end it. If only I had shut up and paid attention, Nate might be alive right now.

"What happened is awful, Judith. But it's not your fault."

Tears fall as I stare at her. I want to believe her, but I can't stop thinking about how angry I was. How ready I was to walk away if he didn't agree to try harder, to change, to become the person I wanted him to be.

She steps close and puts her arms around me, holding tight while I cry.

"I haven't even read the book. I haven't been able to read anything at all." I say this as if it's the worst thing that has happened. When everything that's happened is the worst I've ever known.

"You know that doesn't matter," Meena says gently. "You're coming for the company. To be with people who care about you."

This, of course, is exactly what I've been trying to avoid. Because sympathy from strangers is bearable. Sympathy from people who really know you just opens the floodgates.

"What will everyone think if I'm out so soon? Drinking wine and talking about books as if they matter when . . ." I can't finish the sentence or the thought.

"Assuming you take a shower first, and maybe put on a bit of makeup, all they'll think is how great it is to see you."

"But . . ."

"Judith. Honey. You have been through a lot. And I know it has to hurt like hell. But you can't stay in this house forever.

"We may not have passed the Equal Rights Amendment yet, but we are, fortunately, living in a time when a woman's life does not end because her husband's does. No one expects you to climb on a funeral pyre. Or wear black for a year. Or close yourself off from the world."

Meena places her hands on my shoulders and holds me away from her so that she can look me in the eye. "We don't have to stay for the whole discussion. I'll bring you home whenever you want. But I'm not leaving here without you."

"I can't," I say miserably. "I just can't." New tears leak out of the corners of my eyes. I no longer know whether they're for Nate or for me.

"You can." She pulls me close for one last bracing hug. "We'll go, we'll have a glass or two of wine, eat something chocolate, and hear what people thought about the book. Then I'll bring you home."

"But I don't think . . ."

"Fortunately, thinking isn't required at the moment, either. Come on. You jump in the shower. I'll lay out something for you to wear."

Sixteen

Sara

It didn't take as much convincing as I expected to get Dorothy to come to book club with me. To my knowledge, it's the first time she's left the house since Mitch confessed his sins, except for occasional forays to retrieve bits and pieces of his possessions I threw outside.

She hasn't spoken since we got in the car and is still staring straight ahead, clutching her purse as we pull into the parking lot of Between the Covers. I'm no longer certain that the fact that she agreed to come is a positive sign. It could just be a desperate need to get out of the house for more than five minutes or be around someone who isn't me.

"Will everyone there know what's happened with . . . Mitchell?"

I would have thought the theft of her home would trump all else, but this seems to be her greatest fear, that strangers will know what her son has done. My greatest fear is that despite his reprehensible actions, Mitch might somehow end up with our house or manage to force its sale. Until I know what lies ahead, that fear is a mushroom cloud hanging over me.

"Only if you tell them."

"Not even your boss?" Doubt etches her face and infuses her voice.

"I've told Annell some of what's going on, but no one else is likely to pry. It's a book club, not an inquisition."

"Yes, well, I've never been to a book club before." Her voice drops as if even saying "book club" is somehow dangerous, and I have to remind myself that she's never even read in public. "Is everyone required to speak?"

"No. No one's going to force you to expound or argue about themes or meanings. But I find hearing what others think and how they reacted to different parts of the book and the characters brings a lot to the reading experience."

She nods but makes no comment. As we cross the parking lot, her eyes are pinned on the building. Despite the warm yellow light that spills out of the windows, her shoulders are rigid, and her chin is set in its most determined angle. Her pocketbook, which hangs in the crook of one arm, is held tight to her body, as if she's afraid someone might attempt to take it off her person. Or maybe it's just an additional protective layer.

At the front door she hesitates, and I have to fight back my huff of impatience. Her son has turned out to be a liar and a cheat and has stolen her home out from under her, and she's worried about going to a book club?

"There's absolutely nothing to be afraid of," I say a little more forcefully than intended. "It's just a group of nice people who really like books."

She nods again, but her shoulders remain stiff. Her smile is small and tight. She steps through the front door with all the enthusiasm of a prisoner approaching the gallows.

Inside, the scent of books wraps around us in welcome. I glance at Dorothy and note her quick intake of breath, and what might be a slight easing of her trepidation. Annell hugs me, and for a moment I'm afraid she's going to ignore the invisible "do not hug" sign Dorothy keeps pinned to her chest, but as usual, Annell does exactly the right thing and offers a warm smile and a hand clasp. "I'm very glad that you could join us tonight. I'm a big fan of your daughter-in-law. It's wonderful to finally get to meet you."

Dorothy manages a small smile as she takes in the seemingly endless shelves of books. "This is . . . this is quite nice." She says this almost primly, but her eyes are bright and her breathing has kicked up a notch.

"It is, isn't it?" I lower my voice to a stage whisper. "Don't tell Annell, but I'd probably work for free."

"I heard that." Annell smiles over Dorothy's head. "I'd worry that I was overpaying you, but we both know how lucky I am to have you."

As we make our way back to the refreshments, I watch Dorothy take in the children's section, the cozy reading nooks, the signed book posters on the wall, like a castaway catching a first glimpse of a rescue boat on the horizon. Some of my foster parents grew impatient with me always having "my nose in a book," but at least none of them tried to dictate what I should and shouldn't enjoy like Dorothy's parents did.

At the drinks table, Meena offers a smile and a choice of red or white wine. Judith stands next to her, here but not. Her smile, when she's introduced to Dorothy, doesn't quite reach her eyes.

"I'm very sorry for your loss," Dorothy says as I wrap my arms around Judith and hold her close. I have never understood why we use that word when someone dies. As if she's somehow misplaced him. I'm the one who "lost" a husband. Or, more accurately, allowed him to be stolen.

"So, you're Mitchell's mother," Meena says.

"Yes," Dorothy replies, and in that one word I hear her fear. That Mitch has truly jettisoned her along with me and is not, as I suspect, just giving her time and space in which to forgive him. Because while she has every reason to be hurt and angry, when the dust settles, she will still be Mitch's biological mother while I will be little more than a footnote in his personal history. The *first* wife. The one who didn't even know she'd been cheated on for years. Ultimately, I will be a divorcée. Like Meena.

I'm still processing all of this as we move on to the food table, where Jazmine Miller offers us chocolate chip cookies from a bulging bakery box and introduces us to her assistant, a young, petite blonde named Erin Richmond. Nancy Flaherty, who's also new to the group, stands behind a platter of cupcakes decorated to look like golf balls, complete with white dimpled frosting. Golf tee earrings swing at her ears. Her sweater reads KISS MY PUTT. Angela McBride and Jazmine's assistant are nibbling on cookies and cupcakes.

The first bite of cookie helps push back visions of myself as a more studious, less outgoing version of Meena. The second bite elicits a smile.

"They're great, aren't they?" Erin says. "I've already had two, and I think there's a third in my future."

"And that's why those of us who don't bake, buy," Jazmine points out. "But I'm definitely going to have to try a golf ball cupcake." She turns to Nancy Flaherty. "Did you make them?"

"Yes. They're a specialty of mine. In fact, it was because of my balls that I first got to meet Tiger."

Dorothy's eyes go wide at this. They go wider still when Carlotta, Wesley, and Phoebe join us around the food table, along with a guy in an EMT uniform named Chaz. Perhaps I should have warned her that we're not your garden variety book club.

I sip wine and nibble on a cupcake, comforted by the sounds of conversation and laughter and the simple pleasure of being surrounded by people who love to read as much as I do. By the time Annell claps her hands and tells us it's time to get started, my shoulders have relaxed and my breathing has slowed. Even Dorothy looks less rigid, as if being surrounded by books has softened her sharp edges or maybe ripped a small hole in her normally impenetrable protective layer.

"I haven't actually read the book," Erin admits, her face screwing up in apology as we refill our plates and Judith and Meena top off our glasses. "I didn't know I was coming."

"Neither did I." Judith clutches a bottle of red to her chest as we merge into a bit of a herd and begin to move toward the breezeway. "Until *someone* dragged me out of my house without warning." Her usual teasing tone is a ghost of its usual self, but I'm relieved that she's making the effort.

"Quite a few of us seem to have ended up here unexpectedly," Dorothy says with a glimmer of humor I've never heard from her. "Who knew book club impressment was so rampant?"

"That's how they used to man British naval ships," Chaz says, and I'm kind of impressed that he not only knows what impressment is but showed up for a discussion of a book titled *City of Girls*. "Press gangs rounding up Americans to serve on British ships was one of the causes of the War of 1812."

"Well, I'd rather be pressed into a book club than the Royal Navy any day," Carlotta says, tossing back her hair with impossibly long fingernails and smoothing the long fuchsia sweater over distressed black jeans. Somehow, she is once again eating fruit while the rest of us have piled our plates with baked goods.

"That's for sure," Wesley agrees.

"Given how seasick you get," his twin adds, "I don't think you would have been of particular use to the Royal Navy."

Our herd thins into more of a column as we pass through the breezeway and into the carriage house. I claim two spots on the window seat while Dorothy peers out the glass doors into the lit garden, a smile hovering on her lips. We've only been here about twenty minutes, and she's already smiled more than I've witnessed in the last twelve years.

"Now then, how many of you have read the book?" Annell asks once we're all settled.

All hands but Erin's and Judith's go up.

"Good. Remember that you're always welcome whether you've read the book or not. However, we don't tiptoe around the details, so there may be spoilers." Annell smiles. "We do have a few new faces, so let's run around the circle and introduce ourselves."

I sip my wine while I listen to intros. Chaz and Nancy are new to me, and although I try to focus on the details they share, my mind wanders back, once again, to Mitch and how utterly he has trampled on my life and his mother's. When it's Dorothy's turn, I tense up briefly, like I do when one of my shakiest students has to address the class, but Dorothy doesn't wobble or falter. "I was once an efficiency expert," she says, quite efficiently. "My favorite book is *To Kill a Mockingbird*. This is my very first book club discussion. Thank you for making me feel welcome."

I'm still pondering my mother-in-law's choice of such an emotional read as her favorite given how steadfastly she's avoided the messiness of true emotion for as long as I have known her, when Jazmine's assistant stands.

"I've never been to a book club before, either. I'm not really a big reader if you don't count the sports pages, but I did love the Harry Potter books and always wished I was as clever and strong as Hermione." She glances down as if weighing her next words. "I kind of needed a distraction from my real life tonight, so I'm glad that Jazmine invited me."

Annell beams. "I'm glad all of you are here tonight. And I want to remind everyone that not liking a book doesn't mean it was a bad book—it just means you didn't enjoy it. I'm always fascinated by how differently readers react to the same story and characters. How much of ourselves we bring to the experience someone else has crafted."

With that the conversation begins, pinging from person to person. Tonight, I let the words flow over and around me, like perfectly heated bathwater that both soothes and buoys. I'm pretty much floating until Phoebe brings up the "awful" way Vivian, the main character, lost her virginity but nonetheless fell in love with sex.

"Did anyone have an incredible first experience?" Meena asks. "I mean, everything takes practice, right?"

This elicits some laughter but, mercifully, no actual answers. Once again, I'm drawn inward. Back to my first time with Mitchell. How he treated me as if I were made of spun glass. The joy I felt the first time he told me he loved me. My tears of happiness and relief when he asked me to marry him and I knew, finally, I wouldn't live my entire life alone.

Dorothy shifts in her seat beside me, and I remember the first time Mitch took me to meet her, right after he proposed. How I assumed our mutual love of him would be a bond and how excited I was to finally have a mother who was not provided by the foster care system, a mother who would love me because I loved her son. Only she always held me at arm's length, found fault wherever she could, withheld whatever warmth she had to give.

"Well, I thought it was nice to read a story about female promiscuity that didn't result in death." There's a teasing lilt to Dorothy's voice I've never heard before. "I mean, Vivian does end up a lot better off than Anna Karenina."

I blink at the laughter that follows. My mother-in-law has proven herself to be many things over the years; funny has never been one of them. I look at her face, the smile on her lips. Who *is* this woman?

"Well, I didn't understand why a big star like Edna would have stayed married to that young actor who was such a buffoon. And I don't think she should have been so nasty to Vivian," Meena says.

The warm bathwater I've been floating in turns to ice. "Seriously?" The word slips out before I can stop it. "You think Edna should have just ignored the fact that Vivian and Celia

Ray slept with her husband? And everyone knew it? Edna *was* the injured party after all."

Dorothy shoots me a cautioning look. As if I should not be raising the subject of infidelity. As if I'm about to cast aspersions on her son. Or let all of those assembled in on the sorry state of my marriage. Mitch's other life. His children. The beautiful and fertile Margot.

An uncomfortable and slightly confused silence follows.

Annell ends it, steering the conversation in another direction, then keeping it going longer than we ever would have on our own. I begin to relax again—not enough to be warm and floaty, but enough to appreciate the way Annell offers insights and prompts discussion without lecturing or taking over. How she gives me just enough time to rein in my emotions. I do not meet Dorothy's eyes.

"All right, then." Annell nods decisively as she draws the discussion to a close. "Any suggestions for our next read?"

Chaz, the EMT, suggests Bill Bryson's *The Body: A Guide for Occupants*. Angela McBride proposes Malcolm Gladwell's *Talking to Strangers*.

"I originally hoped we might read and discuss *121 First Dates*, the book I mentioned last time?" Meena says. "I'm having a blast with online dating. In fact, I've met someone pretty special. And I thought you all might enjoy it."

"I'm on singlegolfers.com," Nancy Flaherty offers with a swing of her golf tee earrings and a suggestive smile. "It's a free site, but I'm pretty sure it's just for *players*."

We look at one another, and I know I'm not the only one trying to figure out if this is a double entendre or she's simply saying that the site is only open to golfers.

"I bet Erin's got lots of experience swiping left and right and setting up profiles," Phoebe says.

"I've never, um, actually tried online dating." Erin shifts uncomfortably in her seat.

"Really?" Meena leans forward. "I thought all young people did that today instead of blind dates and that sort of thing."

Now I wonder if Mitch met Margot online or in person. How long they dated before she got pregnant. Whether he took the job in Birmingham to be with her.

"No. I . . . I've only really dated one person." Erin swallows. "I fell in love with him in elementary school."

Dorothy sniffs in surprise. Erin blushes.

"Oh. Sorry. I thought you were joking." This may be the first time I've heard Dorothy apologize. Ever. She's having quite the night.

"We were supposed to get married on New Year's Day," Erin continues. "Only . . ."

"Erin, you don't have to share anything you don't want to," Jazmine begins.

"Only he changed his mind." Erin's voice is stark and flat.

My eyes tear up. I know what that kind of rejection feels like. The loss. Judith drops her head.

"Wow. That sucks," Chaz says.

"Big time," Phoebe adds.

"Yeah." Carlotta nods. "Men can be real shits. And I'm allowed to say that because I used to be one."

"Can't argue with that," Meena says. "And I totally get that this might not be the right book for us. Especially not right now." She sends Judith an apologetic smile, and I'm grateful she doesn't know that what I really need to read right now is a primer on divorce. "So, I withdraw that suggestion. At least for the time being."

Annell nods in agreement, and I am, as always, comforted by her good sense. "Let's go with Bill Bryson's *The Body* for March. I'll order copies and let you know when they arrive."

This elicits a whoop of victory from Chaz.

"And I'll order copies of the online dating title, too. In case anyone would like to read it," Annell adds.

We're about to adjourn when Phoebe raises her hand. "Were there any book club names in the suggestion box?"

"Oh, right. I almost forgot." Annell rummages through the folders on her lap, then takes out a stack of once-folded pieces of paper and puts on her reading glasses. "Let's see." She glances down. "We have Best Cellars, that's C-E-L-L-A-R—as in where wine is kept." One eyebrow goes up. "Second is Reading Between the Wines." She glances at the group. "Followed by Waiting for Merlot and Wines and Spines."

Angela McBride titters. There's a snort of laughter from Chaz.

"There does seem to be a certain emphasis on alcoholic refreshment," Annell observes. "Because we also have Books & Booze and Bookaholics." She peers at us over her reading glasses, a smile hovering on her lips. "The last sort of sums up the rest." Her smile grows as she reads, "Drinking Club with a Reading Problem."

There's a low belly laugh from Carlotta. A hoot from Jazmine. Soon the whole circle erupts in laughter.

"Well, at least we know where your customers' priorities lie," my mother-in-law says with yet another glint of humor.

"We are a thirsty crowd!" Meena crows.

"We *are* a prime example of a Drinking Club with a Reading Problem!" Jazmine grins.

Annell waits for the laughter to die down. "It seems keeping the suggestions anonymous has inspired a certain . . . creativity. Let's give it another month and see what else comes in. All in favor?"

There's a resounding "aye!"

"Hmmm, sounds like it's time to step up the competition," Jazmine says, eyeing Angela.

"You better believe it," Angela shoots back.

"Nothing like a little mental challenge to keep one's wits sharp," Carlotta observes.

"Some of us need less sharpening than others," Meena retorts.

"Very true," Judith agrees.

"I'm in," Chaz says.

Phoebe and Wesley grin.

Dorothy and I exchange a look as we all tidy up and gather our things. There's that glint again.

Let the games begin.

Seventeen

Judith

Rosaria, our cleaning woman of seventeen years, is disappointed in me.

"I think you don't need me anymore."

"Of course I need you." For the last four and a half weeks, Rosaria has been the only other human being in the house for more than fifteen minutes at a time, which is how long it apparently takes to pay a condolence call or check in on a widow. *Widow!*

"No." She looks around the family room, her eyes both sad and accusing. "You don't."

I follow her gaze. Every knickknack is in place. The area rug still appears freshly vacuumed. The wood floors gleam. The kitchen is no better. Or worse, depending on your view. The wineglasses are washed and in the cupboard. The stainless-steel appliances sparkle. I can see my reflection in the chrome cabinet pulls. Even the barstools are pulled up to the island in a perfectly straight row, just the way she left them two weeks ago. Although I wouldn't have believed it when Ethan and Ansley were still living at home, it's not that easy to trash a home that's been professionally cleaned. At least not when all you do is wander from room to room in the oppressive and never-ending quiet that even a television laugh track can't fill.

"Come sit down. Have a cup of coffee," I say hopefully, moving toward the coffee maker.

"You don't want to pay me to sit and drink coffee."

Although it sounds ridiculous when she says it, I am willing to do this. Just to have some noise, another human being breathing the same air.

"Would you like something to eat? I still have . . ."

"No." She shakes her head. "No more casserole. Not even the breakfast kind. I'm getting fat."

Ironically, after a lifetime of unsuccessful attempts to lose weight, my clothes are starting to feel baggy. Sometimes I actually forget to eat. Yet I can't bring myself to throw out the condolence casseroles—not even the quinoa risotto and brussels sprout tater tot ones—because they were delivered with such kind words and good intentions.

Plus, it might somehow signal that I'm no longer mourning Nate, that while I hate rattling around in this empty house by myself, I'm not sure that I miss *him* as much as I should.

Would I be more devastated if I'd been happier or at least less angry when he died? I honestly don't know the answer to that or to any of the other questions I keep asking myself. I also don't know what I'm supposed to do next. Which is not all that surprising given that I'm not living enough of a life to leave a shoe print in the carpet or fingerprints on the refrigerator.

Rosaria and I are still staring at each other when Ansley's daily text arrives.

How ya doing

OK, I reply, not adding the "ish" that rings in my head. You?

Good

That's great. How's Hannah?

Good

Great!

You need anything

No, but thanks for asking. I add a heart emoji. I do not add that the only thing I really need is a reason to get out of bed in the morning.

TTY tomorrow

Ansley texts every morning before she leaves for the office. Ethan texts each afternoon on his way to the gym after work— a tag-team system they've recently worked out between them to make me feel loved. Don't get me wrong, I am beyond grateful that they both check in daily, even if it's out of duty, but while they think of texting as talking, I'd much rather hear their voices. And frankly, why did we send them to college if they're not ever going to use punctuation?

I look up to see Rosaria watching me. If I don't give her something to do, she'll leave, and I'm not sure I can survive another day of silence.

"Why don't you start down here?" I say. "You know, just give it a once-over. The real work is upstairs. I mean, it's practically a pigsty."

Or at least it will be as soon as I get up there and wreak enough havoc to make her happy.

Jazmine

I arrive at Bistro Niko for brunch on Saturday—my second date with Derrick Warren, the first without Thea and Jamal grinning like they've pulled off a palace coup or the heist of the century. Already seated, he stands and smiles as he watches me walk toward him, then waits until I'm seated before sinking back into his chair. I look up into his eyes, which reflect his interest, and allow him to steer the conversation, which is light and comfortable as we peruse our menus. He asks how my week went and then actually listens to my answers. When I ask about his, he tells me about a faux pas he made in court, then laughs at himself. His self-deprecating humor is refreshing after the oversize egos and insecure neediness that I deal with on a daily basis.

When the waiter returns to take our orders, I go with the herb omelet and crispy potatoes while Derrick chooses the trout amandine. We both order mimosas. The live music lends a festive air and floats above the buzz of conversation. Sunlight streams through the plate glass windows and glints off the mirrored bar.

"So, who are you looking at right now? Any athletes you're hoping to scoop up?" Derrick asks.

"I don't do a lot of 'scooping,' but there's a pitcher at a local community college that I feel has been underrated."

"And what is it about him that makes you think otherwise?"

I tense briefly before I reply, but I can see from his expression and his tone that it's a real question and not an assault on my observation skills or knowledge of the game. "Scouts and agents have dismissed him because he doesn't *look* like a pitcher and his windup is a little bit jerky. His fastball rarely hits ninety, but he's got a great changeup and a killer curveball. A lot of people are so fixated on the radar gun that they overlook someone with skill and finesse."

"Interesting."

"Yes. If I can find a spot for him at a ball club with a pitching staff that will take advantage of his strengths and help him develop, he could be big."

He looks at me with surprise. "I didn't realize there was so much nuance involved. So much long-range planning and strategizing."

"Well, there are those who go for the obvious and prefer to sign players who are already in demand. But I'm not always those players' first choice."

"Because?" He waits, practically daring me to say it.

"Because I'm a woman. And although I'm at a well-known agency and have handled some very successful athletes, that is a strike against me in many players' eyes. I have to work harder than most men. Be smarter."

I wait for him to laugh or pass it off as my imagination or knee-jerk paranoia, but he nods. "I see it in the legal field all the time. One of the women who mentored me when I was starting out was absolutely brilliant. I learned so much from her. But she had to prove herself over and over again. She had this poster of Ginger Rogers on her wall that I've never forgotten, not that I knew who Ginger Rogers was at the time. Had to look her up. It said, 'Ginger Rogers did everything Fred Astaire did. She just did it . . .'"

"'. . . backwards and in heels,'" I finish.

"That's the one." His smile is slow and appreciative. "I started watching old musicals after she explained it to me. I don't admit it to a lot of people, but I kind of liked them. And there's never been any question in my mind that Ginger had the harder role."

Our mimosas arrive, and I cover my surprise at Derrick's admission by taking a long sip, then another. Derrick is a good listener and an even better interviewer, and by the time our food arrives, we've covered a lot of ground.

"Thea and Jamal told me that your daughter is a gifted tennis player. Like her mother."

"Oh." I meet his gaze. "I guess I shouldn't be surprised that they felt they had to tell you every little thing about me." My cheeks flush with heat. "I gather they covered the accident and . . . everything?"

He nods, takes a bite of his trout, and chews thoughtfully. "You've dealt with a lot. And managed to raise a child and succeed in a male-dominated profession. It is impressive."

"We all have to play the hands we're dealt."

His eyes close briefly. "Not everyone manages to deal with their hand. Some people fall apart or abdicate all responsibility." His voice rings with something deeply personal. "My father fell in love with drugs early on, and he never loved anyone or anything as much, including me and my brother. We were raised by a mother who fought for every single thing she achieved. Somehow, she got a nursing degree. Fed all three of us. Made sure my brother and I took our studies seriously. Stayed out of trouble. Got college scholarships. I have a huge amount of respect for strong, determined women."

"That's good to hear." I'm getting why Thea and Jamal are so adamantly Team Derrick. "A lot of men don't see things that way."

"A lot of men aren't as smart as they think they are."

"Can't argue with that." I finish off my omelet and potatoes. Derrick is not Fred Astaire, and I'm definitely not Ginger Rogers, but I'm enjoying the dance and surprisingly glad that neither of us seems worried about who's leading.

"It's nice to see a woman who isn't afraid to eat."

I laugh. "That's good news, because we're going to be ordering dessert."

"We are?"

"Um-hmmm."

"And why is that?"

"Because it would be downright criminal to leave here without sharing an order of their profiteroles."

"I've never ordered them here, but I've always had a weak spot for profiteroles." His grin is infectious.

"Prepare to be dazzled, then. I'll try to make sure you get a bite or two."

Sara

When I get home from work on Monday, I find Dorothy in the living room reading, which is still a surprise. The book is *The*

Body: A Guide for Occupants, which we picked up at Between the Covers over the weekend and are planning to share.

She looks up and considers me for a moment as if she, too, is still surprised to be reading in public. "I've never been into nonfiction, but I do love this author's voice," she says. "I'm not sure how I feel about knowing so much about all the stuff that's stuffed inside me." Her voice carries something unexpected.

I look up and meet her eyes.

"I heard from Mitchell today."

"Oh?" Something inside me deflates. I've been meaning to reach out to Meena, who's the only happily divorced woman I know, but at the moment just getting through the workday and acting normal takes all my energy. Plus, once I have a referral I'll have to make an appointment. Tell a total stranger what my husband has done. Admit how completely I've been deceived and then discarded. I'll have to fight for the house. Fight to get back the money he's already stolen. Just thinking about it is exhausting.

"Yes. He apologized," Dorothy says. "He told me that he didn't mean to do what he did. That he panicked and that everything got away from him and he was very sorry."

It takes everything I have to keep my expression neutral. Even though this is almost exactly what he said to me. As if the whole having children with another woman, living a secret life, and stealing from his mother and his wife to keep that life secret was just some sort of accident.

"He said that if I could just give him some time, he'll sort everything out and find a way to try to get the house back." Her chin is up so high that if she were taller, she'd be looking down her nose at me. "And I'm certain that he will keep his word."

Our gazes lock, and I clamp down hard on the retort that springs to my lips. I desperately want, make that *need*, to let loose on someone. But Dorothy is the only person who knows the truth, the only person I don't have to keep up a front around.

I know exactly how it feels to want to believe the best about someone you love. How much I'd give to be able to erase what Mitch has done or somehow turn it into something less heinous. But that would require a level of denial that apparently only a person who gave birth to the perpetrator could possibly achieve.

"And I . . . I realize you have no obligation or reason to allow me to live here any longer." Dorothy's face is pinched, the words blunt and unadorned. "But . . . if you'll let me stay . . . at least for a while, I can . . . My social security, I still have that. I can pay you rent."

Her chin stays up, and she does not cry despite her obvious fear that she's about to be chucked out onto the street. If your own son doesn't care what happens to you, why should the daughter-in-law you've never gotten on with?

It's my eyes that blur with tears.

Dorothy and I have never had a good relationship or seen eye to eye. The only things we have in common now are books and being betrayed by Mitchell. But I grew up virtually homeless, and I'm not going to be putting a seventy-five-year-old woman who's only just recovered from surgery out on the street no matter who she's given birth to. Which is, I assume, what Mitchell is counting on. Unless he actually cares as little for his mother as he does for me.

"I have no idea what's going to happen next or how long . . . things . . . might take." I'm not going to discuss my plans, or lack thereof, with someone who could so easily aid and abet the enemy. I'm somewhat shocked when I add, "But as long as I have the house, you can . . . you're welcome to stay."

"Thank you." The words come out in a rasp, and I know what they cost her. I'm surprised when she cocks her head and continues, "I expect you'll take this the wrong way, but I went online and put together a list of family law attorneys." She holds up a two-page document. "They're listed in order, based on reviews. The top five look very strong."

When I hesitate, she pushes the pages toward me.

"Thank you." The pages rustle in my hand, which seems to be shaking. "I think I'm going to need a glass of wine before I study this. Maybe two."

"I understand. I just . . . if I were in your position, I would already be looking for representation."

I stare at her in shock; does this mean she's on my side? Her tone is brusque. But her face is ravaged by too many emotions to catalog. It looks the way mine feels.

"Would you like to join me?" I ask quietly. "I don't think I can face drinking alone tonight."

Eighteen

Erin

I drive by Walden High School on my way to work like I have every day since I moved in with my parents. What used to be a rambling hodgepodge of added-on wings and buildings has been replaced by a shiny new multistory structure. The sports fields that surround it, including the hill that houses the Badger baseball complex (sometimes referred to as a "mountain" in an attempt to frighten rivals), remain the same.

I slow down to a crawl as I drive past Badger Mountain. All three of my brothers played baseball here, and I spent most of my childhood in or running around the bleachers. On early March days like this one, I would sit wrapped in layers of wool and my brothers' outgrown Under Armour, breathing in the cold, crisp air and listening for the crack of the bat, which sounds entirely different at the beginning of the season than it does in the sweaty playoff days of May.

My parents were always there to cheer on my brothers and their teammates and to support Badger Baseball. I love my brothers, annoying as they can be, and I do love the game. But what I loved most was watching Josh pitch.

I brace for the pain that follows any thought of Josh. Only this time it's not the crippling blow I'm used to but more of a . . . small jab. I mentally feel around, prodding and nudging, but while there are bruises and tender spots, I'm not fighting back tears or the urge to turn around and go home so that I can climb back in bed. Maybe you really can grow past the pain. Or maybe it's just gone on so long I'm finally numb to it.

Because I've left the house so early, traffic is light. When I arrive at the office, Gayle's not at the front desk yet. I drop my things on my desk and am walking through the half-lit halls toward the break room when I hear voices coming from one of the smaller conference rooms ahead.

Larry Carpenter and an agency scout are seated at the oval table in the glass-fronted room staring up at a large television screen on the far wall, their backs to the glass. I glance up to see what they're watching. My step falters when I recognize the windup of the pitcher on the mound. I've been watching a progressively more impressive version of it since I was a little girl. I hold my breath when Josh releases the ball, which flies over the plate, dropping at the last second, far too tempting for the batter not to swing at. Strike one.

Frozen, I watch the next pitch. There's less movement on the ball this time, more velocity. Another swing and miss. A close-up of Josh's face shows his concentration. The calm, focused look he gets when he's in the zone.

The batter strikes out on a perfectly placed fastball. The truth hits me with all the power of that ninety-eight-mile-per-hour pitch. While I've been drowning in a well of self-pity and sadness, Josh has been going about his life, doing what he loves, achieving his dream.

I wait for the unhappiness to rise up and drown me, but the well is nowhere near as deep as it used to be. Somehow my feet have found the bottom, and I realize that if I push off strongly enough, I will break through the surface and shoot up into the air. Where I can finally breathe again. Where I can be *me*. I close my eyes briefly as I imagine it, see it. I am not some wussy princess who can't get up until the prince comes back to kiss her awake. I am one of Disney's newer kick-ass kind, who can wake up her damned self whenever she wants to.

"Erin?" I turn and see Rich Hanson striding down the empty hallway toward the conference room. "You're quite the early bird, aren't you?" He flashes a smile that I'm far too happy to dissect.

"Yes." I smile back. Even though I'm more of a kick-ass princess with an impressive set of wings than a bird. "As soon as I chug some caffeine, I'm going to go catch a whole bunch of worms."

He chuckles and reaches for the conference room door as I soar past.

I spend most of the morning happily working my way through the list Jazmine has left for me. By eleven, I'm completely caught up, so I check in on the group chat that I've barely even opened since everything happened with Josh. Every time I looked at my phone, there seemed to be a million messages, but I couldn't bring myself to read through all of them—the updates, the invites I never responded to, the gossip. More often than not, I'd just open the chat and close it to rid myself of the annoying notification icon and constant reminder that everyone else's lives were still moving along and mine, well, wasn't.

Now that I'm paying attention, I see just how often and for how long my friends reached out and tried to include me.

In those early weeks, I was so humiliated, so ashamed at having held on so hard to someone who didn't love or want me the way I loved and wanted them, that I couldn't face my friends. I never even considered that they might have needed me for some crisis of their own.

The person who shows up the most often and held on the longest is Katrina.

I consider texting her an apology right now, but I don't know if she'd even open it. After the way I've behaved, the way I cut her out, she deserves the chance to reject me in person.

It's almost eleven thirty—late enough to take my lunch break. Jazmine isn't due in until one thirty. Before I can chicken out, I walk out of the office building and across Lenox Road to Phipps Plaza, where I buy a Starbucks Grande Caramel Macchiato—Katrina's favorite—and walk toward the entrance to Saks Fifth Avenue, where she works.

I'm in the mall . . . usual spot . . . pls come for just a minute? I text. While I wait for what would have once been an instant response, I offer up a small prayer for forgiveness.

Seriously??? thought you probably blocked me.

No. Sorry! We used to text and speak a million times a day, and now I don't know what to say. Pls come down.

I wait with the macchiato in my hand for what feels like forever. I'm about to give up when she comes out the glass door and sweeps into the mall wearing a black jumpsuit that shows off her figure. Her makeup is flawless. Her blond hair is pulled back in the perfect messy bun. We are both blondes, but I have always been a miniature Daisy Duke to her Grace Kelly.

Heart pounding, I hold up the macchiato.

She ignores it.

"How are you?" I ask in a wobbly voice, hoping we can maybe work up to the hard part. But she's not having it.

"I tried to be there for you, Erin. But you just ignored all of us like we didn't even exist anymore."

"I know. I'm . . . sorry." Although I came here to apologize, I'm having trouble getting the words out. "I've been so stupid."

Her stare is long and hard. I have no idea what's coming next or what I'll do if she turns her back on me and walks away.

"Then I tried to let you know that I got that job in New York."

"Oh my gosh!" My brain can't quite pivot the way it needs to. Katrina has wanted to move to New York and work in fashion since we were kids. She majored in Fashion Merchandising while we were at Georgia, studied abroad in London, and did a New York study tour. For the last two years, she's worked in the designer department at Saks. She was the one who helped me and my mom pick out my wedding dress and got us her employee discount. "That's . . . oh my God, that's incredible!"

"Yeah." I see the flicker of pride in her eyes, but she is still totally pissed. Forgiveness is not a given. "It would have been even more incredible if you'd bothered to respond. Or congratulated Amber on her promotion. Or Kelsey on her engagement. I mean, Josh was an asshole for waiting till the last minute like he did. But if it were me, I'd rather know before I walked down the aisle. You just ghosted all of us like he was the only person on earth who ever mattered."

I flush with shame at the truth of it. "I'm so, so sorry." I have been a needy ball of self-centeredness. "I . . ." I swallow. "I've been such an incredibly shitty friend."

"The shittiest," she agrees without hesitation. "You just threw us out like we were nothing to you. Everyone's been so afraid of upsetting you, but Josh wasn't the perfect man or anything. If *you* hadn't worked at it so hard, you guys would have been done after graduation like most everybody else." Her voice breaks.

Tears stream down my face. "You could never be nothing. I just couldn't think. I was afraid to think. It was like all my brain cells got sucked out and . . ." My voice trails off. "I lost it. I lost my frickin' mind. And I am really, truly sorry."

She doesn't say anything, but she doesn't leave, either. Tears slide down my cheeks. I feel people staring, but I don't even swipe at my cheeks while I wait for her to speak. "Would you . . . could I maybe take you out for a drink after work before you leave town?"

There's a huff, and I think she's going to blow me off completely and there will be nothing I can do about it. I deserve to be kicked to the curb. But I'm not going to be the first to move or leave. I'm still standing there, holding on to the Starbucks cup, when she takes it out of my hand and says, "Let me check and see what's being planned. There might be a going-away party. *If you're feeling up to it.*"

Relief gushes through me. While I'm not exactly forgiven, she didn't tell me to f-off, either. "If there is one, I would totally love to come and celebrate with you."

Another huff. Softer this time. The road back into Katrina's good graces can be long and winding. Before I can react, she turns and walks back into Saks.

I owe a lot of people apologies, and there will be many butts to kiss, but for the first time since Josh called off our wedding, I feel equal to the task. More importantly, I want my friends back. And my life. And this job.

Just before Jazmine's supposed to be in, I place a copy of Bill Bryson's book on her desk as a thank-you gift for taking me with her to book club. And hiring me. And everything.

I picked it up at Between the Covers over the weekend, and I got one for myself, too, because I want to give book club a try. Everybody there was pretty cool. And if I'm going to move on and let go of the idea of Josh, I'm going to need to stay busy. Plus, the more friends the better.

I might even go back and buy the online dating book. My stomach feels kind of funny at the idea of kissing—or even going out with—someone who isn't Josh. But I'm going to have to start somewhere, right? I don't know if the advice will apply to me—I mean, I'm pretty sure Meena's even older than my mother—but it couldn't hurt to practice around people who don't know what they're doing, either. And it's not like we'd be competing for the same guys. Okay, that thought makes me laugh out loud.

I'm still smiling when Jazmine arrives on the dot of one thirty.

"Please get that scouting report to me by . . ."

I hand her the hard copy before she finishes. "It's also in your inbox. And I've updated your schedule—you have drinks this evening at F&B at eight. Also, your father called to say that . . ."

"I know, I'll be at Maya's match at four thirty and . . ."

"Her match has been moved up to four o'clock, so I rescheduled your two thirty to tomorrow right after a twelve thirty lunch at New York Prime just to be safe. There's a fresh latte on your desk."

She doesn't stop or comment, but a small smile appears on her lips. Which is high praise from Jazmine.

An answering smile tugs at my own as her office door closes behind her.

"Impressive."

I jump at the sound of Rich Hanson's voice. The guy does have a way of materializing out of nowhere.

I look up and meet his eyes, which are always kind of probing even when he's being friendly. I'm not the only one wondering why he's even here at StarSports Advisors, which is way smaller than the LA agency he came from, with its legions of star agents; worldwide offices; and fashion, event, and marketing divisions. Their baseball, tennis, and golf academies have turned out some of the biggest-name athletes on the planet.

Hanson was at the top of the heap there, and football and baseball were his things. Now he and a handful of his biggest clients are here, and nobody knows how Larry Carpenter lured him away or even if that's how it went down.

He nods toward Jazmine's office. "Please buzz her and let her know I'm on my way in to talk with her."

Jazmine

"Tell him I'm not in," I reply when Erin buzzes me. The last thing I need today—or any day—is Rich Hanson.

"He just watched you walk into your office."

"Then tell him I'm on the phone. Tell him I'm . . ."

". . . busy?" Hanson asks as my office door swings open and he steps inside.

I grit my teeth. I am not going to engage in a conversation about knocking before entering. Or get into tit for tat or any other cat-and-mouse games. Because he will automatically assume that he's the cat, and I'm not about to scurry out of his way or look for a hidey-hole. I just wait quietly, allowing my irritation to show, while he looks me and my corner office over, taking in its view of the traffic down on 400 and what locals refer to as the King and Queen Buildings in the distance.

"You don't have a single memento of your playing days," he observes, as if he just stopped in to chat.

"I was a college athlete. That was a long time ago." He's the last person I would ever tell that I threw out virtually every reminder of my brief career the day I came home from the hospital. Xavier was gone, and I knew I'd never play competitively again. I didn't want any reminders of my former life.

"I've known people who pitched maybe one inning in Double-A ball and milked it forever," he says as he takes a seat that I have not offered and he hasn't asked for. "But then I guess that would have been a reminder of everything you lost." It's said almost gently, but my blood goes cold. I can't seem to find the words to tell him this is not his business.

"I understand you have a daughter who may be as talented as you were."

I blink in surprise. "Is there a point here somewhere? Or are you working on a psychology degree in case the agenting thing doesn't work out?"

He smiles. "I fell in love with sports during my first T-ball game. I played three sports in high school—everyone else picked one to excel at, but I wanted to play everything. I was pretty good, but I was never great." He looks down. "I have a huge amount of respect for people who have the talent and the drive. All I had was the drive."

"And the ego. I think you got plenty of that."

He smiles, not at all offended.

"Are you here for a reason or purpose of any kind? Because if not, I am, in fact, busy."

"Right." He straightens. "The wide receiver I mentioned, he's good and he needs the right kind of representation. But I can't take him on because I've got . . ."

". . . Cosgrove."

He nods.

"So, you want to have your cake and eat it, too. And you want me to pretend to bake that cake for you."

"No, I want to do everything I promised for the client I already have. But I hate to see a really promising player get overlooked. He's not ready for the draft right now, but I think he can go pretty high next year if he can be convinced to wait."

"So, you want to use me to convince someone else's prospect not to enter the draft. After you stole Tyrone Browning's endorsement deal for your client."

"Someday you're going to have to explain why you always see me in the worst possible light." He looks at me with an earnest expression I don't recognize. "But for now, I'll just say that if you'd had Verizon locked up for Browning, no one could have taken it from you. He was counting his chickens, and he wouldn't have embarrassed you both if he'd kept his mouth shut like I'm sure you warned him to."

I resist the urge to argue, which has become practically automatic whenever I'm around him. I'm not sure where all that sincerity he just served up came from, but even though he's right about Browning mouthing off, that doesn't mean I'm not looking forward to rubbing his nose in the Sony PlayStation deal. Or that I'm going to take on the wide receiver he claims he's just trying to help.

He hands me a file folder that includes Isaiah Booker's photo and stats. The name is familiar. "Didn't he take over for Juran Holmsby up at Appalachian State at the end of the season?"

"Yeah. He's a junior. Didn't get much playing time until Holmsby got injured. I saw him at a small pro day. He's five-ten, smart, agile. Knows how to run a route. Ran the 40 in 4.45.

"The only agent interested in him is urging him to declare for the draft, which would be a mistake. The kid needs more time and opportunity to develop. Someone needs to convince him to stay where he is another year." He's watching my face. "If it would make you more comfortable, I could introduce you . . . and maybe offer help from the sidelines once he's eligible to sign."

"If I sign an athlete, he's mine." I stare into his eyes, but they're not giving up much. "Tell me the real reason you want to bring me in, and I'll consider it."

"I don't know what you're looking for here. This kid's good, and he needs representation. You're the right person for the job."

"Why me?"

"Because I like the fact that you always bring your A game." Eyebrow up, I wait for the rest of it.

"All right . . ." He shakes his head, puts his hands up in surrender. "And because he was raised by his aunt, a lovely but no-nonsense woman who . . ."

"Would probably tell you to get lost."

"I doubt it, but she'd probably listen better to you."

"I don't actually specialize in athletes raised by single women," I snap, annoyed.

"Well, you kind of do. I mean, I can understand why they'd trust you."

"And they would be right."

He puts a piece of paper with contact info in front of me. Then he picks up his phone and sends me a text with links to Isaiah's most recent game videos. "I told his aunt she might be hearing from you and that we'd like to come out and talk to her and Isaiah." He shrugs as if the whole thing doesn't really matter, but I can tell that it does. "Just think of him as a peace offering."

"A person is not a peace offering."

"Then what is?"

I sigh. "Why don't you stop beating around the bush and tell me what you really want."

There's a brisk knock on the door. Erin pops her head in, takes a quick look between me and Rich. "I was, um, just checking to see if I can get fresh coffee for either of you?"

"Thanks. I'd love some." I'm careful not to smile at her clearly protective tone. "Rich was just leaving."

After she backs out and closes the door again, I stand. "Was there anything else?"

He stands, because otherwise he'll have to look up at me. "We can discuss it when you have more time, but I just wanted to give you a heads-up that Larry and I had a conversation about creating a new tennis division."

I look into his eyes. But I can't read them. "I brought this up when I first joined the agency, and he wasn't interested." I study him as I think it through . . . "But a lot of players are making moves to smaller boutique firms."

"Bingo."

"But we'd need to take on at least one or two top players."

I stare at his face and all the way into his eyes, which is something I typically avoid, and realize that he's far more interested in this subject than he's letting on. What I don't know is why. "Or we'd have to invest the time and money into building them."

His eyes glitter. "I was thinking we might do both."

Nineteen

Sara

I have now read, highlighted, and sticky-noted the copy of *The Empowered Woman's Guide to Divorce* that Annell tucked in my tote bag when I wasn't looking last Saturday. A lime-green sticky note with the words "I'm here" scrawled across it was stuck to the cover.

The book is written by a female therapist and a male lawyer who practices family law and is meant to cover both the emotional and legal aspects of what they describe as "your divorce journey." Which was a little discouraging, since I was hoping that given the fact that Mitch is a liar, a cheat, and a thief, it might be a short trip.

Apparently, my hurt, anger, and fear are a part of this journey for everyone. So is my sense of loss. I thought I'd finally found a partner who would share my life and prove once and for all that I am not unlovable and therefore destined to spend my life alone. I was wrong.

Every night after work I pick up or throw together some kind of dinner for Dorothy and me. Then I sit down to do my divorce "homework," which includes surfing county court, state bar, and judicial websites as well as attorney blogs and articles. As a result, I now know that Georgia is an "equitable distribution" and "no-fault" state. I also know that Mitchell doesn't actually have to agree to a divorce.

The book claims that hardly anyone can really afford a divorce attorney without going into debt and has sections on less-expensive options, like mediation, negotiation, and even self-representation—something I consider for about five seconds until I remember Abraham Lincoln's quote about a person who represents himself having a fool for a client. I already feel deeply stupid for not realizing what my husband was up to.

Today, I have free initial consultations with five family law attorneys. Happily, because of the homework I've done, I can use these appointments to ask more specific strategy-oriented questions. Not so happily, I now know a lot of things I wish I didn't. By the time I get to my last consultation at four P.M., exhaustion has set in. Ditto for hunger and thirst.

Bonnie Traiman appears to be somewhere in her late forties or early fifties. Her brown hair is parted down the middle and hangs in waves to her shoulders. Her calm, appraising brown eyes and her genuine smile are the most comforting things I've seen all day.

Given how wilted I feel at the moment, I'm relieved that she's not wearing a suit, like the sharp-eyed, perfectly turned out lawyers I've already met with. Or heels like some of the other female attorneys.

An eyeblink after we've shaken hands and introduced ourselves, I'm seated on a sofa and she's handing me a Kind bar and a bottled water, which she pulls from a mini fridge built into a bookcase.

"Go ahead. Please." She nods to the bar and drink on the coffee table. "You look like you've had a long day. We're not on the clock until you at least finish the water. I'll be right back." She leaves me alone just long enough to devour the bar and gulp down the water. By the time she comes back and takes a seat across from me, I feel almost human.

"So. How many lawyers have you talked to so far today?"

"You're number five."

"Wow, that's a lot of legalese for one day."

"Yeah. And most of it's been pretty disheartening." The sofa, on the other hand, is pretty comfortable. If it were an option, I'd curl up in a ball right now and never get up again.

"I know this isn't the kind of conversation anyone ever really expects or wants to have. Tell me what brings you here." She's definitely warmer than almost all of the "suits" I've spoken to today, and I appreciate that she doesn't dillydally.

"Well, my husband has been working and living in Birmingham during the week and mostly coming home on the weekends for a little over eight months now. On New Year's Day, I found out, completely by accident, that he has a . . . girlfriend . . . and they have a four-year-old child together and . . . she's pregnant again."

She winces. "That's rough."

I wince at the understatement, but she's the first lawyer today, male or female, to offer what feels like actual sympathy. "I thought that we were happy. Or at least okay."

"So, he asked for a divorce so that he can marry her?"

"No. In fact, it's really weird, but I'm getting the impression that he'd be perfectly happy to stay married and just keep things the way they are."

"Interesting," she says, not at all shocked. "I'm assuming that's unacceptable to you."

"Yes."

"So, here's the thing. If we were to work together, you'd have to decide what you care about most. Raking him over the coals or getting this over with in as equitable a way as possible."

"I was kind of hoping for both. I mean, shouldn't he be punished for what he's done?"

"Yes, he should. But the courts aren't going to do that. In Georgia, you're looking at irreconcilable differences. What he's done is abominable. Unfortunately, judges hear stories like this every single day.

"I prefer to represent women because I think they often get the short end of the stick. Women and children tend to come out of divorce worse off while men tend to walk away better off. If we work together, I will help you win your freedom. Because your freedom is the ultimate win. His punishment is not getting to be your husband anymore."

"But he's used *our* money to support another woman, another *family*." My eyes well with tears that I've been holding back all day.

"That's something we'd have to document and prove." She pushes the box of Kleenex gently in my direction. "Judges want to see a father supporting his children regardless of who mothered them, and frankly, I think that is as it should be." Her gaze is direct and unapologetic. "Is there any one asset that matters to you above all others?"

I dab at my eyes; as always, I'm uncomfortable crying in public. Most of the foster parents I lived with tended to equate tears with ingratitude. "I know Georgia is all about 'equitable distribution,' but I never had a home growing up. The one Mitchell and I bought is my first." My throat clogs with emotion when I think back to the day we took possession. The bottle of champagne we shared sitting on the bare floor of the empty living room. "All I . . . I'd hate to lose the house."

"Once we have a complete list of assets and debts and so on, we'll have a better sense of what's possible." She meets my eyes. "I am extremely cost conscious—otherwise things can really snowball—and I'll save you money wherever I can as long as it doesn't jeopardize the outcome. If your husband hires an attorney, we have a much better shot at reaching a settlement. Going to trial can quadruple the cost."

I watch her face as she talks. I like that she's sympathetic but not soft. I hold my breath while she explains the required retainer and a ballpark of what I can expect to pay at her rate of $350 per hour. That ballpark, like all the others I've heard today, is far more expensive than I'd hoped, but at least she has addressed the issue head-on and promised to keep expenses in mind. Gut level, I feel comfortable with Bonnie Traiman in a way I didn't with the others. I just hope my gut knows what it's talking about.

We both glance down at our watches. I have only five free minutes left and plenty of other questions, but Dorothy's situation has been in the back of my mind all day. For the first time, I bring her up.

"Are you and your mother-in-law close?" she asks after I explain the situation.

"No, not really. At least we never have been. But . . . what Mitchell's done to her is just . . . wrong. And lying to the lender to make sure communication came only to him—wouldn't that be illegal?"

"This isn't my area of expertise, but we do have someone in the firm who deals with elder abuse." She goes to her desk and comes back with a business card. "Just remember to be careful what you share with anyone who might not be completely in your camp."

When I get home, exhausted and oddly hollow inside, I'm shocked to smell food and even more shocked that the tuna casserole and leafy green salad waiting on the table were made by Dorothy. A bottle of wine sits open, and presumably breathing, between our place settings.

"Wow, this looks great." I wash my hands at the kitchen sink, wondering whether to be grateful or suspicious, then join her at the table.

"So, how did it go?" Dorothy asks, dishing salad and casserole onto my plate while I down half my glass of wine. This may be the most motherly gesture Dorothy has ever offered, but Bonnie Traiman wasn't the only attorney I met with today who warned me to be careful about who I took into my confidence.

Dorothy may be living in "my camp," but this was not her

choice. The fact that she's a voracious reader does not automatically make her a kindred spirit. She could be a very thin and somewhat frail Trojan horse.

"Okay," I say as I drink an entire glass of water, then take a bite of salad. "I think I found an attorney." I am careful not to offer details. Mostly I eat and drink—a Kind bar can only go so far—but neither the food nor the wine I wash it down with can wipe out this day or the realities of my life.

Her expression is tight-lipped, and I'm not sure whether it's because I'm drinking too much or because I'm keeping the day's details to myself. But she hasn't exactly shared any of the conversations I've overheard her having with Mitchell. I have no real idea whether she's friend or foe or somewhere in the middle, and I don't know how to ask.

My wineglass is empty, and I'm trying not to dwell on how grossly and painfully unfair life is when Dorothy sets down her fork. She's only eaten a few bites, and *her* glass of wine is untouched. Despite the tight lips and her faint air of disapproval, I see a shadow in her eyes, a vulnerability that reminds me that I'm not the only one of us battling fear and uncertainty.

"When I told the attorney I'm planning to hire what happened to your house, she said that it could possibly qualify as elder abuse."

Dorothy does not meet my eye, but she's clearly listening.

"She gave me the card of a lawyer who specializes in that field. For you. If you're interested."

Dorothy bunches her napkin in one hand. "I'm not that old. And I am *not* going to sue my son." She sniffs. "He's made mistakes. But I know he'll come through. He's promised to talk to the mortgage company and I guess I just have to believe he's telling the truth."

I beat back a rush of disappointment. Was I really expecting her to take my side over her own flesh and blood?

"Thank you for dinner." I stand and reach for my plate.

"Leave it. I'll take care of the dishes."

"Thank you," I say again. "I appreciate it." My words are heavy and oddly formal. The time for pretending that Dorothy and I are ever going to see eye to eye on her son is over.

So is my marriage. There's nothing Mitchell could say or do that would erase what's happened. It's time to find the money to pay Bonnie Traiman's retainer and file for divorce.

"I'm going to turn in early. I'm beat." I turn and head to my bedroom.

> lu·gu·bri·ous
> loo-GOO-bree-əs
> *adjective*
> 1. sad or gloomy
> 2. exaggeratedly mournful
> Ex: "I am far too lugubrious due to the state of my marriage and my life to sit here a moment longer."

Judith

I'm curled up in a chair reading Bill Bryson's *The Body: A Guide for Occupants* and trying not to picture the bazillions of bacteria that reside in my belly button, many of which modern science has yet to identify, when my phone rings.

The sound is jarring. While I'm used to the daily ding of texts from the kids, it's been a while since I got a call from anyone not trying to sell me something.

"Hey. What are you doing?" Meena's voice is even perkier than usual. I'm pathetically happy to hear it.

"Reading our book club book pick and realizing how miraculous our bodies are even though we have a lot of spare parts we don't really need anymore." I flush for the thousandth time at the memory of what happened the last time I used my entire body.

"You gotta use it or lose it, girlfriend." Meena is the only person who knows just how much guilt and anger are mixed in with my sorrow. Not to mention what a horrible comedy of errors Nate's death was. This makes her the only person I can share my emotional roller coaster self with.

"Use it or lose it? What exactly are you suggesting I do with mine?"

"I'm suggesting you shower it, put clothes on it, and bring it over here so that we can hang out. Frank's in California," she says, mentioning the man she met on match.com and is now seeing regularly. "I thought you and I could walk somewhere for dinner." Her voice drops a bit. "After we drop by the building happy hour."

"Sorry, I didn't hear that last part."

There's a pause and then, "My building has happy hours at nearby restaurants every other month. The restaurant puts out appetizers, and we buy our own drinks. This time it's at Del Frisco's—it's just a five-minute walk up the street."

"Happy hour?" It sounds so far removed from my current reality that it takes me a moment to respond. "First of all, I'm in mourning." I consider myself in the family room mirror. Ratty pajamas. Wild hair. Luggage-size bags under my eyes. "And even if I weren't, it would take me hours to get presentable."

"I doubt it. Come on. It'll do you good. It's not healthy to spend so much time alone."

"Thanks, but I don't really feel up to it. I don't think I'm ready for strangers."

"Jude, seriously. You can't sit in the house forever."

At the moment, I'm pretty sure I can. It's one of the few things I feel capable of.

"Sitting there isn't going to bring Nate back. And it sure as hell isn't doing anything positive for you."

"But it would be disrespectful of his memory. He's only been gone six and a half weeks." I have been counting the days. One day, I even used the calculator on my phone to add up the hours and minutes. "People will think I'm . . . that I've forgotten him already. No, I don't want to." Only, some part of me actually does.

"No one here knew Nate, Judith. And they don't know you from Adam's house cat. It's not a crime to do something that might be *fun*."

"Fun?" Surely, this word does not belong in my current vocabulary.

"You're *allowed* to have fun. All you have to do is come, have a few drinks, and meet some of my friends from the building."

Drinking alone takes the edge off and can blur the misery. But it is most definitely not *fun*.

I could go to Meena's happy hour and just have one drink so that I can drive home. Only, I'm not sure one drink is enough anymore.

I've spent a month and a half just trying to get through each day. My biggest accomplishment has been making it until four o'clock—well, sometimes more like three thirty— before I pour the first glass of wine. As if that's some sort of badge of courage. Or proof that I am not an alcoholic.

"Or better yet, spend the night," Meena suggests. "You've seen the guest suite. We can have a pajama party. Then tomorrow morning we'll go to Buttermilk Kitchen for breakfast. They have a pimento cheese omelet that is truly to . . . that I know you'll love."

"I don't know." I'm dug in so deep that I'm not sure how I'll handle the bright light of day. The idea of going somewhere new, of being around strangers with no preconceived notions about who I am or how I should act, is both exciting and frightening.

"Just say yes, Judith. Honestly, I really think this will do you good."

I don't actually feel all that good the next morning when I wake in Meena's guest room with my face pressed into the mattress and my head buried under a pillow. My mouth is dry and cottony. I drag the pillow off my head, pry open one eye, and see my clothes in a heap on the floor.

A brisk knock sounds on the door. Meena's voice precedes her into the room.

"I've been debating whether to wake you up or not, but I was starting to get worried." She places a cup of steaming coffee on the nightstand and plops down on a nearby chair.

"Holy shit." I manage to prop myself up on an elbow and reach for the coffee. My hand shakes slightly as I lift it to my lips. My brain is filled with odd fragments that I can't quite piece together. "Did I get run over by a truck?"

"Not exactly. But you did have quite a lot of . . . fun."

I take another sip. But my memory of last night remains sketchy. "So, I didn't do anything . . . embarrassing?"

"Nope."

"You're sure?"

"Yep."

"Could you stop grinning like that and give me a recap?"

"Okay, let's see. First, we had drinks and appetizers at the happy hour as planned. Then we stayed for dinner and drinks with friends from the building." She smiles. "Then we moved elsewhere and had a couple of nightcaps."

In my muzzy brain, I hear laughter and music and see a large round table crowded with people. "Did I . . . I didn't dance, did I?"

"You did."

"With whom?"

"Everyone!" Meena's still grinning. "We all danced together. You also danced with Chris and Scott, who both thought you were a hoot. And there was this guy at the bar who tried to talk you into going home with him."

I blush with embarrassment, but I am also secretly pleased and oddly impressed with myself.

"Everyone really enjoyed meeting you. And you seemed to be having, dare I say it . . . quite a lot of *fun*."

"I know I'll never hear the end of it, but it appears that you might have been right."

"I'm sorry, what did you say?" she teases.

"Fine. It was *fun*." In truth, I still feel a residual sense of well-being. It was the only evening other than book club that I laughed and smiled. A night that wasn't all about me. Or Nate. Or my guilt. Or the loneliness. "Everyone was very welcoming."

"It's what I love most about the building," Meena says as she puts her feet up on the ottoman with a satisfied smile. "I mean, the location's great and my condo and its views are fabulous. I enjoy the walkability. But it's being a part of a *community* that makes it so special.

"It reminds me of how it was when we moved into River Forge and we all first got to know one another. We became friendlier with some people more than others, but we always had the neighborhood in common. It's like that here, only it's not the 'bubble' we raised our kids in. I like the diversity. The different ages and ethnicities. It reminds me of book club, only I get to see these people more than once a month."

She beams, and I think how much Nate would have liked this place if he'd been willing to let go of the familiar and try something new. Maybe our marriage would have been enhanced by the infusion of new people and experiences. Or maybe we would have been over faster, unable to coexist in the smaller square footage, like Meena and Stan. For the first time since I overheard Nate's "good egg" conversation, I don't feel that pressing weight of unhappiness on my chest. The need to fix my marriage. My life.

"When we got back it was after eleven and you, well, you were having some difficulty getting your pajamas on," she says, and a picture forms in my mind of Meena and me giggling hysterically while I try and fail to get my feet into the legs of my pajamas.

"You were a little *rubbery* last night. It was a miracle you figured out how to get my nightshirt over your head. Lucky for you, I made you take aspirin so you wouldn't have a hangover." A last grin. "You're welcome."

Sunshine streams through the floor-to-ceiling windows. I look around the bedroom, taking in the room's crisp white walls covered with brightly colored artwork, the thick pile rug, and the clean-lined furniture. All so Meena. No sign of the dark woods and heirloom furniture that filled her home in River Forge. No sign of Stan.

"Frank called after I was in bed." Meena lights up at even the mention of his name. "I wish he didn't have to travel so much for business, but it does make the sex spicier." She winks.

We both blush—her in anticipation, me in embarrassment at even the idea of having sex with someone I haven't spent a lifetime with.

"I think we both need more coffee," Meena says. "After that, shall we go out for breakfast?"

My stomach rumbles in response. This is the first time since Nate died that I actually feel hungry. "That would be great."

She reaches for my empty cup.

"Is there time for a shower?" I ask as I get out of bed and stretch.

"Absolutely. As far as I'm concerned, we have all the time in the world."

When I come out showered and dressed, my overnight bag is sitting open on the ottoman. Meena is standing next to it with a copy of *121 First Dates* in her hands. "I hope you don't mind. I took the liberty of buying you a copy."

"Oh, there's no way that's going to happen."

"Just read it. You know, so you'll know what's going on in the world. You don't have to *do* anything."

"Said the snake in the Garden of Eden."

"I don't think either of us is Eve," Meena replies. "And I promise I'm not going to push you to start dating. But one day you might be ready. You were not responsible for Nate's death, Judith. And thanks to you, he did die with a smile on his lips. A lot of men would be glad to go that way."

"But I was lecturing him while he was dying."

"Based on the medical examiner's report you shared, he was probably already gone before you got out of the bathroom."

"So, you think lecturing a dead person and not noticing is better? After all those years of complaining that he wasn't paying attention?"

"Okay. It's a little ironic. And I'm not trying to belittle the loss. I liked Nate, and I'm sorry he's gone. I know you miss him. You built a life and raised children together. But you're still alive. And hiding in the house afraid to come out because of guilt or what someone might think or say isn't going to bring him back.

"It's not an insult to Nate's memory for you to move on with your life. You never have to tell your children that you considered leaving their father. You didn't do it, and believe me, they don't want to hear it. I know that from personal experience. You need to go a little easier on yourself. Nate's heart attack should be a reminder that there are no guarantees in life. None of us know how much time we have left.

"It would be a damned shame to waste your life dwelling

on the past rather than figuring out what to do with your future. I hope one day you'll be as happy as I am right now."

I agree with this in theory, of course; it's exactly what I would say to someone else. But in my experience, giving advice is a lot easier than following it. And making it through one happy hour is not necessarily a harbinger of happiness to come.

Twenty

Jazmine

My daughter has a backhand that could make the angels weep. I mean a serious, God-given backhand that a million years of lessons might never produce. Her forehand is gorgeous, too, and her serve will be a serious weapon one day. She has it all. Everything I struggled and worked so hard to master seems to come easily to her.

She's smart and intuitive, with her father's speed and power and my timing and agility all wrapped in her DNA and tied with a silver ribbon, hers to command. With all that athletic ability that she can unleash at will, she's gotten used to winning.

It's a beautiful March morning, and the sky is bright and clear as I sit between my father and my sister watching Maya play. As an agent, I'm careful to school my features and reactions, but when I'm watching Maya compete, I am every bit as emotionally invested as any other parent.

"Jamal and Derrick had lunch yesterday," Thea says. "And Derrick couldn't stop talking about you."

"That's nice." My eyes remain on the court. It's match point. For the third time. Maya has lost her focus and seems irritated that her opponent refuses to give up. This is when mental toughness becomes even more important. An ace would be nice. But that's never something you can count on. She has to aim for that but also be prepared to play out and win the point.

"He thinks you're really great."

"That's nice." Maya steps up to the service line. She bounces the ball once. Twice. I hold my breath as she begins her serve. As soon as she releases the ball, I can tell that her toss is too low.

The return slams right up the line just out of her reach. She's muttering to herself as she moves into the ad box. Even before she tosses the ball, I know she's going to lose. Because her opponent is laser focused and Maya is clearly angry. At herself. At her opponent. At the world.

I watch her double-fault. Then I watch her fail to return her opponent's first serve. Her second return is long. She has pretty much handed her opponent the game.

The winner jogs to the net and offers her hand. Maya doesn't even attempt a smile or offer congratulations as she shakes it. She's scowling as she stomps off the court.

If Thea wasn't clutching my arm, I'd already be headed for my daughter right now. Her lack of focus lost her the game, but it's her poor sportsmanship that troubles me the most.

"Let Dad talk to her. You're too upset right now."

My sister holds my arm. Somehow, I manage not to shake it off while I watch my daughter stuff her racket into her bag, her movements jerky with anger.

Her coach steps over to speak to her, no doubt a recap of everything that went wrong, and while she doesn't turn away, her face is a thundercloud. I attempt to distract myself by coming up with positives to acknowledge, a practice I've all but abandoned lately, but it's hard to be grateful when your head is about to explode.

Okay. Let's see. It's a positive that Maya's so talented. There, that's one.

Her face is still dark when my father, who has given so much of himself to all of us, hugs her and speaks quietly to her. No doubt pointing out what she needs to work on in a much calmer and kinder manner than I could manage right now.

I force myself to take a deep breath.

Maya tosses her head while my father is talking to her, and if my sister wasn't still holding tight to my arm, I'd already be down there reaming Maya out, something I don't believe in but am dying to do right now.

Instead I search for another positive and come up with the fact that we can afford coaching and tournaments and everything my father struggled to pay for, for me.

When my father shakes his head almost sadly, I've had it. I rip my arm out of Thea's grasp and stride down the bleachers, my sister on my heels, to where my daughter stands, chin out, scowl still in place.

"You need to apologize to your grandfather right now." Somehow, I keep my voice low.

Maya does as instructed, glaring at me the whole time, which, of course, negates the whole apology. Anger and disappointment bubble in my veins like lava in a volcano. It takes every ounce of control I have not to erupt as I hug my father and Thea goodbye.

When they're out of earshot, I turn to Maya. "Lose the scowl. Let's go."

"I'm not . . ."

"Now." I say this quietly, but it's a command.

In the car, I buckle my seat belt and sit with the car idling. "I am incredibly disappointed in you."

She shrugs. "I lost a match. It's not the end of the world."

"No, it's not. And it's not losing that's the problem, although I'm not a fan of the practice. It's giving up. Not staying focused. Not caring enough. Not playing to the end. There's no point in competing if you're not going to give it your all. You handed it to her, Maya. And then after she took the gift you gave her, you acted like a spoiled brat."

She says nothing. But the car is hot with emotion and anger.

"You were born with immense talent. But talent alone is not enough. You have to want to win every time. You have to *commit* to winning."

"Well maybe I don't care about winning as much as you do. Maybe I don't even like tennis all that much."

The words are a knife to the chest. It's hard not to double over. But I am the adult here. "Then quit. No one is forcing you to play. End of story. There's no point in playing if you're not willing to give it your all."

A car horn honks, and I look up to see my sister and father pull out of their nearby parking space. I wave, but I don't put the car in gear. Maya refuses to wave or meet my gaze.

"Should you choose to continue to play," I resume, "being a poor sport is not an option. I know Poppy's told you stories about Arthur Ashe and what a gentleman he was on the court. And how Björn Borg's father taught him to control his temper. Your behavior today was unacceptable. *And* it prevented you from winning."

"You think you know everything." She sounds about five.

"No, I don't. But I do know what it takes to excel at sports. I also know how quickly it can all be taken away from you. You need to respect and honor the talent you were born with. A lot of it came from your father. If you only want to use it for fun or as a hobby, that's your business.

"But if you choose to compete, then you have to *be* a competitor. *And* a good sport."

She doesn't argue. Or speak at all. As I put the car in reverse and back out of the space, I give myself permission to count that as positive number three.

Sara

Dorothy and I haven't spoken much since she shut down the subject of elder abuse the other night. Neither of us has brought up the topic of Mitchell.

I've left several messages on Mitch's cell phone, hoping that maybe we *could* discuss our next steps in some civilized manner, but while I'm angry that he hasn't called back, I'm not incredibly surprised. My husband has always sidestepped, and apparently this is no exception. As if not talking about his secret life and family will somehow allow me to pretend that they don't exist. *If only.* But I will never be able to unsee the sight of Mitch standing in the foyer of that Birmingham apartment with his son and the pregnant Margot at his side. It is imprinted in my brain forever. The caption reads: "My greatest wish denied and handed to another woman."

He's left me no choice but to act. Yesterday, I transferred $3,500 to Bonnie Traiman out of my savings account to cover her retainer so that she can get started. Then I took out another thousand in cash just so I wouldn't feel as broke as I am.

I have always handled our money and paid our bills—or believed I did.

Now I live in fear that Mitch will halt the auto-deposit of his paychecks into our household account before Bonnie can file my petition for divorce or freeze our assets. The only thing that allows me to sleep at night is the knowledge that with Dorothy's "rent" added to my paycheck, I can handle the mortgage payment and household expenses without him if I have to. At least for a while.

Late Saturday morning, I walk through the kitchen on my way to my afternoon shift at Between the Covers and find Dorothy sitting at the table staring out the window. Our copy of

The Body: A Guide for Occupants lies open on the table. She's already close to the end.

"Good morning."

"Good morning." Her tone is polite but reserved. Though she rarely initiates conversation, she always responds.

"How's the book?"

"Interesting," she says. "But I never realized how much scientists and doctors don't yet understand about how we work."

"It looks like you're almost done."

She nods.

"Well, have a good day."

"Thank you. You, too."

As I turn to leave, I tell myself there's no reason to feel bad about leaving Dorothy on her own. She's a grown woman. I've offered to take her wherever she'd like to go, invited her to come with me when I run errands or go to the grocery store so that she can choose what she'd like in the house, but the only time she's taken me up on an offer since Mitchell's confession is to book club, and I practically had to drag her there. Evidence to the contrary, I am not my mother-in-law's keeper.

I'm almost to the garage door when I turn. "Would you like me to bring back anything on my way home from work?"

"No. But thank you." Her smile is polite, her answer precise.

"Okay." I turn. A few more steps and I'm out of here. It's not up to me to entertain her. I make sure there's food in the house. I am here for emergencies. I've even helped her "out of the closet" as a reader. But when I glance back over my shoulder, her hands are gripped tightly together on top of the book. The polite smile is frozen on her face. She looks small and alone.

Before I can stop myself, I turn yet again. "Do you have any book club name suggestions you'd like me to put in the box for you?"

Her laugh is short and surprising. To both of us. I'd never

even known she *had* a sense of humor until that night at book club.

"As if I'd turn them over to the competition so easily." Her smile is close to teasing.

"As if I'd stoop to snooping," I reply with a mostly straight face. "For all I know you just haven't come up with anything."

"Ha! Wild horses and all that," she says.

"Well, then why don't you come to the bookstore with me and put them in the box yourself?"

Once again, Dorothy looks as surprised as I feel. "But then I'd be stuck there all afternoon."

I flush at her response. But now that I've put the idea out there, I feel compelled to defend it. "Spending an afternoon surrounded by books and other people who love them doesn't sound too bad to me. Saturdays are busy. You might even see some of the people you met at book club."

She looks skeptical, and I remind myself that I no longer have any reason to try to turn her into a mother figure. Once Mitch and I are divorced, I'll probably never even see Dorothy again. The thought is not as cheering as it should be.

"It's very nice of you to ask," she says in a tone that borders on gentle. For her. "But I believe I'd prefer to stay here and rest."

"Okay." I swallow. "Right." I'm shocked at how much the rejection stings. I do not ask what she would be resting from. "No worries."

I'm at the door with my hand on the knob when I hear a chair scrape back.

"Wait."

When I turn, she's on her feet.

"I mean . . ." She takes a step toward me. "If I *did* come, what would happen if I wanted to leave before you're finished for the day?"

"I don't know." I'm careful not to smile or look the least bit triumphant. "I guess I'd order you a Lyft or an Uber."

"Oh. Well, then." She smiles almost timidly. "In that case, I guess I could come along and give it a try."

I wait while she retrieves her coat and shoves a stack of folded pieces of paper into her purse, making sure I can see. Clearly, I'm going to have to get on the stick with the book club names. I wouldn't want her to win by default.

Even I am surprised at how warmly Dorothy is welcomed when we arrive at the store. Charm, who I am relieving, flashes her a smile. Annell comes out of the breezeway with the tow-headed Holcomb twins following in her wake and heads straight for us, smiling the whole way. Annell may be small, but her hugs are large and meaningful; her smile is like a bowl of hot oatmeal sprinkled with cinnamon on a cold winter morning. When she releases me, I'm smiling.

"Oh, how great that you've come," she says to Dorothy, still honoring my mother-in-law's invisible "do not hug" sign. "We always have a crowd for story time, and I'm thrilled to have an extra adult on the premises." She looks down at the twin girls who are each clinging to one of her legs. "This is Stacy and Lacy." She cups a blond head with each hand while I reach down to high-five with them. "Their mother had to run out to take care of something."

"People just leave their children here without supervision?" Dorothy is well and truly horrified.

"No, of course not." Annell smiles. "Adult supervision is definitely required. But I've known the twins' mother since her mother brought her to story time as a little girl. So, she felt safe leaving them in my care."

"Oh." Mollified, Dorothy peers down at the little girls, but she doesn't crouch down to their level or attempt to engage with them. Not for the first time, I try to imagine Mitchell's childhood. I know that Dorothy loves him, but she's one of the least demonstrative people I've ever met. (And given that I was raised by a succession of strangers, that's saying something.)

Could that be why he needs extra affection and attention? Or am I just looking for proof that Mitchell's behavior is not my fault? Or due to something I lack?

Determined not to spoil the afternoon, I shove thoughts of Mitch aside and step behind the front desk to stow my purse beneath the counter. "I can hold yours back here, too, if you like."

"Still trying to scope out the competition?" Dorothy asks, clutching her bag to her chest as if I'm going to steal it.

"I swear your entries are safe from me. But here." I grab the cardboard box and set it on the counter in front of her with a huff of exasperation. "Go ahead and stick them in."

Dorothy doesn't make a move. If you don't count the twinkle that flickers in her eye.

"Oh, good grief! Annell is the only person allowed to open the box. Right, Annell?"

"Absolutely. I am the keeper of the box." She lifts it and shakes it so that we can hear the rustle of paper inside. "And no one will be opening it until I read the new batch at book club."

"Fine," Dorothy says. "Turn around." She motions me to turn my back. "No peeking."

"You certainly are serious about this," I observe. "I mean, there isn't even a prize. Is there?"

"Hmmm. Never thought about it. But I don't see why there couldn't be." Annell bends down to Stacy and Lacy. "Do you think we should have a prize for the winner?"

Both blond heads bob up and down. One of them, I'm not sure which, puts her thumb in her mouth. The other says, "I'm liketa win a prize!"

"Even without a prize there will be bragging rights," Dorothy says. "And it's a competition. There's nothing wrong with wanting to win, is there?"

"Of course not," Annell replies. "I can hardly wait to hear this month's entries." She looks down at the twins. "Okay, let's go set up drinks and snacks."

"Yippee! I wanna cupcake!" They race ahead toward the children's section.

"When you're done here, would you like to come help us set up, Dorothy?"

Dorothy flushes with what looks like pleasure. Then she opens her purse, pulls out a wad of folded pieces of paper, and begins to stuff them through the slot in the box top. I've really got to get on this or she's going to win by sheer volume.

Thirty minutes before story time, the jangle of the front bell grows louder and steadier. The store vibrates with color and laughter and . . . life. The steady hum of adult conversation is punctuated by high-pitched squeals of delight and the occasional screech of protest that squeeze my heart and make me wish that every single one of these children were mine.

The brightly colored pillows and floor cushions are strewn across the floor of the kids' section. A low table near the story time stage holds a bright-yellow plastic bin filled with juice boxes and small bottled waters tucked into the ice. Boxes of raisins and individual bags of goldfish curve across the tabletop like dominoes, leading to a plate of cupcakes beautifully iced and topped with sprinkles that I know are Annell's handiwork.

The adult table holds silver urns of coffee and tea along with cups and saucers and a tray of Annell's cream cheese brownies.

I ring up sales and answer questions while parents help their children choose snacks and get them settled. Straws are poked into juice boxes and handed over with instructions to be careful. Tea and coffee are poured. Saturday afternoons at the store are my favorite time of the week.

"Hey, there." Chaz comes in the front door still wearing his EMT uniform. "Just getting off shift, and I wanted to get started on the new book. I think Annell has a copy of *The Body* set aside for me?"

"Yes, she said you might stop in." I go to the hold shelf and retrieve it for him.

"Have you started reading it yet?" he asks as I ring it up.

"No. Dorothy's reading our copy first." I nod toward where my mother-in-law is helping one of the Holcomb twins unwrap a cupcake, something she does with the focus required for defusing a bomb.

"You've got a ton of munchkins here," Chaz says. "It looks like fun. I'll have to bring my niece one Saturday."

Wesley and Phoebe arrive, literally two peas from the same pod, and the three of them greet one another. As always, I am fascinated by how the twins mirror each other, how on the same wavelength they appear to be. I don't really know anything about their larger family scenario, but it must be incredible to be that close to another human being. To share DNA. To have shared their mother's womb.

The three of them go over together to speak to Dorothy. And though they seem to carry most of the conversation, Dorothy smiles in an almost motherly way. When Chaz departs with a cheery wave, Phoebe and Wesley take seats not far from her.

Then Annell claps her hands for attention, and the moms and dads decamp to their space, which is far enough away to speak quietly to one another and not feel "on duty" yet close enough to keep an eye on their children and to swoop in if necessary.

Those with the youngest children settle in near the stage, with their little ones in their laps. One girl leans back, twirling her hair and sucking on a thumb. I feel the pain of want in my chest.

The room begins to fall silent as Annell ascends the two small steps to the stage.

"Welcome to story time," she says. "Please be courteous of others. Remember, if you need to go potty, please go get your adult as quietly as you can. We don't want to disturb others, so there is absolutely no snoring!" Annell snores and snorts aloud in demonstration. The children imitate her snores with snorts of their own.

When the laughter dies down, she continues. "I'm going to read three stories today. *The Very Hungry Caterpillar*, *The Hiccupotamus*, and *Grumpy Monkey*. Which one should I read first?"

There are shouts and chatter. There is no possible way that Annell can discern a favorite, but she does this every week. Because children like to have a say in what happens as much as adults do.

"Good, thank you. That's exactly what I thought." She grins in delight. "Is everybody ready to listen?"

There are happy affirmatives and final shouts. Children wriggle more deeply into laps or cushions or pillows. I sit down on the stool behind the register, put my elbows on the counter, and rest my chin in my hands. And then, like I do every week, I lose myself in the stories and Annell's marvelous voice.

When the last story is over, mothers and fathers gather their children. A line forms at the register. Annell joins me there, placing each purchase in a bag, offering a smile and a thank-you, and helping to keep the line moving.

When the last purchase has been paid for and the store is finally quiet, I notice that Dorothy is still sitting in the same spot where she listened to story time. I'm about to walk over and make sure she's all right when a frazzled blond woman comes racing in the door.

"Oh, Annell, I'm sorry to be so long. It took forever to get a tow truck and then . . ." She looks around. One of the twins comes running toward her. "Mommy! I thought you forgotted me and Lacy!"

"Oh, Stacy, honey. That could never happen." The woman bends down and lifts her daughter in her arms. "But where's your sister?" She swivels, eyes searching the empty store.

Annell takes Stacy's hand and leads her toward the children's section. A gentle smile suffuses her face. "Shh . . . she's just over here. Slept through all three stories."

Curious, I follow them. Annell stops in front of Dorothy.

Who is sitting still as a statue. The other twin is curled in her lap, her head resting on Dorothy's bosom, her thumb planted in her mouth.

The twins' mother steps closer, then peers down. "Goodness," she whispers in what might be awe. "I've never seen her get so close to a stranger before. Ever. She's never been one to go to just anybody."

Dorothy's face suffuses with pleasure. There's a serenity about her I've never seen before. "I hope you don't mind. She didn't ask. She just climbed up and made herself at home." Her voice, though hushed, is gruff. But her eyes gleam.

The mother lifts the little girl gently out of Dorothy's lap. "Mind? I can't thank you enough for taking such care with her."

Dorothy doesn't move as the woman bids her goodbye and leaves, with one daughter still sleeping in her arms and the other at her side.

"Are you okay?" I ask Dorothy as the front door swings shut.

"Of course," she says, straightening. The serenity evaporates. "The child climbed up without invitation. I couldn't toss her onto the floor, now could I?"

Twenty-One

Erin

Jazmine comes in on Monday morning in a really different kind of mood. She's not rude or unusually demanding or anything. But she's definitely strung more tightly than usual.

"Do we have the scouting information on the wide receiver I . . ."

I hand her the file on Isaiah Booker before she finishes.

"And what about the contracts from Sony for . . ."

Ditto for the file on Tyrone Browning's endorsement deal. "Ready to be signed."

This gets r   smile and the nod of surprised approval that I'm always wc ing for.

"You're set for lunch at South City Kitchen and a three o'clock coffee at Seven Lamps," I say. "And your father called and said that he'd take Maya to practice and have her home in time for dinner."

She sighs, which is not her usual response to a mention of her father or her daughter. She doesn't dismiss me or give me anything else to do, so I stay where I am.

"Did you play sports at all?" she asks.

This is not a question I'm expecting, and I have no idea why she's asking it. I take a second to consider how to explain the role that sports played in my family. "I'm kind of athletic, and

I've got good hand-eye coordination—my whole family does. But I'm short and I'm a girl. I started gymnastics when I was in kindergarten, and I'm practically built for the top of the pyramid—so I went with cheerleading. I enjoyed the competition, and it wasn't like I didn't know how to cheer others on— I'd been watching my older brothers play one sport or another since I was in the womb, you know?"

I don't mention how much I've always envied my brothers' size and athletic ability. I think it kind of goes without saying.

But Jazmine says, "Mother Nature can be a hard lady sometimes. The gifts she bestows on us aren't always the ones we want or even know what to do with."

She studies me long enough to make me brace for whatever's coming. "Did you talk back to your mother when you were thirteen?"

I almost laugh before I realize that she's serious. It's a little bit world rocking to see Jazmine, who's always so strong and opinionated, seeming unsure. Not to mention speaking to me as if I'm an adult or a peer. "Absolutely. I think it's a requirement, isn't it? I mean, I can do a mean eye roll and a pretty withering death stare. I've even refused to speak to my mother a couple of times. But most of the time my mother and I were so glad to have another female in the house that we were more of a team."

Jazmine nods in understanding because of course she and Maya must feel the same. "What did your mother do when your behavior wasn't up to par when you were a teenager? How did she punish you?" She's staring past me, to something I can't see, thinking about something she's uncomfortable expressing.

Wanting to lighten the mood, I say, "She locked me in a cage and refused to feed me until I begged for forgiveness."

Jazmine's head jerks up.

"Sorry. I was just trying to pull you back from wherever you were."

One eyebrow goes up, and I know I need to offer a real answer. "Let's see. Usually, I got grounded. Or assigned extra chores. Or I had something I cared about taken away for a while. You know, like my phone. Or driving privileges. Once, I wasn't allowed to go to a sleepover."

"And did those punishments help you to change the behavior?"

"Well, I was always upset that I had so many rules that my brothers didn't—there was a total double standard in our family. I used to get pissed off that I had a curfew when my brothers, and a lot of my girlfriends, didn't. And I hated always having to finish my homework before I could go out or meet up with friends. But, honestly, I'm glad my parents didn't let me get away with stuff.

"They've been there for me during this whole thing with Josh, and even when we've argued, I've never doubted how much they love me. So, although I wouldn't have said so when I was thirteen, I appreciate that they set rules and boundaries. I think discipline and consequences are important."

She's studying me now, and I get how much this matters to her, so I try to pick my words with care.

"If I ever get married and have kids—and that's not looking like a slam dunk anymore—I'm going to be a tough-love mom like mine." I meet her eyes. "And like I think you are."

Her smile is kind of sad at first, but the way she looks at me is different than in the past. I hope that's a good thing. I'm never going to be Louise. But maybe, just maybe, there will be other kinds of things that I can bring to the table.

Jazmine

It's a beautiful mid-March evening, but it is possible that hell has, in fact, frozen over. Because at this very moment, Rich

Hanson and I are in my BMW—*together*—on the way to the home of Yvonne Booker and her nephew, Isaiah.

I have agreed to this meeting because the man in my passenger seat has sworn that our only goal is to urge the wide receiver not to declare for the draft this year. We're in my car because letting him drive might make him think he's in charge. Plus, if anything doesn't play out as promised, I will be free to go and leave his ass behind.

"You are absolutely certain that we have no motive other than what's best for this player at this time?" I ask for what may be the hundredth time.

"Yes, I'm certain."

"And if I had a stack of bibles in the back seat for you to swear on?" I press.

"I would be impressed that you own a stack and carry them with you. But the bibles aren't necessary. You are a damned hard sell, Jazmine Miller. I never thought you of all people would need this much convincing."

"And why is that?"

"Because you're an intelligent, highly educated former athlete and successful sports agent whose personal history is a perfect example of why it's important to have an education to fall back on in the event of injury."

I can't argue with this answer, either. Which is kind of disappointing. I do enjoy a good argument. Especially, I am discovering, with Richard Hanson. "I'm assuming there's a reason we didn't ask them to come to the office?"

"Yes. Yvonne has a lot on her plate already, and I didn't want to ask her to have to come to us. Plus, we're not going to be saying anything Isaiah is going to want to hear. I'd rather not bring him into the office under what might feel like false pretenses."

I make no comment, but I'm almost surprised by how carefully he seems to have thought this out. There've always been so many rumors and stories about his ability to outmaneuver other agents or strike better deals or opportunities for his clients that I've always ascribed his success to underhanded tactics and a willingness to cross the line to get what he wants. But maybe that's just sour grapes on my part.

Yvonne Booker's home is in a neighborhood called Bedford Pine in the Old Fourth Ward, an area that's become increasingly popular as the BeltLine—built on what was once old railroad track—has begun to link city parks and neighborhoods in the southwest corridor of Atlanta. It's not far from Collier Heights, where I grew up and where my parents still live. The tennis court I first learned to play on is maybe ten minutes from there.

I pull into the driveway of a 1950s brick ranch-style house with a small picket-fenced garden in the front. Two massive cherry trees are just beginning to blossom. A basketball hoop hangs above the double garage door.

Isaiah answers the door and invites us in. He's a nice-looking young man of twenty with a shaved head and a wiry, streamlined body that is built for speed. His aunt, who is built a lot like her nephew, is waiting in the living room, which has been recently vacuumed and cleaned within an inch of its life. I can't quite pin down her age, but I'm thinking late fifties to early sixties.

"Thank you for coming out to see us." Yvonne Booker shakes both our hands before inviting us to sit, side by side, on a floral chintz sofa.

A pitcher of iced tea and what look and smell like homemade chocolate chip cookies fresh out of the oven sit on the coffee table. "May I offer you a glass of tea and a cookie?"

"Thank you. That would be great." I learned long ago to never turn down offered food or drink. Especially not something someone has taken the time to bake for you.

"Richard?"

"Absolutely, thank you."

She nods and pours tea and passes the plate of cookies while I try not to look surprised at Rich Hanson's manners. She and Isaiah sit in chairs directly across from us. She does not invite us to call her Yvonne.

There is silence while we sip our tea and take bites of the cookies, which are truly heavenly and well worth the calories.

"Thank you for seeing us, Miz Booker," Rich begins. "As you know, I've watched Isaiah play, and I think he's got a bright future ahead of him."

"Yes," she replies, her eyes on Rich Hanson's face. "I'm very proud of my nephew. He's always been a good boy and has grown into a fine young man. Earned himself a college scholarship. In another year, he'll have a degree. I'm not keen on anyone trying to talk him into doing anything that might jeopardize that."

I barely breathe while I wait to see whether Rich will keep his word or reveal some less noble agenda. I brace as he smiles and leans forward. Relief courses through me as he says, "I couldn't agree more. In fact, I believe it would be a big mistake for him to declare for the draft as a junior. He's not ready, and there's no reason to rush things."

Yvonne's face reflects only mild surprise and something else I can't quite make out. Her nephew's is mottled with shock and anger.

"What?" Isaiah glares at us. Whatever he was expecting, this is not it. "Then what in hell are you doing here? Grant Peters at AMI told me I can make good money if I go high enough in the draft *this* year," Isaiah sputters. "And I think it's time I pay back some of what my aunt has done for me."

"Oh, Isaiah," his aunt sighs. "I did not work two jobs all these years for you to leave college before you graduate."

"I know what's going on here," Isaiah says, his gaze, and fury, focused on Rich. "You're just here to make sure I don't compete with your boy Ellis Cosgrove; he's a client of yours, isn't he?"

"Yes, he is," Hanson says smoothly. "And you are not in his league right now. But you will be."

"That's not what Grant Peters says."

"Have you researched Grant Peters? Read about what's happened to most of the athletes he's signed?" Rich asks.

Isaiah's chin juts forward in anger. His body is tight, as if he's holding himself back.

"Because Grant Peters is all about grabbing up low-lying fruit. Selling young talent that hasn't ripened yet for ten cents on the dollar. What he is *not* about is fertilizing and pruning and watering and helping the fruit get bigger and stronger."

"I don't care about all this fruit shit. I am not fruit! That is a damned stupid example."

I'm actually enjoying watching Rich Hanson get swatted around. Except of course for the ways in which Isaiah reminds me of Maya. All headstrong and sure of her talent, with no idea of how easily it can all be smashed to pieces. Or yanked away.

"I'm talking about the fact that there is no reason to rush this, Isaiah," Rich continues calmly. "Juran will be gone next year, and you will be starting every game. People that matter will know who you are and what you can do. Teams will be fighting over you. You will be invited to the Combine and not some small pro day. If you go now, some team will pick you up just to have you around, and you'll get a pittance compared to what you could command next year. Plus, if you wait, you'll have a degree to fall back on."

"I don't plan to be falling back a single step." Isaiah folds his arms across his chest.

"No one ever does. That doesn't mean it doesn't happen," Rich replies with a depth of feeling I've never heard from him before.

Isaiah's aunt turns to me. "I'm curious. What do you think, Miz Miller? Why are you here today?"

"I'm the cautionary tale. The person who discovered first-hand how important a college degree can be. I was a college athlete—I played tennis at Georgia Tech and was looking to turn pro as soon as I graduated. I was on my way, dreaming about being the next Serena Williams, when I . . . I was involved in a car accident. My chance to compete professionally was over in an instant. I lost somebody I loved." I don't mention that I lost the love of my life. Or that I also became a single mother. "Fortunately, I had a degree. And I went on to law school. I represented a few athletes who needed help with their contracts, and ultimately, although I hadn't planned it, I became an agent. So, as far as I can see, I'm here to make sure Isaiah understands how important it is to have a degree when and if the ability to play football is taken away. And frankly, it doesn't even take an injury to make that happen. According to the NFL Players Association, the average career of an NFL player across the league is 3.3 years. For wide receivers, it's 2.81."

"Aw, hell!" Isaiah says. "Those are just numbers. I'm not worried about any of that shit. Nothing's going to be happening to me."

"You're not the first athlete to believe that. That doesn't make you right," I reply as calmly as I can.

He snorts in disagreement. The only reason he hasn't stormed out of the room is the hand his aunt has placed on his shoulder.

"And if Isaiah was your son?" Yvonne's voice breaks on the last word. "If you'd raised him up and you knew how much he wanted to be a professional football player?"

"I'd be every bit as proud of him as you are, Miz Booker. And I would absolutely want him to have a college diploma.

Once he'd earned that diploma, I'd want him drafted as advantageously as possible."

I glance over at Rich, who's watching Isaiah's face carefully, almost as if he's searching for something in it.

"There are a number of really strong receivers in this draft class. Next year, there are only one or two. If Isaiah has as good a senior year as we think he can"—am I really presenting Rich Hanson and me as a team?—"he'll be much more valuable. He'll be totally ready and in the front of everybody's minds. Not an afterthought. *And* he'll have an education no one can take away from him."

I'm starting to wonder why Rich isn't chiming in as I wrap up.

"I think that makes a lot of sense. We're only talking about a year," Aunt Yvonne says quietly.

Isaiah's chin juts angrily. His body language is as closed off as it's possible to get. "With all due respect to you, Auntie, this is total and complete bullshit. I don't want to wait and waste this time on a degree I'm not ever going to need."

The young man glares at me and then at Rich.

Yvonne cups his cheek with one weathered hand. "You need to listen to what they're saying, son. You need to stay in school and get that degree and show all those scouts who you are and what you're made of. You do not need to settle for what you can grab right now. That's the easy way, the lazy way. And I know I taught you better than that."

She drops her hand but holds her nephew's gaze. I am so impressed by this woman, I'm barely breathing. This is the very kind of tough love Erin and I were talking about the other day.

Finally, Isaiah nods. He closes his eyes briefly. It's clear he's still not happy about waiting, but he's not going to buck this woman who has raised him and done so much for him.

As we prepare to leave, I notice what seems like a silent conversation taking place between Yvonne and Rich. A relieved smile. A nod of the head. I look more closely as she packs up a small bag of cookies for the two of us and hands them to Rich along with parting words I can't hear and another look I don't fully understand.

"Thank you so much for coming out. And for . . . explaining things," she says as we walk toward the door. "It was a pleasure to meet you, Jazmine."

Moments later, we're outside and heading toward my car.

"That went well," he says. "And you didn't even have to pull the single-mother card. Thanks for coming with me."

While I back down the driveway, I catch a glimpse of Rich Hanson's face. He's wearing a satisfied smile, but there's something more there. Something that doesn't quite add up.

My foot finds the brake as realization dawns. I wasn't there today to impress or convince Yvonne Booker of anything. Just the opposite. This was all a show. Performed for Isaiah's benefit.

"You could have told me why you wanted me to come with you today, you know. Instead of playing me."

"I'm sure I don't know what you're talking about," he says, but his indignation is feigned.

I shake my head, mashing my foot on the gas as I put together the signs I missed. "She reached out to you, didn't she? To try to talk some sense into her nephew. And for some reason, you decided to add me to the cast."

I drive, watching the small, neat houses go by as I try to work it out. "Seriously. How do you and Yvonne know each other?"

For a minute, I think he's going to try to deny it. Then he says, "Her son was an old friend of mine. The very first NFL player I ever signed."

"Hiram Booker." The name slips out of my mouth, the final puzzle piece. "Wide receiver, UNC, two-time All-American.

Went to the Atlanta Falcons in the second round. Injured in a playoff game in 1997 and never walked again. Died in . . ."

"In 1999. Self-inflicted gunshot wound to the head," Rich finishes. The sigh that follows is heavy. "That was the year Isaiah was born. Yvonne took him in when her younger sister died in childbirth. Gave her a purpose and him a home." Another sigh. "Yvonne did everything she could to keep Isaiah from playing football—there's not a single photo of Hiram in a uniform or a plaque or anything else from his football days anywhere in that house. But Isaiah has the same kind of speed and talent. He reminds me so much of Hi."

For the first time, I feel the urge to comfort this man. I push it aside. "You shouldn't have lied to me."

"Not knowing allowed you to be yourself and speak more convincingly."

I take my eyes off the road long enough to give him a steely look.

"And I think it was really more of an omission than a lie."

"If you'd told me that you were doing a good deed and you needed my help, I would have said yes."

"Probably." His smile is a far gentler version than I'm used to. "But where's the fun in that?"

I know I should give him some shit. Tell him how and why I object to the manipulation.

But even as I consider what I might say, I accept the fact that today was not at all about me.

"Let's just say your plan worked. And I'm going to forgive you this one time. Because I understand where Yvonne is coming from. There isn't much I wouldn't do to help my daughter make the right choices. And Isaiah has the makings of a great athlete."

"That's very . . . big . . . of you," he concedes with a far more familiar tone.

"Yes, it is," I reply, glad to be back on familiar footing. "But there's a price to be paid for tricking me into something that I would have done gladly if only you'd treated me like a colleague rather than a mark."

"And what would that price be?" His eyes are on my face. A smile tugs at his lips.

"When Isaiah signs with StarSports Advisors, he belongs to me. You will keep your thoughts about how he should be handled to yourself."

His smile grows. "I wouldn't have it any other way," he says. "Besides, before we left, Yvonne told me that she already likes you better than she ever liked me."

Twenty-Two

Sara

The day Mitchell is served with divorce papers, he does something he hasn't done since taking the job in Birmingham. He braves Atlanta traffic on a weekday afternoon.

When I get home from work and see his car in the driveway, I gird my loins. (A phrase whose origin I'm going to have to look up.) I find him at the kitchen table with his mother, an untouched sandwich in front of him.

Mother and son look up when I enter. Mitch glares at me. Dorothy appears nervous with a possible side of guilt. I can't tell whether they've been arguing with each other or plotting against me.

"I got served with divorce papers today. In front of a new client. Without warning," Mitch says, his eyes narrow.

"How horrible for you," I reply, with every ounce of sarcasm I can muster. In the past, I would have been careful not to upset Mitch or argue in front of Dorothy, but in this moment all I can think about is the indignity and injustice I've suffered. "But then I don't remember you warning me that I might hear from your secret son on your secret cell phone. And you clearly never gave a thought to what you were doing to me. How you were trampling all over our vows."

"This is not the time for recriminations," Mitchell says.

"Oh, I don't know. This seems like a perfect time for recriminations. Did you honestly believe I would just sit here and take it once I knew you were building a family with another woman?"

"She tricked me. She told me she couldn't have children. That she'd had some illness when she was a child that made her infertile." He actually looks indignant.

"Oh. So this was all *her* fault?"

"No. No, of course not. I just want you to know that I didn't intend for any of this to happen."

"Yes, you keep saying that. But it no longer matters what you did or didn't intend. Or that she somehow managed to 'trick' you *twice*. Because for at least a third of our marriage, you've been sleeping with another woman." My voice breaks, and it occurs to me that I'm making a scene, something I've avoided for most of my life.

"But I'm so unhappy. Things got away from me." He sounds like a teenage boy trying to justify how he totaled the car.

"You, more than anyone, knew how much I wanted children. Yet you refused and then went off and impregnated someone else. Twice. You gave *her* the children *I* begged for. Do you have any idea how much that hurts?"

"But I didn't want children. I don't . . . I saw what it took for my mother to raise me, everything she gave up, how small her life became. And I never wanted that kind of responsibility. Not any of it."

Dorothy gasps.

My eyes remain on Mitchell. "And stupid, responsible me respected your feelings."

Dorothy pulls herself to her feet, leaning on the table for support. "When your father deserted us, I swore you'd never want for anything. That I'd make it up to you."

"But . . . you told me you didn't know who my father was." Mitchell stares accusingly at his mother.

"I said that so that you wouldn't feel abandoned." She exhales heavily. "Do you really know me so little that you believed I had no idea who fathered my child?

"I have loved you and protected you from the moment I realized I was carrying you. Yes, I put you before everything else. Yes, I lived a life that wasn't what it might have been. No one *made* me do that. I did it out of love." She shakes her head in wonder. "And all you took from that was to never give that much of yourself to anyone?"

I'm frozen in place as this woman, who has always been so guarded, spills out her lies and her truths.

"I know I'm not warm or *fuzzy.* Neither were my parents. But I never doubted that they loved me. I could tell by their actions if not their words. But you have not learned any of the subtlety of love. Or bothered to look deeper than the very surface." She moves closer, looming over him.

"You're a grown man, but you still behave like a child. Making excuses for what you've done instead of making up for your bad deeds and behavior. And now you expect the wife you've cheated on and stolen from, and who has taken in the mother you've left homeless, to go easy on you? To be careful of you while you moan and complain about the children you've fathered and don't want to be responsible for?"

She takes a deep shuddering breath. Her hand trembles on the table. "Shame on you. And shame on me for allowing you to turn into the selfish, self-centered person you've become."

She turns to face me, her face bleak. "You were right that day when you said that my son isn't good enough for you. And it's clear I'm not going to be winning any 'mother of the year' awards. I was wrong to treat you the way I did, trying to somehow keep his affection, what there was of it, to myself. Horribly wrong."

I'm too shocked by her apology to respond.

"I've turned a blind eye because he has always been all that

I had." She takes another deep breath. "I owe you an apology, Sara. And my gratitude.

"Now, if you'll excuse me, I'll leave you to hash this out. Hopefully, like the adults you are."

I study Mitch's shocked face as his mother leaves the kitchen. I'm still staring at him when her bedroom door closes behind her. Has Mitch always been only for himself? Did I settle for someone who didn't really love me, because I couldn't bear being alone anymore? Or did I imbue him with qualities I wished he possessed rather than see him as he really was? I may never know.

"Have you hired an attorney?" I ask.

"Yes. You didn't leave me much choice, did you?" He says this with quiet fury but not a shred of shame.

"Then I suggest we let them get to it so that we can get this over as quickly as possible."

"You're going to be sorry, you know," he says.

"Oh, I'm already sorry. But not for the reasons you think."

"No, I mean it. Because your precious house will have to be sold and the proceeds divided up. And there's quite a lot of debt that you'll have to help pay off. Both of us will be worse off."

I straighten my spine. Raise my chin. "You just worry about yourself," I say stiffly. "Like you apparently always have. I wonder how long it will take Margot"—the name rolls off my tongue for the first time, no longer a woman to be afraid of but perhaps one to pity—"to realize that the man she's stolen is no prize."

> wish·ful think·ing
> /ˈwɪʃ·fəl ˈθɪŋ·kɪŋ/
> *noun*
> the imagining of an unlikely future event or situation that you wish were possible
> Ex: "Expecting Mitch to grow up and put others first is a tragic case of wishful thinking."

Jazmine

Derrick and I sit at the bar at Valenza, sipping negronis and waiting for our table. The Italian restaurant is packed and noisy, which is how a restaurant should be on a Friday night. I come here often because it's just a ten-minute walk from the house.

This is only my third date with Derrick, and if I hadn't put my foot down, Thea and Jamal would be here, pushing us together and grinning like banshees over their success as matchmakers.

"So, what is Maya doing tonight?" Derrick asks between sips of his drink.

"She's spending the night at her grandparents so that my father can take her to her match tomorrow." I do not add that Maya asked me not to come or that my father promised that he would have a talk with her about her on-court behavior.

"I'd love to come watch her play sometime." He smiles. "Jamal says she's really something and has incredible potential. 'Like her mother.' And that's a direct quote."

"I think she's way more talented than I ever was." I feel the wrench of regret as I think about how proud Xavier would be of his daughter's athletic ability and how much of that ability came from him. "But I'm starting to wonder if it's becoming too big a part of her life. If maybe it would be better for her to pull back and, I don't know, just be a teenager."

"Did you wish that when you were her age?" he asks, his eyes on mine.

"No. I practically slept with my racket. All I wanted was to win as often as humanly possible. To be the best. And, of course, I wanted my father to be proud of me."

"Nothing wrong with that."

"No, but I'm not sure whether I'm pushing her to fulfill my dream because I couldn't. Or if it's really what she wants."

"Maybe you just need to talk it over with her."

My snort is pure reflex and not particularly ladylike. "Said the man who has clearly never had to face down an angry thirteen-year-old girl."

His laugh is easy and uncomplicated. If men were awarded a theme song, and perhaps they should be, Derrick's would be "Don't Worry, Be Happy."

"Completely true," he replies. "But I have no doubt you're up to the task. Maybe it's just a matter of finding the right moment." He smiles again, a flash of white teeth when I roll my eyes. "There. Now, is there anything else I can solve for you?"

At the table, we take our time perusing the menu. Actually, I don't peruse because I pretty much know it by heart. And though our waiter explains the specials and answers all of Derrick's questions, I choose the fritto misto for our first course and the coniglio (braised rabbit) for my main dish like I almost always do.

Derrick tut-tuts over what sort of person could consume a relative of Bugs Bunny, then goes for seafood, with no qualms at all about devouring Charlie the Tuna. I make sure we get an order of the butternut squash ravioli because I can never let anyone leave this place without at least tasting it. I let Derrick choose the wine.

He's remarkably easy to talk to. It's almost like being with a girlfriend who happens to have a hard body and "man parts." We cover a lot of ground while we sip wine and eat our way through some of my favorite foods. I can't imagine him losing his temper or doing anything remotely underhanded like— I'm about to think of Rich Hanson, except that it turns out Rich Hanson isn't quite as big an asshole as he leads everyone to believe. I think back to our visit with Isaiah and his aunt. There aren't many agents who would go to such lengths to save a player from himself.

"Jazmine?"

"Hmmm?" I blink back to the man across the table from me.

"I know you're the expert on desserts. Which ones should we order?"

"I commend you for leaving this important choice to a professional," I tease, then talk him through my three top picks.

"Only three?" he says. "I'm shocked."

"Wow. I'm glad I left the decision to you," he says later as we linger over the final bites of tiramisu and the strawberry crostata with vanilla bean gelato. "These desserts are amazing."

I nod my agreement. "Glad you like them. I can never fall completely in love with a restaurant that doesn't deliver all the way to the very last bite."

"No pressure there."

We laugh again, and I think how easy Derrick is to be with. There's no need to press a point or to argue. No hint of dark secrets or hidden layers. If he hadn't mentioned his father's addiction to drugs, I'd never guess he'd dealt with anything unpleasant.

Unlike Rich Hanson, with whom sparring is not just encouraged but required. Appalled at his second intrusion into what is proving to be a perfect evening, I shove him and his cocky smile right out of my head.

"Would you like to try another favorite place of mine?" I ask as he stands and pulls out my chair.

"I'm up for wherever you want to go, but I'm not sure I have room for another bite."

"How about another sip or two?" I suggest. "Brookhaven Wines just across the street is having a complimentary tasting. It's always fun to try something new."

Others might respond to this with a double entendre or something that hints at intimacy, but Derrick simply smiles as we stroll companionably across Dresden and into the wine store and the happy buzz of conversation.

Jeff, one of the owners, gives me a hug of greeting and shakes hands with Derrick. "Now this one looks interesting," he teases.

"Did my sister call and tell you to say that?"

"Nope, I can see it with my own two eyes. Be sure to try the Barolo and the Cab."

He passes us on to Eddie, who pours us generous tastes. Then we mingle with the mostly neighborhood crowd.

"They have a wine club, too," I explain. "I'm never going to be an aficionado, but I like trying new wines. And on the exceptionally rare occasions when I entertain, I know I'll be safe with whatever they recommend."

"Very cool. I appreciate you sharing your hood with me."

He takes my hand and matches his stride to mine as we amble back to my house in the crisp spring air.

On the porch, we stand in a spill of light. When he leans down, his mouth is curved into a smile, his features are dappled with light, his eyes are shadowed. Slowly, he angles his face toward mine, hovering briefly, and I realize he's giving me time to object or withdraw.

There was no thought of a kiss after that first evening with Thea and Jamal. Our brunch was followed by a quick peck on the cheek before we went our separate ways. He's the first man I've dated in so long, I'm not sure what rules apply—or even if there are any. And this doesn't seem like the right moment to google it.

I close my eyes, eager to discover what he tastes like, how I'll respond. Whether his kiss will sweep me off my feet and allow me to stop all this *thinking*.

One strong arm encircles my waist. I wait for the prick of goose bumps, a shudder of longing, a tingle as he pulls me close.

It's been so long that I'm actually afraid I'll incinerate on contact. To put it in symphonic terms, I want the clash of cymbals. A timpani roll that reverberates like thunder.

When his lips find mine, I brace for Beethoven's Fifth Symphony. What I get is a Brahms lullaby.

When he pulls away, I open my eyes, surprised that it's over.

"Thanks for the lovely evening," he says with a smile. "I had a really nice time."

Twenty-Three

Erin

Everywhere I go, people are talking about Josh.

The name that was virtually never spoken or even hinted at in my presence is now on everybody's lips. And there's nothing I can do about it but pretend it doesn't bother me. Kick-ass Disney princesses don't run around with their hands pressed over their ears trying not to listen.

I'm at the office the day the Braves play their season opener in Houston. I know Larry's at the game. So is Rich Hanson. If Josh and I had gotten married, I would have been there, too.

StarSports Advisors represents four key Braves players and several who are in the Braves minor-league system, so every office television I pass is tuned to the game.

I take my time pouring my coffee so that I can watch the break room television out of the corner of my eye. I'm punished with a camera shot of the dugout that zooms in and lingers on Josh while the analysts discuss the contribution he's expected to make to the team, which has several of its starters on the disabled list. I edge closer just in time for an even tighter close-up on the face that used to be as familiar as my own. My heart pounds as I study him. He's still clean-shaven, and his hair is still cropped short, but now I see subtle differences in the way he holds his head, his awareness of the cameras, the weight of expectation.

The camera pulls out, and I see the leg jiggle that I know signals anticipation, not fear. He's sitting next to Tyler Flowers, a catcher who's almost a decade older but also grew up in Atlanta.

I lean even closer so that I can hear as the TV commentators point out that Braves fans haven't been this excited since hometown boys Brian McCann and Jeff Francoeur were drafted. Then they debate whether Josh is as good as people think. Whether he'll prove his potential or be a disappointment. Brian McCann had a long and successful career. Francoeur not so much.

I feel eyes on me, no doubt both curious and pitying. I know I should act as if this means nothing to me, only I can't stop watching the screen. Can't stop imagining how much Josh must love being compared to McCann, who was always his idol.

They speculate about how many innings Josh might get. Whether they'll give him innings on the road or save his major-league pitching debut for the first home game on April 2, which is just a little over a week away.

I have to keep reminding myself that this has nothing to do with me. That his life and mine are no longer connected. I am moving on, but how are you supposed to push someone entirely out of your mind when you can't even skim through the sports section without seeing his name? Will I ever be able to watch a Braves game and see him as just another player?

At Sunday dinner, my entire family is practically oozing with excitement about the upcoming home opener while trying not to show it. All three of my brothers stayed away from Josh that first month or so after he called off the wedding, and they *did* offer to punch him out on my behalf. But now that the season is starting, hostilities have apparently ceased.

"Josh texted to say he's leaving tickets at will call for the Friday night home opener," Tyler says with a grin that only fades when everyone else's eyes land on me. My oldest brother, Travis, cuffs the back of Tyler's head.

"Oh. Sorry." Tyler shoves Travis's hand away. "I figured now that she's not lying around in bed all day looking like a bag lady it was okay to talk about him."

"Yeah. Isn't it time to bury the hatchet?" My middle brother, Ryan, lifts one arm. He and Tyler break into the Braves tomahawk chop and hum the wordless chant that has been a part of Braves games since before I was born. (And which, despite its recognized and much discussed insensitivity to Native Americans, has not yet been banned. Don't even get me started on Chief Noc-A-Homa . . .)

Travis huffs his disgust. "You two are such cretins. You should know it takes girls way longer to get over shit than it takes guys. You don't want to send her back to bed, do you?"

"Oh my God!" I shout. "I'm sitting right here. Do I look like I'm headed back to bed?"

The Three Stooges consider one another, uncertain.

"How would I know?" Tyler finally counters. "I have no clue what makes girls do what they do." (His recent break-up with his very first girlfriend has soured him on love.)

"Guys, that's enough," our father says. "I'm sure Erin is fine with you going to the game. But there's no reason to rub her nose in it."

"He's leaving tickets for you and Mom, too," Tyler says.

"Oh." Dad's smile is automatic and squashed as soon as Mom gives him the eye.

"He, um, said he was going to leave one for Erin, too. In case she wants it." Tyler adds this more quietly.

All eyes rivet on me. Silence falls. The last time this happened, Ryan was trying to stab the last piece of steak on the platter and Travis's hand got in the way.

"You can all relax," I say as clearly and calmly as I can. "No one needs to miss the home opener on my account." I smile as best I can and excuse myself. I don't mention the extra ticket because while I'd love to say that I have no issue with going to the game, I'm not at all sure that's true. And I definitely don't see how I could sit and watch Josh pitch while surrounded by my family, watching me like I might fall apart.

The dishes are done and I'm still resisting the lure of my bed when a text dings in from Hailey—longtime friend, member of the gang, and supposed-to-be bridesmaid. **Going Away party for Katrina on for Saturday, April 3 8pm at St. Regis.**

I'm telling myself everything's okay, I'm getting my life together, it'll be fun to see everybody, when a follow-up text arrives. **Josh coming, too.**

Great. My immediate future now includes a Braves game I'm not sure I can make myself attend and a party filled with people I've been avoiding, including the guy who decided not to marry me. Take that, Universe!

I wander into my bedroom and eye the unmade bed. It crooks its finger. I've always known that one day I'd have to see Josh again. Only I thought it would be on television or from the stands or at the office, where I could hide my feelings behind a mask of professionalism.

For one very long moment, I consider climbing back in bed, burying my head under the pillow, and becoming the pathetic bag lady my brothers think I am.

Instead, I smooth the sheets, tuck in the comforter, and fluff the pillows. Kick-ass princesses may not come with a manual, but I know they don't lie around and wallow.

Judith

It's been two months since Nate died. That's the equivalent of eight weeks, fifty-six days, 1,344 hours, or 80,644 minutes. Yes, I'm counting!

I've spent a lot of those 80,644 minutes wandering through my empty house (and occasionally messing it up enough to keep Rosaria from quitting), trying to come to terms with what happened. Trying to let go of the guilt I carry. Trying to figure out what I'm supposed to do next.

After a whirlwind shopping trip for resort wear, Meena left for the Mayan Riviera with Frank, so I've had no one forcing me to get out. The kids continue their daily text tag-teaming, but the only phone calls are from Realtors who've learned that I'm widowed and who think I should sell the house.

I've spent much of my life worrying what people think of me, but I'm beginning to realize I'm not at the forefront of anyone's thoughts. (At least no one who isn't trying to get a new listing.)

All the errands I used to complain about, all the grocery shopping, the meals I planned and cooked, the doctor's appointments I scheduled for both of us, the hair and nails and everything else I filed under "personal maintenance," the social life that I organized and kept track of—without Nate, it all feels so unnecessary. What difference do my hairstyle or my nails make? Why cook when I can microwave a frozen meal or pick up or order something delivered? I have no idea how to use up all the time I have on my hands, how to create a life out of all this "nothing."

For those first months, I could hardly make myself leave the house; now, I can hardly bear to be in it. Listening to the echoing silence. Reliving the life I was ready to discard. Cursing Nate for dying. Chastising myself for not saving him.

When I can't take it anymore, I get in the car and go . . .

somewhere. Often lots of somewheres, most of them within a five-mile radius. I wander through the grocery store for an hour and leave with a head of lettuce. I go to the dry cleaner and finally retrieve the carefully pressed dress shirts and lucky ties that I dropped off when Nate got back from Europe; I'd give anything to feel even an ounce of the fury I felt when I left them there. I go to Costco and push the basket through every aisle, which takes up a good forty minutes, ultimately leaving with exactly enough bottles of wine to get me through the week. (In case you're wondering, that's usually three, but I always buy four just in case.) Sometimes I pick up a couple Chickin' Lickin' meals from one of our franchises, even though I rarely open them. I wander aimlessly through Stein Mart and T.J. Maxx and Target and leave empty-handed.

But this morning when I wake up, I have something to look forward to. An actual reason to get out of bed and, I think, to bake. Because tonight is book club. Which means I will be out of the house and going somewhere for an actual reason. To be with people I know and like.

I head for the kitchen and put on a pot of coffee. While it brews, I scour the Internet for inspiration. And voilà! I find the perfect idea for *The Body: A Guide for Occupants*. Because who doesn't love a theme?

For the first time since Nate died, I open the pantry and pull out flour and sugar and food coloring and everything I haven't touched in so long that I feel like I've unearthed buried treasure. I print out pictures from the Internet, then use them to cut out the cookie dough I've made.

I spend the entire day making anatomically shaped cookies—brains, kidneys, lungs, and small and large intestines. I don't tackle the heart, because it's complicated and too sobering a reminder. And no reproductive or sexual organs, because those make me think of Nate and the night he died, too. Plus, our book club *is* coed.

I also make a batch of lemon cupcakes with lemon cream cheese frosting for anyone who balks at eating cookies designed to look like body parts.

The entire day practically flies by. Plus, I create a stupendous mess, which will appease Rosaria when she comes tomorrow. This is a win-win.

When I've got everything packed up in Tupperware, I jump in the shower for the first time in, well, I've kind of lost track. But I'm pretty sure my hair and skin sigh in gratitude.

I close one eye while I blow-dry my hair so that I see only half of the gray roots. I also apply makeup and spritz myself with cologne, then pull on a pair of black pants that now require a belt to hold them up. The black-and-white-striped tunic I pull on to hide the belt hangs on me like a circus tent. Why is it the only time you lose weight without trying is when you're too miserable to enjoy it?

By four thirty, I'm dressed and ready to go. Even though it's rush hour and way too early, I load the desserts into the car and drive to Between the Covers. I'd much rather hang out at the bookstore than sit at home alone, waiting.

"Oh my God, these are great!" Charm laughs when she pops off the top of the Tupperware and sees what I've brought. "Do you mind if I create a sort of display with them? I'd love to get some shots for social media."

"Sure." I've had the pleasure of creating and baking. My job is done. "Have at it. Is Annell around?"

"She's out in the garden. I'm sure she'll be glad of the company."

I wander out to the carriage house, where the French doors are flung open, and find Annell kneeling over some flowering bush I can't identify. Her short salt-and-pepper hair is standing straight up. One cheek is streaked with dirt. She looks incredibly content.

"Oh my gosh!" She glances up and sees me. "What time is it?"

"It's just after five. I thought I'd come hang out for a while. You've got plenty of time before book club. Don't let me interrupt you."

"Phew. Got a little panicked there. Have a seat." She motions toward the concrete bench angled beneath a tree that's bursting with magnolia blossoms. I sit under its branches and inhale the soft citrusy scent.

"Ummm, this is nice."

"Yes, this is my favorite spot this time of year. Actually, any time of year." Annell cuts off another stray branch and wipes her face, leaving another streak. Her fingernails are filled with dirt.

Annell has always been easygoing, happy to talk or respect someone else's silence. She's never been one to pry.

For the first time, I realize I've been so wrapped up in my own life, I've missed out on growing a deeper friendship. I've never wondered if Annell is single by choice or by necessity. Whether she worries about money or is as content as she always seems.

I'm lucky that I have been left okay financially. Not exactly rich or anything. But the mortgage is paid off, and the franchises, under the experienced eye of the manager Nate hired and trained decades ago, throw off income.

"I can't believe I never thought to ask this before, but did you always intend to open a bookstore?"

"Lord, no." She laughs. "I was living in Boston, teaching English at a private prep school, and imagining myself as a Louisa May Alcott when my parents both took ill. I was an only child, and so I came home to nurse them. After they died, I remodeled the carriage house and set out to prove my talent. When I realized I'd rather read books than attempt to write them, I opened Between the Covers." She smiles. "It hasn't always been easy, but I've never regretted it. I've met some pretty wonderful people, and I can read as much as I want.

"How about you, Judith? Are you doing all right?"

"I'm not sure what that means right now. I . . . I think I'm doing better than I was. But getting through the days . . . I don't really have a purpose anymore, you know?" I watch her snip off the tiny branches, tamp down the soil around the base of the plant. "What do you do in your spare time besides garden?"

"Whatever I like."

It sounds so simple. But I have literally never thought about what I do and don't like. I've spent my adult life running around taking care of things. Of my husband. And my children. I've never had a great passion. Or a talent. Or something I wanted to be or do. My single aspiration was to be a good wife and mother. *Huh.*

I mean, I enjoy tennis and golf, and I'm decent at them. But mostly I learned both sports so that I could play with Nate on a vacation or a rare empty Saturday, or with girlfriends when I had the time. And because in my world those things were expected.

But I'm not passionate about them the way a lot of people are. I don't have a burning desire to start a business or get more involved with running the Chickin' Lickin's. The children are self-sufficient.

"How does one choose what to do with one's time when one could theoretically do anything?"

Annell laughs in surprise. "I'm really not sure how to answer that question. I think it's different for each of us. But I'm guessing it could be fun to try to figure it out."

I look at the woman I'm just now coming to fully appreciate. I'm not the first person to have life as she's known it blown apart, and I certainly won't be the last. A once favorite line from *The Sound of Music* forms in my mind: "When the Lord closes a door, somewhere He opens a window." Perhaps it's time to find a window I can fit through.

Twenty-Four

Jazmine

When I arrive at Between the Covers, I'm relieved to see Erin's car in the parking lot. I've been worried about her because the closer we get to the Braves home opener the more intentionally upbeat and relentlessly communicative she's become, as if she needs to convince everyone that she's not the least bit bothered by how excited the agency is about Josh Stevens. Or more to the point, how excited the Braves are about our client Josh Stevens. He and his surprisingly stellar innings on the road are pretty much all the staff's been talking about. I've even held off the announcement of Tyrone's deal with Sony until after these first home games of the season, so that the spotlight can shine completely on him. Even though I can't wait to see Rich Hanson's face when the PlayStation endorsement deal is announced, there's no way I'm going to let Tyrone's pride get bruised again.

I'm imagining Hanson's shock and awe over Tyrone's deal when I reach the refreshments table and find Angela, Erin, Sara, and her mother-in-law staring down, transfixed. I feel a good bit of shock of my own when I see the chalk outline of a body, etched out on the tablecloth as if at a murder scene, with cookies shaped and decorated to look like that body's organs arranged inside.

"These are wild." Erin picks up a kidney-shaped cookie

from a platter that sits beside the body and places it on her plate. "Oh, and look at this one," she says in delight as she reaches for another. "This is the closest I've ever been to an internal organ. I've never seen anything like them. Have you?"

"No," I reply truthfully. The cookies are incredibly detailed, but while I did read the book, I have no idea whether they're exact reproductions or have been placed in their correct locations within the outlined body. I appreciate a theme as much as the next person, but the brains and kidneys are more than a little unsettling. So are what I think are supposed to be intestines.

Still chatting effusively, Erin adds a cupcake to her plate, helps Dorothy choose an assortment of cookies, then pours herself a glass of wine, falling silent only long enough to take the first bites and sips. I remind myself that she's not a child and that we all react to stress and unhappiness differently. I'd rather be around upbeat and chatty than Maya's surly and silent any day.

"Wow. These are awesome." Chaz circles the body outline before reaching out and picking up a brain. "Did you really make these, Judith?"

Judith nods and smiles. "I saw a decorated cake online that was made for a medical school graduation, and it got me thinking. I made the cookies. But Charm came up with the chalk outline."

"They look pretty anatomically correct to me," he says, taking a large bite.

I don't think I'm the only one trying not to gag as he pops the rest of the brain into his mouth. But then I guess you can't have a delicate stomach when you spend your days in an ambulance racing from one emergency to another.

There are no anatomically detailed hearts, and I wonder if Judith's loss made her shy away from reproducing the organ that failed her husband. Did she think of him while she baked?

Or were these cookies an attempt to escape what must be constant thoughts of Nate and the life they built together?

Dorothy's also studying the body, though her gaze has dropped lower. "Am I allowed to say I'm relieved there are no reproductive organs to nibble on?"

Sara, normally so quiet and self-effacing, emits a snort of laughter.

Angela and I exchange a glance. Without a word, we reach for cupcakes.

"I'm kind of hoping the catering at the StarSports suite at the Braves opener will be a little less body-centric," Angela says as we move to the drinks table and fill our wineglasses.

"I'm counting on it. Chicken wings are about as close as I plan to get," I agree, holding up my glass in toast.

"I'm pretty excited to have a whole weekend to myself," Angela says.

"I hear you. I really appreciate Perley taking Maya along on the Destin trip." At the moment, this is an understatement.

"Well, Lyllie's not happy that her father and both of her sisters are going to be in the same state let alone the same town, but it was the only way he'd agree to let her go there for spring break with her friends." Angela smiles somewhat wickedly. "He's promised to be invisible, but you know Perley. He's not really built for shrinking into the background."

"No. Neither of them ever were." I can't help smiling at the memory of Xavier and Perley when we double-dated. "They always looked like bouncers no matter what they wore."

We share another smile as Phoebe and Wesley come through the front door in matching skeleton costumes that make it even more difficult to tell them apart. Carlotta struts in behind them in a flesh-colored dress that not only hugs her curves but outlines them in stitches of white thread. Nancy Flaherty brings up the rear, still clinging to her own personal theme. Tonight's sweater is a grassy green and reads QUEEN OF

SWING. A golf club topped by a crown is bedazzled beneath the letters.

We mingle. Food is piled on plates, and drinks are poured. Judith accepts compliments on the refreshments with a smile we haven't seen from her for a while. The hum of conversation grows until Annell leads us to the carriage house, where we formally—and loudly—applaud Judith's efforts, then dive into a discussion that becomes a bit of a free-for-all, possibly because we already know one another. Or perhaps it's the result of having confronted, and in some cases ingested, sugar cookies masquerading as organs.

We all agree that the book was fascinating and that while we enjoyed the author's deft touch and occasionally droll tone, most of us, with the exception of EMT Chaz, are shocked and somewhat horrified by all the things medical science doesn't understand about how and why our bodies work the way they do.

When the book conversation begins to wind down, Wesley says, "Phoebe and I are ushering at the Braves game Friday night. Anybody else going?"

Beside me, Erin goes still in her seat.

"The press has been going crazy over Josh Stevens," Phoebe adds. "They're saying he'll probably get at least an inning because of the way he's been performing on the road."

"Yeah," Annell nods. "It'll be cool to see a hometown boy get a chance in an opener."

I put a hand on Erin's arm and give it a soft squeeze. I don't think either of us is breathing as we silently will the topic to change.

"Gosh, I hate to miss it," Nancy says. "But I'm going to be at a tournament out in LA that Tiger's hosting."

Erin and I begin what feels like a joint sigh of relief that the topic is actually changing when Dorothy cocks her head and asks, "Isn't Josh Stevens the boy you were engaged to?"

Erin manages a smile, but I can tell how much effort it takes. "Yes, he is."

"Are you going to the game?" Carlotta asks the question I haven't yet raised, partly out of respect for her privacy and partly because I haven't wanted to undermine her vow not to cry at the office.

"Well." Erin clears her throat. "Josh offered tickets to my whole family. Including me."

"Are you going to take him up on that offer?" Annell asks carefully.

There's a part of me, the mother part of me, that wants to change the subject and spare Erin from the attention now focused on her. But I've known since the first time Angela dragged me here, still raw from the loss of not only the man I loved but the sport I'd devoted myself to, just how much this group, disparate as it is, cares about the individuals who make it up. There is warmth at its core and concern for even its newest members. Kindness, and unconditional support, are unwritten bylaws that we all somehow know and follow. I believe that anyone who comes more than once comes not just for the book conversation but because they can feel it.

Erin hesitates just long enough for me to wonder if she'll take the leap of faith required to answer truthfully. "My family assumes I don't want to go. But this is the thing Josh and I always dreamed for him. There's no way I'm missing it." She swallows, and the last of the false cheeriness disappears. "But I don't want to sit with my family. Or with my oldest friends. They know the gory details, and they'd all be sitting there feeling sorry for me instead of being happy for Josh." She looks down at the hands clasped in her lap. "I've been thinking I might just go on my own. You know, buy a ticket and sit around strangers who don't know anything about me or my connection to Josh." There's a slight quiver in her voice, but so far no sign of tears. She is so much stronger than she knows.

"Watching him pitch could be the most painful thing ever. Or maybe it will prove I'm ready to move on. I don't know. It could go either way." She shrugs, and I have the oddest desire to stand up and applaud.

There's a silence then, and just when I'm thinking it needs to be filled, Annell says, "Well, I have an extra ticket if you'd like to come with me."

I've always known that Annell's a Braves fan, but we've never really talked about how often she attends games. I've never run into her at Truist Park.

"So do I." Judith sits up in surprise. "Nate has . . ." She swallows. "*I* have season tickets. Four of them. Nate used to take key employees and potential franchisees. But we went as a family, too, when the kids were still at home. I'm sure the tickets are in . . . Nate's office somewhere." She stumbles a bit on the last mention of her husband. "You could come with me if you like. And I bet Meena would join us—she'll be back from Mexico on Thursday. And someone else from book club could sit with us. That way you wouldn't be with people who know you *too* well. But we wouldn't be complete strangers, either."

"Hey, if I can get someone to cover for me Friday night, I'd love to go," Chaz says.

"So would I," Sara chimes in. "I don't want to speak for Dorothy, but . . ."

I see the surprise on Dorothy's face but also a flicker of interest.

"I'm sure I could round up some extra tickets for anyone else who'd like to go," I offer, feeling small for not thinking of any of this. "Angela's going to come to the agency suite with me, and it's pretty full because Josh is our client. But maybe we could all meet up for a drink after the game. The Battery's fun, and it's a good way to wait for the traffic to clear."

Erin looks up. This time her smile is not forced or overlarge.

It carries traces of gratitude and relief. "That would be great. Thank you. You guys kind of rock."

We decide to make *All the Ways We Said Goodbye: A Novel of the Ritz Paris* our April read. It's written by three authors who have come to Between the Covers on a book tour, and it's been a huge hit with historical fiction fans.

We're draining the last of our wine and getting ready to disband when Dorothy raises her hand. "Are you going to share the book club name suggestions?"

Sara blinks in surprise.

"Gosh, I'm glad you reminded me." Annell laughs, opens the folder in her lap, and pulls out a stack of creased pieces of paper. "Okay, let's see." She unfolds and leafs through them. "Hmmm. They are a little less alcohol related than last month's. This time out we have the Biblio Files, the Happy Bookers, Book Enders, Page Turners, and Not Your Mama's Book Club." She lifts another handful, her expression bemused. "We also seem to have quite a few blanks."

"Entirely blank pieces of paper?" Phoebe asks in surprise. "Do you think someone dropped them in by mistake?"

"It seems hard to imagine why anyone would put them in on purpose," I say.

"Yes." Sara spears her mother-in-law with a look. "Why, it's almost as if someone was trying to psych someone else out or something."

Dorothy looks innocent. Sara continues to look suspicious. When neither of them speaks, Annell, who doesn't really try to hide her smile, moves on. "All right, then; any feedback?"

"I like all of them—but especially Not Your Mama's Book Club," Erin says. "Because we so aren't."

"Yeah. It's got some attitude going for it," Carlotta says, crossing one long curvy leg over the other. "Definitely sets a tone."

"Hear! Hear!" Judith raises her glass. "Even though some of us could actually belong to *your* mama's book club."

Annell laughs. "It's all a state of mind."

"Page Turners is clear and practical," Phoebe says. "So is Biblio Files."

"I'm not sure I want to be a Happy Booker," Wesley says.

"Have to agree, man." Chaz pops a final cookie into his mouth. "People might get the wrong idea."

Annell grins. "So, what do you think? Have we heard one we want to go with? Or do we want to give it another month?"

"I say we take another month . . ." Phoebe begins.

". . . because it deserves more thought," Wesley finishes.

"I agree." A small smile plays on Sara's lips. "After all these years of namelessness, there's no need to rush. We want to pick something really special."

"Sounds right," Dorothy agrees. "I'm still eager to hear what the prize for coming up with the winning name is. You know, just to help with inspiration."

"Good point," Annell concedes. "Let me think about that and get back to you. Now that we're doing this, I'd love to have lots of entries to choose from.

"Oh, and before you go, let's get a count of how many available tickets we have for the Braves game and how many people want to go."

I steal a last look at Erin as a count is taken. I'm proud of how well she appears to be handling it all, but I'm glad that she'll have us holding her hand, both figuratively and literally, on Friday night.

Twenty-Five

Erin

It's Wednesday night, and my brothers, who have no doubt already consumed the casseroles and potpies my mother regularly stuffs into the freezer of the rental house they share, which looks and smells like a frat house, are here for a midweek home-cooked meal.

We're devouring my mother's justifiably famous buttermilk fried chicken when I mention that I've decided to go to the Braves game after all.

"Oh, that's wonderful news. I know Penny and John will be thrilled to see you. We have seats right behind home plate."

For a minute, I think the chicken I've just swallowed is going to come back up. Penny and John are Josh's parents. Whom I once thought of as second parents.

"Actually, I'm planning to go with some people from book club."

"You joined a book club?" My mother looks as if I've just admitted I joined a cult. "You never said."

"I only went the first time because Jazmine invited me, and I couldn't really say no." I don't mention that it was a pity invite to pry me out of the ladies' room. "I didn't say anything because I wasn't sure that I would keep going. But I . . . I kind of like it."

"You'd rather go to the game with strangers than with us?" my father asks, unable to hide his surprise.

"No, not strangers. Just new friends that you don't know. Yet." I consider telling them exactly what I admitted last night at Between the Covers, but to them I'll always be the baby of the family. Their little girl who needs protecting. They don't know that I'm working on becoming a genuine kick-ass Disney version of myself.

"I'll be fine. I already said I'd go. I'll . . . I'll let you know where I'm sitting. After the game, we're meeting up for drinks at the Battery. But maybe I'll see you all before then." I take another bite of chicken and chew really slowly so that I don't have to say anything else.

"You're sure you wouldn't rather be with us?" my mother asks. "In case you find it . . . challenging?"

There's no seat that's going to make this easier, but watching the game with people who expect me to fall apart feels wrong on every level. "I'll be fine," I say in a totally kick-ass kind of way. "Really. There's nothing for you to worry about."

My mother frowns and looks worried. My father looks doubtful and worried. My brothers look ready to do battle over the last piece of chicken.

Sounding kick-ass and being kick-ass are not exactly the same thing. I've spent the last two days grinning like a goon while the excitement over Josh's addition to the pitching roster and how that might impact the team's season builds in the press and at the office. On Friday night, I make sure my smile is in place and pull on what little emotional armor I have left, but when I climb out of the Uber at Truist Park and make my way to where Meena, who's tan and glowing from her beach vacation, Judith, and Chaz are already waiting, I'm feeling kind of shaky.

"Hey! It's a great night for baseball, isn't it?" The three of them are wearing Braves hats and T-shirts and great big smiles that appear way more real than mine. On the bright side, they're not looking at me as if I'm someone who needs to be pitied, babied, or handled. They just look glad to be here, and suddenly, I am, too.

Judith's seats are on the first base line directly behind the dugout at Terrace Level, which means we've got a great view of the field but aren't right on top of it. We get peanuts and popcorn from the vendors, and I tell myself that everything's going to be okay. I'm just another person here to watch the game. There's nothing I have to do or prove. But I'm careful not to watch who comes in and out of the dugout too closely. And I definitely don't use Chaz's binoculars to see who's warming up in the bullpen out behind right center field.

I do see my family and Josh's parents take their seats overlooking home plate, but I'm careful not to be caught looking. I think we're far enough up and behind them to keep them from spotting me. Especially since I'm sitting just beyond Chaz, who's way bigger than me. It takes me a couple minutes to realize that he's noticed what's going on and is giving me a pretty large shoulder to duck behind.

Just after the national anthem, Meena, who's on my other side, hands me her popcorn to hold and gets up. She returns with a cardboard tray of cocktails just as the first batter strolls out of the dugout. "We've got you covered." She winks as we all take a Braves Bramble. "Just sit back and relax as best you can. No one's going to notice you unless you want them to."

I don't want to sound like an alcoholic or anything, but the drink does help. So do the people around me. Chaz seems relaxed, but he's super aware of his surroundings in a way I guess people who are always ready for an emergency are. If a foul tip came this way, he'd catch it or protect us with his body. If I pass out from nerves or hyperventilate while Josh is pitching, at least there'll be someone who can resuscitate me.

Meena and Judith do their part, too. Meena makes sure I'm included as she goes on about the glories of her romantic getaway and how eager she is to schedule our online dating intro. Judith occasionally rolls her eyes at Meena, but she's listening intently.

Judith kind of reminds me of my mother but maybe a couple years older and with an extra layer of sadness underneath her smile. It must be even worse to lose a husband you've had so long than to lose a fiancé. It's another reminder that people deal with all kinds of stuff every day. For about two seconds I try to picture my mom without my dad, but I just can't go there.

Judith's neighborhood is only a couple of miles from the one I grew up in. Sure enough, when I ask, she tells me that both her kids went to Walden. One of them lives and works in New York, and the other one's in Denver.

"My kids graduated from Walden, too," Meena says. "Judith and I moved into River Forge right around the same time. My son, Justin, lives in Midtown. Julie is in Charleston." I listen as they talk and tease each other. Meena has the bigger personality, but Judith's got a pretty wicked sense of humor when she lets it loose.

The game begins and . . . as much as I love baseball, the past runs through my head. All the bleachers in all the places where I cheered my heart out. First for my brothers and then for Josh.

Even my chosen sport of cheerleading was more about urging others on to victory than competition. But I guess that makes me a natural for representing athletes, right? All I need is to develop the killer instinct that agents are supposed to have and that I'm really hoping is hiding inside me, waiting to be tapped.

The first few innings fly by. We're playing the Marlins, and our guys are hitting the crap out of their starting pitcher. In the third inning we're up four to zero. In the fifth, even after a pitching change, it's six to one. I keep my eye on the game as I open my program and begin to flip through it.

My breath catches when I reach the roster. There's Josh's headshot. Clean-shaven. Earnest smile. Official team hat on his head. He's number 45, just like he was all through Little League and high school and college, one up from his idol Hank Aaron. R/R 6'2" 210lb. There he is in black and white. Suddenly, it's completely real. I tell myself to stay calm. That I'm totally okay. But I'm dragging air into my lungs a little loudly. Braves shortstop Dansby Swanson, another hometown boy and former number one draft pick whom Josh used to play against in high school, hits a homer at the end of the sixth inning. We're up seven to one.

"You okay?" Chaz asks.

I look into his face. He's square jawed, and he's got really nice blue eyes. There's an air of calm about him that has to soothe the people he is sent to save, just as it's soothing me.

"Yeah." I nod to reinforce the fact. "I'm fine."

"Good." He peers into my eyes, double-checking. "Because it looks like they're warming him up in the bullpen right now."

I look up at the scoreboard. It's the top of the seventh inning. Then I hear this roar from the crowd. Josh, my Josh, is on the field and jogging toward the pitcher's mound. Tyler Flowers runs out to meet him and hands him the baseball before jogging back to home plate.

Josh digs at the mound with his left toe. Then he jiggles the ball lightly in his hand. Getting its feel. Relaxing his hand around it. As if it's an egg. Getting his breathing under control. I know every habit, every move he'll make before it happens.

Flowers crouches behind the plate. Josh goes into his

windup. Hurls a few warm-up pitches right over the strike zone. Not too fast. Not much movement. Just confirming that he's ready.

The umpire signals the batter to step in. Josh stares at Flowers. Nods that he's got the signal. My heart beats so fast in my chest that I'm afraid Chaz will hear it. And then he sends a fastball flying into Flowers's mitt at 99 mph. The batter swings, but he's way too late. The crowd goes wild.

The second pitch is another fastball. This time it's low in the strike zone, and the batter doesn't even go for it. "Strike two!" Another roar when the speed of the pitch registers on the scoreboard. 100 mph!

"Wow!" Chaz shakes his head in admiration. Every team has its special flamethrower, but not many of them hit 100 mph or more.

Tears form in my eyes. My chest feels so full I'm afraid it's going to burst. People chant Josh's name. A couple of guys in the row in front of us are debating whether the catcher will call for an off-speed pitch. Maybe a slider. But I know what's coming. Even if the batter doesn't. The final strike roars in like a hurricane. 101 mph.

I cry full out while he sits down three batters in a row, then jogs off the field, where Flowers pounds him on the back. The crowd shouts his name. He faces six more batters, ultimately sitting down their entire lineup. No hits. No walks. The whole team surges out of the dugout and wraps itself around him.

This will go down in the record books. *This* is as good as it gets. *This* is exactly what we dreamed of but never really expected.

It's the most exquisitely beautiful and achingly painful thing I've ever experienced.

I can hardly breathe as the crowd goes crazy. Embracing the people around them. Pounding one another on the back. Shouting with happiness.

Here, in the midst of strangers who are unexpectedly turning into friends, the tears slide down my cheeks unchecked. They stain my face and soak my T-shirt. I look around, take in the mass euphoria. I'm not the only one smiling and laughing and hugging. But I am the only one crying.

Jazmine

The celebration in the agency suite is still raging when Angela and I make our way to the door to leave. Larry Carpenter is the happiest I've ever seen him. And possibly the drunkest. Rich Hanson has been matching him drink for drink but barely looks buzzed. Ever since our outing to the Bookers, we aren't exactly what I would call simpatico, but he's not as combative. Or maybe seeing his softer side has made me a little less knee-jerk.

"Where are you running off to?" he asks.

"Meeting up with some friends." In the past, I would have tweaked him about not even knowing what friends are, but our visit with Isaiah and his aunt has proven otherwise.

"Ah, a secret assignation at an undisclosed location." He arches an eyebrow, but there's a flash of something in his eyes that doesn't quite match his flippant tone.

"We're having margaritas at Superica," Angela says for some reason. Then she adds, "With friends from book club."

"Ah, literary ladies who like baseball *and* margaritas. How fascinating. I'd give a lot to be a fly on that wall . . ."

There's the Rich Hanson I know and don't love. Is it odd that I'm almost relieved to see that version of him?

"Have fun."

"Okay, that was weird," I say as we exit the suite and make our way to the Battery, which is jam-packed with happy Braves fans.

"No, that was a man who's interested in you," Angela says,

sidestepping a family that stops suddenly and looping her arm through mine.

"Don't be ridiculous," I snap while we wind through the crowd past overflowing restaurants and bars and shops. I'm about to add that Rich Hanson isn't interested in anyone but himself when the memory of Aunt Yvonne's iced tea and cookies raises its head and compels me to keep silent.

Superica is the opposite of silent. It's a pulsing, buzzing beehive of activity. We find the others already seated at a large round table not far from the bar. Pitchers of margaritas, baskets of chips and salsa, and various colors of queso dot the table. This is what people mean when they talk about perfect timing.

My eyes immediately go to Erin, who's sandwiched between Judith and Chaz, and although I'm not sure exactly what I was expecting, I'm relieved to see her smiling.

Phoebe and Wesley are there with Carlotta beside them. I almost don't recognize Dorothy in the Braves T-shirt and baseball cap, but she and Sara are smiling, too. Annell is Annell. Unflappable. Smiling in welcome as she scoots over to make room.

Annell and Meena fill glasses, then pass them around.

"He had a great outing, didn't he?" I say, leaning toward Erin.

"It was absolutely crazy," she says. Her smudged eyeliner hints at tears, but however many she may have shed, they're gone now. "It's what he worked so hard for. I was . . . I'm glad." Sincerity and wonder ring in her voice. "It was incredible to see him light up the crowd like that."

"I'll drink to that." I raise my glass in Erin's direction.

"To the Braves!" We clink those nearest us and take happy gulps.

"To us! To . . . Boy, we really do need a name, don't we?" Annell muses. But in a content "it'll happen when it happens" kind of way.

We shrug and clink and take another gulp.

"Well, it would make toasting easier," Dorothy says in that unexpectedly droll tone that always surprises.

We toast a lot of things. And grin at even more. I let go in a way I never could or would at an agency function. "To Erin! Who's made of strong stuff and is already making Louise proud."

Erin blushes with pleasure.

"And who figured out how to move on when love didn't go as planned!" Carlotta adds. "You go, girl!"

We finish our margaritas in Erin's honor. Then we refill our glasses. With twelve of us shoehorned around a table for ten, we have no shortage of things to drink to.

We toast with verve and, I like to think, panache. We are at that point where everything seems deep and meaningful. So we laugh and pontificate. On the surface, a stranger would probably wonder what we're doing together. We don't look as if we should have anything in common. But I realize that although the people and the food and drink were fancier in the agency suite and lots of other places where I do business, there's nowhere I'd rather be right now.

The empty margarita pitchers disappear. Before I can register their loss, twelve shot glasses filled with tequila appear, along with a large saltshaker and a plate of quartered limes.

"From the gentleman." The waitress sweeps a hand toward the other side of the room, then looks surprised when she doesn't see whomever she was looking for. "Oops. All I can say is you have two rounds on the house."

Everyone preens just a little—Chaz and Wesley included—but none of us see anyone who's smiling or trying to take credit. No one approaches our table.

"Ah, well." Angela holds hers aloft. "It's been a while since someone I didn't know bought me shots. I say we make the most of it."

"Arriba!" We lift our shot glasses. Then the bravest of us lick salt from our hand, down the shot, slam the empty glass down, and suck on the lime. The rest of the table follows suit. There's a brief, possibly stunned silence.

"Holy shit!" Chaz gives his head a hard shake. "I am clearly out of practice."

Some at the table look lost in thought. Some just look lost.

The second round of shots arrives on the heels of the first. We contemplate one another. "Nobody drove here, did they?" Chaz asks.

Everyone shakes their head. But carefully. The next round goes down more slowly, with breaks for water and chips.

The surrounding noise recedes, as if someone packed a layer of cotton balls between our table and the rest of the room. My thoughts slow. It takes me a moment to realize that a conversation is taking place. And that it's Sara who's speaking.

"In a way, you're lucky Josh didn't wait until you'd been married for a decade before he let you down," she says to Erin. "Marriage is not what it's cracked up to be. And neither are men." She motions vaguely toward Chaz and Wesley. "Sorry. Present company expected. Um, excepted."

We gape at Sara, who is generally the quietest and least argumentative among us.

"Are you . . ." Phoebe looks at Sara in distress. "Is everything okay?"

"No. It's not. Everything is abominable, abhorrent, atrocious, awful. And that's just the *a*'s." She looks at her mother-in-law. "Do you wanna tell 'em, Dot, or shall I?"

Everyone but Sara blinks at the "Dot." Including Dorothy.

"Okay. I'll go ahead and hannel it then," Sara continues. "I am divorcing Mitchell. Because he is a liar and a cheat. And . . ."

"I think that's enough, don't you, Sara?" Dorothy interrupts.

"Oh, definitely. It's way more than enough. But there's a

whole lot more! And I have a confession to make." She turns to Judith. "I'm sorry your husband died. I really am. But I'm jealous, too. Because you stayed married for so long, and you got to raise two children. I bet you didn't find out your husband had secret children with another woman. And I bet he didn't steal his mother's house right out from under her, either. Who does that kind of shit?"

At first, I think I've misheard. I can tell everyone's thinking that. Because Sara is the last person you'd expect to share such private information.

"How could you?" Dorothy gasps, her face so wretched there's no real room for doubt.

"Oh, Sara. I'm so sorry," Judith says. "But if you want to know the truth . . ." She doesn't pause long enough for anyone to tell her that we don't want to hear anything else that's painful. "Just because a marriage lasts a long time doesn't mean it's a good one. I was seriously considering divorcing Nate when he died. I mean literally. While he was dying. Or possibly already dead."

I'm not the only one whose mouth gapes open at this. Shock suffuses every face at the table, including Judith's. I want to applaud her for being brave enough to share something this big, even as I feel us being swept into the unchartered territory of one another's lives.

Angela expels a big rush of air, and suddenly I'm afraid that the one person—other than my parents and sister—that I've always assumed is happy is going to confess that she isn't. I hold up my hand, ready to beg her not to speak, when she says, "No marriage is perfect all the time. I've never considered divorce—not for more than a minute or two, anyway. But no matter how much you love someone, occasionally murder looks extremely attractive."

Wesley and Phoebe nod somberly, their faces, their Braves jerseys, and the angle of their Braves caps set at identical angles.

"He . . . she . . . sometimes is lucky to be alive," the twins say, each pointing at the other.

Judith's face turns white. Meena reaches out and squeezes Judith's hand.

"Wishing someone dead—even for a split second—doesn't make it so. And I know this from personal experience," Meena adds. "If it did, there'd be a lot more women in jail for murder. Or appearing on *Snapped*!"

"Wow." Chaz straightens and looks around the table. "Women sure do have unexpected depths."

"You don't know the half of it," Carlotta adds sagely. "Women are like icebergs. We only let you see the very tip of us."

We're all drinking water now, but once tongues are loosened, it's hard to tighten them back up.

"I was married right out of college," Annell admits in a stunning spray of words. "It barely lasted a year."

We contemplate one another almost warily. But there is no censure, no rush to judgment. For the first time, I ask myself why I've been so guarded—sharing the facts of my loss but not the pain—when this support has always been there for the taking? I realize that my reticence, my constant need to show strength, has been more wall than protective shell.

And suddenly I'm spilling my truths, too. "A lot of you know that I lost my fiancé fourteen years ago. What you may not know is that I'm only just now starting to date again. Mostly because my sister didn't give me a choice. And frankly, nothing that's been said here tonight makes me want to go on another date ever again." I look around the table. "You people are scaring the you-know-what out of me. And probably Erin, too."

"Oh, don't be a baby," Angela scolds. "It's time you get back out into the world and give men a chance." A smile blooms on her face. "But you know what this reminds me of? Did you all ever see that movie *Almost Famous*, where the rock band thinks their plane is going down and they start telling one another what they really think and confessing all the horrible things they've done. Including sleeping with one another's wives?"

"Oh yeah!" Wesley laughs. "And then the plane levels out and . . ."

". . . they're all just left looking at each other," Phoebe finishes as we do exactly that.

The silence is brief.

"Well, I know we've always tried to be there for one another, but tonight marks the move into new, previously unexplored terrain," Annell says carefully. "And . . . I'm glad we feel comfortable enough to share the things we have."

"So am I," Sara adds. Dorothy still doesn't look all that comfortable, but her nod is firm.

"Me, too," Wesley and Phoebe say in unison.

Meena holds up Judith's arm as if she's just won a boxing match. Which in my book she definitely has.

Erin pumps a fist. Angela and I follow suit, while Carlotta and Chaz begin a chant of "woot-woot."

"So, in keeping with the importance of the things we've shared tonight," Annell continues solemnly, "let's all raise our hands just as enthusiastically as we raised our glasses and swear that what's said at book club—or any gathering of book club members, especially those that include alcohol—stays at book club."

We raise our hands and do so solemnly swear. Out of the corner of one eye, I see a man who looks a lot like Rich Hanson ducking out of the way as if attempting to not be seen.

Twenty-Six

Erin

I'm pretty sure I'm not the only member of book club who wakes the next day with a hangover. I lie in bed for a while, taking stock and listening to the creak of wood floors and the faint sound of my parents talking. My head pounds, but it's more a dull throb than a sharp stabbing pain.

Encouraged, I pry open my eyes—which are caked and goopy with makeup I failed to remove. Ditto for last night's clothes. I roll onto my side and land on something hard and flat that turns out to be my cell phone. *Shit.*

Daylight streams through the shutters I forgot to close. I planned to be up early so that I could spend today primping for Katrina's going-away party, but if my cell phone is right, it's already one o'clock, and I'm not sure it's a good idea to get too close to a mirror. I take two aspirin and chug down a full glass of water. Then I scroll through our group chat and Instagram posts and what feels like a million shots of Josh on the mound.

My original goal for tonight was to look so incredible that (a) Josh would be forced to see exactly what he walked away from and (b) no one would feel sorry for me. But even now, tired, hungover, dry mouthed, and dehydrated, trying not to look pathetic seems like a pretty pathetic goal. A kick-ass princess would aim higher.

I stare up into the ceiling reliving last night's game. Josh on the mound. In command. Impressive. Everything I always knew he could be. Such an incredible relief to be able to finally let go of my own unhappiness and be genuinely happy for him.

Afterward at Superica, I discovered that everyone (including my boss, who always seems so totally together) is carrying stuff around, and a lot of that stuff is way heavier than mine. I think about Judith and Sara and Annell and Meena and the rest of the group, so *there* for me even though I've known them for such a short time. I need and want to be there for them.

I breathe in and out, slowly and with intention. Pillowing my head in my hands, I stare upward, listening to the murmur of my parents' voices, a soothing soundtrack that I've taken for granted my whole life. For the first time, I wonder if they ever considered divorce. Or even briefly contemplated murder. The idea seems ridiculous, but then I've never given their relationship any thought at all. I've always thought of them in terms of me. A kind of disturbingly juvenile perspective and not particularly kick-ass.

I drink another glass of water, then doze for a while. I wake rested, clearheaded, and hungry. So I go to the kitchen and wolf down the leftover fried chicken my mother left wrapped in the fridge with a note reading *For Erin ONLY* folded around it to protect it from looting siblings. Who have been known to come here to graze or "shop" instead of the nearby grocery stores.

After two more glasses of water and a really small piece of apple pie, I head back to my bedroom where I shower, wash and dry my hair, then apply makeup.

Tonight is Katrina's night. The only thing I need to do is to show up and celebrate her, her new job, and the adventure she's beginning. It's time to move on. To look ahead, not back.

What anyone else, including Josh, thinks of me is beside the point.

But that doesn't mean I have to fade into the woodwork. After all, we *are* talking the St. Regis on a Saturday night.

I spend the entire drive pumping up my courage and arrive at the St. Regis with a smile on my deep-red lips—which exactly match my dress—and a trip-hammering heart. I accept the valet's hand and use it to rise carefully out of my car, because the Honda CR-V isn't really designed for tight cocktail dresses with discrete slits down one thigh and low, square necks that prohibit bending over.

I balance on stack-heeled snakeskin-embossed sandals that make my legs look longer, then throw in a head toss and a friendly yet mysterious smile. In my head I'm wearing a tiara that would make Cinderella and all her sister Disney princesses proud.

When I walk into the cocktail lounge and into Katrina's hug, I feel every eye on me. With the possible exception of those of my brother Tyler, who's too busy munching on the hors d'oeuvres and unsuccessfully trying to chat up the cocktail waitress.

"Whoever talked you into buying that dress is an absolute fashion genius."

"Yes, you are." Katrina and I hug and sway. "I am so proud of you. You better make sure there's room for me to visit in that New York City apartment you'll be rocking."

"Good thing you're small," she replies. "I won't exactly be living in a penthouse. At least not at first."

We laugh. "I'll miss you. I'm sorry I lost these last months with you." All that time wasted lying in bed feeling sorry for myself. Convinced I had a broken heart when maybe what I couldn't bear to give up was my plan.

I think of all the confessions last night at Superica. Every one of them a plan ripped away. By death. Divorce. Betrayal. Theft. Was it the loss of my plan that shook my world to its core more than my loss of Josh?

"You're not allowed to disappear like that ever again," Katrina says sternly. "But I'm proud of you, too. You look beautiful. And I'm sensing some new big-girl vibes coming off you."

"Very astute of you," I say, realizing she's absolutely right. "I guess it's about time, huh?" I say, because we have always called a spade a spade.

"Totally."

Someone calls her away, and I head over to the bar. Where a very elegant and very flirty waiter makes me a cosmopolitan.

Unlike last night, I nurse my drink, carrying it around and stopping to chat with friends I've known forever and haven't seen in way too long. Most of us went through school and puberty and crushes and pretty much everything else together. I can't remember why I was so embarrassed or why I thought they'd be judging me for Josh's change of heart.

I'm sipping my drink and waiting, while pretending not to, when there's a stir at the entrance. I turn and see Josh hugging Katrina. Slapping old friends on the back. Butting foreheads with Ty. His dark hair is short and spiky. Just the right amount of stubble edges his face. He's wearing jeans with a plain white T-shirt under a really great-looking black blazer. That I didn't help him pick out. Another reminder that he's living his own life and seems more than able to fend for himself.

I don't make a move toward him, but I don't move away, either. I become aware that everyone's watching us, waiting to see what will happen. I don't care.

He looks me up and down as he approaches. His smile creases the dimple that cuts into his left cheek. When he stops in front of me, he gives a slow shake of his head and a low whistle. "You look beautiful."

"Thanks." In the past I would have been talking a mile a minute, smiling my happiness to see him, easing us into conversation. I just smile and mentally adjust my tiara.

"You wore that dress to our engagement party."

"Yes, I did." I tip my head back so that I can look into his whiskey-brown eyes, like I have a million times. I see the confusion in their depths. He came prepared for anger or hurt or, worst-case scenario, tears. It never occurred to him that I might be okay.

"You were a force last night," I say honestly. "I couldn't believe you struck out their whole side."

The dimple flashes. "I couldn't believe it myself. It was like an out-of-body experience." He drops his voice so that only I can hear. "I wasn't sure if you'd be there or not, but I hoped you would."

"I don't think I could have missed it. Not after all those years that we dreamed about you one day pitching for the Braves."

"I'm not sure I would have even had that dream if it weren't for you. You always believed in me more than I did. I was along for the ride." He shoves his hands in his jean pockets. His eyes search mine.

"Are you sorry you took the trip?" I meet his gaze, but my knees are kind of weak. There's an old flutter in my stomach.

"God, no. It's an unbelievable rush. Of course it's not as much fun when you give up runs and hits. I discovered that in Houston and Boston."

"Nobody's perfect." I smile.

"You always acted like I was."

"Couldn't help it." I shrug.

"I'm not, you know." There's regret and a whole lot of other things packed into those four words.

"Yeah, I figured that out when you called off the wedding."

He winces. A totally attractive crinkling of his brown eyes that's hard to look away from. "That wasn't about you. I was lucky to have you. To be loved that completely. I'm sorry that I hurt you. I just wasn't ready. And it seemed wrong to marry you under false pretenses."

I nod. Because really, what can you say to that?

"But you know, last night after the game, you were the person I wanted to tell what it felt like." He barely hesitates before he adds, "The person I wanted to make love to."

His eyes hold mine. I feel a way too familiar pull of what I'm pretty sure is lust. My emotions are less clear.

"After the drinking and celebrating, you mean," I say, trying for a teasing tone I can't quite pull off.

"Well, yeah," he admits. "But you were in my head the whole time. And you'll always be in my heart." He moves closer, close enough to whisper. Everybody else disappears. "Sometimes I wonder if I made a mistake. Calling things off. Giving you up."

My body sways toward his. I inhale his scent. For an agonizing moment, all I want is to bury my head in his chest and feel his arms go around me.

Then I actually register his words, their meaning. They're all about him. What he did. What he wants. What he lost.

I step back. With trembling hands, I smooth down the sides of my dress and look up into his eyes. "No, Josh. You were right. I set my heart on you way too early and held on too tight to something that . . . well, what kind of decision-making can you expect from a six-year-old?"

Surprise is evident on his face. I don't know what shows on mine. Relief? Regret? A newfound confidence? I feel and am no doubt telegraphing all of those things at once.

If this were a movie, the music would swell. We'd give each other one last lingering smoldering look. I'd turn and walk away. The screen would fade to black.

But this is real life. So what actually happens is my brother Tyler walks over, throws an arm around Josh's shoulders, and says, "Come on, man. There are drinks lined up and waiting for you."

Then this brother, who only months ago offered to maim Josh on my behalf, turns to me and asks, "You got a couple extra dollars I can borrow for liar's poker?"

"I got you, man," Josh says as I shake my head at Ty.

"Brothers," I tease. "It's a miracle you don't go out without your head."

I look up and see Katrina standing in the midst of an absolute gaggle of my friends. She waves me over. I turn and walk—it's possible I even strut just a little bit—toward a great big group of my very best girlfriends.

Judith

The front doorbell rings bright and early Monday morning, not long after Ansley's daily text dings in.

I press my face to the front door peephole and see Susan Mandell, Realtor and head of the River Forge Bereavement Committee. Coincidence? I think not. Especially because she's delivered numerous casseroles since Nate died and every one of them had her business card taped to the foil.

She's not the only Realtor who appears to rely on obituaries in search of possible listings. My voice mail is full of calls apologizing for bothering me in my time of sorrow while offering to help take the worry of selling my home off my hands.

Of course, Susan does have the home court advantage, since she lives three doors down and I *am* the only person currently living in River Forge who has a house that's obviously too big for her and no husband to help with upkeep or to argue against listing it.

I open the door a crack and poke my head out.

"Good morning. How are you?" she asks perkily.

"I'm all right, thank you." This has become my stock reply because I've learned that this is all anyone who isn't Meena or a long-standing member of my book club really wants to hear.

We stare at each other. I'm greatly relieved that she hasn't brought another casserole, because Rosaria won't touch them anymore and because the lack of casserole relieves me of the obligation to invite her in. "What's up?"

"I know you've suffered a terrible loss, and I hate to intrude on that. But I've had several clients inquire about homes for sale in the neighborhood."

I wait. Because while I appreciate the casseroles and her concern and all, I'm not remotely ready to even think about selling my house.

"And it occurred to me that you might be considering downsizing in view of . . ." Her voice trails off. "In view of Nate's death. And the fact that your children live in other cities."

She flashes me a comforting yet hopeful smile. "I wondered if you'd consider allowing an out-of-state client of mine to take a look even though it's not listed. Yet."

My hand closes on the knob. It takes everything I have not to tell her just how tasteless her casseroles were and how much her timing sucks.

Instead I put on a "bless your heart" smile, which Southern women are born knowing and those of us who are transplants take years to master. Then I say, "Why, that is so considerate of you to think of me. But I'm afraid I'm just not ready to have strangers in my home. I'll be sure to let you know if that ever changes." I hold on to the smile until the door is closed.

Then I stomp around the house in righteous indignation, which leaves some footprints in the carpet that will no doubt thrill Rosaria. After that I call Meena.

"Oh my gosh, Jude. It was absolutely heavenly," she says when I finish griping about my Realtor-neighbor and ask for more nitty-gritty about her vacation than we were able to get to at the Braves game.

"And Frank? What was it like being together for a whole week?"

"It was amazing. Honestly, we had the most fun. He talks

to everyone, only not because he's trying to sell something but because he's interested. And he wants to explore and *do* things. We went on excursions and tours and . . . he actually *likes* to dance." Her voice lowers. "And I'm just going to come out and say it—the man is really good in bed."

I try and fail to imagine myself naked in front of . . . anyone. But I feel the oddest twinge of what might be jealousy. That Meena is putting herself out there. At how she's bounced back from her divorce and created a whole new life for herself.

"One night he even brought up the idea of being exclusive."

Exclusive. Just one of a whole new set of dating vocabulary.

"Does that mean you're not going to do online dating anymore?"

"I don't think people automatically take their profile down because they're seeing someone. I'm not looking to get married or anything. I don't see why I shouldn't just enjoy his company and see where it leads."

"Goodness. How adult of you." I say it teasingly, but I am impressed.

She laughs. "It's a whole new ball game, that's for sure. But I'm putting myself first for the first time in my life, and I'm having such a good time. I can't see where there's any harm in that. You hear about all these online dating scams and everything, but I think that's just people who don't do their homework or pay close enough attention."

I've always admired Meena's self-confidence. I wish I had even a tenth of her certainty about anything right now.

"Anyway, Annell has offered the use of the carriage house Saturday afternoon for what I'm calling Online Dating 101. I just sent out an email to the whole book club. A young photographer I found has offered to shoot profile pictures for anyone who's interested. I hope you'll come."

"I'm not ready to think about putting the house on the market. I'm even less ready to think about dating. Nate hasn't been gone that long." I shudder. "It's not just disrespectful, but as angry as I was at him . . ." Damned tears blur my vision. "I've started dreaming about him, Meena. And remembering the good parts of him. And our life together. And . . ."

"Aww, sweetie," she says quietly. "There was a lot of good in Nate. And your life was so much more than the way it ended. That's your subconscious working on it for you. You're going to be all right. I know you are. And there's no rush for you to do or change one more thing until you're ready.

"But I think you should come on Saturday. Just to hear what it's all about and maybe to cheer on whoever decides to give online dating a try. It should be fun. And really," she says in true Meena fashion, "what have you got to lose?"

Twenty-Seven

Sara

The appointment with my attorney on Friday afternoon is not the day brightener I'm hoping for. When it's over, I drive home in a noxious fog of gloom. In the garage, I turn off the engine and lay my forehead on the steering wheel, gathering my thoughts, looking for something positive enough to lift that fog.

When I finally enter the kitchen, I'm hit by the unexpected scent of food. Specifically, my nose tells me, Thai food. Dorothy is standing by the kitchen table smiling, which seems to be happening with increasing frequency.

"Is that . . ." I sniff again. "That's not pad thai I smell, is it?"

She nods. "We've got panang chicken, too."

The fact that she pronounces both dishes properly is almost as surprising as the fact that those dishes are here. Ethnic food is not Dorothy's thing. I didn't even know whether she'd eat Thai food or not until I ordered in from my favorite place the other night.

"I used the Uber Eats app you set up on my phone," she says proudly. "You were right. It did come in handy. And it wasn't as intimidating as I thought it would be."

I'm not sure what stuns me most. Her acknowledgment that I was right. Or the fact that she actually used the app that she professed to see no need for. But as she steps aside, I see the takeout cartons on the kitchen table along with plates and silverware. And even more importantly, given the day I've had, an open bottle of wine.

"That's so great. Thank you. I'm starving and I . . . I really appreciate you organizing dinner."

"Can't have you getting hangry." She smiles again as I wash my hands at the sink. "I think that's actually quite a clever portmanteau," she says, using the French word for combining two very different words. "Don't you?"

"Absolutely. And I'm glad to be sharing a meal with one of the few people I've met who not only knows the word 'portmanteau' but how to pronounce it."

"If you read enough books, you learn all kinds of things." She laughs, once again emitting a sound that's becoming almost as frequent as her smiles.

We take our seats, and although I've been careful to keep my wine consumption to one glass a day since our supercharged Superica experience, I pour us both a full glass, then raise mine in her direction. "Thank you for the meal and the company. This is by far the best thing that has happened today."

"My pleasure." Our eyes meet, and I see a camaraderie in her gaze that warms me almost as much as the first swallow of wine.

We fill our plates, and I take the first few heavenly bites. For a time, we eat and sip our wine in silence.

"How was your appointment with the attorney?"

I study Dorothy's face. I'm still not sure whose side she'll be on if and when she's forced to choose. But I'm too tired to be hypervigilant, and I can't live expecting betrayal or waiting for the rug to be pulled out from under me. And it's not as if there's anything really left to hide.

"It was a bit of a mixed bag. The good news is that Mitch's attorney has responded to my petition for divorce," I say. "The bad news is that Mitch has run up way more debt than I expected, and unless I can find the money to buy him out, we'll probably have to sell the house."

My voice breaks on the last word. I drop my eyes to my plate and push around the noodles I no longer have an appetite for. When I'm able to speak again, I search for a less distressing subject.

"So," I finally manage. "I was wondering if you'd like to come to the bookstore with me tomorrow?"

"Oh, I don't know." Dorothy's protest is automatic. I listen as she lists all the reasons this isn't a good idea, but what I'm seeing is Dorothy's face when we found her cradling the little Holcomb twin.

"I'm sure Annell would be glad of your help. I know she really appreciated you being there for story hour last time."

Dorothy pinkens. "I guess I *could* come along to help Annell out." She eyes the glass of wine I lift to my lips. "But if you ever call me Dot again, all bets are off."

Somehow, I don't choke on my wine. I lift one hand and swear as solemnly as I can manage that those three letters will never pass my lips in that particular order ever again.

On the way to the bookstore late the next morning, Dorothy tries to act as if the whole outing is no more important than a run to the grocery, but her smile betrays her when Annell, who has somehow discerned that Dorothy's invisible "do not hug" sign has been removed, greets her with an especially warm embrace.

Moments later, I catch my mother-in-law slipping pieces of paper into the book club name suggestion box. "I hope you're not padding that thing with blank entries again to try to scare people off."

"Whyever would I do that?" Dorothy asks as seriously as a person can when their eyes are twinkling.

"I have no idea. But it isn't working," I declare as I pull out my own wad of folded papers and stuff them into the box one by one, keeping a challenging eye on Dorothy. Never mind that I was up until almost midnight coming up with them. And that I may have googled just a bit when my brain ran dry.

Dorothy hums happily under her breath while she helps Annell set up the food and drink. She brightens even further when the kids and parents begin to arrive.

The Holcomb twins are barely through the front door when they drop their mother's hands and race over to Dorothy with happy shrieks. Lacy, who spent the last story time Dorothy attended in her lap, wraps both arms around Dorothy's leg and refuses to let go until my mother-in-law picks her up. This is further proof that children can sense those things we try to hide. That little girl knows a "Dot" when she sees one.

Jazmine

I don't know if it's the size of her personal cheering section—both my parents and Thea and Jamal are with me in the stands of the tennis center where Maya is playing her singles match—or something her grandfather said to her, but my daughter is completely on today.

She moves in anticipation before her opponent's racket is even back. Aims deep and devastating forehands and punishing backhands from the baseline. Places the ball with military precision. Charges to the net, where she is a human backstop.

I hold my breath when she races for a drop shot and manages to tap it back over the net, catching her opponent flat-footed.

"Lord, that child is on fire today," my mother says.

"She surely is," my father replies with justifiable pride.

Maya's up five games to four. It's her serve. Her chance to close her opponent down.

Today there is no double-faulting. No hesitation. No letting down. I barely breathe as she fights for and ultimately wins the first point. Fifteen-love. Her next serve spins into the corner of the box and bounces away from her opponent. Ace. Thirty-love.

My heart thuds in my chest. I know just how important calm is when you're serving for the match and how hard it is to maintain. This is where the pressure builds. This is where focus is everything.

Thea reaches for my hand, and I'm glad of the contact. My father always appears calm, but I know from experience that his stomach is churning every bit as much as mine. *Come on, Maya. You can do it*, I will silently.

I hold my breath as my daughter bounces the tennis ball on the service line. Once. Twice. The toss is perfect, and as her racket loops behind her head, I know exactly where the ball is going. I squeeze Thea's hand as the ball zooms in right at her opponent's feet and skids away. The girl flinches, but that's the only move she makes. Forty-love.

"That's our girl," my father practically whispers. "She's in the zone. She's got this."

I breathe but only because I have to. I've got a pretty great poker face, a necessity in my profession, but this is not a client I'm watching; this is my daughter. It's personal. *Oh my God. Oh my God. Let him be right. Let her win it right here.*

I watch the bounce. The toss. I keep my eyes wide through the thwack of the racket on the ball. Maya is already racing to the net. Somehow, her opponent manages to get her racket on the ball and whack it down the line just out of Maya's reach. Forty-fifteen.

Maya is rattled. This is that moment when a player is most vulnerable. But if she lets the girl score another point, she might become emboldened and tie things up. Maya needs to end this here and now.

Maya's serve is hard and deep. It lands in the backhand corner of the box, but her opponent manages to return it.

Come on, Maya. It's almost a prayer. *You can do it.*

And today she does, running her opponent all over the court with long, wicked ground strokes. When she's tired the girl out, Maya feints slightly, then smashes a crosscourt backhand that sails right past her opponent.

Maya's arm and racket go up in victory. Her smile of joy lights up her face. Then the two girls are reaching over the net. Shaking hands. We all jump up in excitement and applaud as Maya strides happily off the court.

We hug one another and jabber about Maya's best shots, the aces early in the last game, her gorgeous ground strokes, the crosscourt winner, how happy she looks. We're heading down the bleachers to say all those things to her in person when a man steps out from beneath a shade tree and approaches Maya and her coach, Kyle Anderson. They shake hands. They're too far away to overhear their conversation, but the man is clearly congratulating Maya. Kyle is practically bowing and scraping, as if the man were royalty. That man is Rich Hanson.

I step up my pace and get down there in time to hear Hanson ask Maya, "Does Serena know you stole her backhand?"

Maya grins at the compliment.

"Not everyone can pull that off. Going straight back without the loop. You hit early and on the rise, just like she does. It's a beautiful thing." He shakes his head. "Pretty sure she didn't have that down at . . . how old are you?" Rich asks.

"Thirteen."

"My Jazmine had that shot down early, too. Gotta coil the shoulders—get that extra torque," my father says knowledgeably. He is, after all, the person who taught us that backhand.

Still grinning, Maya looks me in the eye with a warmth I haven't seen in a while. "My mom's been an even bigger inspiration than Serena Williams. She's the real reason I love this game. Even if I don't always show it, I want to be a champion one day."

My eyes blur with tears, and I wrap my arms around my

daughter. Not caring whether I embarrass her or not, I crush
her to my chest.

"Do you know who this is?" Kyle asks, motioning toward
Rich.

"Afraid so," I reply. "Mom, Dad, Thea, Jamal—this is Rich
Hanson. He recently joined our firm."

"But he's . . . he's big-time," Anderson says.

My jaw locks, which is the only thing that keeps me from
saying things I know I shouldn't.

"Not any bigger than Jazmine," Rich says with a surprising
flash of irritation at Maya's coach. "Especially not since she announced her client's new endorsement deal with Sony PlayStation. It set all kinds of records." He bows to me and does a roll
of the hand in that "your wish is my command" way, and somehow manages to pull it off without appearing silly or insincere.

"Gee, Mom. That's cool."

"Well done, Jazz." Jamal ruffles my hair as if I'm still the
child I was when he first started dating my sister.

"That is for sure," Thea adds, eyeing Rich suspiciously.

"That's our Jazmine for you," my father says. "All do and no
brag. Most people got it the other way around."

"Too true," Rich says to my father. "It's nice to meet you,
sir." His respect seems genuine, no bullshit attached. The only
question I have is what he's up to.

"Well, we have to get going," Thea says. "You coming with
us or staying with your mom, Maya?"

"We're going to the bookstore to learn how to do online
dating," Maya announces, choosing this moment to forgo her
normal surly silence.

"It's tied to a book that's been suggested for book club," I
say way too defensively. "Some of us are just going there to . . .
support others."

"But you said there was going to be a photographer there to
shoot profile photos and all," Maya exclaims.

I close my eyes and huff out a breath of what I'd like to believe is something other than embarrassment.

"Listen, I'm sorry to intrude on your Saturday," Rich says to everyone, "but I could really use Jazmine's input on something."

"Now?" I ask. "A little warning would have been helpful."

"I'm sorry," he says as my family looks on. "But I've been trying to reach Craig, who manages this complex for the current owners, all week. I only heard back from him about an hour ago, and he's leaving town again tomorrow. I'm meeting him at one thirty. I figured I'd have to fill you in later, but when I saw you were already here . . . I thought you might want to take the meeting with me."

"Of course I would. But I have plans."

"Yes, I heard." Rich bites back a grin. "But we're only talking an hour or so. Maybe you could fit it in before you go pose for those photos?"

I roll my eyes. But I am hardly going to engage here and now, and I am definitely not going to argue the relative merits of online dating. Especially not when Thea is wearing that little frown she gets when something is off but she's not sure what it is.

"Jazmine does not need to go online to find a man." Thea spears Rich with a challenging look. "Not when the man she's already dating is absolutely perfect for her."

"Thanks, Thee. But I really don't think Rich cares who I'm dating." I glance down at my watch, mulling how to make it all work. "We don't have to be at the bookstore until three. I assumed we'd all go to lunch first, but . . ." I sigh again, though I couldn't say exactly why. "Would you mind taking Maya out to celebrate her win, then dropping her off at Between the Covers?"

"Cool! Can we go to Flower Child?" Maya asks, not at all bothered by the idea of my absence. "It's not too far from the bookstore."

Rich smiles his thanks and says his goodbyes to my family. "Congratulations again, Maya. That was a truly impressive victory. You, too, Kyle."

"Thanks." Kyle Anderson reaches out to shake Rich's hand. "Great to meet you, sir," he says with a level of enthusiasm he's never showered on me.

We stand and watch my family disappear into the parking lot. I am annoyed at the late notice, the change in my plans, and all kinds of other things I can't really articulate. I do what I learned to do long ago when I stepped onto a tennis court for a match. I shove all the noise out of my head and focus on what I have to do right now. In this moment. "All right, why don't you tell me what the purpose of the meeting with Craig is?"

"You know Craig?"

I give him a look that says I know he knows I know Craig and that I also know his being here in time to see at least part of Maya's match was no accident.

"Okay," he concedes. "What do you think of this complex as a base for a StarSports Academy?"

I glance around, trying to hide my surprise that this has gone this far without my involvement. "I guess it could work, but don't you think we should sit down with Larry before we start looking at facilities and talking to people?"

"We'll sit down with him soon enough. He knows I'm here, and he's made moving forward contingent on your involvement," Rich says.

"And if I choose not to be involved or don't think it's a good idea? What then?"

"I don't know," he admits. "But I figured it was worth taking a look when the opportunity presented itself and talking it through afterward."

Hanson is trying to treat this like it's no big deal. That he just happened to come when I was already here. As if there's no urgency. Only I can feel that there is.

"What's the rush?"

He opens his mouth, but I'm looking into his hazel eyes and I see them shift. They go just a little cloudy.

"No. No lying or bullshitting or fudging or whatever you want to call it," I say. "You give me a straight answer or I'm out of here and on my way to lunch with my family."

It's Hanson's turn to sigh. He does it loudly enough that it could qualify as swearing.

"I heard that IMG is looking at expanding into Georgia, and if that goes well, possibly into the Carolinas."

IMG sports academy in Bradenton, Florida, began in the late '70s as Bollettieri Tennis Academy. It's grown into a behemoth sports training destination for athletes who play baseball, basketball, football, golf, lacrosse, soccer, tennis, and track and field. It's spread over six hundred acres and even includes a preparatory boarding school for students in K–12.

The academy makes tons of money and creates an important pipeline of athletic talent that keeps their sports agents at the top of the heap. They've staked out Florida as their own. Letting them get a toehold here in our own backyard would not be in StarSports Advisors best interests.

"Okay, I get it," I say. "But we have to be careful not to get pushed into something just to keep them from having it."

He smiles. "Well said. Pretty good piece of dating advice, too. You might want to remember that when you're putting together your online dating profile and all that."

I ignore this. "Assuming we wanted to build something, we'd have to really think it through. Proceed with caution. Take care not to overextend. Stick to two, maybe three sports we have expertise in.

"What?"

His eyes are riveted on my face. A small, pleased smile plays on his lips.

"What's wrong?" I've never seen him look this way before.

"Not a thing," he replies, as if he's almost surprised at what he's saying. "You can be a real pain in the ass sometimes, Miller. But I knew you'd get this. I frickin' knew you'd understand."

Twenty-Eight

Judith

When I arrive at Between the Covers for Meena's Online Dating 101, the children's story time is just breaking up. I linger for a few minutes to watch the little ones and their parents, swamped by my own memories of those early years with Ethan and Ansley, which felt like they would last forever and then somehow flew by.

This is our first gathering since last Friday's drunken confessions, and I steal a glance at Sara, afraid to see censure of my story or a flash of discomfort over her own, but she smiles and waves from behind the counter, where she's ringing up a large stack of children's books. Nearby, a young mother attempts to pry a small, squawking, cherub-faced toddler out of Dorothy's arms.

"Wanna stay wit Dot-Dot!"

I expect a flush of annoyance from Sara's mother-in-law, who made it clear she wasn't okay with one "Dot," let alone two, but her face and tone are surprisingly gentle as she helps transfer the little girl to her mother with promises of a special surprise next time. The smile she sends me is unencumbered. Methinks some people are a lot softer on the inside than they've led others to believe.

Annell hugs me hello and points me toward the carriage

house without the slightest hint of embarrassment or regret, and I relax further. "Meena and her photographer are already here, and Carlotta's setting up a whole makeup and wardrobe section. Refreshments are out. As soon as we get everybody rung up here, we'll head back so we can get started."

It's a gorgeous day, and with the French doors thrown open, the carriage house smells as fragrant as the garden outside. There's a table with wine and nibbles. Meena is huddled with a young woman who has chin-length blond hair and oversize bright-pink glasses. Several cameras hang from straps around her neck.

Carlotta's makeup and wardrobe stations are tucked into a corner near the bathroom, which is now a "changing room." Angela; her daughters, Lyllie, Mollie, and Kerina; and Jazmine's daughter, Maya, are checking out the makeup and looking through the rack of clothing, which includes some pretty out-there designs but also some simpler pieces in soft, flattering colors.

"This is so beautiful." I reach for a pale-violet tunic with three-quarter sleeves and a boatneck that's cut in deceptively simple lines.

"I designed that for you, Judith," Carlotta smiles. "I knew that color would be just right with your dark hair and eyes."

"You designed this just for me?" I hold it up in front of me, hardly able to believe it.

"Um-hmmm. You know I enjoy things that sparkle, but I've been thinking that I could bring some more subtle 'pop' to people who aren't looking to make a huge statement. Especially now that I've learned firsthand how hard it is to find things that fit and flatter when you're not a size zero."

Jazmine arrives and is surrounded by her daughter and the McBrides. Wesley and Phoebe grab glasses of wine and huddle around Carlotta with the rest of us. Soon they're oohing and aahing over matching white linen button-down shirts,

Phoebe's sleeveless, Wesley's long-sleeved, topped off by beautifully tailored navy blazers with oversize gold buttons.

"Hey, everybody. What's going . . ." Erin skids to a stop just through the doorway. I'm not sure how Sara and Dorothy, who are right behind her, manage not to slam into her. "No one said we were dressing up." She looks down at her black jeans and plain white top.

"You just leave that to me," Carlotta says. "I brought things for everyone to wear for photos today. I'm kind of practicing on y'all. Plus, I thought we could get a group shot at the end—as a memento and something I could use to show off my creations."

"I'm in. I cannot wait to put this tunic on," I say truthfully as Carlotta presents Jazmine and Angela with denim wrap dresses—Jazmine's is brushed light-blue denim that sets off her honey-brown skin, while Angela's is in a stonewashed black that contrasts perfectly with her pale skin and blond hair.

Chaz is the last to arrive. "You don't really have something for me, do you?" he asks skeptically when we point him toward the rack.

"You better believe I do." Carlotta pulls out a T-shirt with a hand-painted American flag that covers the entire shirt.

"Wow. That's awesome," he says, reaching for the hanger. "Is it okay to put it on?"

We all suck in a breath when he pulls his plain white T-shirt up over his head, exposing pecs and abs you generally only get to see in Peloton commercials. We are careful not to ogle or make him uncomfortable, but I don't think I'm the only one who's sorry to see the flag T-shirt cover him back up.

The photographer, who Meena introduces as Vicki, shoots candids of all of us yammering and modeling our designer pieces. No one displays the slightest hint of embarrassment or regret at having confessed such personal things at Superica. No one brings up what I admitted about the night Nate died. Or that Sara is getting divorced because her husband has a secret family, or that Angela, Phoebe, and Wesley admitted that they have briefly considered murdering those they love. And then there's Annell's revelation that she was married. It's strange how you can know people for so long yet only uncover slivers of who they really are and what they've been through.

What I do know is that this is a group that only supports and does not judge. And I am lucky beyond measure to be a part of it.

"Is Nancy coming?" Carlotta asks. "I made something for her, too." She holds up a lime-green golf skort with a multicolored striped halter top that would be perfect on Nancy Flaherty.

"That is adorable!" I say, because it is.

"She's in Augusta for the Masters," Annell says. "And then she goes to Hilton Head for another tournament, but she said she'll be back for book club." She glances around the room. "What do you think, Meena? Are we ready to get started?"

"Yes, we are!" Meena steps to the front of the group and in a fair imitation of Annell's usual book club welcome says, "So. How many of you have had a chance to read *121 First Dates*?"

All hands go up, including Annell's and mine. But I only read it out of curiosity, and while I did enjoy dancing at Meena's building's happy hour, I have no intention of going anywhere online that's more personal than Amazon or Instacart.

"Okay then, you don't need me to recap," Meena smiles. "What did everybody think?"

"It was a fun read," Phoebe says. "Except having to go on one hundred twenty dates before you find the right person sounds exhausting."

"The fact that a size 16 middle-aged woman had plenty of dates *and* ultimately found a life partner was pretty uplifting," Annell says.

"And her pole dancing hobby was an interesting choice," Carlotta adds.

"I thought her advice not to date anyone who lives farther away than you're willing to drive three times a week was pretty spot-on," Chaz adds, stretching his arms and making his flag fly.

"And meeting in person as quickly as possible so you can find out whether you have chemistry seems like a time-saver," Wesley chimes in.

I grin. Leave it to men to focus on the practicalities rather than finding true love.

"Okay." Meena holds up a sheet of paper. "Here's a list of dating sites with notes about optimal age range, consumer rankings, et cetera. Everyone needs to decide which sites make the most sense for them. I've gotten the best results with Match and eharmony, but I've heard good things about SilverSingles, too. Bumble and Hinge seem to be really big with younger people. Carlotta mentioned a site called BlackPeopleMeet and one called HER. On the back are some examples of strong profiles.

"I saw a statistic that people who use the word 'whom' correctly in a sentence have a thirty-one percent better chance of a right swipe." At first I think Meena is joking—I mean, I never took dating this seriously when I *was* dating—but she turns to Sara and adds, "Would you be willing to help anyone who needs it with their profile? A little editing never hurts."

"Sure." Sara smiles. "It's nice to know that grammar actually counts in the real world."

"Vicki here"—Meena points to the bouncy young woman who's been snapping photos since we arrived—"is going to shoot photos for us to use when setting up profiles. My treat. And you'll probably want a number of other photos from real life. The sites vary as to how many photos they expect you to include." She pauses and looks around the room. "So—how many of you are going to set up profiles and give it a whirl?"

Chaz, who must already be beating women off with a stick, is the first to raise his hand.

Wesley and Phoebe raise one hand between them, and I wonder if they'll set up one profile or two.

"How about it, Dorothy?" Sara asks her mother-in-law. "Do you want me to help you get started?"

The shock on Dorothy's face is comical. There's sputtering. Eye narrowing. "Of course not. Have you taken leave of your senses?"

"Oh, I don't know," Carlotta says. "You might want to at least get some pictures taken while you're here." She holds up a beautifully patterned silk scarf with brightly colored fringe that she made for Dorothy. "This would be stunning on you, and you can wear it with virtually anything. Besides, a woman can never have too many flattering photos of herself, can she?"

"Goodness, that's beautiful." Dorothy reaches for the scarf, then rubs it against her cheek.

Annell laughs. "I have zero interest in getting married again—saying 'I do' made me realize 'I don't.' But I wouldn't mind a date now and then. And it seems like this way you at least have some control over the situation. Besides, I am not wasting this gorgeous jumpsuit that Carlotta made me." She holds up a green silk one-piece garment with a V-neck and flared leg. "What do you say, Dorothy? Shall we pose for some photos and consider creating profiles?"

I wait, assuming Dorothy's looking for a way to say no. In the end, she says, "Hmph. I guess it couldn't hurt."

Sara's eyes go big, but she doesn't comment.

"Well, I'm going to help Jazmine set up a profile," Angela says. "So I can live vicariously through her."

"I beg your pardon?" Jazmine looks her friend over. "I am already dating. I do not need to put myself online."

"I don't know," Angela replies. "I'm not sure three dates in fourteen years can really be considered dating. Going online will significantly deepen the potential dating pool."

"Oh my God," Jazmine says. "When did you turn into Thea? What if someone who knows me professionally saw it?"

"You don't think people who work in sports use dating apps?" Angela deadpans.

"Angela's right, Mom. You should get set up online. I'll help." Maya is looking at her mother as if she's just realizing that Jazmine is a living, breathing woman. "Aunt Thea says Rich Handsome is interested in her. Only Aunt Thea isn't happy about it, and she didn't like the way my mom flirted with him at my match."

"That's Hanson," Jazmine huffs. "And that was *not* flirting. That was irritation. And, and . . . business."

"How about you, Erin?" Meena asks when Jazmine shoots her daughter a look that finally closes the subject. "Are you ready to put up a profile and see who else is out there?"

Emotions flit across Erin's face far too quickly to categorize. This girl has matured so much in the months we've known her. She even managed to survive watching her ex-fiancé have the night of his life.

Erin steals a glance at her boss. "I will if Jazmine will."

"Huh." This is Jazmine's only comment. But the look she aims at her daughter and her assistant speaks volumes.

"Come on, Mom," Maya pushes, clearly not intimidated.

"And we'll help," Lyllie, Mollie, and Kerina promise.

"All right, then," Meena says. "Maya, Mollie, and Kerina have offered to do makeup for anyone who wants it. Lyllie will help you download your chosen dating app and get you at least started on setup. Carlotta, to whom we are extremely grateful, will serve as wardrobe mistress. After everyone's individual photo shoot, we'll get a group shot for her."

We stand up and get started. Some of us, make that all of us of legal age, grab a glass of wine.

"Oh, I almost forgot! I brought some music to get us in the mood." Meena pulls out her phone, scrolls, and taps a couple times. And we are transported back to the late '70s and the '80s. Carole King feels the earth move. Whitney Houston wants to dance with somebody who loves her. It's impossible to hear these songs and not feel good. Moving is required. Soon even Maya and the McBride girls are singing the bits they know along with their mothers as they apply makeup and arrange hair.

There's noise and laughter. And plenty of faux catcalls when Vicki poses Chaz in the garden leaning against a tree trunk, his sunglasses low on his nose so that he can look over them directly at the camera.

I bob and sing. Annell and I take up positions on either side of the photographer, where we make faces that cause Dorothy to smile a smile that lights up her face. Everyone, even those who have no intention of using the photos online, takes their turn in front of the camera.

Then we pose together, letting Carlotta place and arrange us like mannequins, until the photographer gets the shots she's looking for.

We're about to disband when a new song begins. It's Sister Sledge singing "We Are Family." And every single one of us sings—or more accurately, shouts—along.

Because in this moment and in so many ways, that's exactly what we are.

Twenty-Nine

Erin

It takes most of Sunday to finish my dating profile on Hinge. One of my biggest problems, other than freaking out about the whole idea in general, is how hard it is to come up with six photos of myself that don't include Josh. Or some part of Josh. Or me staring up at Josh. In fact, I can hardly believe how few mementos or memories I have that are only about me.

I already downloaded the app, so now I answer prompts and upload photos—two of them taken yesterday at Between the Covers thanks to Carlotta, Meena, and her photographer, and one of me in the red dress at Katrina's party that she sent me.

I feel like I'm practically naked in front of the world by the time I finish my profile, which will open me and my life up to a whole batch of strangers. Before I can freak out completely, I speed-dial Katrina, who is now an official resident of New York City.

"Hi." She answers, and all I hear are traffic noises, car horns, a siren, people shouting.

"Where are you?"

"I, my friend, just left an incredible fashion exhibit at the Met and am now on my way into Central Park."

"Oh my God! You are an *actual* New Yorker."

"I am. It's a whole other world, and I keep pinching myself to be sure I'm really here."

"Is it wonderful?" I ask.

"Oh yeah. I mean, my apartment is the size of a postage stamp. And there is no dishwasher or washing machine or any other convenience, including an elevator. But the location's great. I can walk to shops and restaurants, and to the park. And the subway is only five minutes away."

"You ride the subway." It's a statement, not a question. The closest I've ever been to Manhattan is *Sex and the City* reruns.

"I do. Personal space takes on a whole new meaning in the subway at rush hour. In other words, there is none."

"Is it awful?" If someone gets within two feet of you here in Atlanta, they're most likely a relative.

"Sometimes. But it's wonderful, too, you know. I just . . . everywhere I look there's something interesting. And life. And . . . remember how the suburbs would be deserted at nine P.M.? Well, things don't even get started here until then. How about you? You all right?"

"I'm okay," I say, trying to sound it. "I'm on Hinge as of, like, fifteen minutes ago. And I'm feeling kind of unhinged about it."

Katrina snorts. "Ha. Good for you. It's about time you experience some of the rejection and heartache the rest of us have been living through for years."

"I think I did that in one great big chunk," I point out.

"True. You always were an overachiever," she says. "Are you really okay?"

"Yeah. Just . . . it's weird. He was such a part of my life for . . . forever."

"I know, Erin. And I know it's hard. But it's time. You're right to move on. Like Josh is."

"I know. Only, I feel kind of like a balloon off its string, just sort of floating along with nothing to hold me in place."

"You never *needed* Josh, Erin," she says. "You know that, right?

You drove that bus, and frankly, he was lucky to be on it. I don't think he'd be where he is today without your drive and ambition for him." There's a brief pause. "You can do that for you now. You can tether yourself. Not so tightly that you can't take off and fly, but not so loose or fast that you can't control where you're going.

"It's called freedom. And it can be totally scary and totally fabulous, sometimes all at one time. I feel that here every time something new happens or I have to do something I've never done before. You just have to take a deep breath and know that everything you need is right inside of you."

"Wow," I say when she finishes. "You're good. A little woo-woo but good. Maybe you should give up fashion and become a therapist."

"Hey, as far as I'm concerned, fashion *is* therapy. It brightens the world. And when you get some time off, I want you to come up and visit. I'll show you around. I think you'd really like it here."

"I'll come up. Just as soon as I can. But . . . I don't know if I can do this whole dating thing right now. Not because I want Josh back or anything, but— I don't know, I'm just not really interested."

"So don't. You don't have anything to prove. Just focus on yourself for a while. Figure out who you are and what you really want—not what you thought you were supposed to want. You're only twenty-three, girl. You have plenty of time to find a man when and if you want one. There are, as they like to say, plenty of fish in the sea."

Sara

When I come into the kitchen Monday morning for that all-important first cup of coffee, Dorothy is already at the kitchen table frowning down at her phone.

"What's wrong?" I ask over my shoulder as I brew my K-Cup.

"It's this dating app. The SilverSingles thing."

"What's the problem? Do you need help setting it up?" I ask, carrying my coffee to the table and hoping Saturday's Dating 101 session was enough to help me help her figure it out.

"No. I think it's working. But now that I have it, I feel like I have to use it. I'm not sure what I'm more afraid of: that no one will be interested in me or that someone will."

I understand this completely. Not having to put myself out there and find out if strangers consider me attractive may be the only upside to my current still-married status.

"No one is going to force you to do this," I point out as I add cream and sugar.

"I know." She takes a long sip of coffee. "Only, I promised Annell."

"Yeah." I join her at the table. "I still can't believe I've known her all this time and never had any idea that she'd been married."

"We all have our secrets," Dorothy replies sagely. "Some are more benign than others." She looks down at the tabletop, then up at me. "I should have told Mitch the truth about his father a long time ago. I . . . shouldn't have babied him all those years, excused the weakness I saw." Her face and voice are tinged with regret.

"You did what you thought was right, Dorothy. He's an adult. And he needs to accept responsibility for his actions." It's my turn to look away, gather my thoughts. "He was lucky to have someone who loved him and who was always in his corner. Even if it wasn't perfect. I would have given anything for that." My hands wrap around the coffee mug, cupping its warmth.

"You haven't mentioned where things stand. And Mitch doesn't want to talk about it," Dorothy says. "He seems to be living in some fantasy world where everything works out exactly the way he wants it to. Are things moving forward?"

I study my mother-in-law's face and think about Bonnie's warning about not sharing with the enemy. But as far as I'm concerned, avoiding the truth, as Mitch has done over and over, is the same as lying. It's a breach of trust. And this woman is as close to a mother as I'm ever likely to get.

"Well, the paperwork has been filed. We hired a forensic accountant at $300 an hour, and it seems that after Mitch ran through everything that should have gone toward paying your mortgage, he began depositing a portion of each paycheck into an account at a bank in Birmingham. He then took out a credit card on that account and used it to pay the rent on Margot's apartment, her monthly allowance, which he classified as 'domestic help,' and their son's private preschool tuition." I take a deep breath because somehow the idea of Mitch paying for private school tuition while I earn a public school teacher's salary feels horribly personal.

I close my eyes. When I open them, Dorothy is waiting quietly for my answer.

"So the bright side, if there is one," I continue, "is that I'm not on that card and shouldn't be responsible for half of that debt. Because having to pay for his other life—well, that would be about way more than money." I take another deep breath and force myself to say out loud the thing that keeps me up at night. "But the house—well, unless the miracle I'm praying for occurs, this house will be sold, and all I'll have left is half of whatever we get for it minus the payback on the mortgage."

"Oh, Sara." The words are filled with apology.

"But Mitch is cooperating, and his attorney's responsive, so Bonnie is certain we'll ultimately reach a settlement. And once that happens, I'll be free, and as she keeps reminding me, that's what this is really about. The opportunity to move on and . . . live whatever life I choose. Maybe even meet someone else one day." That thought seems so far out of the realm of possibility that it brings tears to my eyes. I spent my childhood trying and failing to make strangers love me. Now that the one person who ever loved me has betrayed me, how could I ever trust anyone again?

I'm blinking back tears when Dorothy's phone pings. Once. Then twice. She glances down. An odd look steals over her face.

"What is it?"

"It's . . . I . . . it's the dating app. I'm sure it's not important." She begins to push the phone away. "I'll look at it later."

But I'd way rather focus on someone else's life than think about mine, so I reach for her phone and glance down at the screen. "Oh my gosh! You have four smiles. That's . . . that's men reaching out to you." I tap and scroll. "Here are their pictures." I angle the phone so that we can both see the screen. The first man is balding with shaggy white eyebrows and a beak of a nose. The next two are moderately attractive in a silver-haired, well-groomed way. The last stands out from the others, though it's hard to pinpoint exactly why. He has a square jaw, straight nose, and wide-set green eyes that look straight into the camera lens and thus into ours. His iron-gray hair makes him look older than his seventy-three years, but his smile is the eager, friendly one of a golden retriever. He looks like someone you'd want to share a lifeboat with if your cruise ship went down.

His name is Dean Francis. According to his profile, he's a widower and father of two grown children who's looking for a woman who can "help him find love again." He was an investment banker before retiring to manage his own portfolio.

I tap on the screen to read more. Dorothy leans closer. "Oh, look," she says. "He majored in finance at NYU, then got his MBA at Harvard."

"Impressive," I agree. "The app said that eighty percent of the people on this site have university degrees. But these aren't just any universities."

Another ding. I attempt to hand her the phone. "Dean is chatting with you. He wants to know whether you're interested in meeting for coffee sometime next week."

She looks at me, panic flashing in her eyes. "But . . ."

"According to the book, coffee's safe. But you only want to go to places where there are a lot of people, and you don't have to stay long if you don't like him. And you're never supposed to let him know your address."

"How on earth did you remember all that?" she asks, still staring at Dean Francis.

"It was on Meena's handout."

We laugh, but Dorothy looks way more nervous than excited. She doesn't take the phone I'm still trying to hand her.

"I'm pretty sure you can just chat awhile if you like. You know, to get used to the whole idea and see if he feels like someone you even want to meet." I set her phone on the table in front of her. "But Meena also said you want to meet relatively quickly so that you can eliminate people you don't have chemistry with."

"Chemistry? Oh my God . . . I didn't really think this through," Dorothy says. "It seemed a bit of a lark: the makeup, the dressing up, taking photos. I honestly never considered what might happen if someone expressed interest."

I feel an odd swirl of affection and protectiveness toward this woman I've known for so long but only recently begun to understand. "What do you *want* to do?" I ask.

"I'm not sure." She looks up, and I see fear and nerves but also an odd gleam of excitement in her eyes. "How do I wave and . . . and chat?"

I click through to the instructions, and she scribbles down notes. She may be hyperventilating. But, I think, possibly in a good way.

"Okay. I've got to go. I'll see you after work." I get up and sling my purse over my shoulder.

"Right. Have a good day."

I glance back when I reach the kitchen door, but Dorothy's attention is completely focused on the screen in front of her, the excitement winning out over the fear. I pull the kitchen door closed behind me and get into the car, unable to ignore the irony; my seventy-five-year-old mother-in-law is chatting with an attractive, available man while I slog my way toward the end of a marriage that was riddled with lies.

If that's not irony, I don't know what is.

Jazmine

I arrive at the office after a working lunch to find Erin grinning like a loon.

"What is it? What happened?"

"Louise called me." She grins.

"Louise? My Louise?" I ask, referring to the woman whom I will always love and respect, but for whom, I realize, I no longer pine.

"Yes, she heard that I am"—she does air quotes with her fingers—"'knocking it out of the park.'"

It's my turn to grin. "Oh, I just told her that to rattle her chain."

"You did not."

"Okay. I may have told her that you're doing a good job. I believe I even used the word 'impressed.' But the corny base-ball analogy? That's pure Louise."

Erin's face lights up.

"You can stop going all Cheshire Cat on me. Compliment given and received. Can we get down to work now?"

She holds on to the grin for another few seconds, then nods. "Right. Rich Hanson is waiting for you in the small conference room. All pertinent files and notes on the tennis center are on your desk." She points to the stack. "I'm reminding you this one last time that I have to leave at two thirty for a dental appointment. I tried to change it, but I couldn't make it happen. Your calls will be transferred to the front desk."

I nod.

"Most importantly, you're due to pick up Maya from Chastain Park at four o'clock. They're finishing early today because the younger players are at a tournament."

"Got it. Thanks. Anything else?"

"No. But I did order those mini desserts you like. And I'll bring them in with coffee right before I leave. Early. Before my dental appointment."

"Yes, I heard that part."

"Please, give me your phone."

When I don't hand it right over, Erin takes it out of my hand. Her thumbs fly over the screen. "Okay—there's an alarm set now for three thirty. So you can get to Chastain by four."

"Got it." I give her a look. "I'm not really loving being treated like a child here, Erin."

"Sorry. It's just that I know what happens when you're completely focused on something, and I won't be here to drag you out of the meeting."

"Boy, you're getting to be almost as big a pain in the ass as Louise was."

Erin looks as if I've just handed her a winning lottery ticket.

"Oh, no. Don't get all excited again. That wasn't meant as a compliment."

"Sorry." She shoots me a grin. "It's a little hard to tell sometimes."

I find Rich in the conference room. Graphs, charts, spreadsheets, and athlete photos are spread across the table.

"Hi." He motions me toward the chair next to him. I'm barely seated before he launches into what might actually be rehearsed opening comments. "So, I was thinking we should put together all the info on the tennis center itself. Once Larry approves those details, we can move on to . . ."

"No." I stop him as I settle back into my seat. "Larry's a big-picture guy. He's not going to care about the details of the facility remodel or the exact tournaments we want to host. Or even the specific talent we're looking to attract. If we give him too much up front, I'm afraid we'll lose him."

"So, you're saying the way to get Larry all the way on board is with the sizzle, not the steak."

"Exactly." I'm surprised at how quickly he gets, and accepts, my point.

We consider each other. "That's . . ." we both begin.

"You first," he says politely.

"No, you," I say, eager, possibly for the first time, to hear what he has to say.

"All right." He nods, smiling almost to himself. "I was going to say that that's the exact opposite of what I expected you to say."

"Sorry to disappoint." I open my top folder and drop my gaze to it.

"Never," he says so quietly I almost miss it. Then he clears his throat and speaks up. "What I meant was, I just assumed you'd want to bury him in facts and numbers so that he can't say no."

"He's not going to say no," I reply.

"He did when you originally brought it up," he points out.

"Yeah. But the time wasn't right," I concede, shocked that I'm willing to admit to having made a mistake in front of this man. I hesitate before confiding the rest. "And I was thinking too small."

With that admission, I charge forward, letting one idea lead to another until we're actively brainstorming, arguing and re-arguing, looking for holes.

Rich Hanson knows how to look at an opportunity from every possible angle, and I realize that I'm enjoying hashing this out with someone who knows how to form a cogent argument and doesn't cling to an idea just because it's his.

Erin delivers fresh coffee and desserts as promised with one last reminder that she's leaving. I pop a mini cupcake into my mouth and chew it while I visualize turning the idea I once dreamed of into reality.

"How do you eat all the crap you do without putting on weight?" Rich asks.

I shrug, still thinking about the academy. "Metabolism, I guess. And these are not crap." I hold up a perfectly formed, beautifully iced cupcake. "These are tasty items loaded with deliciousness and energy."

"And sugar."

"Yes, definitely sugar." I lick the icing off my fingers. Then I challenge him on the ratio of coaches to players he suggests. The number of hard courts versus clay. At what point we might need to add an agent who specializes in tennis.

We argue about pretty much everything. I don't think I've had this much fun at a meeting. Ever.

My phone alarm goes off in the middle of a debate about rankings. He knows a lot more about tennis than I want to give him credit for. Clearly, he's not one to shirk on homework.

I'm about to make a point when I remember what the alarm was for. I glance down at my watch and jump to my feet. "Damn. Sorry. I've got to pick up Maya at Chastain." I shove my files under one arm. "We're going to have to finish this another time."

"Sure. No problem." He stands. "Go ahead. I'll clean the rest of this stuff up."

"Thanks." I drop my files in my office and grab my purse. Then I race down to the parking garage, my keys already out to beep the BMW open. I'm reaching for the door handle when I notice that I've got a flat. *Damn.*

I start to speed-dial Erin when I remember that she's gone. I consider calling an Uber or Lyft, but neither are ever as fast as you need them to be. I look down the row of cars and spot Rich Hanson's. It's an Aston Martin convertible. Midnight blue. Sleek and curvy. Even more penile than Kyle Anderson's. I hit speed dial. When he answers, I explain.

"Be right there."

And he is. "How did you get here so fast?"

"I was already in the elevator." He looks down at my flat front tire. Then he tosses me his keys and reaches for mine. "You go get her. I'll change your tire."

My eyes narrow. "I do know how to change a tire."

"I'm sure you do. If you want, you can stay here and prove it while I go pick up Maya." He's grinning.

He follows behind me as I stride to his car. "Just be careful. It accelerates like . . ."

"Men get so protective about their cars." I lower myself into the driver's seat, breathe in that expensive, über-masculine new car smell, and press the starter. The engine roars throatily to life.

He motions to me. I lower the window.

"Seriously," he says. "You barely want to touch the gas pedal."

"Got it. Be right back." Then I smile and intentionally peel out of the parking garage like a bat out of hell.

Thirty

Judith

Meena's already seated and waiting when I arrive at Marlow's Tavern for lunch. It was always our go-to when she lived in River Forge because it's only about five or six minutes from the neighborhood, it's in the middle of a shopping district, and—asparagus fries!

"Thanks for coming out to the burbs," I say as I slide into the banquette.

"No problem. It's good to take a stroll down memory lane now and then. A good chunk of my life took place here. I expect it'll always feel 'homish.'"

"Homish." I repeat the word, letting it roll off my tongue. "That's how our house feels to me right now. Homelike, but not really home. It changed the night Nate died, and it hasn't felt the same since."

Meena reaches over the table and squeezes my hand. "The condo felt that way for a while after Stan moved out. And we hadn't even been there that long." She winces. "And, of course, he wasn't gone completely."

"It's all right," I say when I see her getting ready to apologize. "I know what you meant. Tell me what's going on with the kids."

We catch up on our four until the waiter comes to take our order.

"Okay," I say as he departs, "I want all the juicy details. And I want to see pictures. I've never been on the Mayan Riviera or on a vacation with anyone besides Nate."

She laughs and picks up her phone. "Okay. Here's where we stayed." She scrolls through photos, and I legitimately ooh and aah over shots of sparkling clear green water and fine-white-sand beaches. A private casita.

Then come shots of Meena smiling here and posing there. A selfie shows her grinning up at the camera with a man, presumably Frank, pressed in behind her with his arms wrapped around her, his hands clasped at her waist. His face is buried in her neck.

Another shows her at a crowded table in a restaurant. "Oh, Frank took that one," she says when I see only an empty seat next to her. "He makes friends wherever he goes. And he loves to play photographer."

She scrolls past a few more shots of scenery to one of a man stretched out on the beach. A straw hat covers most of his face, but his chest is bare and tan, with a dusting of dark hair threaded with gray that arrows down a trim stomach until it disappears into the waistband of a pair of bathing trunks.

"Very nice."

"Yeah." She winks. "We had such a great time together in Mexico. He used to go there regularly with his wife. The casita we stayed in belongs to a friend of theirs. Frank hadn't been there since his wife died four years ago. I . . . we got along so well."

"It's not hard to get along on vacation," I point out as gently as I can, even as I think of all the holidays I had with Nate. How he'd stopped inviting me when he traveled for work. How angry I was when he'd gotten back from Europe.

Our grapefruit rickeys and asparagus fries arrive. We sip and munch.

"I'm starting to think I might be ready to put the house on the market."

"Really?"

"Yes. As annoyed as I am with all the cold calls and Susan Mandell for using her casseroles to try to get my listing, the house is just too big. I'm living like a squatter. I sit in one chair in the family room, one barstool in the kitchen. I sleep in a corner of the bed; the only time I pull the comforter down at all is when Rosaria's coming.

Meena snorts. "Do you remember all the time we used to spend cleaning the house *before* the cleaning people came?"

"I do. It feels like a lifetime ago." I sigh and take a long pull on my cocktail. "But I'm afraid of what the kids will say. What if they don't want me to sell the house?"

"You do realize this isn't up to them. If you and Nate had decided to move and the kids didn't want you to, would you have given up the idea?"

"No, of course not, but . . ."

"Don't ask them, Jude. Tell them. This is your decision, your life. They have lives somewhere else. You need to do what's right for you. And if you decide to put the house on the market, you give them plenty of time to come down and go through their things so they can choose what they want to take or keep or store or whatever. I was shocked at how little my children wanted. And the silver and formal china we all got when we married? Neither of them were even remotely interested."

"I can't imagine going through that whole house. Having to look at everything. Remember everything." I take a sip of my drink. "I don't know how you managed to downsize from five thousand plus square feet to . . . how many do you have now?"

"Just under two thousand." She shakes her head. "It's crazy, right? Stan did take some of it, but I had to let the rest go. Purging a lifetime of stuff was brutal. But I have to tell you,

Jude. I don't miss a single thing I got rid of." She grins. Neither of us mention Stan.

We finish off the asparagus fries and our grapefruit rickeys. We decide to split a second cocktail rather than getting two more. (Is that restraint or what?)

When our main courses come, I dive into my fish tacos.

Meena picks at her steak salad. "You know how I told you that Frank had brought up being exclusive?"

"Um-hmmm," I manage around a mouthful. "What did you decide?"

"I've been waffling. I mean, I'm not really dating or responding to new people. He's a great travel companion. And I'm not about to sleep with more than one man at a time."

"At least you don't kill the people you sleep with," I point out after a long pull on my drink. "I feel kind of like a black widow sometimes."

"Hmmm . . . If you do decide to try online dating at some point, you could post a warning."

We laugh, but I can tell there's something on Meena's mind.

"I really enjoy spending time with Frank, you know?" She hesitates. "But yesterday morning, while we were just kind of lounging around, he started talking about how much I meant to him, how he hadn't felt this way about anyone since his wife died."

I try and fail to imagine ever saying that, ever feeling that strongly about anyone again.

"Then he brought up the idea of moving in together."

"Really?" It's a lot to take in.

She nods.

"So, he wants you to move in with him?"

"Actually, no. I think he wants to move in with me."

"Wow." I look at her face, the way she's downing the last of her cocktail. "That's a pretty big step."

"Yeah." She glances down into the empty glass. "I'm just not sure whether I'm ready to take it."

Jazmine

It's Friday night. Derrick and I have braved rush-hour traffic for dinner at Thea and Jamal's house in Candler Park, where all the advantages of wedded and long-standing bliss are on display.

Carmen and Maya are at their grandparents' so as not to spoil the picture with too much reality. I am in the kitchen with my sister, who is worried that Derrick's and my relationship is not moving forward fast enough. For some reason, she's decided that tricking him into thinking I can cook will help.

"There are laws against misleading advertising. And misrepresentation," I point out while I stir what is apparently beef stroganoff.

"There's nothing wrong with letting him think that you know your way around a kitchen."

"Except that the only things I know my way around are the microwave and the toaster oven."

Thea is not fazed. We both know that she can beat me at any argument, having served as captain of her high school and college debate teams. "We're just celebrating the Sony PlayStation deal."

"We already celebrated that at Mom and Dad's. This is just you trying to force Derrick and me together."

"Well, when Jamal asked Derrick how things were going, he said you'd been busy whenever he called."

"I *am* busy."

"Not too busy for Saturday afternoon meetings with Rich Hanson." She shoots me a look. "Or for arriving to pick up Maya from tennis in his British racing car."

I roll my eyes. "Rich is a colleague. We're working on a project together. I borrowed his car to pick up Maya when I had a flat. You've taken all of these things out of context."

"Derrick is perfect for you. Richard Hanson is not."

"No argument there." I set down the spoon and turn to face her. "But I'm not so sure your candidate is all that into me."

"Why do you say that?" She puts her hands on her hips.

"Well, for one thing, our first, and only, kiss was slightly less than enthusiastic on his part. And when he had the opportunity to come in after our last date, he didn't."

"He's a gentleman," she says. "You can't penalize him for that."

"Maya was gone for the night, Thee. I assumed he'd at least come in. He didn't."

"Oh, tosh." She dismisses this, but a small worry crease appears on her forehead. "He's attractive and intelligent and available. And he has a great sense of humor."

"I know."

"So what's the problem?"

I've wondered this myself, and I haven't come up with an answer. I close my eyes and listen to Jamal and Derrick chatting amiably in the living room. Derrick's voice is unhurried, well modulated, ever friendly. And there's that faint island lilt.

I look down at the stroganoff Thea wants me to pass off as my own, trying to put it together. "I don't know. We have a good time together. We're on the same page about almost everything. He's like the nicest guy ever, Thee. That's the truth. But there's just no . . . spark." I wipe my hands on the dish towel and remove the apron she insisted I put on. "You and Jamal would have lasted like five minutes without that."

"Hmph."

We carry the dinner out to the table. Derrick pulls out my chair and waits until I'm seated before he takes his own. His manners are impeccable. He is one of the politest men I've ever met.

"Wow. That smells delicious," he says as we fill our plates.

"You have totally outdone yourself," Jamal says to Thea. At her glare, he amends it to, "Yourselves. Outdone yourselves."

"What's your favorite meal?" I ask Derrick as he takes his first bites.

"At the moment, it's definitely this one." He takes another bite and smiles his approval. "I'm always grateful for a home-cooked meal."

We eat and talk. Laughter comes easy.

When we've finished the main course, Derrick excuses himself to take a phone call from the office. The three of us carry dirty plates into the kitchen.

Jamal looks between Thea and me. "What's going on?"

"Jazz here has already relegated Derrick to friend status," Thea huffs. "She's hardly given him a chance at all."

"I like him a lot," I reply. "He's a genuinely nice guy and really good company. But we don't seem to have any real chemistry."

"That just makes things . . . restful," Thea argues. "And friendship is an important part of any relationship, and especially a marriage. Derrick is smart and kind, and he has a great sense of humor. He's such a *good* man. Shouldn't those things matter more than chemistry?"

"But we have all that *and* chemistry," my brother-in-law points out to my sister. "We've got mountains of chemistry." He waggles his eyebrows. "We got chemistry out the . . ."

"Okay, you can stop right there," I say to Jamal. "You guys definitely got it going on. Sometimes I'm even jealous of how right you are together. How you light up around each other. But it shouldn't be an either-or situation, Thee." I lower my voice. "It doesn't matter if someone's perfect on paper. Or even perfectly nice." I tap Jamal's chest and then Thea's, right where their hearts are. "If it doesn't feel perfect right in here."

Thirty-One

Sara

It feels incredibly weird to even say this, but my mother-in-law is dating. Dean Francis's profile photo is very attractive if you go for men with iron-gray hair, eager smiles, and tortoiseshell glasses. As opposed to men in their, say, mid-forties who have brown hair and secret families.

According to Dorothy, Dean is even more attractive in person than he appears online. She's met him for coffee three times at three different Starbucks. I dropped her off the first time they met and actually watched through the window just in case, as if she were seventeen and not seventy-five. But you hear such awful stories about romance scams and con men who prey on lonely older women that I wanted to have eyes on him. She used her newly installed Lyft app to get to their second and third coffees. Yes, Dorothy is using Lyft, Uber Eats, *and* SilverSingles. So much for "old dogs" and their inability to learn new tricks.

I'm dressed for my shift at Between the Covers and have just enough time to down a bowl of raisin bran and a piece of toast.

"I have my own reusable coffee cup now," Dorothy says. "And I get ten cents off every time I bring it in. Plus, I got a

Starbucks card and I registered it, so that adds another 8.33 percent discount and free refills every time I use it."

"He doesn't buy your coffee?" I look up from the bowl of raisin bran that I'm shoveling in.

"Oh, he always tries to pay," she says. "But I wouldn't want to be beholden. You never know what a man might expect in return."

I am careful not to laugh, partly because my mouth is full of raisin bran. But it's hard to imagine just how much a man might feel entitled to in exchange for a cup of coffee and an occasional blueberry muffin.

"He's made me promise that I'll go to dinner with him next time. And he's already warned me that he'll be paying." She harrumphs and attempts to hide her happiness behind her normal crusty exterior.

"Where do you think you'll go?"

"Oh, I don't know," she says airily. "But Dean is used to dining at the best places. He's had such an exciting life. After *Harvard* he was an investment banker in New York. On *Wall Street*. And then he was in LBOs, that's leveraged buyouts, when they were becoming a thing. He ended up in Atlanta on a deal and never left. Now he serves on charitable boards. And consults. But what I love most is how fondly he speaks of his wife. But then they were married for over thirty years. I think that says quite a lot for his character."

I choke slightly on my cereal at the mention of character, which my own husband, her son, so sorely lacks. "What part of town does he live in?"

"Oh, somewhere up off 85, I think he said. Around Duluth." Her brow furrows as she tries to remember. "Sugar Coat Club? Or something like that, I think."

"Sugarloaf Country Club?" I name the well-known and affluent suburb.

"Yes, I think that's it. Although he has complained about rattling around in the huge home where they raised their children. Now that they're both grown and living outside of Georgia, he's thinking of downsizing."

"How nice." I don't point out that we may soon be forced to downsize to no home at all, if my divorce doesn't go as I hope.

"Did you know Annell met someone online, too?" Dorothy asks.

"Um, no."

Dorothy's hands flutter. A smile flickers on her lips. It's amazing what a real smile can do to a person's face.

"She texted me all about it." This is another new skill my mother-in-law has developed in order to be able to communicate with her online heartthrob. And, apparently, with Annell. "He's divorced, I think." This is clearly not as attractive as being a widower. "But he loves to garden and read almost as much as she does."

"If it's all right with you, I'd like to ride with you to the store." Her smile flickers back to life. "Annell asked if I'd come help with story time. And I'm eager to see photos of the man she met online. It's really quite exciting."

I nod and smile because no speaking is actually required. And because I can't possibly be jealous that Annell and Dorothy are communicating directly. Without me.

When we arrive at Between the Covers, there is no surreptitious depositing of book club names or even blank pieces of paper.

I've barely set my purse on the counter or hugged Annell hello when she and Dorothy make a beeline for each other.

"I honestly can't believe how perfect a match he is," Annell says in delight. "It's almost as if he was made-to-order."

They decamp to Annell's office so that Dorothy can get a look at Howard Franklin, whom Annell is already referring to as Howie, even though they haven't yet met in person.

I hate to sound bitter or jealous, but they remind me of my middle schoolers down to the squeals of excitement.

I stuff a few book club name suggestions in the box, only it's nowhere near as fun as it was when Dorothy and I were psyching each other out.

> jaun·diced
> \ 'jȯn-dəst, 'jän- \
> *adjective*
> 1. affected with or as if with jaundice
> 2. exhibiting or influenced by envy, distaste, or hostility
> Ex: "My view of men and relationships may be slightly jaundiced."

Erin

Early Saturday afternoon, I pull up in front of my brothers' house to deliver a care package from our mother, who, despite the height and weight of her three sons, lives in constant fear that they will somehow waste away to nothing if she fails to provide regular sustenance. Travis's Jeep, which is the largest of their vehicles, is in the driveway, with its back window up and its tailgate open. Duffel bags and camping gear are stuffed inside.

I knock on their front door, which is only a formality because it is virtually never locked. "Mom sent you guys some homemade subs and brownies," I announce as I walk in. I don't mention the salad she's also sent because I know it will never be eaten.

"Perfect timing." Travis is packing a cooler that sits on the kitchen counter.

"It's like she can read our minds or something," Ryan says

as he takes a six-pack out of the open refrigerator and hands it to Tyler, who then passes it to Travis to stuff into the cooler.

"What's happening?" I ask.

"Road trip," Ryan replies. "The Braves are playing a double-header against the Rays tomorrow, and Josh hooked us up with tickets. We're driving down to Florida today and coming back on Monday. We're all going to take sick days."

I would never do that sort of thing to Jazmine or any other employer, but I am not my brothers' keeper. "When are you leaving?"

"Soon as we have the Jeep loaded."

"It doesn't bother you, does it?" Ty asks. "That we're still friends with Josh?"

Travis stops loading beer long enough to cuff him on the back of the head. He's protective that way.

"Of course not." My answer is automatic. I told Josh to his face that calling off our wedding turned out to be for the best, but was it true or was I just trying to save face?

I feel around inside searching for tender spots, hidden bruises. Nada. The well of loss that I once thought I'd drown in? All dried up.

The only thing inside me is . . . me. Which is kind of stunning. "It really, truly doesn't bother me. Not even a little bit." I straighten and examine myself one more time. "I don't think I've ever felt better."

Their faces show various degrees of skepticism. But I haven't felt this good or this clear since the day Josh told me he couldn't marry me. I love learning from and working with Jazmine. I'm building new skills and growing stronger and more confident every day. I can hardly wait to start representing clients of my own.

"In fact, I think it's time to look at apartments." The idea sends a little shiver of excitement darting through me.

"You can live with us if you want," Travis offers generously.

"Yeah," Tyler chimes in.

"Sure," Ryan adds. "There's that extra room just after you come in from the garage. You'd have your own space. All you'd have to share is the bathroom."

My shiver of excitement turns to a shudder.

"It could be sort of like Snow White and the Seven Dwarfs," Ryan says.

"Except there's only three of us," Ty points out.

"And we're clearly not dwarfs." Travis rolls his eyes.

They look at me expectantly.

"That is so sweet of you," I say, going up on tiptoe so that I can kiss each one of them on the cheek. "But I've never really lived on my own, and I think it's time."

I am touched by their offer. Really. But the bathroom thing? Not even a zombie apocalypse could induce me to share one with all three of them. Ever.

Judith

I wander through the silent house, slipping in and out of empty rooms.

Nate's clothes, including decades of lucky ties, still hang in our closet. The kids' bedrooms haven't changed since they were in high school. They're hermetically sealed time capsules of the children they once were. Documentation of the family we used to be.

The all-white kitchen feels cold and sterile. It's no longer a place where meals are cooked or shared. It's a place I walk through or heat something up in, where I make my lone cups of coffee.

In the family room, I sit down in the recliner from which Nate watched a succession of ever-thinner, ever-larger televisions and stare unseeing out the French doors to the backyard, where sunlight dapples the magnolia leaves. I catch a faint buzz of a distant lawn mower as my neighbors go about their lives.

There are things I could do. Places I could go. But I sit here in the silent emptiness. I have to do something, change something. Become something. Because if I continue to try to fill this place up by myself, I'm going to snap.

Before I can talk myself out of it, I do the thing I've been unable to make myself do. I hit speed dial and wait for Ansley to pick up.

"Hi, Mom. We just got home. Can I call you back a little later? We . . ."

"No." I say this quickly, before she can hang up. Because if I don't do this now, I'm afraid I never will. "Hold on. I'm going to add Ethan to the call."

When I have them both on the line, I dive in before I can lose my nerve. "I just called to let you know that I've decided to sell the house. It's too big. It's too full of . . . everything. I need to sell it. And I . . . I just wanted to let you know so that you can come back and select whatever you'd like to keep before I put it on the market."

Silence follows. I warn myself not to overreact. But I'm not remotely prepared for what comes next.

"Oh, no," Ansley cries. "You can't do that!"

"Why would you even want to?" Ethan asks. "Dad loved our house. He always said he'd never move, that he'd have to be carried out . . . feetfirst." His voice falters as he realizes what he's just said.

I blink back tears as I remember the EMTs pulling the sheet up over Nate's face. I steady my voice, determined to sound stronger than I feel.

"As horrible as it was to lose him, your father's gone. But I'm . . . I'm here in this huge house all alone, and it's . . . I just don't want to do this anymore."

"But giving up the house would be like losing him all over again," Ansley declares. "It would be the end of . . . *us*."

"Why are you in such a hurry?" Ethan demands.

"How can you be so selfish?" Ansley adds.

Am I being selfish? Was I wrong to think they'd understand?

Silent tears stream down my face as they berate me. My heart aches in my chest. Their anger is hot and scathing, but it's their anguish that pierces me to the core. I have loved my children beyond measure since the moment of their birth. I've spent my entire adult life cherishing and protecting them. I have always put them and their well-being first. How can I possibly do something that will inflict more pain?

"I've got to go." I can barely get the words past the ball of hurt and disappointment that clogs my throat. "We'll . . . we'll talk about this later."

I hang up quickly, then sit and stare through the scrim of tears. I've spent these months living with Nate's absence, but Ansley and Ethan haven't processed their loss. Will time help? Do I owe it to them to give them that time? I don't know how much longer I can stay in this house and on this same path without losing my mind. But if I do move forward, will they forgive me?

My sobs are the only sound that breaks the silence that surrounds me. When the tears finally subside, I call Meena in desperate need of one of her pithy pep talks or at least some sympathy.

"Aww, Jude. I'm really sorry to hear that. Your kids are only thinking of themselves at the moment, and that's so unfair to you. Life can be so . . . unpredictable." It's only when she pauses and takes a shuddering breath that I realize she's crying, too. "Just when you think you have it figured out . . . things just . . . fall apart."

"What's wrong, Meena?" I ask, my own voice faltering. I've heard Meena cry maybe two or three times in all the years I've known her. "Did something happen to the kids? Or to Stan?"

"No." She sniffs. "I'm so embarrassed to be crying over something so silly, especially given what you're dealing with."

"What is it? Can you tell me on the phone? Or do you want me to come over?" Meena has always been there for me. I don't know how I would have survived any of what's happened without her.

"It's Frank."

"Oh my God! Was he in an accident? What happened?"

"I don't know. Everything was so great. We had that wonderful vacation, and he's been so sweet. I even told him that I was willing to be exclusive. You know, to see how it went."

"So, what's the problem?"

"I really don't know. But when I told him I didn't want to live together, he just . . . ghosted me."

"He what?"

"He disappeared. He doesn't answer my emails or respond to my texts. I tried reaching out through his profile on Match, but it's gone. He's taken it down."

Her drama somehow helps distract me from my own, at least for the moment.

"Can't you go by his house and try to talk to him?"

There's a silence. "I don't know where he lives. I've never been there."

"What?" Now I wonder if Frank is married. If Frank is even his real name. He could be anybody.

"He told me he lives in Alpharetta. But like I told you, he has an office here in Buckhead, so we just always made plans around my place. Because there's so much more to do here in town."

There's more sniffling.

"I'm on my way, Meen. I'm coming over and we can talk about it. Make some kind of plan for both of us. And cry on each other's shoulders."

"But promise you won't tell anyone about the Frank thing, okay? Not yet anyway. God, I feel like an imbecile. After raving about online dating and talking everybody into trying it, I feel completely ridiculous."

Thirty-Two

Jazmine

"You ready, Andretti?"

Rich Hanson has been referring to me as Mario or Andretti ever since I borrowed his car to pick up Maya from tennis. There was a time when this would have irritated the crap out of me, but he says it with such relish that it somehow comes out feeling like a compliment.

He is without a doubt one of the most maddening people I've ever known, and given the egos I deal with on a daily basis, and even some of my family members, that's saying a lot. But it's hard to be angry with someone who argues with such good humor and remains respectful even in disagreement.

We have argued over virtually every detail involved in purchasing, converting, and staffing the tennis center, as well as its role in the ultimate creation of the StarSports Academy, including the things we agree on. He believes we have to "go big" in terms of facility and amenities, much bigger than I think advisable. And when it comes to identifying and attracting talent in both students and instructors, he's far more inclined to go after top names than identify lesser-known but equally talented choices.

"You can't *be* the best if you don't *have* the best," Rich insists.

"Yes, but I'd rather identify potential and build on it than try to steal existing talent from others."

"That's nothing but semantics," he says with a laugh. "Is it really stealing if someone else's boyfriend thinks you're smarter, funnier, and more attractive than the woman he's with? Should you be judged poorly for being born with more beauty or brains or a better sense of humor and then not hiding those things?"

His eyes twinkle as he looks into mine. The hazel turns a deeper amber, and the green is reduced to flecks, but I'm not sure if this conversation is as personal as it feels.

"I've been accused of stealing since I first became an agent, but in a lot of cases I just made myself more attractive than the competition."

"And how exactly did you do that?" I ask.

"I took a smaller percentage than the other agent was willing to consider. Or I agreed to a sliding fee based on my performance, not theirs. Sometimes I just worked harder to prove myself, sold more convincingly. It's not so different from what you do. Only people, especially women, don't trust me as easily as they trust you."

"I can't imagine why."

"See? You just don't want to trust me. You don't want to believe I could have become successful from working my ass off rather than poaching off others." His eyes deepen further. The smile remains on his lips, and his tone is light, but I can tell how strongly he feels. "I think it actually bothers you that I'm not the bastard you thought I was."

I burst out laughing. "You're assuming I don't think you're a bastard anymore. Maybe I'm just better able to deal with you."

"No." He searches my eyes as if looking for something. "You are desperately trying to hold on to your dislike. You don't want to believe I'm a good guy. So, you look for examples of bad behavior."

"I think you think I think about you way more than I do."

"Do I?" His grin is infectious. In fact, he uses humor more effectively than almost anyone I know. He's quick. And opinionated yet able to argue from multiple sides, sometimes all at once.

Dueling with him keeps me on my toes. And although I'm not planning to admit it anytime soon, having to defend my positions and being forced to seriously consider his has helped hone the presentation we're about to make to Larry in ways I never would have expected.

By the time we settle on the sofa and chairs in Larry's office that Tuesday after lunch, another choice we hammered out together, finally agreeing it would be more effective than a formal presentation in the conference room, I don't even need the notes I always have as backup.

"Okay," Larry says. "Go!"

Without actually planning it, we present as a tag team. I explain our intention to stick with tennis and baseball, with the focus on tennis first, including the role of the Tennis Center. Rich lays out our overall strategy for recruiting staff and coaches and players, but there's a lot of back-and-forth and filling in with background on how decisions were reached.

We spend a lot of time on why we think this is the moment and the importance of getting started as quickly as possible to prevent IMG from getting a toehold here on our turf.

We summarize, then hand over two possible budgets—one with all the bells and whistles and one that contains compromises—partly because you almost never get everything you want and because the bottom line will ultimately depend on Larry's enthusiasm for the project. Which based on the size of his smile and the nodding of his head is looking pretty encouraging.

"Jazz brings a lot to the table. You were right about not even attempting anything of this scope without her," Rich says in closing, startling me not only with the compliment but with the use of the nickname my sister bestowed on me long ago.

Every time I think I know exactly who he is, he pulls out some shiny new facet.

"I'm glad you're finally seeing the light," Larry replies. "You two are even more impressive when you're pulling together."

When we leave Larry's office, I'm jangling from the whole presentation, the ease of communication, the flow of our pitch, how clearly Larry seemed to get it.

"Did that go as well as I think it did?" I ask as we round the corner, headed, by unspoken agreement (a first!), toward my office.

"Better. It was a beautiful thing. If he doesn't approve every penny of every bell and whistle, I will be shocked to the very depths of my being."

"I didn't realize your 'being' was all that deep." But in truth, he has depths I never expected, and I have never been part of a better, more cohesive experience. I am high on it.

"Very funny. Tear me to shreds if you must, but we definitely need to celebrate. And no, we're not waiting for a formal approval from Larry. Can I buy you a drink? Unless you need to pick up Maya or something. You could take my car so you can get there and back faster."

"My dad's picking her up. She's spending the night with her grandparents," I say as we near Erin's desk. "I am not opposed to a drink. But I'll do the buying."

Erin's eyes are bigger than I've ever seen them. They blink in surprise.

"If you're waiting for me to go all macho or something, you can forget about it," Rich replies. "You can definitely buy me a drink. Hell, you can buy me two."

Erin looks between the two of us. "So, it went well?"

"It went better than well," I say.

"Your boss is a genius. I mean really, she's that good," Rich adds.

I drop my files on my desk and grab my purse. "We're going

to celebrate. See you tomorrow." I can't seem to stop smiling. "Hold down the fort."

Rich gives her a salute and links his arm through mine. "Come on, Mario. Time's a-wasting."

We decide on Mission + Market because it's in the next building and are ordering a drink and "bar bites" by 3:20.

"I always wondered what kind of people went drinking at three thirty," I say as our cocktails arrive.

"Smart people. People who have things to celebrate." Rich raises his glass to mine.

"We are both of those things, aren't we?" I say with relish as we clink glasses.

I buy Rich the two drinks I promised, but I'm too busy talking and laughing and arguing to order a second for myself.

When we move to Kaleidoscope on Dresden, close to my home, he insists on reciprocating. I'm sipping a glass of my favorite rosé when I ask the question that's been on everyone's mind. "So why *did* you leave Pinnacle Partners and LA for Atlanta? I mean, I think StarSports is a great agency—Larry's built something impressive—but it's pretty small potatoes compared to Pinnacle."

"It's a lot simpler and less interesting than all the rumors going around." His eyes snare mine. "My daughter started at Emory in the fall. She's a freshman, but a young one." He hesitates. "And I, uh, know it sounds a little old-fashioned, but I didn't want to be all the way across the country from her."

"You have a daughter."

"I do."

I try to picture Rich as a father and husband. "You're not married, though." It's a statement and a question.

"No." Another hesitation. "I was. But . . . no."

There's something in his tone that tells me there's more but warns me not to ask. I try on the idea of Rich Hanson as a concerned and involved father. One who would pick up and move across the country for his daughter. It flies in the face of everything I've ever heard or thought about him; it adds another layer of satisfaction to what we accomplished together today. And all that lies ahead.

He leans forward and looks directly into my eyes. It's clear that he wants to kiss me.

But I'm the one who disregards my normal aversion to public displays of affection and presses my lips to his. It's my eyes that flutter shut. But I'm not in that kiss alone.

When we pull apart, he looks slightly stunned, exactly how I feel. Without discussion or debate, he pays the bill and follows me home. On the front porch we kiss again. This time our tongues tangle, and I feel the clear, hard pull of desire. I take his hand and lead him inside.

Which is how I awake next to a naked Rich Hanson the next morning. Our clothes are strewn across the carpet. The late-morning sun streams through the wood blinds. I go up on one elbow and reach for my phone on the nightstand. It's almost ten o'clock. "Oh, God!"

"What? What is it?" He sits straight up beside me. Our naked bodies touch.

I yank the comforter up to my neck, which pulls it down below his waist. In this moment, I actually wish I had drunk more so that I could at least pretend that I did not choose to sleep with this man. My colleague. And until so recently, my nemesis.

I shake my head. "I can't believe we did this."

He turns to face me. He's trying not to smile. "But we did. And frankly it was . . . unbelievably fantastic." He sighs. "I don't think I can apologize for something I'm pretty sure I'm going to remember to my dying day."

"But I don't even *like* you!" Somehow, I pull the sheet out from under the comforter and stand while wrapping it around me. "I don't understand how this happened!"

"Well, let's see," he says calmly as he gets out of bed, picks up his boxers and pants from the floor, and steps into them. "You kissed me at Kaleidoscope. I saw you home. We kissed again. You invited me in. One thing . . . led to another." He stands on the opposite side of the bed, bare chested, his hair tousled.

"Oh my God. I can't believe this."

"That's what you kept saying last night. Only you sounded happier about it."

And, of course, I was. Because while I am shocked at my behavior, I haven't forgotten how thrilled I was with our collaboration, how great it felt to bowl Larry over, how much I enjoyed celebrating with Rich. How surprised we both were when I kissed him. How eager we both were when I took his hand and led him inside.

It's the rare man who can make you laugh even while he's making love to you. The rarest of the rare who understands just how great an aphrodisiac humor can be. The only other man I've ever known who got that connection was Xavier.

I shake my head. "I've never slept with a client or a colleague. I don't believe in it. It can lead to complications and . . . misunderstandings." I look him directly in the eye. "I won't be another notch in someone's belt."

"I'm not into notches," Rich says, pulling on his shirt, tucking it in, buckling his belt. "I've never seen the point. But as much as I think we both enjoyed last night, if it's a problem we can pretend it never happened." He says it lightly, but I'm starting to be able to read those hazel eyes. To decipher what he means, what he doesn't.

Nonetheless, I take the out he offers. "I apologize for crossing the line. We're going to be working together, and it would be silly to jeopardize that. As far as I'm concerned, it didn't happen. And it definitely can never 'not happen' again."

Erin

Jazmine arrives at work late the next morning even though she had nothing on her calendar, something that's never happened before. She offers no explanation. Rich Hanson never shows his face. When I ask, his assistant says he's out at meetings all day.

We spend the day on paperwork and researching high school and college tennis players. Jazmine displays none of the excitement or satisfaction of yesterday's presentation. I had never seen her that excited. It's as if some curtain has been brought down and now it's back to business as usual.

It's early afternoon and we're in her office going over upcoming travel plans and discussing her calendar when Larry strolls up, knocks on the open door, and steps inside. He has a huge smile on his face.

"Afternoon, Jazmine. Just wanted to say again how impressed I was with your and Rich's work. I am blown away by what a great team you make, how well you managed to work together and put aside your differences."

Jazmine's head cocks to one side. It's a signal that she's listening, of course, but although there's still a smile on her lips, I can see that she's gone very still. Her eyes are pinned on Larry's face.

"I told him when he joined the firm that the only way he was ever going to make his mark here was to get you on board." He chuckles, wags his head. "I have to admit, I never thought he'd win you over. I was kind of looking forward to seeing you put him in his place."

"Is that right?" Jazmine's smile freezes on her lips. Her eyes go all flinty.

I'm not sure exactly who that look is meant for, but I hope I never find myself on the other end of anything half as lethal.

Thirty-Three

Judith

I've spent the last five days waiting for the kids to call—they haven't. Even the daily texts have stopped. Despite her own meltdown over Frank's disappearance and her disillusionment with online dating, Meena keeps reminding me that whether to sell the house or not is my decision. So is what I do next with my life.

I'm tired of waiting, waffling, and second-guessing. When I get in bed on Friday night, I stare into the ceiling and give myself a Meena-esque pep talk. By the time I turn the light out, the one thing I know for sure is that as much as I love my children, I can't live only for them. It's time to stop beating myself up and set things straight. It's time to reclaim my life. Or, more accurately, begin to build a new one.

For the first time since Nate died, I sleep through the night. At ten on Saturday morning, when I'm sure they'll both be up, I place a call to Ansley. When she answers, I ask her to hold, then quickly add Ethan to the call before she can refuse.

"Yeah?"

At his tone, I swallow back the apology I had intended to lead with. "I hope you're both fully awake, because there's something I need to say to you."

"Yeah." His response is slightly less hostile but nowhere near apologetic.

"Yes, Mother," Ansley says in the tone that has always accompanied an eye roll.

I let go of any hope that this is going to be a poignantly beautiful meeting of the minds and force myself to continue.

"I've been thinking about our last conversation," I begin. "I loved your father. And I love you both more than anything in the world. The last thing I want is to hurt or disappoint you."

Their silence is heavy and unnerving, but I've made my decision, and I need them to understand my reasoning. "But you both live where you've chosen to live, and I believe I deserve the right to do the same. This house is too big and too empty. I can no longer stay here alone, stuck in our past. Somehow, I need to carve out some kind of future. I have to find a way to move on. So . . ."

When neither of them speaks, I expel one breath and draw in another, gathering my courage. "I'm going to begin preparing the house to go on the market. I'd like you to come down over Memorial Day weekend—that's five weeks from now—to help go through things and decide what you'd like to keep." I hesitate, trying to strike the right tone, because as much as I want them to come be a part of this, I am not asking permission. "I would love for us to do this together."

I wait, barely breathing, as the silence spools out.

I'm about to hang up when Ansley breaks the silence. "I'll be there, Mom. And . . . I'm sorry for carrying on the way I did. It's just . . ."

"I know," I say softly to them both. "Everything about this has been so hard."

"And I'll see if Hannah can come with me."

"Oh, that's wonderful," I breathe, still waiting for my son, afraid he won't speak. Even more afraid of what he might say.

"And if I can't make it?" Ethan finally asks.

I close my eyes. "I hope you'll come, sweetheart. Truly, I do. Otherwise, I'll . . . I'll have to assume there's nothing here you want." I swallow. "Or care about."

Another silence, one I'm careful not to fill. I've said what I needed to say.

"I'll think about it," he says. Then they both hang up.

Sara

Mitchell and I no longer have a need to communicate, not that we've done much of that since our attorneys took over. And there's not all that much to divvy up. The biggest plus for me was the ability to dodge part of the debt Mitch ran up. The biggest loss will be the house, but at least I'll get enough from its sale to start over in something smaller. Which is just another word for 'cozy,' right?

I also get Dorothy. She has nowhere else to go and not enough funds to get there, so as far as I'm concerned, she's mine. We're pooling our resources, and when she's not chatting with or mooning over Dean, she's surfing real estate sites, looking for houses that we can afford and open houses we can attend.

Bonnie Traiman says all that's left is for the paperwork to make its way through the system. Apparently, the average divorce takes about nine months from filing to final decree. Exactly the length of a pregnancy. The ironies certainly do keep piling up.

It's Saturday night, and I'm more than a little surprised when a text arrives from my soon-to-be ex-husband asking to come by next weekend to pick up the rest of his things. (I didn't manage to throw everything out in the yard.)

Come while I'm at work. You can schedule with your mother. She there now?

No. I actually smile as I type, She's on a date.

The cursor blinks. There is no sign of typing. I enjoy what I assume is a stunned silence. But that's life for you. Even the seventy-five-year-old mother you abandoned might have something better to do than sit around waiting to hear from you.

A date?????

Yep.

How?

How does anyone meet someone new? (Yes, that's a dig.) Online. I don't mention his name or Harvard or the big house out in Sugarloaf, because that might make Mitch think Dorothy has access to money, which might make Mitch think his mother has something left to steal.

Holy shit.

I make no comment. Watching Dorothy evolve has been inspiring. It reminds me of the George Eliot quote, "It's never too late to be who you might have been." God, I hope it's true.

Like to see you, too, Mitch texts.

I consider responding "not if I see you first." I can't imagine what we could possibly have to say to each other. Perhaps now that he's almost free of me he imagines we can be "friends."

Or maybe there's something he still wants.

I settle back on the sofa, in a spill of light, and go back to reading this month's book club pick, which is set in three different time periods at the Ritz in Paris. I'm grateful not only for the escape from real life, but not to have to huddle in the bathroom or hide from Dorothy while I'm escaping. Sometimes Dorothy and I sit here in the very same room reading. In our own worlds, but not alone.

I'm at the end of a chapter when a car pulls into the drive. I glance at my phone. It's only nine o'clock. Thinking I might be about to meet the infamous and fascinating Dean Francis, I uncurl myself and straighten my clothes. But I hear the car back down the drive at almost the instant the front door opens. The door closes. No footsteps sound on the floor.

"Dorothy?"

"Yes?" Her voice wobbles. "I'm just . . . I'll be right there."

She walks into the living room. Her shoulders are back, her chin is up. She's wearing a lovely lilac dress with nude low heels, but the smile she left with has disappeared.

"Are you all right?"

"Yes, I suppose so." She lowers herself onto the chair facing me. She looks as if she's trying not to cry.

"You don't look so good."

"Why, thank you." Her attempt at sarcasm falls flat. It's completely lacking in energy.

I wait, but she still doesn't speak. "Did something happen?"

"I . . . I'm not sure. It felt like something went wrong, but I can't think why."

"Tell me what happened." I close the book and set it beside me.

"We went to dinner at Il Giallo, you know, the Italian place that Meena mentioned. Dean had never been there, either, and he seemed up for trying it. At first everything seemed fine." She hesitates as if running it through her mind. "I thought things were going well. But . . . I don't know." She pauses again. "We were having dessert when he mentioned putting his house on the market and possibly looking around here in Sandy Springs or in Dunwoody for something smaller. He said he thought it was time to let go of the past and to stop mourning. He even brought up the idea of us taking a weekend trip up to the mountains this summer."

Her hands clasp in her lap.

"He's so attentive—it's one of the things I enjoy about spending time with him. And he's had such exciting life experiences. I told him I'd like to introduce you and that we were going to be looking for a new house, too. That led to a conversation about Mitchell and his . . . his behavior. I hadn't brought it up before because I didn't want to come off as too needy or sound as if I hadn't tried to be a good mother and raise him properly."

Her face reflects her uncertainty. Her teeth worry at her lip. "He listened to everything I said. He seemed sympathetic at first. But then he got the oddest look on his face. He demanded to know why I hadn't told him any of this before." She swallows before forcing herself to continue. "He told me that he was hurt that I hadn't been honest with him. That he didn't know if he could continue to see someone who would keep so much of herself a secret." She lets out a jagged breath.

"The worst part was the way he looked at me. Perhaps he holds me responsible for Mitchell's actions. I know I do."

Her lip trembles. I have the oddest urge to reach out and take her in my arms and tell her she's not to blame. That everything will be all right. But I'm not sure how she would react. And I'm not at all sure that everything *will* be all right.

"It certainly sounds as if he overreacted," I say in a measured voice. "You're a victim, Dorothy. In many ways even more than I am."

We sit in silence for several long moments.

"I don't know," she says finally. "His expression was . . . it was like a light switch turning off. He barely spoke on the way home. When I was getting out of the car, he said he'd be in touch, but he sounded so different. I don't know what it was that I said or did. But I clearly did something wrong."

Thirty-Four

Judith

Although I haven't heard anything more from Ethan, I remain hopeful that he'll come around. In the meantime, I've made a list of Realtors to interview, reached out to the estate sale company that Meena and Stan used, and plotted out a plan of attack and a timetable I intend to stick to. It's such a relief to have a reason to get up in the morning. I am a woman on a mission.

I'm not yet ready to empty Nate's closet or face his lucky ties, so I've decided to start at the bottom of the house and work my way up. In the basement I tell Alexa, who is no doubt stunned at being summoned after being ignored for so long, to put on my favorite playlist. Since Meena and I are serving refreshments at book club tonight and are discussing a Paris-set novel, I begin by pawing through the boxes filled with costumes and accessories we've been accumulating since Ethan's and Ansley's first Halloweens.

When I arrive at Between the Covers, Annell envelops me in a hug.

"That's quite the mustache," she teases, eyeing the black cardboard number affixed inside my nostrils and dangling above my mouth. A droopy French chef's hat perches on my head. (I briefly considered dressing as the French mime Marcel Marceau, but there's no way I'm making it through book club in silence.)

Meena has already set up the food table, which is covered with platters of macarons, éclairs, and petits fours that she picked up from a favorite French bakery. (A definite step up the food chain from my homemade body-part cookies.)

She's wearing a pin-striped chef's coat and starched white toque. Her mustache is drawn on in what looks like black eyeliner. We are extremely careful not to smudge or dislodge as we hug hello.

I pour champagne into plastic flutes that Meena hands out with a deep-throated and yet nasal, "*Hon, hon, hon,*" delivered in a truly horrible accent, which may or may not be intentional.

She hams it up, pretending to be a woman without a care in the world, but her eyes are troubled. I know she's fretting over Frank's vanishing act and the pall it's cast on the realities of online dating. But we all have our secrets. If I learned anything from the tequila-induced revelations at Superica, it's that other people's lives look easier and less complicated only because we don't know the burdens they carry.

Jazmine and Angela stop for pastries and champagne and stay to chat, showing off their French manicures. Chaz, Erin, and Carlotta join them along with Wesley and Phoebe, who arrive in matching black berets. Nancy Flaherty is back and absolutely thrilled with the golf skort and halter top Carlotta presents to her.

Dorothy and Sara are the last to arrive. They stop off at the register, no doubt to stuff the box with book club name entries, then come over to join us. Conversation and laughter swirl around us. Everyone offers a cheery "merci" and an extra "oui" or "mais oui" as they fill their plates and accept glasses of champagne.

When everyone has been served, Annell escorts us into the carriage house, where Meena and I settle next to each other on the window seat. Each time I check, Meena is smiling or "*Hon, hon, hon*"-ing, but I can feel the effort even a bad faux French laugh requires.

With no newbies in the group, we skip introductions and give ourselves a round of applause for our mostly terrible French accents. I pass a champagne bottle around the circle for refills as Annell kicks off the book conversation with insights into how deftly the three authors wove three very different characters into three separate time periods and also managed to turn the Paris Ritz into an important fourth character.

The discussion has barely ended when Angela raises her hand. "I'd like us to choose *Becoming* by Michelle Obama as our next read as a birthday gift for Jazmine, because it's her favorite and our May meeting falls on her birthday." She shoots a smile at her longtime friend. "I'll bring the birthday cake."

"I like eet," Annell says in a terrible French accent. "All een favor?"

The vote is unanimous. Jazmine stands up, smiling, raising a now-empty champagne bottle aloft. "Thank you! I can't wait to discuss it with you all. It might even help soften the blow of getting older."

Annell is about to pull out a stack of book club name suggestions when Meena stands.

"If it's okay, there's something I'd like to say before we wrap up."

"Of course." Annell sits.

All eyes turn to Meena, who has ditched the "*Hon, hon, hon*" and the last vestige of her smile. "How many of you put a profile on a dating site for the first time after I presented Online Dating 101?"

Dorothy, Annell, and Chaz raise their hands. Erin's goes up halfway.

Angela gives Jazmine a look. "You promised."

"Sorry. I've been busy," Jazmine counters.

"I think most everyone else who's single was already using dating apps?" Meena's going somewhere with this; none of us know exactly where.

"You know that's right," Carlotta says.

"On occasion," Nancy replies with a knowing smile.

Wesley nods. Phoebe grimaces.

"Yeah, turns out it's a mixed bag of an experience." Meena looks around the circle. "I . . . want to apologize for making it sound like it's all sunshine and roses." She drops her eyes for a moment, then meets our gazes again. "I was matched up with a man named Frank who seemed perfect for me. Remember, I told you we spent that week together on the Mayan Riviera?" She swallows. "Then he wanted to be exclusive, and in the end I figured, Why not? But as soon as I agreed to that, he started talking about living together. He wanted to move in with me."

All eyes are on Meena as she hesitates once again. "When I told him I just wasn't ready for that, he ghosted me."

"What does that mean," Annell asks. "Ghosting?"

"It means disappearing without a trace," Wesley says.

"It sucks," Phoebe adds. "Especially when someone's been really responsive and then they're just . . . gone."

"Yes," Meena says slowly. "It hurt a lot. Plus, I felt so stupid, you know. Because if he'd really cared about me, he wouldn't have disappeared the minute I said I wasn't ready for that." Her face is filled with regret. Her cheeks flush with embarrassment. "Anyway, I just wanted you to know. It just seemed like so much fun that despite the book's disclaimers, I didn't give any real thought to how easy it is to get hurt. Or how you open yourself up to people you don't really know."

"Lots of people out there got an angle," Carlotta says. "Or they're lookin' for something they're keeping to themselves."

My heart thuds in my chest. I've finally found the courage to try to move on and change my life. But what am I opening myself up to?

"There are people who target divorced women or widows of a certain age," Chaz adds. "They'll put on a show so they look super successful. Then they flatter and act like they want to build a relationship. They tell you that they're swept off their feet. That you're 'the one.' Scammers that are focused solely on getting money out of a mark tend to operate from a distance over a longer period of time. They may live in another country and use someone else's photo for their profile shot, often a man in uniform because that inspires trust."

We have all fallen silent.

"But then there are the scammers in our own backyard who don't waste any time wanting to meet. Sometimes moving in and mooching off someone can be the goal, though that's almost never stated. They want to charm you into asking them. If you have other assets, that's just icing on the cake," Chaz says.

"How do you know so much about this?" Meena asks in a whisper.

"Because I have friends in law enforcement. And . . ." He hesitates. "Because last week I caught a 911 call at a woman's house who'd been a victim of a guy like that."

We wait. ˮ clear the ending to this story is not going to be pretty.

"He lived off her for a year. Took pretty much everything she had. Distanced her from friends and family. When there was nothing left, he moved on. She was so humiliated when she realized how she'd been played, and so heartbroken that he'd never really loved her, that she slit her wrists." Chaz's warm French vibe is long gone. "She bled out just before we got there."

There's a hush. Every last bit of fun has fled. If there were a drop of champagne left, I'd be drinking it.

"She'd documented the whole thing on her computer," Chaz says quietly.

Without a word passing between them, Wesley and Phoebe pull laptops out of matching messenger bags, set them on their laps, and tilt open their screens so that we can see.

"Your Frank may just be a bozo without feelings. But it couldn't hurt to do a search on his name and his email. That'll lead to an IP address, which will tell us the exact computer his emails came from," Wesley explains.

"We can also do reverse email and image searches and check for aliases," Phoebe adds.

"Aliases?" Nancy Flaherty shifts uncomfortably in her seat. "Is it really that easy?"

"I'm sure he doesn't have aliases," Meena says, not sounding sure at all.

I can tell she's already sorry she brought this up. But we are all leaning in and listening intently. This is that car wreck you can't quite look away from.

"If that was Frank's game, Meena, you're well rid of him," Chaz says. Either way, in today's world, these are steps everyone should probably take before going out with someone they don't know. I'm only sorry I didn't think to suggest it when we had our online dating class."

"What's his name?" Wesley asks as both twins' fingers fly over their keyboards.

"Frank Vincent," Meena answers almost reluctantly. "FrankieV at gmail.com."

A few more keystrokes. Some scrolling. Photos pop up on both screens. The face is attractive and clean-shaven. Dark hair threaded with gray. The eyes are a brilliant blue, their expression trustworthy. The square chin has a comma-shaped cleft in it. He looks to be in his mid-sixties.

"That's Frank's profile photo from match.com. But he already took it down," Meena says.

"You can take a photo down; that doesn't make it disappear," Phoebe explains as their fingers continue to fly. More photos pop up. I see the shot of him Meena took on the beach in Mexico. The group photo at dinner. "There are quite a few different email accounts using the same computer," Wesley says.

The carriage house is completely quiet except for the sound of the twins' fingers tapping on their laptop keyboards. No one makes a move to leave. Even Erin, who's probably far more computer savvy than most of us, is spellbound. I may have stopped breathing.

Other photos of what looks like a completely different man pop up. This one has iron-gray hair, an equally gray mustache. Mossy-green eyes are partially hidden behind a pair of rectangular tortoiseshell glasses.

"Oh my God!" Dorothy gasps. "That's Dean, Dean Francis. The man I met on SilverSingles."

Sara looks over her mother-in-law's shoulder at Phoebe's computer screen where the new photos line up next to those of Frank Vincent. "The chin is the same, but if you didn't see these photos together and weren't looking for it, you'd never know it was the same man," Sara observes. "He looks early seventies like he told you."

"I haven't heard from him since last week when I told him that I live with Sara and don't have a house of my own." Dorothy shakes her head. "He actually told me off for not sharing that information sooner."

"This guy's got a lot going on." Once again, the twins' fingers are on the move. Photos of a third man appear beneath the others. He has close-cropped brown hair and eyes that are partly hidden by narrow black-rimmed glasses, a stubbled face, and a chin with a cleft that is beginning to look very familiar. His name is Howard Franklin.

"Oh no," Annell breathes. "That's Howie."

"Are these really all the same person?" Sara asks.

"The facial structure and the chin are identical. He's using colored contacts and glasses and wigs and hair dye . . . but it's the same man," Wesley says.

With a stroke, Phoebe pulls up the three men's bios. Once again, she places them next to one another. "They all have very impressive backgrounds. Harvard. Yale. Big-name firms. Most of which seem unlikely to hold up to fact-checking."

"Did 'Howie' ask you about your living situation?" Chaz asks Annell.

"Not exactly." Annell can't seem to drag her eyes away from the growing number of images. "But he seemed intrigued by the fact that the store was in a historic home. He said he'd like to come over and look at the carriage house and especially the garden. He sounded so sincere . . ."

"He is sincerely pretending to be at least three different people," Jazmine observes.

"And he's sincerely looking for a relationship. As long as she's willing, has a home of her own, and no one else is there to object to him moving in," Nancy posits.

Dorothy's shock has not faded from her face, but she's fallen quiet.

"I don't know what else he might have on his mind, but three different identities on three different dating sites? Frank/Dean/Howard is making an extremely calculated effort," Chaz points out.

"He used 'Frank' in some form in all three profiles. Do you think it could be his real name?" Angela asks as Wesley and Phoebe continue to tap away on their keyboards.

"His name is Frank all right. Frank Anderson," Phoebe says, pulling up a shot of the same man taken at some sort of charity fundraiser. The face is the same, only his hair and eyebrows are white and he's not wearing glasses of any kind. His eyes are a bluish gray.

"Why is that name familiar?" Angela asks.

"Because he was a well-known money manager and an

Atlanta A-lister who married into a prominent family," Meena says. "I used to see photos of him and his wife in the newspaper."

"That's right." I peer at the photo. "Nate met him once or twice at charity golf tournaments. I think he ran for a state seat a couple years ago."

"Yep." Wesley opens another file. "Apparently, his wife divorced him. The money was hers. It looks like he's still trying to act like he's big league, but . . . that doesn't exactly jibe with his actions."

"What about his children?" Dorothy asks. "What does it say about them?"

More keystrokes. "Frank Anderson and his wife never had children," Phoebe says.

Dorothy inhales sharply.

I look around me, my stomach churning. The world is such a different place than it was when I was last single. How could someone treat these women, my *friends*, this way? And what if we'd never had this conversation? Would one of them have ended up saddled with this man? Would he have stolen their possessions and their self-respect? "What can we do about this?"

"Can we at least report him to the authorities?" Sara asks.

"You can report him to the dating sites, but he hasn't harmed anyone that we know of, at least not physically. And if he hasn't stolen from any of the women he dates, it's not illegal," Wesley says.

"Well, he's stolen people's trust," Annell says. "We can't let him continue to get away with lying to and manipulating people."

"That is for damned sure! We need to teach this creep a lesson." Carlotta stamps her foot. "Anybody got any ideas?"

"I read about a woman in India who strangled her husband and buried his body in the kitchen and then built a mud stove over it," Nancy Flaherty says.

"If only we had dirt floors here," Jazmine says dryly.

"There's plenty of dirt in the garden," Nancy replies. "We could bury him there and then . . ." A smile spreads over her face. "I know! We could camouflage his grave with a putting green."

We all blink at her in surprise. I'm not entirely sure she's joking.

"I just finished reading a book about black widow spiders," Angela says. "They eat their partner after sex. They don't even *need* dirt."

"Yeah, that's why women who kill their husbands or lovers are called black widows," Carlotta, who is wearing all black and looks gorgeously dangerous, points out.

"I read about those black widows, too. Apparently, women tend to prefer antifreeze followed by dismemberment," Angela adds. Her eyes get big. "One woman fed the remains of her lover to neighbors at a barbecue."

"I'm starting to feel like I should call Perley and warn him about your reading material," Jazmine says with a teasing glint.

"Dismemberment would be too good for this guy," Meena pronounces. "Running around trying to find women to live off."

"Did you guys see the episode of *Good Girls* where they hog-tie Boomer, the attempted rapist, and stash him in the kids' tree house in the backyard?" Erin asks. "I bet we could stash Frank in the garden shed—or in the storage room—and no one would ever know."

Chaz folds his arms over his chest. "I'm all for teaching this guy a lesson, but we are not going to break the law. There will be no tarring and feathering or tearing from limb to limb, which I believe qualifies as dismembering," he says. "I think we should just scare the crap out of the man, expose his bad behavior and true identity, and prevent him from targeting other women."

"I don't know." Dorothy is our lone dissenter. "Maybe we should consider ourselves lucky that none of us fell all the way for it and let it be?"

"Hell, no," Meena says. "I say we at least have to out him like Chaz said."

I look at the angry and determined faces around the circle. We are smart, and we are here for one another. "I agree with Meena," I say. "I don't think we should just let him walk away."

"Okay," Phoebe says. "If we're going to make sure Frank/Dean/Howie, forevermore to be known as FDH, sees the error of his ways, we need to expose him as widely and completely as possible."

We all lean forward to see what she's pulling up on the screen.

"What do you think of this . . ."

Thirty-Five

Jazmine

It turns out it's not all that easy to pretend that you haven't had sex with someone. Especially when that sex was so good.

You know how as soon as you decide to cut out caffeine and sugar, all you want is a Caramel Macchiato? Rich Hanson is kind of like that. I did just fine without sex for most of the last fourteen years, and now I can barely look at him without thinking about it. It's like all of a sudden my body woke up, realized what it's been missing, and wants to make up for lost time.

The only thing that keeps me from dragging him into a broom closet is replaying Larry's advice to Rich about "getting me on board." Even the thought that he might have slept with me in order to solidify his position makes me sick to my stomach; the fact that I'm the one who kissed him and invited him into my bed only makes it worse.

If only he would disappear now that he's "won me over," I think I could get my equilibrium back. But he's invited me to lunch, out for drinks, and has even asked to go with me to watch Maya play. I keep saying no, but it's all I can do to treat him like I would any other colleague when I want to avoid him completely and fall back in bed with him all at the same time. The man isn't even my type. Or shouldn't be. And why on earth am I so attracted to him when the perfectly perfect Derrick Warren barely crosses my mind?

"Rich Hanson is here to see you." Erin's voice squawks on the intercom on my desk because apparently even thinking about him causes him to appear.

"Sorry, on my way out," I say, jumping up. Because now I need to go somewhere so that I don't look like I'm avoiding him. "Can you schedule something toward the end of the week?"

I'm shoving files into my tote bag when Rich strolls into my office. "You never struck me as the kind of person who would run away."

"I'm not running away. Something has come up, and I need to get to an unexpected meeting."

"Erin said your calendar was clear."

"Erin doesn't know everything."

His eyebrow goes up, indicating that he knows that to be a lie. He moves closer. I fight the urge to step back. Or maybe I'm just trying not to walk into his arms. I hate the way standing too close to him clouds my thinking.

"Larry told me he advised you to get me on your side if you wanted to make your mark here." The accusation in my voice is clear. So, no doubt, is the jut of my jaw.

"I didn't need Larry to tell me that. It was obvious the first time I saw you in action. I wouldn't have even considered trying to create the academy without you."

I blink. "So, you admit you were using me."

"Using you? Of course—I was using your brain, your experience, your . . . you. And I assumed we'd use what I bring to the table, too. It's called collaboration. We formed an alliance—it's only smart to do that with colleagues you respect. We work well together when you're not pissed off at me, or afraid of me, or not trusting me. Which provides a very short window in any given day."

"We shouldn't have slept together."

"No," he says, closing the gap between us. "We probably shouldn't have."

"Oh." I feel a distinct twinge of disappointment. "So, you're sorry it happened, too."

"I didn't say that. I refuse to be sorry about anything that felt that good." He steps closer, which is theoretically not possible, and lowers his voice. "I don't believe you're sorry, either. I think you're afraid because you lost control, which is something you almost never do." I can smell his cologne and his intention. If I don't stop him, he's going to kiss me.

More appallingly, if I don't get out of here, I might kiss him first. *Again.* "You said we could pretend it never happened. We agreed we wouldn't let it happen again. And I meant it when I said I'm not interested in being a notch on someone's belt."

"First of all, I am doing my best to *pretend* it never happened." His voice is ragged. "But I can't seem to actually *forget.* And I meant it when I promised you no notches. Seriously, Jazz, I don't even *own* a belt."

I snort. But I don't linger. The longer I stand too close to him, the less willpower I possess. "Fine. But that doesn't change anything. We stick to our promise, and we keep our relationship strictly professional. I have never seen a workplace romance end well. There's no reason why we can't work together, but there's every reason why we can't slip up and sleep together."

Judith

Meena is here at the house helping me sort through what to keep and what to let go. Or more to the point, she is sitting on the basement couch, talking to me while I pull things out of closets and shelves.

I've been working down here for three days, and it's amazing how many ordinary, everyday things now cause a lump in my throat.

"Ethan used to love Monopoly," I say when I open the bookcase doors and pull out the battered game box. "Nobody wanted to play with him because he always won." I open the lid and pick up the silver-colored Scottie dog piece, and the past wafts out. "Nate taught him to buy everything he could, even if he had to mortgage something later." I remember how daringly he played and how much he wanted to emulate his father. "I think he went into finance because of this game. Is it silly to keep it when we haven't played it in years?"

"There is no silly," Meena says. "You keep what matters to you. Or you can set it aside and offer it to him when he comes home," she says, even though Ethan hasn't yet said he'd be here Memorial Day weekend. "He might feel as nostalgic about it as you do."

I look around the finished basement with its ping-pong table and second living room that surrounds a flat-screen TV. It has two guest bedrooms and a Jack and Jill bath. No one but Rosaria's been down here since Christmas.

"I can't believe I'm actually going to sell the house." My hand squeezes the game piece.

"It'll be a lot of work, and there'll be times you think you can't bear to leave after all," Meena says quietly. "But I think it'll be good for you to try to start fresh. Have you given any thought to where you might want to live?"

"My only thoughts so far are small and low-maintenance. I think there'll be plenty of time to look around once I choose a Realtor. Susan Mandell has been giving me the full court press. And someone in the real estate office where Nancy Flaherty works reached out."

I plop down on the couch beside Meena.

"There's a two-bedroom like mine coming up for sale on

my floor and a couple other floor plans in other parts of the building already on the market. I'd love to have you for a neighbor again," she says.

"That could be fun," I say. But it's almost impossible to imagine. Right now, all I can think about is purging and straightening and tidying. It's sad but comforting to touch and look at all these pieces of our past. I can feel myself saying goodbye to the life I lived and the person I used to be.

"Who knows, maybe once I finish going through the house, I'll be qualified to put out a shingle and give Marie Kondo a run for her money. Or maybe I'll take a cruise around the world. Or hike the Appalachian Trail.

"The very idea that what comes next is entirely up to me is exhilarating and horribly frightening. From now on, everything I do, everything I choose, will be up to me. I won't have anyone to blame if I'm not happy."

"It's true," Meena nods sagely. "Growing the rest of the way up, coming into your own, can be scary no matter how old you are when you do it. So is freedom. Sometimes it comes wrapped up in loneliness."

I meet Meena's eyes. "How are *you* feeling?"

Her exhale is loud and slow. "I'm looking for closure and a chance to hit back. I slept with that man, Jude. And I fell for his bullshit. I don't even know who that cottage on the Mayan Riviera belonged to." She shakes her head. "I'm not gonna lie: I'm looking forward to seeing his face when he sees all three of us and realizes that he's not as smart as he thinks."

"Too bad we can't do it in costume," I say, reaching for yet another box filled with Halloweens past. "Hell, maybe I should open a costume shop. Remember this?" I pull out a single-breasted three-piece suit and a large striped tie. Then I locate the gray felt fedora that Nate wore with the suit and set it on my head at a rakish angle.

"How could I forget?" Meena says. "That's the year the guys

went to the neighborhood Halloween party as Gondorff and Hooker from *The Sting* and they kept flicking the bridges of their noses all night, like Newman and Redford and the rest of the con men did in the movie. Stan even wore blue contacts, which is as close to Paul Newman as I ever got. Until Frank." She sighs in disgust. "I can't believe his blue eyes may have been the only 'real' thing about him."

"You do realize that our sting may not be as satisfying as we're hoping. There's only so much we can do."

"I don't care," she says as I instruct Alexa to play the theme song from *The Sting*. "I just can't bear letting him think he got away with it."

Thirty-Six

Sara

"Are you sure you're all right?" I ask Dorothy yet again as we tidy up the children's area at Between the Covers post–story time.

"Of course. Why wouldn't I be?" Her voice is steady, and her smile appears real. But there's an odd sort of energy coming off her.

"Well, he did lie about pretty much everything. Even if he pretended to be different people while he was doing it. The same person who sat with you over coffees and pretended to bare his soul is the same person who spent a week in Mexico with Meena. And is coming here today to meet Annell."

"I'm well aware of that. But perhaps Annell should have just ghosted him. I'm not sure why we're going to all this trouble when we should just be glad to be done with him."

I consider my mother-in-law. "He hurt you and Meena. And if we do nothing, he'll just keep lying and attempting to mooch off other women."

"Perhaps it's our own fault for being so naïve. To want so badly to be loved that we open ourselves up to the wrong people." She says this quietly, but her eyes are cloudy with pain. Caused not only by this stranger but by her own son.

"Maybe we do need to pay more attention and stand up for ourselves sooner, but it's never right to blame the victims." I squeeze her hand, then head up to the front desk, where we receive jangly hugs from the rest of the book club as they arrive. Soon the store reverberates with nervous chatter.

"I'm so angry at this fraudster, I'm not sure how I'm going to be polite when he gets here," Annell says.

"Maybe we should just hit him over the head as soon as he walks in and stuff him in the potting shed," Meena suggests.

"I wouldn't mind laying a little whoop-ass on the man," Carlotta agrees.

"I still like the putting green idea." Nancy twirls, showing off the golf skort Carlotta designed for her. "My clubs are in the car."

Jazmine and Angela laugh. "It is tempting, isn't it?"

"Okay, everybody!" Phoebe and Wesley raise their hands for quiet. "The video camera is set up and tucked out of sight in the carriage house. It's voice activated, but we want to be careful not to block its view from between the open shelves in the kitchenette. We'll be using our cell phones to stream audio and video. Is everybody clear on what's happening?"

There are nods and nervous smiles.

"What's the signal?" Wesley asks.

"I say, 'Right this way'!" Annell calls out.

"Then I do the nose thing." Judith demonstrates. "And once Annell and 'the mark' are in the breezeway, we fall in and walk as quietly as possible into the carriage house."

"That's right," Phoebe confirms. "Don't be nervous. He may have multiple fictional personalities, but we still outnumber him."

Chaz steps forward. "Everyone needs to stay calm and remember our objective. I do have an off-duty cop friend standing by just in case, but we will not go into *Thelma and Louise* territory. Everybody clear on that?"

We respond with a resounding "Clear!" but I don't think any of us are anywhere close to calm.

At exactly four P.M., Meena glances out the front window. "There's his car," she stage-whispers. "He's here."

"All right, everybody." Annell's smile is tight. "Let's take our places. It's showtime."

Dorothy swallows a large gulp of air and clasps hands with Meena. After a last look over their shoulders, they retreat to the carriage house, where they'll keep out of sight until it's time to reveal themselves. The rest of the book club scatters around the store to pose as customers, which is fortunately not a stretch of anyone's acting abilities.

I move behind the counter and glance out the store window. Beside me, Annell takes a yoga-size breath, then releases it quietly.

My heart races as I watch a trim brown-haired man dressed in khakis and a short-sleeved black polo emerge from a silver sedan. He smooths a hand over a stubbled face and slips on a pair of rectangular dark-framed glasses, then walks confidently through the parking lot. Just outside the building he glances up at the living quarters. A small smile plays on his lips.

I drop my eyes, pretending to look something up on the computer for Carlotta. I only glance up as the bell jangles and "Howard" walks in, his gaze taking in the store and the crowd of customers. He does a brief double take when Carlotta shifts her weight, hiking her short skirt higher, revealing the legs of a WNBA player.

"Howard?" Annell walks out from behind the counter. An eager smile lights her face. "Is that you?"

"At your service." He smiles a friendly, everyday guy kind of smile, and I have to remind myself that this man has proven himself to be a consummate actor. "It's hard to tell from people's profile pictures sometimes. But you look exactly as advertised." It's clear he means this as a compliment.

"Why, thank you. I think it's terrible how some people use

old pictures or try to pretend they're someone or something they're not," Annell says. "It's so silly. I mean, it's not as if people don't figure out the truth once they meet you."

"Nice place you've got here," he replies, ignoring Annell's "arrow of truth."

"Thank you." Annell's smile gets bigger. "I'm fortunate to have a large base of loyal customers."

His gaze strays back to Carlotta, who is a good half foot taller than he is and considerably more muscular. Chaz stands in a nearby aisle, an open book in his hands. Wesley and Phoebe are on opposite sides of the store, glancing down at their phones and, I assume, recording this initial exchange.

"So, you live above the store?" Howard asks.

"Oh yes. The whole upstairs is private living quarters. It's so convenient."

He doesn't comment, but he looks very pleased.

"I have to say I was shocked at how much we have in common," Annell observes as she shows him around the store. "It's almost as if I'd ordered you up. What did you do in publishing?"

"I ran a medium-size educational publishing house for a time. When it got swallowed up during all the mergers that took place in the industry, I founded a small press and ultimately sold it to a strategic buyer." His voice is affable, his tone self-deprecating. "I still do some consulting, but I'm mostly retired."

They come to a halt in the children's section, which he compliments profusely.

"Thank you," Annell says again. I know her well enough to see how hard she's working to approximate her usual warmth, but so far she's managed to speak only the truth.

"Every now and then I almost start writing a novel that's been in the back of my mind for some time." He chuckles.

"What can I say? Even those of us who should know better believe we have a book in us." His laugh is low and companionable. I can see why Meena and Dorothy were so excited by his attention.

"I'd love to see that garden of yours."

"Of course." Annell takes a quick breath, then adds more loudly, "It's right this way."

We aren't exactly a well-oiled machine, but Judith nods in acknowledgment of our verbal signal, then flicks her index finger over the bridge of her nose. The others quietly fall in behind her while I put the CLOSED sign out and lock the front door, so we won't be interrupted.

Annell and "Howard" are in the carriage house before the rest of us enter the breezeway. As we tiptoe through it, I hear him exclaiming over the carriage house and its historic charm. Then he praises her camellia and magnolia bushes. His words stutter to a stop as we move into place at the same time that Dorothy and Meena emerge from the opposite direction.

Annell steps away from our "mark" and comes to join us, her face harder than I've ever seen it.

He falls back a step as we assemble. Then he glances over his shoulder as if considering making a run for it, but the garden is surrounded by a brick wall on three sides. His eyes widen as Meena and Dorothy walk forward and take their places on either side of Annell. Worried about the way my mother-in-law is trembling, I step up to flank her other side.

"What's the meaning of this?" he blusters. "What's going on here?"

"Hello, *Frank*," Meena says in a clipped matter-of-fact tone. "You've been awfully busy, haven't you? Does your ex-wife know what you've been up to?"

"I have no idea what you're talking about," he says, quite earnestly.

"I'd ask about your children, *Dean*." Dorothy's tone is seething, and I realize that her trembling is not from fear but from fury. "Only it turns out you don't have any."

"I'm sorry. But you obviously have me confused with someone else."

"You are looking a little pale, *Howard*. Some might even say worn-out," Annell adds, her voice amazingly calm. "It's probably all the house hunting and woman juggling. All those disguises and personalities. All those *lies*." She shakes her head. "Maybe you *should* write that book. You've got quite the imagination."

"What in the hell is this? Who *are* these people?" His eyes dart about like the cornered animal he is.

"This," Meena says, "is our book club, though really we're much more than that. You have unfortunately, and I would think against great odds, targeted three women who belong to it. You then pretended to be three different men, all of whom seem to have been looking for a woman to move in with and presumably live off."

"That's preposterous. You don't know what you're talking about. You girls are crazy." He scans the crowd, still looking for someone who might take his side.

Dorothy straightens further beside me. "We're not girls. We are women. And we're not stupid. Or helpless," she states with a strength I've never heard from her.

"You don't know anything about me," he sneers.

"We know more than we ever wanted to." Dorothy's tone is sharp and biting, her anger no doubt stoked by Mitchell's betrayal and all that she's been through. "We know your real name is Frank Anderson. And we know you deserve to be punished."

"You can't *do* anything to me," he sputters.

"You probably won't get locked up like you deserve," Meena agrees. "But we've reported you to all the dating sites. And we're putting the word out about you."

"Right. Like you know so many people," he scoffs, his expression turning ugly. "I have clearly been scraping the bottom of the dating barrel."

"Well, we are streaming live right now," Wesley says, holding up his phone. "And we've been recording video just so we don't miss anything. Would you like to wave to your audience?" He turns to his twin. "How many do we have watching right now, Phoebe?"

"We're still building, but we've got a good six thousand eyeballs already. We're also sharing every profile photo and alias we've discovered . . . so far. We've reached out to some influencers we know. Plus several local TV and radio stations and the *Atlanta-Journal Constitution* have expressed interest in our group's personal experience with fraud in the online dating world." Phoebe grins. "You're going to be an even bigger name than you ever imagined, Frank."

"This is bullshit!"

"When did you first come up with this scam?" Wesley asks. "Just out of curiosity."

"There is no scam. And I really have no idea what you're talking about!" He glares at us even as he ducks his head in an attempt to hide his face from a camera he can't see.

We glare back.

"I . . . I think I'm having a heart attack!" He clutches at his chest and goes down on one knee, but he sounds more hopeful than frightened.

"No, you're not," Chaz says with confidence, from out of camera range. "But if that should change, you won't need to call 911 to get a trained medical professional to the scene. Lucky for you, I happened to be browsing in the bookstore."

"What do you think?" Meena asks the group. "Anyone besides Chaz want to offer CPR?"

"Hell, no." Carlotta moves in closer, legs wide, fists on her hips. She looks a lot like a taller, more muscular Wonder

Woman. "What do you think, Dorothy? You think we should do a Bobbitt on him?" She smirks at the reference to Lorena Bobbitt, who severed her husband's penis while he was sleeping.

"I know it's not nice to kiss and tell," Meena says. "But it's not all that big, so I'm not sure how satisfying that would be."

"I don't think we'd even need a knife." Dorothy gives Frank Anderson a murderous look. "It would be far more satisfying to rip him apart with our bare hands." She breaks away and charges toward him, her outstretched hands reaching for his neck.

In that moment, I believe my mother-in-law is capable of anything. So, apparently, does Frank Anderson.

"Oh no, you don't! Don't you dare come near me!" He gets to his feet and stumbles toward us as Carlotta reaches out and plucks my mother-in-law out of his path. Is it wrong that I'm happy to see a wet patch spreading across the front of his khakis?

"You are crazy people! You are completely out of your minds!"

At a nod from Annell, we part, kind of like the Red Sea.

He skids through the opening we've created, then turns and races out of the carriage house, through the breezeway, and into the store. We follow, grinning like the crazy people he accused us of being, while he fumbles with the front door. We break into applause and laughter as he finally yanks it open and flings himself outside.

Thirty-Seven

Sara

"God, that felt good!" In the car on the way home, Dorothy is like a prizefighter exulting at the end of a championship bout. "I'm so glad we didn't just let him off the hook without at least having our say. Don't you feel empowered?"

"I do," I say truthfully. "But you're the one who landed the knockout punches, Dorothy. You were impressive as hell."

She raises one fisted arm like the prizefighter in my head. "I would have chickened out if not for you . . . and the others. And I would have regretted it."

"I think that's true for all of us, Dorothy. But you, my friend, are a formidable woman."

"So are you," she says.

We smile the whole rest of the way home, completely in accord.

Some of the joy dissipates when we arrive and see Mitchell's car in the driveway. I'd hoped he and his things would be gone before we got home. Now I have no choice but to face him. Hopefully, for the last time.

We come in from the garage and find him standing at the kitchen window looking out at the yard.

His presence dredges up the memories that I've buried under my hurt and anger. I loved him. In some ways, I always will. He was the first person who loved me back. Not out of pity or duty—which I've learned the hard way are not his strong suits. But because he saw things in me that no one else ever had.

It was with him that I first felt and recognized desire. He was my first and only.

Dorothy's eyes narrow. She nods at her son. To me she says, "I'll be nearby if you need me."

I watch Mitch's face as her footsteps recede.

"Do you remember how small the magnolia was when we got it?" He points to the now towering tree that we planted the day we moved in. My very first tree in my very first house.

His eyes meet mine. For the first time in a long time, I see the man I married, and I believe he sees me.

"I really fucked things up, didn't I?" he says.

"You did."

"I'm sorry. Honestly. I don't know what got into me. I just . . . If I could go back and undo what I've done, I would."

I study his face. Try to read what's in his eyes. I see love and sorrow and regret, all the things that have churned inside me. My heart aches for who we were, for what I thought we'd always have. I wish that everything that's happened—Mitch's secret life, the divorce, all of it—was just a bad dream, something conjured out of my own fear and insecurity.

He moves toward me, reaches out as if to cup my cheek.

"No. You no longer have the right to touch me." I step back and shrug away from him. "What do you think you're doing?"

Dorothy materializes in the doorway and walks toward us. "What *are* you doing, Mitchell? I certainly hope you're not trying to get her into bed."

"This is none of your business." He scowls at his mother. "Leave us alone. We're just . . . saying goodbye."

"Your attorney did warn you not to sleep with him before the divorce goes through, didn't she, Sara?" Dorothy's tone holds a clear warning.

"Yes." I think about that first appointment. "She said that it could . . . derail things. But I assumed that was for emotional reasons." I stare at my husband. "I promise you I have absolutely no intention of sleeping with him."

"Good." She steps up beside me just as I stepped up beside her when we faced Frank Anderson in the carriage house. "Because my son, as usual, appears to have his own motives."

"What motive could there be?" I ask.

"Do you want to tell her, Mitchell, or shall I?" Dorothy asks.

"Go right ahead, Mother," Mitchell exhales angrily. "You seem to have it all figured out. I didn't realize you'd taken the bar exam."

Dorothy's eyes remain on me. She's still in prizefighting mode. But this time she's fighting for me.

"If you were to have sex with each other and either attorney found out, they'd be legally bound to tell the judge that you were not living in 'bona fide separation.' It would cause your divorce to be dismissed."

"Dismissed?" Fear wraps itself around me like a heavy blanket. "You mean the divorce wouldn't go through?"

Mitchell exhales sharply. He closes his eyes.

"Ultimately, you could file again," Dorothy says. "But it could take an additional nine months and more money that I know you don't have."

"So, you hung around until we got home, thinking you'd somehow lure me back into bed one last time so that you could get the divorce dismissed?" I ask, trying to work it through.

His jaw is tight.

"But it makes no sense. We've agreed on everything. The paperwork's been filed. You're the one who chose someone else and built a family with her. Why would you want a dismissal?"

His gaze drops.

For the span of a heartbeat, I think he's going to tell me that it's me he loves and that if I'll only forgive him and take him back, we can start fresh and live happily ever after. I let myself forget that there are children involved. Another woman.

But what he says is, "I'm just not ready. Margot's changed. She's so anxious about everything. All the fun is gone."

If I had access to a weapon, he would already be dead. If I weren't so shocked and horrified, I could probably do exactly what Dorothy threatened at the bookstore and rip him apart with my bare hands.

"What is wrong with you?" I demand. "How can you care so little for the people in your life?" I look him directly in the eye. "I wasn't interesting enough, so you cheated on me with Margot. Margot, the woman who is carrying your second child, isn't *fun* anymore so you think maybe you can have sex with me so that you can put off marrying her and accepting responsibility for your children? And if that keeps me from getting the divorce I deserve, too bad for me?"

Dorothy places an arm around my shoulders. "I'm sorry, Sara. I can hardly believe I raised such a monumentally selfish and conscienceless human being."

"No. This is not on you. Mitchell's failings are not your fault. He is who he is. And I know you well enough now to know that you tried your best." I look at Mitchell. "You need to get out of here right now. And don't ever come back."

"We don't actually have to sleep together, you know," he taunts. "I just have to tell my lawyer that we did."

Mitchell's face is flush with triumph and satisfaction. He believes he's "won" again.

"You'd do that just to buy yourself some time? Knock yourself out. I'll just file again." I refuse to shed a single tear in his presence.

"Mitchell isn't going to say anything to his attorney or anyone else," Dorothy says evenly.

"This has nothing to do with you," Mitch says dismissively. He turns toward the door.

But I hear the determination in Dorothy's voice; I can see it on her face. She's not one to make idle promises or threats.

She smiles at me, then takes Mitchell's shoulder and turns him back around. "If you attempt to use this lie to stop the divorce, I will sue you for elder abuse. Then I'll call your employer and tell them just how untrustworthy you are and that you're a thief who stole from his elderly mother and left her homeless."

"You wouldn't do that," he chides her. "Not to me."

"Unfortunately, you have a tendency to underestimate others while overestimating yourself," Dorothy replies evenly. "This ends now. You will finalize your divorce, marry Margot, and raise your children. I'd like to know my grandchildren and their mother. But I'm grateful to Sara, and I'm glad I've finally come to know her. I consider her a friend and the daughter I never had." Dorothy smiles and takes my hand. My heart is fuller than I've ever felt it.

"You're bluffing," Mitch huffs. "You'd never sue me. You'd just be making yourself look ridiculous."

"Ah, darling," Dorothy says. "I'd rather not have to. But don't fool yourself." She slings an arm around my waist. "Sara and I both have better characters and bigger balls than you do."

His shock is almost comical, but ultimately, Mitchell Whalen does what he does best. He cuts and runs.

Through the kitchen window we watch him climb into his car, fire it up, then back down the driveway.

When the sound fades into the distance, Dorothy and I turn and face each other.

"I think I might need a glass of wine," she says.

"Me, too."

I go to the refrigerator and pull out a bottle of prosecco that I've been saving for a special occasion while she lowers herself into a kitchen chair and folds trembling hands on the table.

I feel awful inside but wonderful, too. I've lost a husband

but gained a formidable friend who's beginning to feel like family. I fill two champagne flutes and carry them to the table. "We have foiled two nefarious plots in one day. I think that might be a record."

I raise my glass. We toast like the bookworms we are. "To the end of a chapter."

"To turning the page," Dorothy adds. "And starting a new one."

> for·mi·da·ble
> /ˈfôrmədəb(ə)l, fərˈmidəb(ə)l/
> *adjective*
> inspiring fear or respect through being impressively large, powerful, intense, or capable
> Ex: "I hope to one day be as formidable as my mother-in-law."

Thirty-Eight

Jazmine

I'm not sure where May has gone, but as of today I am now officially thirty-six years old. Maya serves me a cup of coffee and a cupcake with a candle in it for breakfast in bed, then grabs my phone to FaceTime Thea so they can sing "Happy Birthday" to me together, with Jamal chiming in. After I blow out the candle, Maya races off to get dressed. Jamal departs for work. Thea gives me grief about dumping Derrick Warren.

"I didn't dump him. I just told him that I didn't think we were a good fit."

"A good fit? The man is not a pair of jeans. I cannot believe you are not interested in him."

"I told you, Thee. He's a great guy, and I'm sure he'll make some woman very happy. It's just not going to be me. You can't manufacture chemistry."

"Monsanto does. You could if you wanted to."

I take a bite of my cupcake and chew carefully. Then I take a sip of coffee.

"I see you rolling your eyes at me," Thea says. "I do not understand how you can *not* feel some serious movement of the earth with a kind, gentle, and fine-looking black man like that. She cocks her head. "It's that Rich Handsome, isn't it?"

"It's Hanson, and no, it doesn't have anything to do with him." Because I will not let it. Because one great night does not make a relationship. And because even if it did, *having* a relationship with a person you work with on a daily basis cannot be a good idea.

Thea has quite a lot to say about the size of the mistake I'm making. When she finally pauses to draw breath, I slap a smile on my face, wave merrily, and say, "Gotta run! See you at Mama and Daddy's on Sunday!"

"Wait, I'm not . . ."

I'm sure I'll hear the rest of this on Sunday, but I can't listen to it right now. Tonight, I'll get to celebrate my birthday at book club, where we'll eat cake and discuss my favorite book of all time. All I have to do is get through this day without crossing paths with Rich. I have always prided myself on being clear and straightforward. Pretending that I didn't and never again want to sleep with him feels inherently dishonest.

At the office, another cupcake waits on my desk. "Thanks for everything, boss," Erin says after she sings "Happy Birthday" to me. "Working with you is a great adventure. Oh, and, uh, Rich said he needs to see you."

"No. That's not going to happen today," I say as a knock sounds on my office door.

Erin and I look up.

"Sorry," she whispers, even though she doesn't sound sorry at all.

"No," I smile and whisper, trying not to move my lips. "Go tell him I'm busy. Don't make me call Louise and beg her to come back."

I give her my steeliest look, but it doesn't seem to be working. I blame it on the icing I'm licking off my lips.

"He just wants to wish you a happy birthday." She smiles brightly.

"Fine." I raise my hand and wave him in. "But if you ever get confused about who you work for again, you won't have a job."

"Right, boss." She turns, nodding, and possibly winking, at Rich as they pass.

"Happy birthday." He smiles, places a tiny bakery box on my desk, then takes a seat. "It's a cupcake. But I see you're already wearing one." He points to the other corner of my mouth. Then he pulls a tissue out of the box on my desk and hands it to me.

"Thank you." I dab where he's pointing. Exposing my tongue while he's nearby seems foolhardy. "How can I help you?"

"Actually, there are a few things I'd like to clear up." His tone turns serious as he shifts uncomfortably in his chair.

"O . . . kay." His discomfort just adds to mine. I make myself wait while he gathers himself.

"You seem to think that I'm some sort of party guy. That I sleep around and date indiscriminately." He looks me in the eye. I'm not sure what he's waiting for.

"Um-hmmm."

"Well, I wanted to make sure that you know that's not true." His eyes do that thing where they turn kind of amber. It's almost as if he's willing me to see something, only I don't know what.

"Listen, I know you're just trying to make our sleeping together seem less . . . awkward," I say. "Which is really kind of awkward in itself."

His eyes are pinned to mine, but he doesn't interrupt. I can't seem to look away.

"But it doesn't matter because it won't be happening again. And we did agree to pretend like it never happened. So, I'm not sure talking about it is going to be helpful."

He's still watching. Waiting. I'm just not sure for what.

"So, I'm thinking that since we're doing what we agreed, we're good. Right?"

"Right," he says. "I mean . . . we are good . . . *together*. Better than good. So, I've decided I just need to be honest here. About myself. And my marriage."

Between the looks he's giving me and the discomfort I feel, I can't think of a single thing to say.

"When I told you about my daughter and you asked if I was married, I . . . I left a few things out."

My stomach drops. "Oh?"

"I pretty much never talk about my wife because . . ."

I brace for some ugly divorce story. Complaints about how she didn't understand him. How she "took him to the cleaners" or tried to poison his daughter against him.

But what he says is, "It's my fault she's dead." He stops and closes his eyes, opens them.

When I don't speak, mostly because I have no idea what to say, he continues, "We were on our way home from picking out baby furniture for the nursery. She'd chosen this beautiful crib that cost what felt like a fortune at the time, but she'd just fallen completely in love with it, you know?" He swallows. His smile is a painful thing. "I remember she couldn't wait to be a mother. I was kind of freaked about the responsibility, the cost, the way our life was going to change, but Amelia was over the moon about it. She had this incredible glow, practically from the moment she found out she was pregnant."

I brace again because it's clear that whatever's coming is going to be hard to hear.

"I had leaned over to kiss her. I only took my eyes off the road for like a second, but when I looked up, this car was coming straight at us going the wrong way. It hit us almost head-on."

His eyes cloud with memory. "I barely had a scratch. Amelia didn't make it. But they managed to save Amy."

"Oh." I stare at him, trying to absorb the tragedy and pain that plays out on his face. "I can't believe I've never heard even a hint of this."

"That's because I don't talk about it. I was twenty-four when it happened. And not the most mature twenty-four. I was just starting out in a field that required lots of travel and crazy hours, and . . . it took a long time to even start to get over it. Fortunately, Amy's grandparents on both sides stayed involved."

My eyes blur with tears. I know exactly what that kind of loss feels like.

"As you know, even with family nearby, being a single parent of a newborn is totally overwhelming. Add in the grief and the guilt, and . . . all I could think about was making it up to my daughter. That's what drove me to sign the biggest names, climb the ladder as fast as I could, and make the most money. Sometimes I've cut corners and been more ruthless than I should have been. I have poached other agents' clients. As if money and success would somehow fill the void of the mother I took from her." He hesitates. "Why are you looking at me like that?"

"Because all this time I had no idea who you were or what you'd been through." I blink back tears.

"It's not the sort of thing you just bring up in conversation or mention at a meeting or during happy hour. I've always respected the way you handle yourself and your clients. And given your own loss and your . . . Maya . . . I knew you'd understand how huge a part of my life my daughter is."

I stare into Rich's eyes. I've judged him so harshly, having no idea we'd walked in each other's shoes.

"My point is, I'm about as far from a notcher/player as it's possible to get." He pauses once again. "I haven't felt this kind of connection since . . . since Amelia died. And I'm fairly certain you feel it, too."

I continue to stare into Rich's eyes, shocked at the honest emotion I am only now recognizing in them. Moved by the courage he's just shown when I, who have always prided myself on telling the truth and doing the right thing, have worked so hard to hide my feelings even from myself.

He leans across the desk. "So, here's the thing. If you really want to pretend there's nothing between us, I'll do my best. But it won't be easy. Because that's the total opposite of what I want."

I lean forward and meld my lips to his. It's a long, thorough kiss meant to convey all the things I can't bring myself to say. When it finally ends, both of us are smiling.

"I'm glad you shared your story with me." I swipe at a stray tear.

"Me, too." His smile gets bigger. "But there is one more thing."

"Really? Because as much as it means to me that you've taken me into your confidence, I might need a small break before the next revelation."

"Oh, I think you're going to want to hear this."

I study his face. Then I pull the box of Kleenex closer. Just in case.

"It's a good thing. I promise."

"Okay. But I'll be the judge of that." I take a deep breath. "Shoot."

"Larry came to me to talk about the new StarSports Academy and the tennis division."

My eyes narrow slightly.

"I know, I know." He raises both hands, palms out. "The three of us should have talked about it together."

"Damn straight."

"What can I say?" He shrugs apologetically. "Not everyone is as enlightened as I am."

"And?"

"At first, he thought you and I should share both positions."

I brace yet again. Afraid that Rich somehow ended up as the head of both.

"But I told him in no uncertain terms that given your background and knowledge of the sport, the tennis division should be all yours." He hesitates. "But I'm hoping you might be open to building the academy together." He's watching my face carefully. A small, hopeful smile lights his eyes. "What do you think?"

Relief rushes through me. I want to believe in this man and trust in that smile. "I think I might be able to live with that. But only after I give Larry grief for not discussing this with both of us."

We grin. Our eyes on each other.

"I'm with you on that," he says. "We need to make sure Larry understands that we're a team and not to be played against each other."

"Agreed," I say.

"Told you it was good." His eyes crinkle.

"I kind of hate it when you're right," I reply. "Is there anything else I should know?"

"Nothing that can't wait," he says softly. "Well, except for this." He leans over the desk so that we're eye to eye. We're both smiling as our lips meet.

Judith

I've been so busy getting the house ready to go on the market that time has begun to fly by. The kids—yes, both of them!—will be in this weekend to go through their things and to celebrate the life we lived here. I know Nate will be with us in each memory and story that we tell. (Who knows, maybe Nate came to Ethan in a dream and helped convince him to come home and help me to move on.)

Every once in a while, I imagine I see him just ahead in a hallway or out of the corner of my eye when I slide into bed.

His presence is comforting. It's almost as if I can feel him smiling.

As I climb in the car to drive to our last book club meeting before the summer break, I feel a little like the religious renegade on that ship headed for the Massachusetts Bay Colony; I don't know where I'd be right now if it weren't for my book club and the friends who make it up. I wouldn't even mind being banished to Rhode Island as long as they could come with me.

When I arrive, the store is ablaze with light and filled with conversation and laughter. The gang is all here, and I hug my way back toward the refreshments, where Annell is preparing to light the candles and prosecco is being handed around.

"Happy birthday!" I throw my arms around Jazmine, who is wearing a pink plastic birthday crown as if it were a diamond tiara. Her smile is quick and easy. Her hug is warm. I see something new, more open in her eyes. "Thirty-six seems to be agreeing with you so far," I say.

"I'm surprisingly good with it," she says as Meena hands us glasses of prosecco. "It's been quite the day."

"Do tell, girl," Carlotta sashays forward in a chartreuse mesh handkerchief hem dress that does incredible things for her figure and her dark skin. "Something's got her all lit up, and I don't think it's the candles."

"I'll never tell," Jazmine insists with a flash of white teeth. "All I'm going to say is sometimes people can surprise you in a *good* way."

Carlotta eyes Erin, who mimes a locking motion over her lips. "I like my job way too much to tell."

"Good thinking." Jazmine grins and taps her forehead.

"There's a lot of good thinking going on here," Chaz says. "Some of my coworkers like to tease me about being in a book club, but they don't have any idea what they're missing." He raises his glass. "You all are the best. Thank you for letting me be a part of this group."

"Hear! Hear!" Wesley and Phoebe raise their glasses. "To the best book club ever. And to the birthday girl!"

"Because she knows how to make thirty-six look good!" Nancy Flaherty adds with a toss of her head that sends her golf ball earrings swinging.

Angela arrives and takes one look at Jazmine before breaking into a grin. "Good Lord," she says, laughing. "I never thought I'd see that look on your face again." She throws her arms around Jazmine. "But I am so happy to see it!"

Sara and Dorothy raise their glasses, and we all gather around the cake, egging Annell on as she lights the candles. Then we're singing "Happy Birthday" to Jazmine, belting out the words as loudly as we can without the slightest concern for pitch or key or anything else but letting her know how much we love her.

We cheer when she blows out the candles. And then we are carrying heaping plates of birthday cake and sloshing glasses of prosecco into the carriage house, where we settle in for the discussion.

We watch Jazmine tear off the wrapping of what turns out to be a first edition signed copy of *Becoming*. As she clutches it to her chest with joy, I feel the warmth of friendship and belonging envelop me.

We discuss the book thoroughly. (I'm not going to go into detail here because I don't want to spoil it for you.)

I know I'm not the only one who is *becoming* more—more myself, more adventurous, more the person I'd like to be. We've all changed and grown and adapted.

When the conversation dies out, Annell settles back in her chair. "So, I hope to see you all in the store over the next few months. There are copies of the books we're reading over the summer at the front desk. Before we vote on a name for our group, I'd like to address the question about what the person whose suggestion is chosen wins. I've given it a lot of thought, and the lucky winner will get"—she points to Chaz, who does a mock drumroll on his thigh—"a free lifetime membership in our book club."

"But isn't membership already free?" Erin asks.

"True," Annell replies. "Hmmm. I know, how about a twenty percent discount on all book club reads?"

"We already get that, too," Wesley points out.

"True." Annell smiles. "How about free food and drink at every meeting?"

Jazmine laughs. "So, this is basically you reminding us what we already get by being a part of the Between the Covers book club?"

"It is." Annell's smile widens. "Can anyone think of anything they want that's not already included?"

"I'm willing to settle for bragging rights when I win," Sara says, aiming a glance at Dorothy.

"Ha! You mean when I win," Dorothy retorts.

"Hey, you two aren't the only ones competing, you know," Chaz points out.

"That's right," Angela adds.

"Now, now, children," I interject. "Why don't we let Annell read the new entries and worry about prizes when and if we choose a name?"

Everyone seems on board with this. No one disagrees.

Annell pulls sheets of paper out of a file folder and passes them around. "These are the book club name suggestions we've already heard. These"—she holds a stack of more ragged sheets of paper—"are all the latest entries."

Annell lifts the first.

As a group, we do a drumroll on the closest hard surface.

"We have Better Than Therapy, which is, of course, true."

There is agreement and laughter.

"Second, we have Nerd Herd."

"Hey," Chaz quips. "Speak for yourself!"

There are snorts of laughter. Meena rouses and offers an extra throaty *"Hon, hon, hon."*

"On a slightly more serious note, we have Cranial Crunch and Rabid Readers." Annell pauses for a sip of prosecco. "We've also got the Bookies, Spine Crackers, and Better Read Than Dead." Annell laughs. "Is it me or are these starting to feel a bit aggressive?"

There's chatter and more laughter as we contemplate one another. I'm sure I'm not the only one wondering who submitted what.

"Okay, we have . . . Literal Hotties, the Witty Worms, the Eclectic Bookworms, Cover2Cover, La Literati, and Litwits." Annell grins at the last. "It's fun, but I'm not sure if that's a compliment or not."

"La Literati has a cool secret-society vibe," Wesley points out.

"I still like Reading Between the Wines," Meena says as she pours the last of the prosecco. "Because we do."

We read over the list of earlier entries. We ponder. We make jokes. We all have our favorites. But once again, there's no clear winner.

"Can't we just call it Book Club and call it a day?" Chaz asks, looking for a compromise. "Or table it until fall?"

"We could," Erin says. "But I was just thinking how Jazmine brought me here when my wedding got called off. And my life was in the toilet. And how much it helped me."

"It *is* an incredibly welcoming place when your marriage ends," Sara says quietly.

"Or your world falls apart," I add.

"Damn straight," Dorothy agrees.

"What are you suggesting?" Annell asks.

"Well, breaking up wouldn't be a requirement or anything because I mean then who would want to join? But what if we called it the Break-Up Book Club? You know, as in it can help you survive almost anything?"

At first, we assume she's joking. There are snorts of laughter. And some of disbelief. We look at one another and then at Erin, who has this sweet, sincere, yet hopeful look on her face.

For possibly the first time since the group was formed, we are in complete and total agreement.

In unison, and with no—or at least not much—disrespect intended, we all yell, "Naaah!"

Acknowledgments

As always, a huge thank-you is due to longtime friends and critique partners Susan Crandall and Karen White. I can't imagine being on this journey without you.

To my editor, Kate Seaver, and the great team at Berkley/Penguin Random House.

To my agent, Stephanie Rostan of Levine Greenberg Rostan Literary Agency, for providing sage advice and for telling it like it is even when I'd rather not hear it. And for her wicked sense of humor.

To Courtney Paganelli, associate agent at LGR Literary, for her insights into how a twentysomething female talks and thinks. Because my sons were no help at all with this . . .

For sports detail, I relied on Kristi Dosh and Kevin Adler, whose passion for and encyclopedic knowledge of sports came in especially handy this time out.

For legal, I turned to Max Ruthenberg-Marshall, founding attorney at Porchlight. Mike Madsen and Realtor Andi Stein fielded questions about mortgages and real estate.

Thanks also go to:

Nick Adams, EMS division chief at Cobb County Fire & Emergency Services, for answering all my questions and for not being shocked at the details that made me blush.

Veronica Wilder, who inspired the character Jazmine Miller, who became so much more than I'd originally imagined.

Angela and Perley McBride and family and Nancy Flaherty, who made generous donations to Curing Kids Cancer, which put their names in this novel. And to Bonnie Traiman, who lent her name in support of the St. Pete Beach Library.

Close friends Dana Barrett and Annell Gerson, for allowing me to borrow their names and meld them into one fabulous character. And a great big shout-out to all the book clubs that shared their group names for this story.

The
Break–Up
Book Club

Wendy Wax

Discussion Questions

1. Have you ever been part of a book club? What is your favorite part of book club? (Did someone say wine? ☺) Have you read books you wouldn't normally have tried if not for the group? What's your favorite book you read with the book club? Do you tend to read more fiction or nonfiction?

2. Jazmine, Erin, Sara, and Judith are very different and yet they become friends through book club. What do you think draws them together despite their varied ages and backgrounds? Have you made unexpected friends through your book club or at another time in your life?

3. At the beginning of the book, Erin, Sara, and Judith all experience a major upheaval in their lives. What are the similarities and differences in how they all handle their altered circumstances? Did you identify with one woman more than the others? Which character, and why?

4. Sara and her mother-in-law don't get along at the beginning of the novel. What draws them together? How do both of their perspectives change throughout the book?

5. Judith struggles to figure out what to do with her life. Has there been a time in your life when you were unsure of your next step? Were you scared, excited, or a combination of both? What helped you make a plan for your future?

6. Jazmine's sister wants her to get married, but Jazmine isn't very interested in dating. She's happy on her own. Do you think women still feel more societal pressure to get married than men?

7. Erin views Jazmine as a professional mentor, a role Jazmine embraces. How does Jazmine help Erin? What lessons do you think Erin learns from Jazmine? Do you think it's important for women to support one another personally and professionally? Is there a woman you admire, someone who has helped you navigate difficult times?

8. Sara's mother-in-law tries online dating. Jazmine starts dating at her sister's encouragement. How are their attitudes toward dating different and similar? What factors contribute to these attitudes? How do you think dating differs in your twenties, thirties, forties, fifties, and sixties? What do you feel is the best way to date—online, setups from friends and family, or other possibilities? If you're in a long-term relationship, how did you meet your partner?

9. What's your favorite book, and why? What was your favorite book club name mentioned in the book? Which character did you most identify with, and why?

Photo by Beth Kelly

Wendy Wax, a former broadcaster, is the author of sixteen novels and two novellas, including *My Ex–Best Friend's Wedding*, *Best Beach Ever*, *One Good Thing*, *Sunshine Beach*, *A Week at the Lake*, *While We Were Watching Downton Abbey*, *The House on Mermaid Point*, *Ocean Beach*, and *Ten Beach Road*. The mother of two grown sons, she has left the suburbs of Atlanta for an in-town high-rise that is eerily similar to the fictional one she created in her 2013 release *While We Were Watching Downton Abbey*.

CONNECT ONLINE

AuthorWendyWax.com
f AuthorWendyWax
𝕐 Wendy_Wax